Siege Perilous

BAEN BOOKS by P.N. ELROD

Keeper of the King (with Nigel Bennett)
His Father's Son (with Nigel Bennett)
Siege Perilous (with Nigel Bennett)
Quincey Morris, Vampire

The Adventures of Myhr

Siege Perilous

NIGEL BENNETT

P.N. ELROD

SIEGE PERILOUS

This is a work of fiction. All the characters and events portrayed in this book are fictional, and any resemblance to real people or incidents is purely coincidental.

A Baen Books Original

Baen Publishing Enterprises
P.O. Box 1403
Riverdale, NY 10471
www.baen.com

ISBN: 0-7434-8854-7

Cover art by Jamie Murray

First printing, October 2004

Library of Congress Cataloging-in-Publication Data

Bennett, Nigel, 1949-
  Siege perilous / Nigel Bennett, P.N. Elrod.
     p. cm.
  ISBN 0-7434-8854-7
  1. Vampires—Fiction. 2. Revenge—Fiction. I. Elrod, P. N. (Patricia Nead) II. Title.

PR9199.3.B3782S54 2004
813'.54—dc22

                                                          2004014349

Distributed by Simon & Schuster
1230 Avenue of the Americas
New York, NY 10020

Production by Windhaven Press, Auburn, NH
Printed in the United States of America

10   9   8   7   6   5   4   3   2   1

DEDICATION

To Hannah.
And a special thanks to Rachel Caine.

Chapter One

Sharon Geary crept unsteadily up two dozen of the ninety steps leading to the top of El Castillo, her supposedly fit and toned muscles already cramping from monotonous effort, her lungs fighting for every breath of the thick, still air.

Something doesn't want me here, she thought.

Apart from supernatural factors, she considered the supreme lack of wisdom in scaling a pyramid at any time, but particularly now, in the dead of night.

Not my choice. His.

She'd lost sight of Neal Rivers hours ago when the sun was strong, while tourists swarmed, oblivious to his threat beneath its glare. No matter. She knew he was not likely to leave until he'd accomplished his errand.

Errand, indeed. She repressed a snort, using the energy to haul up another few steps, legs pushing, arms pulling. God, but the angle was steep, and you didn't dare look down or the sharp pitch would make you dizzy. You didn't dare look out across the vast esplanade below or the height would . . .

Shouldn't think too much. Shouldn't think about it at all.

She hated heights. Airplanes were not a problem, and just as well,

1

but to be on something tall that was so solidly connected to the ground gave her a sick-making sight line straight to disaster. Better not to look.

Sharon paused to rest, reminding herself that thousands of sight-seers made this climb and were no worse for the wear. And long before *their* chattering, guidebook-oriented, camera-toting modern-times invasion the ancient priests of the Mayans had done exactly the same. The show-off buggers had probably clambered the harsh steps at all hours of the day or night, nimble as mountain goats. Well, if they could do it—

Thirty-eight, thirty-nine . . .

She perversely counted steps. It both distracted and annoyed her, ideal factors to keep her moving and from wondering too much about what awaited at the top.

Oh, but wonderful old Stonehenge was a much easier tour. Flat. Not as exhausting, not nearly as perilous.

Well . . . not precisely. That had been a different kind of peril, more hidden than the obvious threat here of taking a bone-breaking tumble. When she'd seen Rivers' work at the Henge, seen what he'd done to it, what he'd left of it, the physical risk she courted now was negligible. Compared to some things, it was wholly preferable.

She whooped in a viscous draught of the heavy air and gained another few feet. God, it was like moving against the wind, only there was none stirring to cool her. The stones were still warm from the day's sun, the heat working through her bare hands into her arms, weighing them down. Sharon ignored the added burden and the sweat pouring from her and kept going, up and up and up.

Forty-four, forty-five . . . there. The halfway point, that wasn't so bad. People handed over fortunes to posh gyms to get this sort of workout. Wasn't she the lucky one?

Forty-six, forty-seven. No reason to turn back; she'd finish it out for sure now. Have a little rest at the top, find out how and why the bastard does it, but above all stop him. Oh—very important—try to forget about the increasing distance to the ground. What was it to the top? Seventy-five or eighty feet? That wasn't much, no, not when one was *inside* a building. Outside it's a whole different perception of vertical distance. And was it the actual height of the structure or the measure of the length of the steps set into its slanted sides? The guide books she read on the plane flight from London hadn't been consistent, nor had they mentioned just how difficult a climb it would be.

But they all agreed it was ninety steps times four sides, with the top being ninety-one, a nice, tidy Mayan year. Imagine building this great bloody thing just to keep track of the planting season. Combine the stifling heat here—even in the winter—with the hangover humidity that was part and parcel with the surrounding jungle and she wondered why a sane person would want to raise so much as a lean-to in such a climate, much less anything so massive. Simply climbing the thing was intense, exhausting work, what must it have been like to *build* under such conditions? Sharon didn't want to visualize that depth of detail. Too humbling.

Fifty-seven, fifty-eight. The backs of her thighs and calves burned. Oh, yes, she was now the pride of every aerobics instructor and film star who had ever put out a keep-fit video. They were always fresh and bouncy in their skin-tight costumes and perfect hair, not a hint of damp about them. Sharon would have been driven in disgrace from the video set in her faded black T-shirt, baggy-kneed, sweat-crumpled army surplus BDU pants and sturdy combat boots. Hardly Hollywood chic, but very practical for hanging about in jungles, particularly with the green camouflage pattern. The Yanks weren't using this style anymore for their active military, but it still worked well for concealment. She'd not expected to have to hide, but had come prepared. Just in case.

Earlier that day she'd drifted in with a tourist group, moving at their speed, but searching for *him* in the other groups. Futilely, as it happened.

Neal Rivers—the name by which she knew him; he had others—should have been easy to spot with his crooked arm and the eye patch, but a number of men matching his general build were clad in loose, long-sleeved shirts and sunglasses. And hats. Everyone sensible wore a hat against the sun. Certainly she'd kept hers on to conceal her too-memorable mane of red hair. She'd never had direct contact with him, but he might wonder at seeing the same tall redhead so soon after his gutting of the Henge.

She'd slipped from the main swarm of vacationers to pick a hiding place within the trees and settled in to wait for nightfall. If he repeated what he'd done at Salisbury, he would want darkness.

Except for the stifling heat and keeping an eye out for snakes and unfriendly insects, she'd been almost comfortable with her spare canteens of water and protein bars. The hours until sunset had gone slowly, but she could be patient for a sufficiently worthwhile goal. From cover she searched the knots of wandering tourists with her field glasses for a recognizable if unsettling face and form.

And finally spotted him.

He'd been at the northeastern foot of El Castillo, standing disrespectfully close to one of the carved stone snake heads at the base of the steps. During the equinoxes, when the sun was right, angled shadows cast from the main body of the pyramid onto the outside wall of the steps created the illusion of the serpent god's undulating back as it descended from the top. Quite an impressive slow-motion show it was, too; must have pulled in droves of worshipers, same as today.

Rivers stood nose-to-snout with Kukulcan's head, almost as though speaking to it, which was ridiculous. Perhaps he'd made faces. She'd heard that sort of cheek was to be expected from him.

Then he abruptly straightened, turned in her direction, and for a few awful seconds seemed to look straight down through her field glasses into her soul. At such a distance he couldn't possibly see her, but it was startling enough to make her jump. By the time she refocused, he'd vanished into the mob and never showed again for the remainder of the day or during the after-dark light show. Quite inconsiderate of him to be sure.

No matter. Though he was out of sight, she *felt* his presence. Very odd, that. This particular quarry was dangerous, far more so than any other she'd ever gone after, and on levels well beyond the ordinary.

His touch was cold, the only hint of chill possible in this climate, and rather than sensed as a freezing whisper on her skin, she felt it in her *heart* and beyond. It went down to the marrow, that feeling. Sharon took it to be a serious warning and gave it her most strict and unsmiling attention.

She never used to trust in such insubstantialities. That eccentricity began only after the business with Richard Dun, her one-time friend and lover.

And teacher. In his own way. He'd opened other doors for her besides the one to his bedroom. Not on purpose, that had happened simply by being with him.

Sixty-five, sixty-six . . . keep going . . .

You'd think there'd be some wind by now. But the night sky was stingy even at this height. Or holding its breath? She could believe it. In the last few years she'd come to believe in quite a number of extremely improbable things.

It was all Richard's fault, of course.

Well . . . not completely. He'd been more of a catalyst than an instigator. It was as though contact with him had awakened a strange insight in her. Sharon had always had intuition a-plenty, combined with boundless common sense, but nothing like this. It was right out of her gram's stories of the women in their family having the Sight. The old lady did possess one hell of a sharp shrewdness about people, though. She'd always been able to tell truth from a lie, know when someone was in pain or happy, and whether it would be a boy or a girl long before the mother knew she was expecting. Both blessing and curse, Gram had said, mind how you wear it.

Sharon thought the idea quaint, a way of making an old tale more interesting. What a shock it had been the day she first noticed auras on people. They were exactly as Gram described, so it wasn't too terribly frightening. Took a bit of getting used to, that, but Sharon had adapted with curious quickness. It was as though she'd always held the potential within and only just needed to be reminded to make use of it.

He had brought it out. Unknowingly. Richard. A very pleasant distraction she'd chosen not to linger with for long. He'd asked her to stay with him having freely confessed—wonder of wonders in a modern man—that he was in love with her. She believed him, but weeks before their parting she'd determined she would have to eventually move on.

Sharon tried to let him off as gently as possible, putting on a bravado face mixed with tenderness and giving him her "itchy feet" speech. Richard wasn't the first man who'd ever wanted to settle down with her, so the words came easily and smoothly, but with a hollow tone to them. They'd sounded so painfully brittle and false and overly rehearsed in her own ears. She half expected him to tell her to shut up and come out with the real explanation, but he'd quietly bowed to her reason to leave. No denials, no anger, no demands, no insisting that she reconsider, no offers of a home and security and true-blue hearts-and-flowers devotion for life . . . just sad disappointment. And acceptance. That was the amazing part of it. He accepted her decision and off she went.

She'd finally met a man who understood her need for freedom and by the time she comprehended the rarity of that quality it was too late to go back to him. She boarded the plane and returned to her previous existence, giving herself a wobbly inner congratulation of having made a successful escape.

A rather narrow escape. He was one hell of a man, after all.

But *no* regrets she'd told herself. Richard was a warm and happy pause in her life, nothing more. If they ever met again, they would still be friends, and, if he was still available, perhaps again become lovers. For a time. Always and only *for a time*. She neither needed nor desired anything permanent. "Wandering Star," her Irish gram had pronounced over her more than once, smiling.

It was only after Sharon had left Richard that she came to realize his crashing and unexpected impact on her life. That little adventure they'd shared had *changed* her. Seeing auras wasn't the half of it.

After auras on people, she began to see them associated with places. It took a bit of practice and study to sort out the accumulation of colors, feelings, and even shapes. Some were terrifying, while others were a delight. That spot in Canterbury Cathedral where Thomas á Becket had been cut down—nasty place, all muddy black and blood red, but then there was that lovely shining glow around the main altar, as though in some way they balanced each other out.

So she'd taken to visiting other historical sites, reading the truth of messages absorbed by earth, brick, stone, and wood, seeing the feelings left behind by thousands of others. She liked the holy sites the best; it didn't matter what religion, they all had something going for them, like . . . well, like different flavors of ice cream. She wanted to sample them all.

Then toward dusk only yesterday she'd gone to Stonehenge on a whim. She'd been there before, drinking gratefully from its energy, and finding comfort in its ancient strength. Having finished up a minor problem for Lloyd's of London ahead of schedule she could spare the time from her freelancing to loaf. It was on her route back, so why not? She pulled off the A303 into the car park and walked in with other late arrivals to the monument, her inner senses open and receptive.

But she'd found something was happening there, a wrong kind of something. The sonorous visual music coming from the ancient stones competed with a powerful instrument playing determinedly out of tune. An alien element had been introduced into their chorus that made her skin crawl. She first took it to be a weather problem, having seen similar disturbances before, but soon concluded this was nothing to do with the voice of wind and cloud over the land. There was a specific source to the problem, which she eventually tracked to one of the lingering tourists, a stockily built balding man standing casually next to a Saracen stone. His hair, combed straight back from his high brow, was shot through with gray and not a few streaks of pure white, the same as his beard and moustache.

His black eye patch and the scars under it were the most immediately noticeable differences setting him apart from the crowd. Then she noticed his crooked right arm, as though it had been badly broken and never properly set. The shape of the twisted bone showed through the sweater he wore.

That's what tripped her memory. She'd never seen him, but knew him from Richard Dun's description. The man could only be Neal Rivers, professor, an expert on Arthurian legend—the Holy Grail in particular—and when going by the name of Charon, one of the most successful and deadly assassins on the planet. He'd spooked even the mostly unflappable Richard, which was saying a lot.

Rivers in person was quite a few steps beyond what she'd heard about him. The impact of his presence was extraordinary to her changed senses. He wore human form like a disguise. It concealed the truth from the unaware. His flesh was a flexible shell, protective coloring allowing him to blend with the rest of humanity. A hunter herself, she instantly recognized another predator—or as she came to learn—a predator and parasite in one.

Sharon shut down her Otherside hearing and kept her distance, observing. Now that he had her attention she noticed small things about his body language, the sort of nuances that set off her internal alarms. She finally identified them as an absolute and overpowering *confidence.* Certainly it was attractive, but somehow askew by a few crucial and creep-making degrees. Richard Dun had a similar eerie confidence about him, but in a positive sense. This man was his opposite number and into overkill about it.

And sometime or other during her otherwise careful surveillance Neal Rivers vanished.

That nettled her. She was *good* at trailing people; having a standout, oblivious subject giving her the slip in such a controlled and confined area was unacceptable. He'd not left, of that she was certain.

Visiting hours came to a close, and the tourists were herded out, but if one was clever and quick one could hide from the caretakers. Sharon avoided them, finding concealment in one of the long ditches outside the stone circle.

She lay flat and very still, invisible as early winter darkness rolled over the land, and she ruthlessly ignored a voice inside that said this was a fool's quest. The worst that could happen was to be discovered by the management; embarrassing, but survivable. Or she might catch pneumonia. Her lumpy bed in the chalk was damp and icy cold despite her well-insulated clothes. To keep circulation going, she made scouting forays around the circle, taking it slow, her senses extending to pick up his presence.

But he must have been concealing himself. In more ways than one.

The car park was empty now, but for two vehicles: her own, and what looked to be a nondescript rental. Perhaps it belonged to a watchman, but she doubted it. She could assume that Rivers was aware another person might be lurking about.

So why was *he* at Stonehenge? Playing tourist? Not likely. He couldn't possibly be after the Grail again. That—according to Richard—was being well looked after in a safe and secret location. If Rivers was on the trail of some other historical holy object, he was flat out of luck. Decades of archeological excavations had picked this place clean. The most he could hope for here was a stray bit of pot shard or perhaps a fragment of deer antler left by the ancient builders. Sharon doubted Rivers would have much interest in their cast-off tools, which were all over the area. As for the stones, well, they were just too *big* for carrying away.

For a bad moment it occurred to Sharon he might be after her, but she dismissed it. Until a few hours ago she'd no idea herself that she would stop for a visit. He'd already been here, so he couldn't have followed her. No, this was one of those mad coincidences that sometimes just happen.

Richard Dun did not believe in coincidences, though. In the short space she'd been with him she'd learned he took such things very seriously, indeed. They were not always portents of grim events, but they were something requiring a certain amount of consideration depending on their level of intrusion and probability. The more improbable, the more important they must be, and how much more improbable could this one get?

I make a casual stopover and run square into a man that several dozen police forces would love to have chained and gagged in a dungeon, which they would gladly build especially for him. What are the odds?

Richard would know the reply to that one. Too bad he wasn't here. He'd said he had certain unfinished and no doubt fatal business to conclude with Rivers.

Perhaps he would have his chance, if Sharon could find out Rivers' business without getting killed. She wished she had her Glock with her. The local law was indecently paranoid about allowing honest people to protect themselves . . .

She froze in midstep, then sank low with only her head above the level of the ditch.

Rivers emerged from his hiding place. He'd been hanging near the stones in the middle of the circle and appeared now as a shadow moving among them. He swaggered about as though he'd just bought the place, apparently unconcerned over discovery and eviction.

Then he climbed atop the Altar Stone in the center. Good God, even the most radical of the "Free Stonehenge" New Agers discouraged that sort of behavior. Not only did it add to the weathering and wear, but it was bloody disrespectful.

Neal Rivers stood tall on the great block and raised his arms to the night sky. Outlined against its leaden press she could clearly see the crooked twist of the right one.

But *what* was he doing?

Belatedly, she turned to her inner sight for an answer. She'd shut it down completely on the off chance he might be sensitive to it and notice her.

When she opened up, it was almost too much.

Instead of the occasional rush of cars passing on the nearby road she was all but flattened by a terrific Otherside howling that hit her ears like a *basso supremo* air-raid siren. It boomed and roared over and around the whole area of the monument, yet she could see no source. The stones shook from it, and smoke seemed to rise from them, though they couldn't possibly be on fire. Streamers thick as storm clouds flowed from their surfaces to rush in a clockwise current around her.

And there were *things* in that river of darkness.

What she glimpsed she had no description for: swirling shadows and sparks of light and half-perceived shapes flowing swiftly around and—alarmingly—*through* her. Some seemed to be human in form, others were like animals, but they shifted too fast to be identified. She felt that many were harmless while others were beyond dangerous, both caught up by this strange squall. It was like a rout from a forest fire, where rabbits and deer fled next to wolves and mountain lions.

A few of the more nightmarish monstrosities, for they did not resemble anything familiar to her, slowed enough for her Sight to focus on. They seemed to see her in turn. They reminded her of the big predators in a zoo held safe behind their bars, and all is well until one of them picks you from out of the crowd. Those all-knowing and hungry golden eyes carry you back to the dangers of the ancient plains, and you know that your once important strivings in life are about to end, you've just been turned into food.

So it was here. Whatever those things might be, they were not only caught in the maelstrom, but held back by some barrier yet invisible.

It took an enormous amount of willpower to wrest her awareness from the Otherside gale to look at Rivers. Only then did she perceive that he was at its center.

He was laughing. She couldn't hear him for the row, but little else could account for his head being thrown back and his arms spread high and wide as though to receive . . . what?

The chaos menagerie, apparently.

Sharon gaped as the overwhelming and gigantic flow of raw power whirled around and around to finally sweep right *into his chest*.

It did not pass through; it went in and stayed.

He was . . . was *feeding* on it.

Oh, now that just wasn't right.

She thought she should do something, but didn't know what that could possibly be. Jump up and yell at him to stop defacing a national monument on the metaphysical level?

And get flattened into jelly. If he could cause this sort of disruption with the enormous primal forces of this place he could do just exactly that to her. Much as she wanted to stop him, this would have to be a strictly intel-gathering operation. Watch everything, then get out and decide what to do about it later. When he was locked up in a cell.

Make that "dungeon." Yes. For people like him a dungeon was just the thing. The only safe place to contain his threat was yards-thick impersonal stone with bars made from cold iron.

Of course, this assumed Rivers was up to no good, but she knew in her soul that evil was afoot—real evil—the kind that couldn't be spin-doctored away with lawyer-speak excuses about an abusive childhood or disadvantaged environment or temporary insanity. This evil was the sickening, deliberately cruel, self-absorbed, old-fashioned kind that made dedicated atheists cross themselves.

So Sharon kept her head down, waiting out the storm, until the terrific howling diminished and finally died.

She wasn't used to absolute silence, in either world she walked in. The ordinary Sussex countryside was mute, with not even the swish of a passing motor to break the hush. She tapped one ear to make sure she'd not gone deaf and heard the light thump, but nothing else.

The same went for her Otherside hearing. She knew that wasn't right, but just *how* wrong was it?

Then Rivers crowed, letting rip a shout of triumph and joy mixed with laughter. It was like a drunk cursing in a church, so loud as to make her wince. She lifted just enough to see.

Sweet heavens, but he was *glowing*. It was an unhealthy light, though, like something from a fifties scare-cinema to show radio-activity. He was happy enough about it, positively gloating before he hopped down from the Altar Stone and went striding off toward the car park. Good. Her cell phone was in her own vehicle. Once he was gone, she'd start the police to tracing his plate numbers. With any luck they could nab him before—

She ceased planning as the surrounding devastation gradually impressed itself on her inner eye.

Of course the Henge on this Side was intact. There was damned little that could influence those monuments into moving.

But the Otherside . . . She blinked, disbelieving.

It was utterly gone. The great stones were crumbled to rubble and dust no more than ankle high, as though they'd been struck square on with a bomb, lots of bombs—or one really big one. The destruction was so thorough that she couldn't tell where anything had stood before; she had to superimpose the view of one world atop the other, and they still didn't match. Everything was *gone*.

And dead. Whatever life, good, bad, or neutral, had been in the circle was missing. The lights, the shadows, the movement of existence itself—had been sucked into that . . . thing. Rivers. The disguised thing in a suit of flesh.

No number of police would be able to stop him. Rivers wouldn't even be slowed, not with that kind of power to command. She could make a call, but it would only get people needlessly killed. Her intuition told her that if he could drain life from a *place* he could just as easily take it from living beings.

Richard Dun might know how to deal with him on such a level, but for that to happen she'd need Rivers's location.

As soon as it was safe—a relative term, now—she dashed shakily to her car and followed his rental as it ran toward London. She kept her distance, but never quite lost sight of his taillights, not that she needed them. All she had to do was lean into her Sight and there he was blazing away like a Guy Fawkes effigy.

Rivers went straight to Heathrow, which did not bode well. He was apparently booked and all the arrangements made. He turned in his car, collected a bag from a storage locker, and headed for an overnight flight with the final destination being Cancún in the Yucatán.

Seventy-two steps, seventy-thr—oh, hell . . . relax a moment. Her heart was making a good run of it, but another break wouldn't hurt. If only the air wasn't so souplike in her straining lungs. Good grief, she'd seen flabby old ladies weighed down by suitcase-sized purses and shopping bags going up this thing at a faster pace. All she had was a single canteen, a machete strapped to one leg, and the Glock.

What's your problem, girl?

Jet lag, perhaps. After the chaos at Stonehenge she'd hardly paused, booking on the next flight out. There'd been barely enough time for a hasty stop at an airport shop to snag some necessaries, then pelt away again. Tight timing and a lot of speeding, but she'd done it, making her plane and arriving in Cancún only hours behind him.

There'd been no spare moment to phone Richard then. She'd eventually managed that from the plane, but he'd not been home. This was not the sort of news one could easily leave on an answering machine. *Hallo, love, I've found Charon. He's off to a tropic vacation in Cancún after metaphysically destroying Stonehenge. Would you mind dropping everything and come lend a hand down here? His aura looks like a black hole on steroids, so I wouldn't mind the help. You can reach me at this number . . .*

What a look she'd gotten from her seatmate. Who had asked to be moved to another part of the plane. Stuffy cow. No matter, Sharon made herself at home on both seats and tried to sleep.

It hadn't worked. She kept seeing the Henge turned into moon-scape. The things that had lived there, that had given the place its—well—magic, were gone. Were they dead? *Could* they die? She was very vague about Otherside life, if that's what it was. Energy, perhaps?

She could use some for herself. The summit of El Castillo seemed miles above her.

But she was used to swift air travel; her body had to be reacting to something other than a different time zone and latitude. She clung tight to a step, drew a deeper breath than normal, and went still, her eyes half shut.

It only took a moment to see, then several more to even begin to take in the magnitude of it.

Though the heavy air pressing close upon her was statue-still, on another plane, in that place where she could see auras, high winds were ripping about the pyramid in a hurricane turmoil the same as before but on a vastly larger scale. Enormous shapes rode the currents, spinning so quickly she could only see their trailing shadows. Her imagination supplied images to fill in the blanks, an inhuman eye here, a gaping mouth there, like a moving Rorschach test constantly turning itself inside out.

Dear God, what was going *on* here?

It was growing in power, too. Energies from the other monuments in the area were being drawn in, stripped violently away from their accustomed place in the universe.

If there was a source for the disturbance it was at the top of El Castillo. She thought she saw a more stable, slower patch of shadow there, but when she blinked it went away. Rivers? Had to be. He would have climbed the pyramid from the northeastern side, the only one with the twin serpent heads flanking the stairs. After all, hadn't he been talking to one of them earlier?

Right. So . . . what were her options?

Ordinary world: Take herself down from here as quickly as possible, get hold of someone in authority and see about pulling Rivers into custody for trespassing after hours, then fix him in place with the international warrants for his arrest. She liked the option of putting some distance between them. It made the bit about possibly being arrested herself seem rather attractive.

Otherside world: She could complete her trip to the top and see what the devil he was up to and this time stop him. Oh, yes, bags of fun trying that, but after the devastation at Stonehenge she couldn't let him get away with it again. She had no doubts he intended to commit the same ravaging here. Her instincts told her he was only just getting warmed up for . . . whatever it was he did, and *that* would be something very bad indeed. What next? The Vatican? The Wailing Wall? Ayers Rock? No, that couldn't be allowed.

One thing in her favor—she hoped—was that flesh-suit he wore. Obviously he needed it to function on this plane, and a body was a body was a body. Vulnerable to damage . . . and death.

Of course the locals here were almost as paranoid about fire-arms as the place she'd come from. She never transported a gun on flights anymore, too much trouble and forms and delays and notice. When needed, it was better to buy one upon arrival, whatever the legality or lack thereof, which she promptly did. Sharon had a wide experience dealing with all sorts of people on both sides of the law and in between, and she knew how to ask the right questions in four different languages. Within hours of reaching Cancún she had a Glock comfortably weighing down the cargo pocket on her right hip, along with spare magazines of ammunition. For good measure she also purchased a third- or fourth-hand machete and scabbard, well used, but with a sharp edge and decent weight. It even fit into her backpack without showing. The shady gentleman she'd bought it from had overcharged her outrageously, but he'd not asked questions, so she chalked it up to being part of the service. God, but it was good to deal with professionals on her own level. Almost homey.

Rivers, she had to be honest about it, was very much beyond her in a number of areas, though she still had surprise on her side. Maybe.

When he was busy . . . feeding . . . she'd have her opportunity.

First-degree murder the Yanks called it, though she didn't see it that way. The chance had fallen to her to deal with this threat, and she wasn't the sort to flinch. It was like those times when Gram went into a "what if" mood. What if you had the chance to shoot Hitler or Stalin before they really hit their stride. Would you do it?

Not of that generation, Sharon was unsure about either of them because of historical impact factors, but she had no hesitation over this particular target.

It was *that* important.

Enough rest, get going.

Seventy-three, seventy four . . .

And on and on. Passage was marginally easier now, as though opening her other senses allowed in a fresh breeze. Maybe in a very small way she was also feeding on the power here. The way it's supposed to be done, in small polite sips, not a gluttonous frenzy.

Eighty . . .

Near-invisible things screamed around her. Whatever was out there was in a panic. She couldn't blame it. Them.

God, I'm really not prepared for this kind of emergency; just thought you should know in case this doesn't turn out well.

Then pace it, one step at a time. Literally. Don't look down.

Eighty-four, eighty-five . . . take it slow. He could have armed himself, too.

She moved quietly. Just because the row had deafened her, didn't mean Rivers was similarly restricted. She lowered the volume on her perceptions. The noise was really quite over the top. Distracting.

Speaking of the top . . . ninety, ninety-*one*. Wonderful. She'd made it. Give the girl a coconut. She eased onto the flat walkway, adjusting to the change and watching her feet, for the ledge was too narrow for her own comfort. The nine large inwardly diminishing steps that made up the general shape of the pyramid had to do with the regions of death in the Mayan universe. Sharon worked very hard at not wondering what the topmost one symbolized, suspecting it was nothing she needed to dwell upon just now. Instead, she wiped sweat from her brow with her boonie hat, then stuffed it out of the way in a pocket. She drained off the water bottle and wished for another from her backpack, but that was where she'd left it in the trees. At the time it seemed best not to carry its extra weight for the climb.

Creeping over, she put her back against the huge structure that rested on top. She couldn't remember what the guidebooks called it, and you got no sense of the size from mere pictures. The walls rose up perhaps another three stories. On this side a single wide door in the center yawned, and at night the effect was a little too ominous. It would be the worst rotten luck if Rivers was inside and saw her silhouetted against the sky. Since he was more likely to be lurking on the north-northeast face to her left, she edged to the right, intending to take the scenic way.

Sharon pulled the Glock out, tucked the spare magazines under her belt so they'd be handy, and quietly made sure a round was ready in the chamber.

She put the first corner behind her, standing where the south-southwest face of the pyramid overlooked forest. The tallest trees remained respectfully dwarfed in its presence. The steps leading down to them were in a shocking state, not repaired like the other three sides. One whole section had no steps at all, but a smoothed-over surface like a great slide. Dangerous. It reminded her of a stage set for a play. So long as the bits facing the audience—or in this case tourists—looked good that's what mattered.

Another centrally placed door to the inner mysteries was on this side. She slipped past it, her heart in her mouth for a bare second. Damn, the weight and solidity of the Glock in her hand should have been more reassuring.

She paused before taking the next corner in her circuit, listening. Nothing on this side. No birds called from the trees below. They must have known something was up and sensibly bolted. Good for them.

Could use with a set of wings myself. Preferably the rotating kind. Attached to a fully armed Blackhawk helicopter with night-vision goggles and a load of those other lovely, expensive-but-totally-worth-it tech toys and an experienced flight crew to aid and abet her quest. She'd stand for all the beers afterward.

From this vantage Sharon could see across the esplanade to the One Thousand Columns. The pale stones glowed faint in the star-light, a silent army marching in a T-shape toward Highway 180. The columns had supported a roof once upon a time that might have shaded a huge marketplace. Impressive, certainly bigger than the average shopping mall. Maybe it *had* been a mall or a temple or housing. If she knew which, it might put off the nasty feeling that she was looking at gravestones. Clever people, the builders, but really too fixated on that death business for her taste. It was catching.

Smoke—rather, something like smoke—rose from each of those thousand columns, from the ground they rested on, from the buildings next to them. It hurried toward Kukulcan's pyramid, joining with the new-formed Otherside storm that circled its base. Within its shadows and in the air she saw the predator monstrosities again. They were different from their English cousins, but no less dangerous. Again she sensed a barrier holding them back, preventing them from entering her own prosaic world, but now she thought that protection might be getting weaker.

Things were changing. Rivers was making them change. For the worse. She knew it in her bones.

Another wide door, a breath of hot, humid air from the interior, then farther along the outside wall. She drew a mirror from a pocket and used it to get a view of what was around the final corner.

The small image jumped in her unsteady hand, showing a flare of sickly light, then settling. He was there, planted solidly in the center of the platform walk at the top of the steps, looking out over the esplanade. The opening to the temple behind him was much wider here, the span supported by two fat columns, giving the initial impression of three doorways. Sharon thought she could ease close along the wall then use the nearest one as cover. She could hit him at this distance, but wanted to be sure. Point-blank range would make the kill certain. She thought she would only get the one chance.

Shoving the mirror back in a pocket, she put her head around; with any luck she'd be on his blind side. She couldn't remember which eye was covered by the patch. Odd, that.

His attention was outward, his arms up and wide as before. He wasn't taking anything in just yet, only working on the . . . well, it must be a *summoning*. It was one hell of a show. Literally. The wild, spinning dance below began to rise like a pool slowly filling with water. Within this one's depths were curious gaudy colors, shreds of light, and bloodred darkness. Lots of that. The memory of those killed in violent sacrifice seemed to take form as thousands of small shadows merged together into a roiling mass.

Noise. That hideous howling began to build as before. Rivers seemed aware of it and might not hear the scrape of her combat boots on the stone.

Now or never. She inched forward, got within reach of the nearest pillar . . .

And hands like iron grabbed, lifted, and threw her hard against the wall. She managed to hold on to the Glock, but the surprise took the breath right out of her and forestalled the pain.

He had help . . . ? She hastily turned, raising the gun to this second threat.

But the man she faced was Rivers himself . . . but he'd been standing over there—

Gone. No others were on the platform.

Just himself, then. Moving preternaturally fast. Oh, lord.

Rivers broke into a big friendly grin. "Hey! Sharon? It's Sharon Geary, right? You dated Dickie-boy for awhile. You don't mind that I checked you out, I hope? In my line it's a good thing to keep tabs on certain people. I've *so* been looking forward to meeting *you*, sweet cheeks."

She didn't think, only pulled the trigger. He was five feet away, and the bullets hit him square in the upper center of his chest just the way she'd trained. She emptied the magazine.

He rocked back, hands clutching, and staggered dramatically. "Oh! Ouch! Ow! Oh! You got me! Ow-ow-ow! Bang, bang, I'm dead!"

There's no blood, she thought, staring at his insane miming.

He straightened. "Aw, gee, did the bad man sell you blanks when you bought the piece?"

No blanks. There were holes in the shirt—just not the flesh beneath it.

Rivers kept grinning. "Come *on*, Sherrie-pie! Did you think it'd be *that* easy to take me out? I been watching you since Salisbury." He gave her no time to reload. In an eye-blink he was behind her, arm fast around her neck, his free hand pressing her head painfully to the side. "Chill out, little mama, or I'll play exorcist with you. One twist and you'll be able to see where you've been walking from."

She froze against the pressure. Another ounce of force at this angle and it'd be game over, forever. She fought to breathe.

"You know something?" he gently husked into her ear, intimate as a lover. "I *really* liked this shirt, and now you done ruined it. What say you drop the toy? 'Cause if you put holes in my pants I might get cranky."

He shifted his balance. A tiny movement, but it made an opening. She dug an elbow into his gut, rammed a heel into one of his shins, slamming it down hard on his instep.

That made him grunt. Right, he wasn't totally invulnerable. Physical assault could damage him even if bullets didn't, figure out why later. With the slack gained she cracked the empty gun against his knuckles. Though famous for its polymer frame and grip, there was plenty of steel in the weapon to hurt him. He jerked, giving her more freedom of movement, which she used to break his hold.

No time to pause and assess, she spun and crashed her heavy boot into one of his knees, full force, intending to blow it out. He yelped and retreated, but the shock didn't last long. A step, then two, and he was nimbly dodging and dancing like a boxer.

The bastard's playing with me. Whatever hurt she did, he was either faking injury or healing incredibly fast.

He smirked. "Come *on*, baby doll. Let's work up a sweat. I heard you chicks *liked* foreplay."

Trying to make me mad. Which wasn't going to happen. She had the idea anger was exactly the sort of thing that would help him here. She looked around for alternative weapons.

Rivers paused as though reading her mind. "What's next? Handcuffs? No bedposts here, sorry. Maybe a club? Nah, who would join? What about some holy water? You can't beat a classic."

Trying to distract me. From what?

From *that*. Her Sight picked up on the sickly radiation glow that outlined his body, which was otherwise dark. It was much dimmer than she recalled. He was using it up . . . yet replenishing. She glimpsed a spider-thin thread of light leading into one of his hands from the growing storm around them. If she could *cut* that line . . .

Whether her machete was made from cold steel or not, she rather thought in this case the symbolic intent would be as important as a sharp edge. She pulled the weapon from her leg scabbard, swapping it with the Glock.

Rivers struck a defensive pose, but held to a smart-ass face. "Oh, you are *really* getting to me now, warrior princess. I tell ya, I could so *do* that babe. Hope you're not jealous if I fantasize a bit while we—"

He ducked when she made her first slicing attack. Wary about his uncanny speed, she kept her back to the wall to deny him the option of gettting behind her. That was when she noticed the bizarre gleam on her own form. It ran along her limbs and right out to the knife blade. What did it mean? That she had power, too? God, but it was bright. Silvery compared to his corpse-light green.

"Oooh, sweet. How'd you do that, cutie, take a few lessons from Spielberg? Or maybe your last boyfriend's special lady gave you some pointers about converting latent energies?"

What was he on about? Richard?

"Of course you know you weren't the only woman in his life. Or did you believe him about all that 'I love you' crap?"

What? How'd he know that? No, Rivers was guessing. Still trying to rattle her. Shotgunning taunts, hoping to find a weak spot. *None today, thank you.*

"I tell ya, he's batted those baby blues at *thousands* of chicks just like you and fed them the line and, hoo-boy, did they *swallow* it. Know what I mean?"

She laughed. A sound of pure delight in her ears mixed with contempt for him, and not the reaction he expected.

Though he kept hammering. "There's only been one babe for him, though. He ever take you to meet her, get her approval? They got this open relationship thing going, though I don't know what they see in each other. Hey! Easy there! Mind the *cojones*, I'm gonna want 'em later—so will you, I think."

Her feint to his crotch had surprised him. Couldn't blame him for that, but he'd retreated out of range, and she couldn't complete the follow-through upswing toward his hand.

Oh, hell. She *had* let him distract her. Belatedly, it occurred to her that she need not cut the thread close to his body. Any point where it trailed toward him from the chaos should do just fine. Well, then . . .

Another feint toward his head, then she side-stepped and slashed strongly downward. Was there resistance to her blade or had she imagined it? No matter, it worked. Rivers roared pain and this time wasn't play-acting his stagger. He fell against the side of the building, going down on one knee with a grunt. The glow about him faded radically.

"Jeeze, woman, you *nuts*? You got no idea what—aw, shit." He looked past her, eyes wide.

Not about to fall for that one, she backed off a few yards, then spared a glance in that direction.

Holy Mary and all the saints, I SAID *I wasn't ready for this.*

The mad flow of Otherside shadow had risen nearly level with them. Seeming to swim in the strange storm was something . . . big. Really big. Its head was the same size as the stone snake heads at the base of the stairs. In fact, it looked quite a lot *like* those heads. But alive. The huge eyes were jet black and glinting and aware and directed at her. A vastly long body undulated in the stream, the length of its spine topped with a diamond-shaped pattern in bright jewel-colored scales. Each scale was larger than her open hand.

"Now you gone and done it," said Rivers wearily. "You shouldn't of chopped my control. Kukulcan is one god you *don't* wanna piss off."

The serpent—"snake" just didn't cover it—swung its attention toward Rivers. Its jaws opened, showing impossibly long fangs, and it rose high, apparently to strike and swallow him.

"Oh, no you don't." Rivers raised one hand, then the other. "No hissy fits from you, wormy. You hump back to your little hole in the wherever. Misbehave and I will *so* burn your ass."

Sharon gaped, every hair of her body on end as the thing kept rising from the chaos. She shrank toward the temple doorway, thinking to hide in the shadows there.

Daft idea, this is its HOME.

With all that size would it be able to squeeze inside?

It's a god, why not?

But for the moment it was interested in Rivers, who seemed able to hold it at bay. It swayed around him as he faced it, countering each of its moves with a smaller one of his own. Must have been work for him, too. Sweat poured off his face, which was pinched and pale with concentration. She used the breather to drop the machete and reload the Glock, which took twice as long because her hands shook so much. There, a fresh magazine and a round in the chamber. Certainly useless against the serpent, probably useless against Rivers, but it made her feel better all the same. She picked up the big knife again and thought about throwing it at him, but she'd never been much good at that parlor trick.

Perhaps while he was involved with company . . . she could try a head shot. He might not shrug it off so easily.

Brace, balance, two-handed grip, and *squeeze*, don't jerk the trigger, double-tap, double-tap again.

What the hell . . . ? The ejected casings arced clear, tumbling . . . *slowly*.

She saw the *bullets* individually tearing from the muzzle, bright as tracer fire.

So did Rivers. He threw a glance her way, gave a short chuckle, and simply moved clear of their spinning path. They continued out into the night sky, vanishing in the distance.

The serpent made a try for him then. It was amazing anything that huge could move so fast, but he was faster, and as the head overshot him, he slapped it, his bare hand cutting the scales like a hot razor, making a long deep wound that bled . . . light? The glow around it dimmed; Rivers was absorbing power from its streaming blood. The creature made no sound as it convulsed clear, but Sharon recognized pain.

And rage. It arched high, and a thickening of the skin behind its head suddenly flared into a great feathered crest of many colors almost too brilliant to look at. Light came from the thing like a beacon in fog. Sharon felt its heat.

"Come on, who's the big Chee-ken in Eetza?" Rivers called, laughing. He'd resumed his connection to the energies, but instead of a thread, it was a thick rope as big around as one of his own arms, leading right into his back. The serpent's *white* blood dripped from his hand and down. He flexed his fingers.

His crooked arm was straight again.

Rivers stared at the healing. "Whoa, buddy! Didn't know you could do that. Thanks a mil for the favor! Guess I was taking the long way around." He tore off his eye patch and swiped his hand over the damage there. "Oh, yeah, talk to me, baby! Go for the money! That's it. That's *it*. That's so IT!"

Not only was his ruined eye restored by the blood, but the gray fled from his hair and beard, turning them black again. Some of the weathering melted from his face. He drew the length of his arm across his mouth, tasting the blood. His body flinched and shuddered as if in orgasm, and he threw his head back. His laughter boomed across the esplanade.

"Wormy, *you* are my new best friend!" he yelled up at the god.

Who wanted no part of it. The huge being shifted swiftly around and lashed its tail at Rivers like a whip. Sharon ducked and rolled as the wall of scaled flesh slammed against the pyramid, shaking it. Otherside stones shattered to dust, pelting her. She missed what happened next, but when the thing moved off it showed fresh wounds, while Rivers was still on his feet, making a banshee-like scream of triumph.

Where gods and angels fear to tread, then send in the Irish, she thought, shifting the machete to her right hand again.

Rivers, busy gloating and feeding, didn't see her. He felt her attack, though, if his shriek was anything to judge by. She cut through the cord leading into his spine, then made a swift back-handed slice at his kidneys, connecting. The blade bit deep into his side and was almost pulled from her grip when he whirled on her.

Her turn to grin at *his* bafflement.

Which was only temporary. He fell away, yanking clear of the knife. Once the steel left his body he regained his shark's smile. He put the back of one hand to his mouth and licked at the glowing blood until another spasm of shuddering tore through him. His eyes took on that same glow, but not in a wholesome way. The wound she'd caused knitted up.

"Whoa. The blood of a god. Now *that's* a rush! You oughta try it sometime, chickie-girl."

Extending one arm sideways a tendril from the chaos leaped to his hand, merging with flesh. The power poured into him and bolstered him up. His outline was almost too bright to look at, but the bulk of his body remained stubbornly in shadow.

He clapped loud, rubbing the palms together. "Okay, honey, sorry to keep you waiting, business, y'know, but now I'm all yours. What say we skip the dinner and a movie part and get right to the screwing over?"

She'd tried to take advantage of the machete's design, using it as a chopping rather than a thrust weapon, but her fencing training was with epée, not saber. *Well, too bad and do the best you can.* For an effective hit, she had to get in close. Perhaps if she cut his hand off along with the cord . . .

And then he was behind her again, moving too fast to track. How the devil—

Something hard banged against the side of her skull, there was a hot stabbing in her lower back then shoulders, and her legs abruptly stopped working. She hit the stone surface like a bag of sand. When her mind cleared she could hardly stand the barrage to her senses. They were wide open, no barriers to shield and filter; the assault of noise and sight and touch and smell from the Otherside were drowning her. Everything was too sharp, too loud, too much, and ongoing. She shouted, trying to negate at least the sound with her own feeble voice.

It was a relief when Rivers framed her face in his two hands and smiled lovingly down at her. His chill touch seemed to blunt the worst of it. Or absorbed.

"Oh, baby, I just *knew* you'd be a screamer not a moaner."

She tried to raise a weapon, either of them, but couldn't feel her arms. All her strength and the adrenaline that had been pounding through her system to feed it were gone. He lifted her up—had to *hold* her up—his arms strong around her as he took a step toward the edge of the platform. She couldn't fight him, her legs dragged loose. It wasn't paralysis, that implied being frozen in place, this was absolute bonelessness.

Her head drooped to her chest, lolling. He grabbed her hair and pulled so she could look at him. "Sweetheart, this has been fun, but the plain truth is when it comes to mayhem, I've just had a lot more practice at it than you."

Looking into his cheerfully mad eyes, she could believe it. He turned her so she could see out. Her Sight showed her the ordinary esplanade and the Otherside version at once.

He whispered in her ear again, as though sharing a secret. "You are so privileged. Do you know that? What you're getting now is what the old priests used to see, layers on layers. They kept adding to it the same way their builders stacked a new building on top of an old one. With every heart they cut out, with every drop of blood that flowed down these stones, they added to the darkness—all with the very *best* of intentions, of course."

Where was the serpent god? Had it left, or had he fed on it as well? She thought she saw a green and blue shimmer under the faux-water of the encircling storm. Its level was lower than before. How can one man burn up so much power? Where was it going?

"They'd get their best and brightest—which is a good way to prevent some upstart from taking your job—fatten 'em up and promise 'em paradise, then—wham-bam—cut out their plucky little hearts while they were still beating. Ah, the good old days!"

Something warm against her cheek. He let her see it: the flat blade of the machete, wet with his blood.

"So . . . what do you think about staging a revival? Glory hallelujah! Gimme some of that ol' time religion!"

She found she could still speak even when the blade kissed her throat. "Bite me," she grated.

"Yup, you're *my* kind of woman. Maybe a couple years ago I'd have taken you up on that, but I got bigger things going." He walked her closer toward the center.

The steep steps were just in front of her. If he let her go she'd—
Don't look at them, then.

"But there's no need to cover old ground. I just get such a *kick* teasing people, one of my better qualities. A little terror energy is okay, and Death Magic has its uses, but you're not the most cooperative bitch I've ever been with. I don't think you'd digest too well on either count."

She looked beyond the stairs, trying to see past the creatures writhing in the storm. There was the serpent, worse for wear, drifting down, heading away from them—or rather toward something else of interest. There were soft but very intense lights at the edge of the esplanade. They had form, were vertical, like the Thousand Columns . . . only these were slowly moving toward El Castillo.

He spun the machete one-handed like a juggler. "Don't get me wrong, this has been a trip, but I'm gonna have to leave, and I don't think wormy would like that. It's been ages since anyone bothered to wake him up, and sweetie, *you* did that. You shouldn't have severed my lines; it messed up my shields, threw things into red alert, and sent him slithering out to see who was messing around on his turf. I worked very, very hard to get myself to this point, and I'm not going to waste all that I've gained fighting my way out through the local guardian. I'm gonna need some help from you, like it or not."

One of those distant lights . . . figures . . . walked closer. It was a man, apparently unintimidated by the gigantic serpent coming toward him, much less the other strange beings that swarmed above him. Fewer of them now, and the wind was dying. Soon it would be the Henge all over again, but with dust and rubble and silence spread for miles.

Rivers went on. "You're not still a virgin are you? Nah, no way. Not with Dickie-boy Dun for your boyfriend. He does love the ladies. Virginity might have been an added plus here for an offering. On the other hand, I heard it has more to do with purity of heart than whether or not you dropped your cherry."

The man below was almost to the foot of the pyramid steps. He was big, with a short-cropped brush of blond hair. Hope leapt in her. She *knew* him, would know his face and form anywhere, even through Otherside veils. She took breath to call down and only at the last instant stopped herself. Rivers hadn't noticed him yet.

"But, sweetie pie, no one's fed old Kukie in so long he'll probably like just about anything. I think you'll taste pretty good regardless."

Other individuals coalesced out of the column-shapes, more and more; they shimmered ghostlike against the darkness. She didn't know them, but her heart told her they were here to help in some way. But they only stared up without any obvious reaction to her situation or to each other. Rivers *had* to see them now; there were so many down there.

She shouted at the foremost figure, who was facing the serpent. "Richard!"

Rivers jerked in reaction, turning her. "What was that? Wishful thinking or do you see something?" He looked out. There must have been hundreds standing below. His gaze passed right over them. "What is it you *see?*"

"'Birnam wood do come to Dunsinane,'" she muttered, chuckling. The quote was not quite accurate to the circumstances, but close enough to shake him. Feeling was returning to her limbs. She knew the symptoms; he'd struck specific pressure points to certain nerve clusters. Nothing permanent. Given time she'd get that knife from him and ram it sideways down his throat.

Given time.

Rivers held his hand out and a last howling sliver of the wind raised high, tugging at them. Stinging sand was in it, debris torn from the other monuments . . .

Which were *gone* now on Otherside. Oh, bloody hell.

"Richard!"

But it was Kukulcan who responded, seeming to leap, riding the wind as it gathered itself for a rush up the sides of the pyramid.

"Oh, no ya don't," said Rivers.

She almost had control over herself again, and if she could break free, she could hinder him.

Only Rivers didn't seem to know that. As though anticipating her move he swept her lightly up like a bridegroom ready to cross the threshold. She clawed at his face.

He pulled back and hit a nerve on her neck. She went slack, arms dangling. "Uh-uh. Not again. Been there, done that. You're a great date, Sherrie-pie. I'll call ya next week, okay?"

She tried to dredge up more fight, but he'd stolen her strength.

There was no way Richard could reach her in time to help. Why hadn't he moved? What was wrong with him? With any of them?

Then it was all up. With unnatural strength Rivers lifted her over his head. She got a ghastly view of the stairs swinging unsteadily below with the serpent god charging up their length, feathered crest flared with rage, mouth open.

Oh, God, no, not now, it's not my time—

Rivers hurled her strongly toward it.

The stairs rushed at her...

Until the wind caught and swept her high into Otherside madness. She glimpsed the serpent god suddenly looming, diving toward her. Sharon screamed to Richard as she plunged into a glittering well of green, blue, gold, and red, but all she heard in return was Rivers.

"Hasta la Winnebago, baby!"

Chapter Two

Toronto, Winter, the Present

"You're different, all right, I just haven't figured out what it is yet," said Mercedes White.

Richard Dun smiled, projecting interest and no small measure of charm across the candlelit dining table, all part of the foreplay begun two days ago in his office when they'd met in person for the first time. Their previous phone conversations had been business oriented, but pleasant and professional, a theme that continued during their face-to-face meetings. However, he had been fairly certain there was an extra dimension to Ms. White's warm cordiality that had nothing to do with their finalization of a sales contract. Since the deal was completed she had nothing to gain by continuing to flirt with him; besides, she did not strike him as being a woman who would stoop to such tactics to further her career.

Take it to the basics, old lad, he told himself. *She gave off the right vibe, you felt it, and she knows you felt it.*

The lady was a stunner with a hell of a brain, and had made a decisive opening move a few hours ago when she suggested dinner at her hotel. It was eye contact and the light touch of her hand on his that told him something more than mere food might be in the offing, so he readily accepted. He'd learned long ago that when a woman took notice, it was best to lie back and enjoy the ride.

In *every* way.

"What is it you do besides sell successful oil companies to larger firms?" she asked.

He was reasonably sure she wasn't all that keen to hear his autobiography. Even a short summary would take days. "Well, if I'm very fortunate I get to take an outstandingly beautiful woman to dinner."

The flash in her eyes told him he'd said the right thing and then some.

A sleek waitress in the hotel's corporate colors came for their order. Richard dealt with the ritual, asked for what he assumed would be the right wine for the meal, and refocused on Mercedes.

Who was curious. "No dinner for you?"

He gave a deprecating smile. "I'm cursed or blessed with an odd metabolism. Sometimes I don't eat for days." *Or even centuries.*

"That is odd. What do you call it?"

"An easily ignored distraction." Eye contact, a smile. But there was no need to press the point, she got that a subject change would not be out of place. "You've not had much chance to see Toronto, have you?"

"I learned how to correctly pronounce Yonge Street and Spadina Avenue and did some shopping in Eaton Centre, but no real tourist stuff."

"Not even the CN Tower?"

She made a mock shudder. "Just looking at it makes me dizzy. I prefer my heights to be less in your face. Have you been up?"

"Oh, yes. It's a fantastic view, especially when you stand on the glass floor and look straight down. Puts you in perspective about the builders."

"They have my respectful admiration. From afar. At ground level."

"Will you have time for other things besides shop? There's a lot to do around here."

"I've a morning flight out."

"That's too bad."

"It need not be." Eye contact, a smile, and her hand touching his across the table. "There's lots to do even when one sees only the hotel."

Indeed. *No* mistaking that message.

If later asked about their conversation, Richard would not recall a single word; his focus was on her dark eyes and dusky skin and how they hypnotically contrasted with her short silver-white hair. It was too light to be natural, of course, but he liked the effect and wondered if she bleached it as a not-so-subtle mnemonic to coincide with her last name. Perhaps if things continued well he would discover just how far she carried out the peroxide treatment.

Mercedes was from Texas, one of the CEOs of an oil company to which he'd just completed the process of selling his own comparatively small operation, Ahryn-Hill. The actual contracts and details had been hammered out by their respective lawyers; she was here to finalize the signatures. Richard put his current name on an inordinately high stack of papers (in triplicate) which were then swept away by yet another lawyer for God knows what purpose. He had the vague idea the accountants would have a turn with them. Fine. Richard's last business ties to Texas were severed, his former employees retaining their jobs without the threat of being sacked by the new management, and the shockingly high profit he'd made would go into other investments and a generous trust fund for his godson.

With all that out of the way, he and the lovely Ms. White were able to shed their executive roles and resume being consenting adults with free time on their hands.

Out of necessity, since he wasn't dining, Richard carried a bit more of the conversation load, allowing Mercedes to eat in peace. He kept things as light, neutral, and amusing as possible. She seemed unconcerned over telling him all about herself, which was refreshing. Most Americans couldn't wait to share things with strangers they'd never divulge to their therapists. He had only the general knowledge that she was divorced and sufficiently recovered from the trauma as to have no need to recite a litany of her ex's faults.

Of course, he did have the passing thought that she might be more than she seemed. In his long and checkered past he'd come under official scrutiny from a number of governments and private interests, some of which were not above using attractive women to ferret out information. Mercedes wasn't the type, though, for even the best, most careful of operatives will give away their training sooner or later. The lady was exactly as represented; single, available, and looking for recreation.

She turned down dessert, preferring to linger over her second glass of wine. "I think I've figured it out," she said.

"A plan for world peace?"

"You. Your difference from other people. Other men, I mean."

He spread his hands slightly. "Please tell."

"It's many things. For one, you have patience."

"That makes me different?"

"Yes. It's a very rare quality in these circumstances. There have been times when I've shown a man this level of attention and he takes it as a done deal and can't wait to stampede into bed. That's told me he's less interested in me than he is in having sex, and I just happen to be the means to provide it. Confidence is one thing, but assumption is quite another. You have the confidence, but seem perfectly willing to continue letting me seduce you at my own pace. Which tells me you have regard and respect. I like that."

"I'm delighted." He was a touch nonplussed as well. He'd been a happy participant in the countless variations of the games of seduction for a very, very long time, and there were always surprises to be had. Mercedes was certainly one of them.

"I am too. My being frank hasn't put you off."

"It's refreshing."

"And a two-way street. I only ever want to be with a man who's . . . enthusiastic . . . about *me*. Anything less . . . well, a girl can just tell."

"Ms. White, you have my undivided attention. And if it pleases you, you will continue to have it for as long as you wish."

"You won't mind if I test that out?"

"Not at all."

A slow smile from her, very white teeth against her naturally dark skin, lovely lips. "Well, then."

An elevator ride, a sedate walk down a carpeted hallway, she was very collected until she swiped the electronic key to her room the wrong way. A cool and calm woman, but deliciously stirred up inside. She reversed the plastic card without fuss, the little light on the lock flashed green—rather symbolic, that—and they were inside. The room was dark, the curtains wide, showing a slice of Toronto from ten stories up and gray night sky. The distant streetlights gilded everything in a warm yellow sheen. His eyes adjusted to the dimness so it was like day to him, but Mercedes navigated more slowly, not bothering with the room lights. Out of long habit he listened for surrounding sounds that might indicate what other hotel guests were doing in their respective accommodations, but all was silent. Apparently they had this part of the floor to themselves for the present.

"Shall I order up champagne?" she asked, slipping off her heels.

"Only if you want some." In the insulated hush of the room his sensitive hearing also picked up the low thundering of her heart, the quickening of her breath.

"What I want, Mr. Dun . . ." She faced him, getting between him and the view. The faint radiance from the window touched her white hair, frosting it even more, yet her skin remained rebelliously dark. She barely came to his chin, how was it that she had such long legs? Her hands slid up his chest to loosen his tie. She did so smoothly and even got the top button of his shirt freed without choking him.

"Yes . . . ?"

"I want you to help me break the damn bed."

Well, put like that—

He obligingly swept her up.

Their initial encounter did not damage hotel property, though it wasn't for lack of trying. To compensate, they made quite a mess flinging their clothes about. Once committed, Mercedes held back nothing. She seemed to have an excess of energy to burn, but not to the point of foolishness. When the time came she produced that which was needed for their mutual protection in these sad modern times, but it was not such as to detract from the build of a roaring momentum. Richard chose not to mar the moment with explanations about his various immunities and joyfully got on with things.

Mercedes acted and reacted to his touch in a most gratifying manner. He responded to her in kind, one thing leading to another in the ancient dance that brings male and female to merge and be whole for a few precious moments.

It was then that he caused Mercedes to discover what else there was that made him different from other men. Her resulting cries might well have disturbed their neighbors had any been around to hear. In the dimness she'd not seen the change coming over him, but as she breathlessly exhorted him to press harder, as the throes of her climax began to engulf her, that's when he buried his unnaturally long corner teeth into the hot velvet of her throat. He broke fragile skin, swiftly, efficiently, and drew strongly on her heat, her life, actually *tasting* her ecstasy as it flowed through her and into him.

God, but it was incredible, triggering his own explosion.

Her response—a mirror to his—was . . . dynamic. Her body arched violently under him with a sudden strength nearly a match to his own, her hands holding him in place as he rode her, her voice gone rough as tearing silk, first urging him on, then failing, then rising to a suppressed shriek, until she lost all control.

He kept his. Barely. It was more than enough on every level and for every sense, but he was careful. Too much of a good thing and he could hurt her. That would *not* happen. But he took himself to the dangerous edge, for she seemed to demand it; he was more than willing to provide. She'd all but ordered him to split her in two. It had been a long time since he'd been with this exigent and vigorous a partner.

Richard held fast to her, prolonging their climax, and, after considerable lingering in that exultance, gradually bringing them down. With some women, if he ceased feeding without that adjustment period, they could go into a kind of light shock. Nothing injurious or lethal, but alarming. And preventable. Besides, it was another aspect of their shared pleasure, a way of drawing it out for that much longer. There are other means to descend from a mountain peak than taking a headfirst fall. He knew he'd gotten it right when she slipped into a light doze. The long sigh of her breath and slower heartbeat told him all was well.

He lay back in the tangle of pillows and sheets, weary and invigorated and thoroughly sated at the same time, and counted his blessings. His goddess had ever been generous, particularly in providing him partners.

Some of Richard's past liaisons were disastrous, some desperately euphoric. He had played the games of each new generation, seduced, was himself seduced, with any number of variations in between. At times, turn-upon-turn, it could be glorious or appalling, frustrating or extraordinary, too ridiculous to bear, too beautiful to endure, but for the most part, wholly wonderful. He had literally bedded thousands of women over his long life, going through the forms of love, more often than not falling in love, again and again, for good or ill, year upon year, *centuries* of it.

And for all that . . . it just *never* got old.

He lay half curled around her, savoring her warmth, not quite asleep, when she wakened and slipped from the big bed. He felt the firm touch of her lips on his naked shoulder, an affectionate signature perhaps, before she padded off to the bath. That was nice. Women were so very, very lovely.

She wasn't long, not to his reckoning, but then his time perception was also frequently different from normal humans. After fifteen hundred years of walking the night, it'd be strange if it wasn't.

He used the pause to gather his clothes, draping them more or less over a chair, and troubled to pick up her no-doubt designer dress and do likewise. For safety's sake he located her discarded heels, kicking them well out of the way. Tripping on those lethal things was just too ignominious. Not that her own bare heels weren't deadly enough. His calves were quite bruised from where she'd dug in with them.

By the time he'd sorted the sheets into a semblance of civilized order she emerged warm, clean, patted dry, and powdered smooth from her shower. Without a word, only smiling, she came over and pushed him back onto the bed. Chuckling, he let himself sprawl crossways on the wide mattress, and she climbed on top of him, the heat from her skin radiating onto his own.

Her scent was delightfully and unexpectedly that of baby powder.

"Isn't it my turn to shower?" he asked as she hovered over him, looking intently into his face.

Mercedes bent low, lips against his neck, nuzzling sweetly with her tongue. "After," she said when she worked up to his ear.

"But—"

"After. You smell like a man. I want that."

"Absolutely, whatever you—ah—" Damn, that tickled. The insatiable houri had turned into a playful imp. Laughing, they wrestled a bit until the tempo changed and kissing began in earnest. His lips brushed the wounds on her throat once more. The nerve endings there were still sensitive, and she gave a strong involuntary tremor from his touch, almost a climax in itself that left her panting.

"What—what *is* that you do?" she wanted to know. Her dark eyes were sharp, very aware. He knew the love play would go no further until she got a reasonable explanation. Or an unreasonable one.

He gave a deprecating shrug. "I'm a vampire, that's all."

What a look on her face. First the disbelief, a short laugh for being teased, then the dawning of comprehension that he might, just *might* be speaking the truth.

"But don't worry about it." There was enough light from the window for her to see him clearly. He fixed his gaze on her until her eyes dulled. "You'll forget that part. Forget it completely and only remember the rest. In the morning you'll ignore what you see here . . ." He touched her throat, tracing his fingers lightly over the fresh wounds. She shuddered again in reaction, gasping. "Ignore them, and remember this."

He pulled her on top.

They were slower, more savoring now. Richard liked this almost stately rendering of the dance as much as the wild rutting version. He tasted every part of her, seeking out her distinctive differences from other women, tested and learned and experimented while she did the same. He carried her to a peak several times, hardly needing to drink, and when he did it was naught but a drop or two. More than enough for his own climaxes, certainly beyond enough for hers. It took hours.

When finally she slipped into true slumber, he was near-exhausted as well, but in a good way. A little nap and he'd be fine. Mercedes would likely sleep heavily on her flight home. She'd be vague about the mark on her throat, but very definite on the fact she'd been well and truly bedded.

God, but women were lovely, particularly the confident ones like Mercedes. No fretting about the future, just taking the moment and running with it. Forceful when needed, but still essentially and undeniably *feminine*.

There was nothing quite like it.

Encounters like this—being able to make love *and* feed—were rare for him, especially of late. Usually he had no time to spare for the hunt or opportunities just never occurred. It made him most appreciative when they did happen. It had been a long time since he last combined the two. These nights he usually he had to separate his fleshy pleasures from his feeding, taking nourishment on the fly from women hypnotized into complete unawareness of the act. Satisfying to his appetite, but emotionally sterile, which annoyed him.

Seeking alternatives against a dearth of prey or lack of time to hunt, he'd necessarily explored the alternative of storing human blood since the invention of refrigeration. The early decades of that type of technology had been uneven in terms of success. Lately, as in the last fifty years or so, he'd enjoyed a certain consistency acquiring and keeping expired stuff from local blood banks. Cold blood was never quite as good as that taken living from a vein, but it served, saving him time and the inevitable frustration from constant casual, and even wholly one-sided encounters.

Perhaps I need to un-busy my life.

He'd done that frequently in the past, shedding complications that stole time from other needs. Certainly this sale of one of his companies could be counted toward such an end. There was no reason why he couldn't strip away a few more. Money wasn't an issue, it was time.

Richard wanted more of it. Though himself ageless, he'd touched his own icy mortality on several occasions in the last few decades. That business with the Grail, in particular, had set things off. Since then he'd gotten the feeling that there might, just *might* be an ending to his life.

Not from age. The face in the mirror when he shaved was ever the same, for good or ill frozen at thirty-five. He recalled when that had been considered old. He'd been ready to die then. On the night of his first and worst defeat in battle, when he'd lost all, that's when Sabra of the Lake came to him and changed everything. She'd taken his blood and replaced it with hers. Passing on the dark gift of the Goddess she served changed his world, that, and her boundless love.

He'd been so *young* then. And innocent, compared to what he knew now, extraordinarily, dangerously innocent. Events and experience in a harsh world eventually had their way with him, destroying and eating bits of his soul, even as new layers formed under the scars to restore what was lost.

But when he was with Sabra that feeling of youth and innocence was born anew. Sabra, the one woman with whom he could utterly lose himself, his constant star to companion him through the centuries. Linked by ties of blood and passion she was his lover, mother, sister, and friend at once and forever.

Well . . . not forever.

She was mortal now. Fully human. Fragile.

Though still youthful looking she had but an insignificant span of time remaining. Unless her Goddess gave her another miracle Sabra would be taken from him in only sixty or seventy years, if that long. Not enough. Not fair.

They'd talked about it, but Richard had not really accepted what Sabra saw as inevitable.

As he lay in the dark he considered that the sale of this company might have been his subconscious at work, giving him a start on that which had to happen. There'd been additional reasons, of course, but the possibility was there.

Very well. He would see about ridding himself of further distractions. Life was too short to waste time. *Her* life. Her time.

There were others as well who needed his whole attention, other frail mortal souls he loved. His godson, Michael, his friend and Michael's adoptive father, Philip Bourland. From them, the circle widened outward to other families and friends. Yes, he wanted to be there with them for as long as they lived.

Mercedes shifted, turning, one arm slipping over him, a smile on her lips.

This too. He wanted more freedom for this kind of sweetness.

He wondered if they'd have time for breakfast before her flight, not that he'd eat, but her companionship was extremely pleasant. Then he wondered if he could simply take some days off to fly down with her. He hated planes, but she'd make the misery worth it. Perhaps he'd take a week, give himself a break from the winter snow. He'd cut his business ties in Texas, but still maintained the penthouse flat in that outrageous pyramid building in Addison. Mercedes would enjoy a visit to New Karnak. He'd see to it.

Richard drifted gently into sleep, exhausted, yet superbly satisfied in every sense, wrapped close around Mercedes, her warmth and scent soothing him. What a woman.

Not long after he became aware of leaving her and trudging in a strange Otherside landscape. Here the pyramids had stepped, not smooth sides, and their purpose was not to preserve life but to end it. The scent of blood was everywhere, soaked deep into each stone and the very earth under his feet. He sensed it came not from past battles, but violent sacrifice. The guardians and gods of this place were dark. Countless thousands had bled to feed them, making them strong. It was a terrific distraction, but something drew him toward a tall structure in the near distance. Though it was night and safe for him, there were lights playing at its top, bright as suns. He thought they must be important, that he should investigate.

Around him were the remnants of a black and blasted forest. The tree shapes were twisted, as though they'd died in agony from their burning, but he smelled no smoke or charring, only blood and baked stone. A sere wind dried his lungs; flying sand flayed his exposed skin. He shielded his eyes with one hand, trying to see through the dust. Ahead came a boom like ugly laughter, and in the sky he glimpsed hideous creatures thrashing about in frenzy. Darkness and lightning fought for supremacy of the sky.

What in hell's name was he *doing* here?

He became conscious of other presences close by, other . . . people? They were like columns of pale light, and there was a stillness about them, but more like the patience of waiting than inherent tranquility.

He could almost discern faces in their glow, and they seemed familiar. Who was that? Michael? Another looked like the boy's mother, Stephanie, who was dead now. That one over there . . . Bourland? Impossible. He was as pragmatic as they come. Why would he be on this Side of things? Standing next to Sabra no less. She was in her element in a place like this.

He looked to her for an answer, but she gave no sign of being conscious of him, only looked past him to something else.

Richard understood he was in a dream, so it was all right to walk unafraid here. Otherside matters were Sabra's domain, though. If he remembered this one upon waking, he'd certainly tell her about it.

Ahead of him, huge even at this distance, was the tall structure, a pyramid looming out of the obscurity of spinning dust. It had nine large steps to the summit and was topped by a kind of block-shaped building. All the uproar was centered there. He walked toward it, struggling against the wind, which dipped and eddied in powerful gusts. The other . . . people? . . . seemed to come with him en masse like an army, but they suddenly ceased to be of importance. He stopped at the sight of a gigantic snake that was half flowing, half floating down the central steps on this nearside of the pyramid. The thing's head was as large as the enormous stone ones flanking the stairs, with a body proportional to that impossibility.

"Oh, Lady, what have we to do here?" Richard muttered, trying to quash his justified alarm.

His Goddess deigned not to reply, and he wished very hard for a sword to materialize in his hand. To hell with that, he wanted a rocket launcher loaded with an explosive warhead. None appeared, dream or otherwise, and still the monster rolled toward him. Running would be futile. Its many-colored scales flashed like fiery gems in the uneven light; the storm had torn its proud feathered crest to tatters and apparently the thing was wounded. The damage was clear but the bright glare oozing from the savage gashes in its flesh was like no blood Richard had ever seen.

The hinged jaws opened wide, but no sound came forth, drowned by the vicious, howling storm. Arching up, it looked directly at Richard, then turned toward the pyramid.

Two figures were struggling at the top in front of the blocklike structure, a stocky man and a tall woman, her red hair flying in the wind like flames. There was a keen silvery glow about her, even as a concealing shadow seemed to envelop the man. The maddening gale echoed their fight.

The man got the upper hand and held the woman's limp body close to his own, but facing outward. He was speaking to her. She looked groggy—until her gaze fell on Richard and kindled with recognition.

He thought he heard her call him by name. The voice, her form, familiar, but how . . .

The snake turned back on itself, returning to the top of the structure, moving astonishingly fast for something that size.

Not fast enough.

The man raised the woman's body high overhead, then hurled her strongly away, but instead of striking the stone steps, she was caught by the storm and lifted. She fought feebly against it.

As did the snake. When it rushed up to her the hurricane wind seized that vast form as well. They spun in a ghastly dance. To Richard's horror, the thing wrapped itself around the woman in one gigantic knot. There was no way she could survive such a crushing, but apparently she lingered. Between the coils he glimpsed her face and one arm out flung toward him, her lips framing his name.

For an instant only. A blackness tore open one whole section of sky in a silent explosion, and both were pulled toward it. The snake tried to thrash clear of the trap, but could not hold its prey and still escape.

The howling eased as though drawing breath, and that's when he heard Sharon Geary's voice, clear, unmistakable.

Richard—help me!

It was a terrible wail, straight out of hell.

Cut short. She and the snake vanished abruptly into the darkness, which then vanished of itself, folding and refolding into nothing.

They were quite gone.

Richard Dun jolted awake.

Heart hammering, he sat bolt upright in bed, sweat-soaked and trembling, so out of breath his chest hurt.

"What's wrong?" Mercedes sleepily asked from her side.

He stared at her as though she was a phantom come to haunt him. The shreds of the dream were just a little too close about him yet.

"Richard?"

Help me.

Sharon. God, what's happened to her?

"Hey, what is it?" Mercedes roused from sluggish curiosity to concern. "Bad dream?"

He nodded. He couldn't quite speak yet.

She made sympathetic sounds and held his arm, which was rigid as steel. Her comfort was wasted. What he'd experienced was far too intense to have been anything but an Otherside vision. He'd had only a few of those in his long past, and they never boded well. Was it a portent of what was to come, or something that had already happened?

Sabra would know. He must call her . . .

Mercedes groaned when his cell phone trilled, muttering a curse about modern times. He'd switched it off. How the devil had it—

Ah. Sabra. She had a way around barriers, whether they were magical or electronic.

"Sorry," he said aloud to Mercedes and quit their bed. What time was it? Bloody late. He fished for the tiny phone in his discarded overcoat and fumbled the button.

Sabra's voice on the other end, saying his name. Relief washed over him, but not for long. She sounded very shaken.

"Richard, did you see?" she asked without preamble. She could only be speaking of one thing. Though no longer sharing the dark gift of vampirism, Sabra still retained the other talents bestowed on her by the Goddess.

"Yes. What does it mean?"

"I saw you in the vision, standing ahead of me. You saw the snake god?"

"That thing was a g—" He bit off the word, mindful that Mercedes was present.

"Yes, a powerful one. He mostly sleeps, but some catastrophe has stirred him."

"What would that be? The storm?"

"The one who caused the storm. I know that something great and terrible has taken place. Until now I've only had hints that trouble might be afoot, that someone's at work disrupting balances. Whoever is causing the disruptions has been very careful to shield them and himself. I didn't know things were this bad. He got careless this time."

"You know it's a man? The one we saw?"

"That could have been a cloak of skin used as a disguise, but yes, it was male energy, but don't ask me how I know."

"What about Sharon? Was that real?"

A long pause from her. Not good, not good. "Sabra . . . ?"

"Richard . . . I'm sorry. What we saw were Otherside events that have happened already."

"Oh, God. You're sure?"

"Yes."

"But—" There could be no argument against it, though. It took a moment to master himself. He pushed the pain hard away.

"I know you loved her," she said in the old tongue.

He could make no reply to that in any language, though he almost felt Sabra's own love for him humming through the cell, offering comfort.

"Sharon is lost, but not in vain. The man behind it, his protections were shattered when he fought with her. She gave us that much. The vision was a warning. We have a chance to find him—"

"What do you mean 'lost?' Is she dead?" It was like a fist in his gut to say the word.

"I-I don't know."

This uncertainty wasn't like Sabra; she was always self-assured.

"Are you all right?" he demanded.

"I'm . . . afraid."

His mouth went dry. Sabra was *never* afraid. Not for herself, anyway. "I'll come right over."

"No, meet me at Philip's house. They were both in it. This may involve Michael."

"In what way?" Any threat to Michael . . . Richard felt the creep of fear up his spine and ruthlessly stifled it.

"His ability with visions. We must talk first. Eight o'clock at Philip's?"

"I'll be there." Richard hated going out in the sun, but some things were better done under its face. He rang off, turning to Mercedes, who had clicked on a bedside light. She'd heard his side of the conversation.

"Something very bad's happened." She spoke it as a certainty, not a question.

He swallowed. "Yes. A close friend . . . some sort of accident. I have to leave."

"Can I help?"

"No. It's—it's bit of a family crisis."

"I'm sorry. But if you need anything . . ."

He could tell it wasn't a shallow offer given out of politeness. She meant it. "I appreciate it, but I . . ." This was terrifically awkward.

She seemed to know his thoughts. "Hey—I love that you're a gentleman, but it's an emergency, so go already."

He felt a sudden, intense, and instant adoration for her. "Thank you."

"E-mail me later, though, so I know you're all right."

"I will."

"I just hope things are better than you think they are."

As do I, he thought, reaching for his clothes, his hands not quite shaking.

Chapter Three

From ten floors up the white-trimmed streets looked mellow and romantic under the orange glare of sodium vapor lights. At sidewalk level . . . ugh.

Richard emerged from the hotel lobby into freezing wind and blowing snow—so different from the desert-dry hell-blast of his vision—and cast about for transportation. He'd cabbed over for his dinner date with Mercedes, not wanting to risk his classic Jaguar E-type to the fender-bending of the slick streets. Of course, he could have driven the more sensible Land Rover, but the same argument held. He liked his toys to look new for as long as possible, and besides, parking downtown was always a bitch. No point in berating himself for caution now. How was he to know the world would decide to fall apart tonight?

There was always at least one taxi loitering before every major hotel in the area, usually lines of them. He couldn't believe they'd all scuttled from sight just to annoy him. Bloody hell. He turned north, going as quickly as he dared on the iced-over walk for a few yards before taking to the street itself. The sanding trucks had been through recently, preparing the roads for the coming morning rush. The mixture of sand and salt was somewhat less perilous underfoot. He covered the two blocks to the streetcar stop on Queen without incident, and chafed impatiently in the inadequate shelter. The things were designed to discourage homeless people from taking up residence, hence the narrow, downward-angled seats that prevented anyone from stretching out for a nap and the enclosure being open below to allow in plenty of fresh arctic breeze. At least there was a roof to keep out the wet. Played against the other inadequacies, its effectiveness was more of a symbolic gesture than anything practical.

Richard did not feel the winter as much as others because of his condition, but it seemed determined to take hold of him now. He suffered an unaccustomed shiver in his long leather overcoat, and belatedly remembered to dig out gloves and a thick black ski cap from one of his pockets.

All in your head, he told himself as he pulled the cap on. Cold comfort. Very cold.

He wanted to go to Philip Bourland's house immediately, but Sabra would not be there any sooner for it. It would unnecessarily alarm Bourland and Michael to be turning up at this late—or early—an hour. Let them sleep.

Richard resisted the temptation to phone Sabra back. If she sensed anything of import she'd let him know.

The next eastbound streetcar rumbled up, and the doors opened. He swung inside, dropped coins in the box, and tore off his flimsy ticket, taking a seat not far behind the driver. Richard had his pick, only two others for company: a comatose kid with too-black hair and a nose ring and a sleepy woman in nurse's shoes.

The ticket's flip side advised him of the availability of gay and lesbian services and gave a number. It struck him as being a rather ambiguous message. If one was gay or lesbian, would calling that number get you serviced? Would that were also true for straight people. He'd never have to worry about hunting or courting his next meal ever again. Just ring a number and hopefully a willing young lady would arrive on his doorstep, rather like ordering pizza . . .

He shook his head, knowing he'd retreated into absurdities to avoid the horrors of memory. God, but it was frightening how swiftly things could shift and go bad.

The line of linked cars trundled forward, pausing at the stops, moving steadily along the length of East Queen's eclectic mix of neighborhoods. Modern flats and century-old houses in varying states of preservation or decay stood cheek and jowl with tiny gas stations, and on almost every corner either a flower shop or a veterinary clinic. With the long drab winters and brutal cold the locals needed the color of plants and the distraction of pets to maintain their sanity.

But there were worse things to threaten the mind and soul than an occasionally difficult climate.

Amid these prosaic surroundings, Richard felt secure enough to dredge his memory concerning the vision. What recollection of it lingered—besides the anxiety it inspired—remained stubbornly elusive to insight. He'd walked in the Otherside, seen something terrible happening, and done *nothing* to stop it.

That infuriated him. His unthinking instinct was ever to rush in, and there he'd stood watching like a spectator at a staged show waiting to see what the actors would do next.

He most feared that because of his uncharacteristic inaction Sharon Geary might be dead. That would be unbearable. Unforgivable, however mitigating the circumstances.

He couldn't and wouldn't be one hundred percent sure, though, until he saw her body himself. There were degrees of death, and wasn't he the proof of at least one of them?

But Sabra said Sharon was "lost." There was a difference between that and death. Being lost implied that one could be found again. Richard held hard to that tiny little flame of hope. If there was a way to find her, bring her back, he would make it happen.

Sharon, with the bewitching smile, the strange but workable mix of charm and stubbornness and bold confidence . . . and why in God's name had he let her go? He could have persuaded her to stay. Without resorting to hypnosis. Bloody hell, but women, lovely as they were, could be damned frustrating.

He had not heard from her in over a year now; she'd been busy. Yet another he'd loved and lost. Now lost perhaps forever . . . but how and why? What *happened* to her? Who was that man she fought? Swathed in shadows, he had been too far distant to recognize.

In the face of Sharon's (possible) loss Richard's other concerns were frivolous and futile. Things had been stable and damned good lately. His businesses running well, and in between their demands he'd kept a fairly close eye on his godson, Michael. The selling of the oil company had also ended the boy's last links to Texas and the tragedy there where he lost his whole family. He seemed to be recovered from the violence and was getting every possible attention. Bourland, friend, almost a second father, to Michael's late mother, had adopted the orphan, and was an excellent father. With his grown daughter off practicing law someplace Bourland had gladly taken on the responsibility. He'd welcomed Michael into his home and heart so thoroughly it was almost as though the boy had always been there.

Sabra had moved to Toronto to be Michael's mentor and counselor, and sometimes mother surrogate, when needed. Richard had been very pleased about that. He'd nearly lost her once and preferred her close.

Michael, they had learned, possessed some very unique gifts, requiring unique help. The boy was blessed—or cursed—with Sight, which was Sabra's specialty, so who better to prepare him to deal with it?

All three adults maintained tight, affectionate ties, linked by their charge. For the first time in decades, Richard felt that he was part of a family again.

He'd had that before, many times, but it always ended in sorrow because of his agelessness. The humans he loved grew, withered, and died seemingly in an instant. It was worth the price, though. He knew too well what life was like without connection. *Treasure it while it lasts and don't dwell on what awaits in the future.*

He pulled the signal cord so the streetcar paused right at Neville Park Boulevard, and ventured into the chill and ice again. The sanding trucks hadn't gotten this far, nor would they bother with residential lanes. Richard forsook the dangers of concrete and walked across his neighbors' small front yards. Snow on dead grass was much safer underfoot. Others had done the same, to judge by their overlapping trails.

His house at the Beaches was the last one on the left, two and a half tall stories with a basement, a narrow drive to a small backyard that was mostly filled by the detached double garage. The side yard was much larger, with a high board fence and a gate that opened directly onto the beach. The splash of waves from Lake Ontario was a constant presence. Though free-running water was deadly to him, he did quite enjoy its music.

He stamped snow on the doormat from his wet shoes and let himself in to silence. The house was at least seventy years old— thoroughly modernized of course—but haunted by its own creaky voice. Tonight it seemed to be pulled in on itself, smothered and waiting. An echo of his own feelings. It would be a long while until six o'clock.

The answering machine in his office blinked patiently at him as he passed the open door. The thing was always doing that. He only ever bothered to check it at the end of the day since most of the calls were the phone equivalent of junk mail. He shrugged from his coat and pressed the play button. Nothing but importunate advertisements, recorded halfway through their pitch then cut off. Idiots. Did *anyone* ever buy anything from some mechanical stranger interrupting their dinner? Perhaps. Just enough to keep the fools dialing other, more resistant types like himself.

Then:

"Hallo, love, I've found . . . henge . . . dropping everything and come lend . . . this number . . ."

His heart rate shot high. The message was garbled through and through with static, but that was *Sharon's* voice. He noted the recording time. This morning, long after he'd left home for business meetings with Mercedes, and he'd not noticed it on his way out for their date. The caller ID screen said UNKNOWN so there was no return number to track. Useless damned thing. If he'd just *been* here or bothered to check his messages . . . for all the good it might have done her. Almost everything important came to him through e-mails or his cell. But Sharon hadn't had that number.

Richard worked very hard at curbing a desire to rip the machine out and fling it through a window. He'd missed her message, and something or other had buggered up the recording. Deal with it. He listened again.

What had she found? And why had she out of the blue phoned

him about it? Where the devil had she been, anyway? If not for the vision he'd have had no clue of anything being amiss for her.

He tried her cell phone number. Hoping against hope. The recorded reply stating the customer had switched off or was out of range was no great surprise.

The memory of the Otherside pyramid nagged him. He'd seen it before. The style was Mayan. He sought out one of his many bookshelves. About fifty years back he'd purchased encyclopedias, the kind with thin paper, small, dense printing, and picture plates. Much of their information was still good and more detailed and faster than delving the Internet. He pulled out *M* and flipped pages. There. A stark black and white photo, but it matched his vision. What in the name of hell had she been doing on top of El Castillo in the Yucatán? On another recovery mission for Lloyd's of London? There was a thriving black market in New World antiquities, perhaps that was it.

He glanced at a clock. Wee-hours morning here, full-blown business day in London. Richard phoned Sharon's employers and was eventually passed to a woman who acted as her supervisor when needed. The nature of the job required that lady be discreet, but she did finally say that Sharon's last report had originated in Bath, where she'd been working. She'd concluded her errand successfully and would call in Monday to inquire after any fresh assignments, apparently taking a long weekend.

Richard then explained that Sharon had gone missing—certainly the truth—and asked the woman if she could check on things from that end. She made it clear she was not too terribly interested in doing so on the word of a stranger, even if he was phoning all the way from Canada, even if he did suspect foul play might be involved. From her tone, she'd decided he was a crank.

Richard held his temper and thanked her and carefully rang off. He had friends in higher places who could help, after all. Within ten minutes he was speaking to one of them, lighting fires, getting things moving. He hoped the woman at Lloyd's would have an interesting time of it under the eye of one of the senior men from Scotland Yard. The man owed Richard a hell of a private favor from ten years back and had ever been ready to return it.

There, that wheel in motion, what next?

"Henge" the recording had said. Salisbury Plain lay between Bath and London. Sharon would have taken the A303 for her drive back, and both Stonehenge and Woodhenge were on that route. He could not guess why she might stop at either of them or why from there she'd suddenly gone flying off to Mexico. What was the connection?

He'd get the recording into professional hands. There had to be some way to extract sense from under the static. Bourland would know useful contacts for that who wouldn't ask questions.

Next Richard called Sabra's cell. His information about Sharon's activities was thin at best, but might shed some small light. It was nothing that couldn't be covered when they met later, but he wanted to hear her voice.

Not so long ago she'd been happy enough in the isolation of her Vancouver wilderness. Sabra loved the touch of primal earth; it was part of her strength, but she was no stranger to accepting change and readily embraced it for Michael's sake. Hers was a compromise, though. She lived miles north of Toronto in a mostly undeveloped area. Her home had all the mod-cons, but the land it sat on was virtually unchanged since the indigenous natives last hunted there. It took some doing on Richard's part to secure her a usable identity and a bulletproof background history, but now she had what she needed to continue comfortably in the twenty-first century.

Each age they lived through possessed its own special minutiae one had to know to survive without drawing undue and often inconvenient notice. For all its high-tech snags, this one is no different. Low tech could be very complicated, too, after all. It was just as demanding to know how to make a bow and arrow from scratch as it was to learn to use a new computer program. Richard and Sabra could do both.

She was breathless when she answered.

"Something wrong?" he asked, coming alert. "Are you all right?"

"I'm fine, just digging my car out from the latest snowfall. It stormed tonight and the snow's still coming down. I'll be running late because of this, but don't worry."

"Look, I can come pick you up."

She laughed. "Please, it's an hour's drive even when the weather's good, don't bother. I'll be in when you see me; I'm going to take my time if the roads are bad."

"Very well . . ." He told her the little he'd learned of Sharon's last whereabouts and the phone message.

"Can you play it for me?"

"The sound will be atrocious, but—" He held the receiver close to the machine and hit the play button again. "Did you get any of that?"

She didn't answer.

"Sabra?"

"A moment." He heard a door open then slam shut. The ambient noise of wind, which had been coming through, ceased. "I'm inside now. Let me hear that once more."

He repeated the playback. "Well?"

"It's not static. It sounds like it, but I heard . . . there were voices, other voices besides hers."

"Whose? Saying what?"

She sighed. "Nothing nice."

"Look, she's already missing, perhaps dead, you can't make me any more worried than I am."

"Please, Richard. Don't say that."

He pulled up short. Tempting fate was always a bad idea. "Sorry. This has me rattled."

"And I as well. Usually things are clear, even if there's a dozen outcomes to choose from." Her Sight again.

"What *can* you tell me?"

"When Sharon made that call something was doing its best to interfere and mostly succeeded. To anyone on this Side, it's static. To someone like me it's was both warning and threat and was very graphic. I'd rather not get more detailed if you don't mind."

"A threat to Sharon?"

"To anyone helping Sharon. Anyone opposing it."

"Which would be us."

"Yes."

"And it can reach us from Mexico?"

"To forces like that, there are no concepts of distance. However, it does take a lot of power to upset the balance on our Side. Such power is hard to acquire and quickly exhausted. I'm not saying we're completely safe, but we should be fine for now."

"I'm sorry, but that's not good enough. After that vision I'm having a healthy bout of paranoia."

"Yes, it's what you're good at. On the other hand, whoever's behind that vision has been compromised so far as I'm concerned. There's cracks in his ability to conceal himself, enough for me to know ahead of time if and when he makes any kind of move against anyone under my protection."

"How far ahead of time?"

"Enough. More than enough."

Richard relaxed only marginally. He knew the tension between his shoulders wouldn't ease until he saw her.

"It will be all right, Richard," she said. "I promise. Go over to Philip's sooner if that will make you feel better. Sit in on breakfast. Keep an eye on Michael. Just be there with him."

"I'll call now. If he had the same vision—"

"Then he would have called me. Or Philip would have. I just want you with them both. I'll get there as soon as I can."

"Is Michael in danger?"

"Not at the moment. That's all I can say at this time, and I'll let you know if that changes."

Richard understood. They were each too well aware that the future was always in flux. "What about yourself? Are you certain you're all right?"

There was a smile in her voice. "I'm being well looked after." This was a reference to the Goddess. "We'll work something out about this, don't worry."

But he sensed a lack of surety behind her words, which disturbed him. She always knew what to do. He very much wanted to ask exactly what was going on and what had become of Sharon, but what would be the point? Sabra would have told him. Perhaps she could use Michael's uncanny gift to find out. She'd be reluctant to involve him, though in the past Michael had surprised her with the power of his Gift. She worried for him. With power comes peril.

"What about the Goddess?" Richard wanted to know.

No answer.

"Sabra?"

"It's . . . clouded."

"What does that mean? A busy signal?" This was getting very annoying.

"For want of a better term. This sort of thing's happened before . . ."

Only when the situation's gone seriously wrong, he silently concluded.

"Richard, the snow's coming down heavy here, I want to dig out the car while I can still see it."

A most unsubtle hint, mixed with a touch of exasperation. "Sorry. This is my own worry showing. I'll shed it and be waiting at Philip's for you."

"With hot chocolate? Double strength?" Since her change back to being fully human, Sabra had become quite the addict.

"A gallon of it. The gourmet kind." Bourland's pantry was well stocked with boxes of the stuff. He delighted in spoiling her whenever she visited Michael.

Hanging up, Richard wanted physical action to distract him. He had hours to fill, a common situation given his penchant for the nocturnal, but he'd long learned how to manage that detail.

Keeping his thoughts prudently neutral if not completely shut down, he trotted up to his bedroom to trade the business suit for more expendable attire. Back down again, through the rarely used kitchen, and out the side door to the garage to fetch the snow shovel. The snow blower would have been faster, but in this part of the Beaches the houses were built close together. The obnoxious noise at this time of morning would not endear him to his neighbors.

Clearing the driveway. After hockey it was Canada's other great winter sport. Not nearly as exciting, but the exercise helped channel his frustrated energy into something more constructive than punching holes in walls. On occasion, he'd been known to do that and was trying to break the pattern.

The Duke of Normandy's son, Lord Richard d'Orleans, later known as Lancelot du Lac, and still later by a hundred other names, worked steadily to free the side of the garage housing his Land Rover. Once upon a time he'd have delegated the humble task to a dozen pages, who would have leapt forward and had a race to see who was fastest. Those days were long past, the young pages gone to dust, their names lost to history. They wouldn't have known what to make of a modern truck anyway, probably taken it for an infernal contrivance and burned it to exorcise the demon within. They'd have assumed success when the gas tank blew . . .

Absurdities. Distraction. Most needed and necessary *distraction*.

Finished, he checked the sky. Snow still tumbled lazily out of the darkness, but had slacked off considerably and didn't seem to be sticking. Mercedes' flight would have no trouble departing then. Damn. For all the abrupt changes that had taken place, forcing him to shift his focus to other matters, he would miss her.

Minutes later in his bath he stripped and stepped into the over-sized shower, the water temperature set just short of scalding and the tap at full force. Mercedes had wanted him smelling like a man. Well, she'd have been most happy with him now with the sweat he'd worked up. He scrubbed it away, along with any lingering trace of her baby powder scent. Pity about that. Her blood was still with him, though. He felt it running in his own veins, almost as hot as the water hammering his skin. What a woman.

Dried and dressed in fresh casual clothes, but with no place to go just yet. More waiting to do before Bourland could be expected to be up and seeking his first coffee of the day. He was an early riser, but not this early.

Richard threw on a jacket and muffler and went out again. His side-yard gate was convenient to the beach, but blocked under a snow drift as high as the fence. He went out the front door, then took the public stairs at the end of the street that led down to the lake.

Ice caked the shoreline; deep snow mixed with sand clung to his boots. The wind was knife-sharp on his face. As far as he could see in either direction he had the place to himself, with not even a psychotically dedicated early jogger to mar the solitude. At times like this he felt that he alone owned the whole of the land and lake. A good feeling, that.

At intervals along the beach boulders had been brought in to serve as breakwaters. People adored clambering on them in the warm months; now they were a deathtrap. He moved past them, wanting an unimpeded view of Ontario's restless water plain.

He slogged east toward a groin, one of the cement promontories flanked by boulders that extended out into the water. There were several of them along the length of the park's shoreline. Their practical use was to also act as breakwaters during storms; the rest of the time locals took them over, especially in the summer.

He took care stepping up onto the broad flat of concrete and held to the center. The edges were trimmed with a footwide band of steel to slow down the weathering that was inevitable with such a harsh winter climate. Slick with ice, possessing no guardrails, they were a treacherous walk. He kept clear of the metal; a fall into the water could be fatal, even to him. It was a big lake; he had a healthy respect for its power.

The rocks and parts of the pier were coated with the frozen splashings from the constant waves. Even if the lake didn't freeze over—he couldn't recall that happening since moving here—some of the more shallow areas could fill themselves with slush. A gray wave rose, washed over the breakers, broke apart into spray, and died, leaving behind another thin layer of wet for the wind to congeal. In the middle of a stand of rocks a small tree had flourished during the summer; now its skeleton was held prisoner by the ice. Would it softly die in its winter sleep or waken to grow taller in the spring? No way to tell, but the odds were against survival here.

At the end of the pier Richard looked westward, barely making out the CN Tower lights in the misty distance. Low clouds dimly reflected the city glow of downtown. So many people there, and who among them was even remotely aware of Otherside matters? Damned few, and probably just as well. There were enough lunatics in the world.

To the east were the Scarborough bluffs, invisible now, and to the southeast, where the sun would appear, he thought he saw the sky lighting a little. It could well be his imagination. The clouds were as thick as sin; it would be a gray and gloomy morning. Good. No need to bother slathering on the sunblock.

A last few random flakes of snow touched his face, and he breathed deeply of the clean lake air. This was a favorite spot for him, and on nights when the water and sky assumed the same shade of dull steel he felt suspended between them, almost floating. Only the lap of waves less than a yard from his boots reminded him how close he stood to the destruction of free-flowing water. It was quite nice here in the summer, looking straight down to the rocks on the bottom a dozen feet below. Now it was an arctic hell. Few ventured out here when it was like this, allowing him much needed outdoor solitude.

Calmer now, Richard thought about Sharon and what had to be done.

Once he and Sabra talked, he would arrange to take the first plane heading to the Yucatán and see for himself what was going on there. Sabra might well come along; she was better able to deal with the tropical sunlight and other, more metaphysical things. What the hell had Sharon been *doing* there? What was the man-shadow thing she fought?

Easy, old lad. You'll find it all out soon enough. Richard knew *that* in his bones. He'd not have been shown the vision in the first place unless the Goddess was certain he was the right person for the job. Of course, it's a most risky business when the gods take notice of one. He'd learned that the hard way, again and again and again.

But . . . anything to help Sharon if he could.

Very, very gently, he touched on his long-suppressed feelings for her.

They were still solidly in place. Dormant, like that tree, iced over, but perhaps ready to waken again given the right circumstances.

Yes, she had decided against staying with him. He'd accepted that. Mostly. Maybe on some level she knew it wouldn't have worked, that she would have been one of hundreds he'd loved before her. Loved, and eventually, inevitably, and irrevocably lost.

How many have I loved and then wept for, how many have I taken to the grave? Taken, but never followed.

Tears flared cold on his face. He chided himself for giving into grief when he still didn't know for sure what had happened. He swiped the chill trails away. They weren't only for Sharon, though, but for the others as well. So many, many others.

To keep himself sane, he'd learned to live very much in the

here-and-now moment, but sometimes the past reared up to over-whelm his heart. A scent, a sound—the little things that triggered the memories, thousands of them, good and bad, the sweetness and the pain.

He brushed his eyes again. Quickly.

Am I getting too old to hold them all?

The Yucatán

The man who had once called himself Professor Rivers sat in the small air terminal, cheerfully waiting for his flight to be called. It was still dark out, but he'd seen no point in hanging around his hotel. Though the chance was small, that redheaded Amazon might have tipped the cops about him being a Suspicious Character, so why make things easy for them? Not that he didn't have perfectly legitimate credentials. God knows he'd paid enough for them.

What was his name today? He tried to remember, failed, and checked his passport. Oh, okay, fine, he could answer to "Daniel Dean" for a few more hours. Jeez, who gave their kid *that* one? Talk about an excuse to get beaten up on the playground. Well . . . they could *try* beating him up.

He preferred his past names over this prosaic example of Western alliteration. The others were more impressive, carried power in their very utterance. Thousands used to tremble and shake-it-up-baby and yadda-yadda way back when upon hearing them. Those had indeed been the good old nights. Gone for now, not forgot-ten, but nothing lasts forever . . .

Whups, don't go there. Think positive.

What was his last favorite? Old Man of the Mountain? Father of Assassins? Apophis? Stuff like that. Charon. One of the good ones. He couldn't use it openly anymore of course, that had been thor-oughly screwed up, but them's the breaks and too bad.

Looong day of travel ahead of him, tiring. He knew it would exhaust him of all the energy he'd taken from Chichén Itzá. If only the hits would last longer; he hated when the buzz left and the pain started barging in again. But he would recharge again, and he'd been through worse. Now he could get out during the *day*, no need to wrap up like a mummy. That was a big plus about being human again, but it well and truly sucked compared to the minus side: the Death Thing.

It's fun to inflict on others, but not so much when the Old White Man is staring YOU in the face.

Charon shifted uncomfortably in the plastic seat and glanced around, half expecting to see that dread specter hanging near one of the terminal boutique shops, maybe wearing a souvenir T-shirt and sipping a cold drink. Biding his time, the gaunt bastard.

Nope, not today. He'd been thoroughly put down, smacked down, tossed out of town.

For the time being.

Might be worth whistling him back, though, to deal with an argumentative young couple trying to get around airline regulations about something or other. God, some of them positively *asked* for it. There were few people in the terminal at this hour, so theirs was the only show to watch. Neither of them or the unyielding gate attendant seemed aware of the thick black and green cloud floating close over their heads, apparently feeding off the rising hostility. The young man with the muddy aura looked ready to explode, but calmed down when another attendant came forward to sort out the mess. The cloud drifted away, its meal interrupted. Like a big jellyfish it hovered over the people scattered about the terminal, probably hopeful for seconds. Who knows how long it had fattened itself up here? Sure had staked out a good hunting ground for heaping helpings of frustration and anger.

No else one saw it. That was such a hoot. They had *no* idea. Idiots.

Then it sank lower. Must have picked up something. An Otherside scent, a feeling. There was no telling how the things knew where to go to find negative emotions. None of them were too smart. A lot simply attached themselves to people for a lifetime of feeding unless the victim got depression therapy and some happy pills or even religion. If not . . . oh, how those things enjoyed contributing to, then feasting on a good suicide, then attaching to the family and friends. Despair followed by a bottomless supply of survivor guilt. *Most* tasty.

It floated toward Charon. With purpose.

Oh, now that was just *too* stupid.

He grinned at it. "Come on, dumb-ass. Gimme your best shot."

But the free-drifting parasite suddenly changed course.

Must not like my aftershave.

Charon stretched forth his will and neatly snagged the thing, drawing it closer. It thrashed and fought every inch. Futilely. He threw a net over its shifting shape and gradually pulled it into himself. The murky green cloud touched his chest . . . and that was *it*. He started feeding in turn and, oh, that was mighty good. It shouldn't have been, considering its diet, but the things were like catfish. Those were the worst of the bottom feeders, but what a nice delicate taste when prepared right.

Damn if the amorphous beast didn't scream as he absorbed it. He'd had no idea they could do that. It was a psychic thing, translated by the mind into a piercing nails-on-a-blackboard screech. Well, live and learn. Charon noticed a woman a few yards away suddenly put her hand to her head and wince. Sensitive types sometimes got migraines from Otherside racket. Aw, wasn't that just too bad, but a fella's gotta eat.

He sucked out the energy until there was nothing left but ash which quickly vanished. That was fun if much too easy, like running down old ladies in a parking lot. Still, Charon relished the tiny refreshment to his power, his Sight resharpened by it.

Absolutely no one in the place saw *any* of the action. Mano-manomano. Wouldn't it be a gas to change that? What looks on their faces if they were suddenly made aware of all the beings and energies floating around their sane and solid world.

I'll be able to make that happen. Then hoo-boy, party night in Bedlam. Xanax anyone? And they thought things had gone crazy when the Black Death hit Europe like a dose of salts.

Uh-oh. He abruptly noticed a dark-skinned man looking at him from across the way, glaring, really. Who the hell . . . ? Charon opened his Sight up a little more.

Well-well, what d'ya know? An honest-to-gawd *ahkin*. The old bastard must have come out of the jungle to look for the cause of last night's big bash at the pyramid and followed the psychic trail to here. Yeah, the natives would have been plenty stirred up by that fracas.

Well, you found me. Charon smiled winningly at him, and got a look of pure hatred in return. *Aw, did I hurt your little snake god? Give it a bloody nose? There'll be hell to pay before you hear from it again. If ever.*

The old man wasn't much to see outwardly: short-limbed, sinew-lean, and pot-bellied, Mayan ancestry strong in his leather-dark face. He wore cheap thin clothes with rubber sandals on calloused feet that looked twice as old as his face. You saw a million others just like him in the towns and villages all through the area, beggars, farmers, merchants, professionals. Their ancestors had been converted or conquered by invaders and disease and time, but the blood still ran strong here. Hell, they shed enough of it so the strain was soaked deep into the very earth.

But the *ahkin*'s astral self was another story—young and damned furious, about twelve feet tall, in full battle gear with sun-bright feathers and one of those fancy clubs, spoiling for a fight. *He* could do some damage and no mistake. Charon didn't want to waste his hard-won energy fending off this self-righteous jerk.

Don't get your loin cloth in a twist, old cock, I'm leaving your territory. You're better off not getting into a pissing contest with me, and we both know it.

The *ahkin* still glared, his lips moving.

Charon felt a gust of heat roll over him. It stirred his hair, plucked his loose shirt, and set his heart to racing. No one else seemed affected. The old boy knew his noodles. Or was it tamales? Key lime chicken? Whatever.

A low, forceful chanting in a language Charon had never before heard, yet understood, rumbled through the whole of the terminal, echoing off the modern walls. Death Magic. One of its countless variations. Here it was, live and in person, straight from the erroneously named New World, a touch diluted by time, but still potent.

The heat shot up, got worse, centered on his heart. Yeah, this bunch had a thing for hearts. *Bet the guy's sorry he can't cut mine out like his great-great et cetera grand-pappy used to do.* That would be his remedy for bringing back his missing god. It just might work, too.

Charon winced against the building fire, but hid it under another grin . . .

Which made the *ahkin* more angry.

Watch it there, daddy-o. Don't get too personally involved.

The astral body of the old man lunged forward, swinging his club, going for the kill. It smashed right through Charon's Realside self. He suppressed a grunt in reaction.

Okay, enough was enough. He'd been very, very patient until now.

Another pass-through. Ow. That one hurt.

So you like it rough, do you? Lemme teach you how it's done, little boy . . .

Charon shut his eyes, seeming to nap, but on another level, on Otherside, he rose up, revealing his true self.

The *ahkin's* weathered face showed shock—about damn time—but the spirit warrior screamed an ancient war cry and attacked again.

Charon wanted this one over fast to conserve energy, so he played it dirty. Oh, hell, he *always* played it dirty; that's how to win. He used a bastardized version of a tai chi move to get in under the club, then drove his hand deep into the warrior's chest. Just like the snake scales did a few hours ago, the magical armor shattered at the first touch.

Be my valentine? Wrong month, wrong culture, but pretty funny. Charon closed his astral hand around that fast-beating heart and pulled for all he was worth. The bodies on this Side could be just as tough as the ones in the so-called Reality Side.

A shriek. Full throated. Satisfying. Loud enough to shake rafters, filled with agony . . . and . . . swiftly over. It should have lasted much longer.

I'm out of practice.

Charon slammed the still-beating heart against his own astral chest and felt the lurch as it was pulled in and consumed.

Whoa, what a rush. The parasite had been cheese on a cracker. This dude was an eight-course banquet, heavy on the cream.

Charon feasted, relishing the nuances of the man's rage and knowledge and power—especially the power. He had a lot of that. Not on a par with the primal stuff of the ruins, but substantial. Made for a nice boost.

When Charon opened his eyes, the old man was facedown on the polished floor, blood flowing from his nose and ears, hands clenched, lips drawn back in a rictus of pain. People were just beginning to notice his collapse. A short man in baggy tourist clothes responded to a call for a doctor and pushed his way through. People in uniforms closed in.

Too late, but you can't say I didn't warn the old coot.

Had anyone else seen the fight? That woman who'd heard the parasite's scream . . . no, she was doing the onlooker thing with the rest of the crowd. Okay, she gets to live another day. Who else?

There. Charon spotted another native man farther along the terminal. Probably the old guy's acolyte. He was much younger, on this Side and the next, and clearly scared. He backed off, turned, and shot out the terminal's glass doors. He'd probably go back to his little grass shack in the back of wherever and mutter chants and burn his herbs and try to figure out what the hell was going on. Fat lot of good it'd do him and the rest of his tribe. Their great scaled protector just wasn't around no more, and manomano, hadn't it felt *good* to take in *its* energy?

Charon flexed his perfectly healed arm. The ache of the break was quite gone. God, but it was great to be free of that pain. For a cure-all there was just nothing to beat the power of a deity's blood. Even his scars had vanished. Jeeze, he'd had some of those old sword and knife cuts from his salad days as a human for so long he'd forgotten how they'd got there. The new skin was fresh and tight, the muscles under it strong.

For now.

The energy rush would soon fade. He could feel it going even now.

Maybe he should have hauled wormy back for a little bloodbath like Siegfried once did with his dragon and hit the reset button on the whole bod. That might have made a huge difference. But it had all happened so fast, and Kukulcan had been a pretty determined fighter, one couldn't think of everything given those circs. Grand Old Snaky had resisted, then gone for the girl. Charon would have squandered all the power he'd gained getting the monster to come to heel, then been too weak for a sanguinary sauna.

The gains were still pretty good, though. Look on the bright side. With *both* eyes. He had stereo vision back, woo-hoo. Charon wanted to shed the now superfluous eye patch, but then he wouldn't match his passport photo. Have to keep up the charade a little longer. Besides, the black patch looked good with the restored color of his beard and hair, positively rakish. *Check out the hot pirate, ladies. Anyone ready to walk my plank?*

To his surprise it was daylight already. Man, the Otherside skirmish with the warrior-priest must have gone on longer than he'd thought. Time was such a *trip* over there. In some places you could stop off for a snack with the locals and emerge twenty years later to everyone else's astonishment. What a handy way to outlive relatives.

The trickle of people coming in for flights increased. Soon it'd be a flood. Charon picked up his flight bag and went through check-in. He produced his expensive paperwork, answered their ridiculous security questions without fuss, and had a few sticky minutes when the clerk commented that he looked too young for his picture ID. Charon grinned, pretending to take it as a compliment, and credited his vacation as being responsible for the rejuvenation. No need to burden anyone with talk about the specific use he'd made of the power taken in from atop El Castillo and the rest of the area.

Happily, no one was overly concerned with the good-humored *tourista*, and he was cleared through for boarding.

The next hitch wouldn't be until he hit customs on arrival and have to explain his collection of prescriptions. The damned things seemed to take up half the space in his flight bag . . . and the cost? Through the roof and into orbit. Hell, buying a gun to end the problem would be so much cheaper.

But he wanted to *live*.

Not an option so far as his body was concerned. Since that mess with the Grail a couple years ago things had been gradually deteriorating. Way back when, at the beginning, when he had his rebirth in blood, men didn't live all that long. He'd been camping on the outside borders of what was then old age, and once turned human again it became just a matter of time before his genetics caught up with him.

The first thing he tried to stave it off was getting himself vamped again. Not a lot of the fang-gang crowd around, and they were good at blending, but he had old friends to look up.

Friends. That was a laugh. Okay, enemies he'd not gotten around to snuffing yet. It was a little tricky trapping one of them, but he'd done it, then starved her into performing a blood-swap, which should have been an end to it.

That had *not* gone well. For one thing it hadn't worked. She'd drained him white, and he returned the favor when it was his turn to drink . . . and waited . . . and waited . . .

. . . and it hadn't fucking *worked.*

After some thought, and the very careful disposal of her headless body so she couldn't come after him later, he decided that perhaps one from his own dark bloodline was needed. He'd made a few rare offspring over the centuries, and they'd early on learned that Daddy Was Not Nice and disappeared themselves, but he knew where to dig. He turned one of them up in Denmark of all places and tried again.

A no go. And another corpse to lose. What was this, a conspiracy?

Or that damned Grail.

Or the whole Vampire Thing being a once-only opportunity. If you were dumb enough to get "cured" you couldn't acquire it again.

Immunity sucked.

Particularly immunity to the one thing that had always kept him alive and healthy.

He'd gone in for a checkup to see about a minor but chronic exhaustion that began to plague him and learned about the bomb ticking in his system.

Make that *growing.* Out of control. Fast. As though it had a grudge on.

The doctor and the others he'd consulted one after another presented him with a number of treatment options. He knew better than to trust their brave "let's fight this together" optimism.

There were other choices outside of modern medicine available to a man like him, though. Of course, you had to have a certain mindset for dealing with them, but he had that down. Hell, he'd lost all ability to be squeamish back when he'd been human the first time around. Piece of cake now.

So Charon sought out that knowledge for his cure. Quickly. As his energy was consumed by his disease, he replaced it with whatever ambient power happened to be lying around. There was plenty of acreage in the Otherside ready to be turned into car parks now, and who would miss a few floating parasites or even place-guardians? Once the place was gone a guardian was out of a job anyway.

It took him a little practice to learn how to feed fully from those energies, but once he got the hang of it . . . wow. Hell of a trip. Way better than anything he'd ever puffed from a hookah. The important thing was that for short stretches he felt better. So far it hadn't reversed or even slowed the cancer that was eating him alive, but he had more energy to deal with it. The pause at Stonehenge had given him enough of an upturn to get him across the Atlantic, and Chichén Itzá would carry him a for at least the rest of today. More than enough time if he worked it right. The snake blood had been a lucky bonus, fixing up his arm and eye like it did. He'd have to see what other of the old gods were hanging around, maybe go calling on them if his next ploy was a wash—

No, don't go there. It will succeed. Positive thoughts.

Gods were pretty damn tough, anyway. Jealous of their power, too. He'd gotten lucky with Kukie, surprised him, used the in-place energy for the fight. The next one down the line might be more prepared. It was getting harder and harder to keep all this veiled. That parasite shouldn't have been able to sense him.

In the meantime, Charon was an old hand at dealing with hypersuspicious customs people and possessed perfectly legitimate (for once) paperwork concerning his ailment and why he needed the miniature pharmacy. It annoyed him to have so many medicines, but perhaps not for long. His next gambit would *have* to heal him. But if not, then he'd hit Lourdes and suck out its power. *That* should tide him over a bit.

But first he had to pick up a little artifact that should have been his ages ago, the one that caused all the trouble for him in the first place and might correct it. He'd also tie up a loose end. Both of them. There were damned few people on the planet who could have the least inkling of what he was up to and he had to keep it that way. The Irish Amazon bimbo damn-near queered the whole scene. He'd done his best to throw a psychic screen around her, to keep her isolated, but chances were she'd gotten a warning out. Charon couldn't risk losing control of the works at this stage.

His flight was called, finally, a morning run due north. Hours and hours of it, but not too bad in first class, and he wouldn't even have to reset his watch. He settled into his seat, enjoying the press of acceleration as they rumbled along the runway, then leapt skyward.

Yes . . . he felt the wind energies outside the skin of the plane. He could use those—if the flight attendant would leave him alone long enough to concentrate.

No such luck. Apparently she thought he was cute. He snarled that he had to sleep, shooing her off. At least he had no chatty seatmate.

Immediate distractions shoved away, he closed his eyes and sank into the kind of trance that was necessary to travel the Low Road. A tricky path, no, make that foolish, especially with his mortal condition, but it would allow him to arrive ahead of his body. He wouldn't have to stay, just drop in for a few minutes' visit, long enough for a peek at what was going on, long enough to maybe do himself some good, then snap back again.

Very few could stop him now. Two in particular, and both of them were in Canada, guarding the souvenir he wanted.

How convenient.

Yes, he'd have a long and tiring haul to Toronto with his physical body. Worth it, though. Once there he would take care of the bloodsucking jock and his witchy-bitchy girlfriend . . .

Chapter Four

Toronto

It was just after six. Richard, sitting in his idling vehicle and ready to leave, called Bourland at last, knowing he would be out of bed by now.

Bourland, apparently reading the familiar cell number from his caller ID, picked up and before Richard could speak asked in a wide-awake voice, "How did you know?" There was an edge to his usually warm tone.

"Know what?"

"Michael . . . he had a rather bad dream last night. Very bad. I sat up with him, half expecting Sabra to call. She always seems to know when he's troubled."

"Is he all right?"

"Oh, yes, he nodded off after a bit. Having his breakfast now. He's right as rain, as though nothing's amiss."

"As it happens, Sabra does know and is coming your way. She expects to get there later this morning. I'd like to leave now, if that's all right with you."

There was no surprise to this unusual request. "Of course, Richard. You're always welcome here whenever you like."

Bourland was quite literal about that. Richard and Sabra had keys and the code for the house alarm. Richard would have gotten both

71

anyway; it had been his security firm that designed and installed the system, after all, but it was nice to have a standing formal invitation.

"There's one thing . . ." Bourland added.

"What?" Richard was already backing from the drive.

"I was going to do it anyway, but especially now with you both coming over. I thought it best to keep Michael home from school this once."

"But I thought—"

"He's just fine. It's for my sake not his. I've called in for myself. The Commonwealth can run on without my help for one day. I think I've earned a long weekend."

"Then it begs the question 'Are *you* all right?'"

"Mostly. We'll talk when you get here."

Mostly. What the hell did that mean?

Bourland had been in the vision, though. Had he also shared it? Remembered it? Not likely, since he had no notion of the uncanny lurking so close to his prosaic paper-driven, bureaucratic world. His realm was the Canadian government—a never-never land of its own, to be sure—but still well removed from metaphysical upheavals. The paranormal was a foreign country with no recognizable flag, and diplomatic relations were quite off the radar.

Unless Sabra had been coaching him. She had a way of making the most insane concepts acceptable. If so, then it certainly might ease things. Best to leave explanations to her.

Richard negotiated the slick streets in his Land Rover, speculating also about Michael. It was probable he had the same vision and heaven knows what he'd made of the frightening images. Children could be unexpectedly tough, though. Michael had lived through and apparently recovered from an overwhelming trauma in his young life. Perhaps the strength he'd gained from that tragedy would serve him here. After all, the focus was not on him this time. Like the others in their glowing shrouds of light, he'd been a bystander, not a participant. Richard hoped it would remain so. *He* was the warrior here, not his godson.

Sabra predicted the boy's psychic abilities would grow stronger the older he got, more so once he began to enter puberty. As though the child didn't have enough on his plate just being a teenager in this day and age. Perhaps to better help she could move into the city for the next few years, and use her more distant house for a weekend retreat. Richard would like that. There was lots of room for the both of them at the Neville Park address. And she would love being so close to the lake. Plenty of primal energy there to please her, in the lake . . . and certainly himself.

Of course, she might just as well move into Bourland's big house. Richard knew they occasionally slept together. But making love now and then with a friend was one thing; lengthy cohabitation always put a whole different dynamic to a relationship. Things between the three of them were well balanced for now. That sort of change either way could create a rather large upset to the status quo.

Richard had been tempted to broach the subject with her, but prudently kept his mouth shut. Unless she asked his opinion it was none of his business. His lady would seek her own path as she'd ever done, and it would be for the best for all of them.

The morning rush was not yet in full swing, meaning the slippery roads were still hazardous. He moved slowly along Queen, hitting spots where other tires had broken a trail on the snow and ice-caked paving, and leaving his trail in turn for others to use. A short but exciting slow-motion jaunt up the Don Valley Parkway, then he thankfully made the exit into the posh environs of Rosedale.

Its curving streets were even more demanding with their nearly unbroken coating of snow, but that's what his vehicle was designed for; he managed not to jump any curbs in his forward progress.

Bourland's house was almost modest compared to his neighbors; but still larger than anything Richard had lived in in some while. The Tudor style looked fine to modern eyes, but Richard had lived through the period and the mistakes made by the architect who built this example in the 1920s were quite hilarious. He never said anything to Bourland, of course; that would have been terrifically ill-mannered.

Richard parked around back, considerately not blocking the garage entry, and went in through the mud room, stamping snow from his boots before proceeding to the kitchen. Bourland's housekeeper was just finishing the washing up for breakfast and smiled a greeting as he came in.

"Some coffee, Mr. Dun?" she asked. "Just brewed it."

Coffee was one of the few things humans consumed that did smell good to him. He'd wondered about its taste since the first houses opened and made it the rage of London way back when. They were nothing like the trendy, sterilized chains of today, but as with the men of business then, Bourland seemed addicted. "Thank you, another time. Where's Philip?"

"In his study. He's staying home, but still working if you know what I mean."

"Indeed I do." Richard speculated that with computers, faxes, and phones Bourland need never venture forth to his regular office ever again; he was not required to be in the public eye, after all. Politicians came and went, but civil servants were a constant. Bourland was something more than an ordinary civil servant though. In every government there are hierarchies operating on all levels; Bourland's was in one of the most rarified areas and he was a senior member. When things needed to be accomplished, invisibly, it fell to people like him to get the job done. The less his presence was seen and felt, the better. Rather like Richard's own work through the ages.

The study was downstairs, but Richard heard electronic music coming from the second floor, indication that Michael was playing at something. Likely not homework, if he had any. Richard went up.

The boy's door was wide open. He had a bath and two rooms to himself. The first room held his bed and a scatter of books and toys and other items indicative of his changing if not maturing tastes. Due to daily patrols from the housekeeper, it wasn't nearly the wreckage it might have been, but his stamp was there, all the same. Trucks and plastic dinosaurs were gradually giving up space to a growing collection of model kits, video games, CDs and DVDs. He had a predilection for Schwarzenegger films, something of a shift from his once valued set of Disney animations. God, but he was growing so fast. In a very short time he'd want a real car, not a scale model.

Richard knocked on the doorframe.

"I'm in here, Dad." Obviously his gift of Sight was not on today or he'd have known his visitor. It was warming that Michael had so readily adopted Bourland in turn as his new father. Some children never bonded to that level of acceptance with their adopted families, but he had, and with an uncanny artlessness. It's what made it seem like he'd always been there.

"It's me," Richard called, going through the door to the adjoining room.

"Hey! Uncle Richard! Come see!" Michael, looking as normal as any thirteen-year-old, was tilted far back in a chair, knees high about his ears, bare feet braced on his computer desk. He wore pajama pants and an oversized hockey sweatshirt and clutched some kind of control device in his hands. He was apparently very involved destroying hoards of green and purple something-or-others with bulging eyes and lots of teeth. He cut them down using either a ray gun or a magic wand that fired bolts of light. Perhaps it was both in one.

"Are you winning?" Richard asked, peering.

"I've almost got it. Ten thousand points and I move up, but the more points you rack, the tougher they get to hit . . . and . . . aaagh!"

There was a magnificent explosion on the computer's monitor, followed by dirgelike music. A sonorous voice from the speakers intoned that because he fought so valiantly he would be accorded a hero's shrine and the bards would sing his name forever. Would he like to play another game?

"Raaats." Michael rolled his eyes in dramatic frustration, though he did not appear to be overly distressed by the defeat.

"What happened?"

"Gas attack."

"Really?"

"They got these fat guys in there full of mega-methane, and if you don't get 'em with a head shot they blow up and take you with them."

"Oh. What are you shooting?"

"Nitrogen bullets."

Richard wasn't entirely at sea with the sciences, but fairly certain such things were impossible. He hoped they were, anyway.

Michael edged his control device onto his overcrowded desk, dislodging a stack of CDs. It was clear the housekeeper never made it this far. Nearly every horizontal surface was covered with several strata of . . . well, there was too much to take in or categorize, but bright colors and plastic seemed to dominate the bulk of the artifacts, that and comic books. The walls and ceiling were completely papered over with posters of current icons of teen worship, including a blond pop princess wearing what appeared to be paint. Closer examination indicated her costume to be made of fabric after all, though it was a near thing. Richard glanced at the boy, one eyebrow twitching. Damn. An early starter. He couldn't recall exactly when he himself had realized that girls weren't horrible creatures one avoided at all costs. Some things were likely better off lost in the mists of time.

Significantly missing from Michael's collection were any toys or mementos from his past in Texas. Those had all been destroyed, of course, though he could have gotten duplicates if he asked. The only reminder of his life before Bourland adopted him just a few years ago was a photo of his much younger self with his late mother and twin sisters that Richard had given him.

There were no pictures of Michael's biological father. Just as well. The therapy was still an ongoing process for that heartbreak.

"Check this out," said Michael. He'd been busy clicking away on his keyboard. Bourland bought the boy a new computer every Christmas in a vain effort to keep up with advancing technology. This latest model, which would probably be hopelessly out of date in less than a week, was sleek and expensive looking, with an oversized flat screen and matching speakers. "There's this way-cool software that came with the computer and it turns any sounds or music into shifting shapes and stuff. See?"

He hit more keys, electronic instruments blared from the speakers, and a window filling most of the screen erupted with the promised show. It *was* rather neat.

"Why you over here so early?" Michael asked, nodding in time to the beat. He had pale blond hair like his mother, cut short, but darker skin than one would expect from her Nordic ancestry. The seemingly permanent tan bequeathed by his father's genes had faded somewhat since his move from Texas to this latitude, and he'd taken to the abundance of snow like a home-grown sled dog.

"I think you know."

He grunted. "Because of why Dad kept me home. That vision. It was gross."

Yes, children were tough all right. "That's all? Gross? Not frightening?"

"Well, yeah, it scared me, but you were there in it, so that made it okay. You were all there. It was cool how you talked to the snake."

"I talked to it?"

"That's what it looked like."

"Did you hear it speak?"

"Nah. Too much other stuff was going on. Look, Aunt Sabra's coming over, too, isn't she?"

"Yes."

"I thought so. Whenever something weird happens you guys gang up. I'll talk about it with her then. Check this—" He cut the music, but the show on the screen continued, reacting to his voice. "You can turn your words into geometric or free forms or abstract designs, and it's got all kinds of colors and styles . . ." He clicked his way through a parade of variations, talking a mile a minute, raising or lowering his tone to bring about an effect. He seemed most pleased at the pattern his own name made.

On one of the shelves Richard noticed a new picture of Michael and Bourland, apparently from their most recent ice-fishing expedition. Red-faced, they looked enormously pleased with themselves, showing off a bounteous catch. Richard felt a too-familiar twinge about missing out on such diversions, but reminded himself that Michael was *here* and alive and that's all that really mattered. Even limited contact was better than nothing.

Make the most of it, he thought, and bent over to inquire about some detail. It didn't really matter what they talked about, just having time together was the important part. He obligingly spoke into a pick-up mic and saw what his name looked like on screen.

"Aw, say your whole name," Michael urged.

"Richard Dun."

"That's not it. Your *real* whole name."

He hesitated. Perhaps Sabra had been giving history lessons. Or it was the Sight at work? "Richard d'Orleans," he finally admitted.

The screen splashed itself with color. Mostly reds. Hm. Coincidence?

Michael grinned and hit keys. Richard's voice echoed and re-echoed his full name, mechanically repeating, making an endless fountain of red against a black background.

He felt suddenly uncomfortable. "That's very interesting, but could you shift it, please?"

Michael made no move; the screen continued active, reacting to the manic repetition of sound.

"Michael?"

The pattern of color changed, giving up its pulsing symmetry to completely random movement. The colors and shapeless blobs began to darken and eventually coalesced into recognizable patterns, stabilizing, becoming a surreal and disturbing picture. Michael went very still. He calmly stared, unblinking and oblivious, at the screen. A sudden shift in color and focus knocked everything from chaos into clear vision. An all too familiar one.

Chichén Itzá.

Heart pounding, Richard felt himself drawn strongly into the scene. It ceased to be contained by the screen, but grew, filled his view . . . and, without fuss, swallowed him.

Laughter . . . booming laughter against the storm raging around him.

He stood at the top of the pyramid, looking down the steep angle of hard steps. Was this what Sharon saw in those last seconds?

Unable to act, only watch, he was raised high by unnaturally strong arms. Who was it? He tried to turn to see the face, but—

A sickening swoop, a cry, but instead of being caught by the storm's force and lifted, he plunged heavily down, crashing onto the stone steps, bones splintering. Spin, roll, rolling faster, gravity and momentum having their way until he was at the base lying twisted on the bare dry ground between the two great snake heads.

From there he seemed to rise from the wreckage of flesh and pull back. Now he was looking down at Sharon's battered form. He reached for her, but possessed no body, only sight. He'd never felt so helpless.

She saw him through her pain, unable to move, struggling to

breathe. Blood bubbled from her lips. Her face changed. The injuries remained the same, but now he stared down at Sabra . . . and then Michael. They shifted in and out of focus, meshing, their voices blending, becoming one.

Richard—help me!

Right out of hell.

Then they were gone.

He gasped awake as though struck with an electric shock; adrenaline hammered sickeningly through his system. But he was only in Michael's study under the harsh but prosaic dazzle of artificial light, and outside was gray winter day.

Michael slumped, pitching to one side from his chair.

Bourland caught him before Richard could even think to move. Apparently he'd been standing there a while. He gathered the boy up and carried him to the next room, laying him gently on the bed. He felt Michael's brow for fever, automatically, the way parents do whether it's likely or not. There was a blanket folded over the footboard. He shook it open and draped it on the boy, who seemed deeply asleep. Only then did Bourland look at Richard, his expression that of barely suppressed anger.

"What's wrong with him?" he whispered. "And what *is* that?" He pointed through the door to the computer, which now showed only an innocuous screen saver and made no sound.

"You saw it, too?"

Bourland nodded. "And its effect on the two of you. He slept the last one off, but—is this *hurting* him?"

"I don't know," Richard answered truthfully. *The last one?* "How long has this been going on?"

No reply, Bourland checked Michael again, then motioned for them to leave.

"You're sure?" Michael looked so very young, painfully vulnerable. The boy's heartbeat sounded normal, regular. Beyond that . . .

"He's just asleep. Come on."

Bourland's study was direct from a decorator's handbook; traditional, sober, projecting a wealth of reassurance and the reassurance of wealth. Warm wood and leather furnishings, dark green walls, some carefully selected antiques, it seemed a century out of date, except that a century ago such rooms hadn't looked quite the same. However, Richard liked it much better than that time Queen Victoria went so ludicrously mad for tartans. This was more like a staid but contented London club than her kilt factory explosion at Balmoral.

Absurdities again. Focus, old lad.

Philip Bourland chose the long tufted leather couch over one of the overstuffed chairs. A big man, he was determinedly informal today in worn slacks, a thick moss-colored sweater over a dark shirt, and sheepskin slippers. Amid the ambiance of his surroundings, he looked more like a misplaced handyman than the lord of the manor. He also looked very tired, his china blue eyes haunted yet blazingly angry.

"That damned dream," he rumbled aloud, as though continuing from an internal dialogue.

"What about it?" Richard eased into one of the chairs opposite.

His friend had shut his face down. In Bourland's line of work it was to his advantage not to broadcast his feelings, particularly the harsher ones. Rarely had Richard ever experienced that aspect directed his way. The two of them were nearly always on the same page. "You were there, square in the middle of it, so you tell me."

This could go very bad, very fast. Anger was a useful weapon, but not between friends. Richard fixed his gaze for a moment until the heat went out of Bourland's eyes. "You know I'm here to help, Philip. I'll do whatever I can. Please trust that."

In a few scant seconds some of the rigidity left Bourland's shoulders. He slumped and rubbed a hand over his face. "God, this has me on the living edge. I don't know what to do so I—sorry, Richard. None of this is your fault."

Don't be too sure of that. "When did it start?"

"I'm not . . . I only began to notice in the last few days. Michael's—well, I call it 'phasing out.'"

"This has been going on for *days*?"

"Maybe longer."

"Why didn't you tell Sabra? Or me?"

Bourland shook his head. "I wasn't sure if this was real or not— his spells, whatever they are. I really don't know why I held back. It was as though there was a hand on my shoulder and a voice telling me to 'wait and see, wait and see,' that everything would get better. It seems completely idiotic now. I must have been in denial, but that's not like me."

Indeed it was not. Bourland always kept them apprized of everything to do with Michael, from his schoolwork to the least bump and bruise on the soccer field or at hockey practice. Had there been some kind of Otherside intervention at work?

He continued. "I'm not one to make excuses, either. You were over Sunday, and he was fine then, wasn't he?"

Richard gave a cautious nod, trying to remember specifics in retrospect. It had been especially cloudy, so he made a rare daylight visit, watching a hockey game with them in the TV room. Bourland's inborn enthusiasm for the sport had grafted onto Michael and their running commentary about the game rivaled that on the television and had been just as constant. An ordinary afternoon together, enjoyable, no hint of looming trouble.

"When did you first notice anything?"

"It was Monday evening. He was at his computer, playing a game, not doing his homework. I was saying the things you're supposed to say in those situations, and he just kept staring at the screen. I thought he'd shut me out, wasn't listening, but he's not like that. Some boys his age start to build up anger and go surly, but not him. Then I saw that there were some damned odd images on the screen. They had nothing to do with his game or homework or anything I've ever seen before."

"What did they look like?"

"I'll get to that. The main point is he was quite fine and then shut down for a few moments. When that happened . . ."

Richard waited him out.

But Bourland gave up. "No, you won't believe me."

"Just say it, Philip. I'll judge for myself."

A longer wait. Then, "All right. When he's like that, when there's things happening on the screen, I seem to see . . . in my *mind* . . . similar things. As though I'm *in* them, surrounded by them. It's because of that I've not taken Michael off to a neurosurgeon for tests. I know in my heart this isn't anything a doctor can diagnose and treat. Please tell me I'm wrong."

"What did you see upstairs?"

"Nothing in my head, but on the screen, those faces . . ."

"I saw them, too. It was just my luck to have a turn to be in it."

"You've gone through this before, haven't you? Experienced it."

"Yes. In Texas. He . . . showed me how his mother and sisters died. There's been nothing since then."

Bourland looked at him a long time, studying, thinking, and not giving anything away. It was this sternness that often compelled others to burst forth with confessions. All he had to do was wait.

But Richard had long been immune to such tactics. He wanted to try to explain, but the odds were very great that Bourland would be unable to accept anything as outré as the truth, about himself, Sabra, Michael, the projected visions, Otherside matters, especially the Goddess. Such concepts simply did not exist for him except as myth.

Then again . . .

Perhaps Bourland's extended contact with Sabra—and Michael—was affecting him on a psychic level, creating a window for him to peer through. Perhaps that's why he'd been able to see certain things. Sabra often kept herself removed from the general crowd of humanity because the press of their emotions wore at her, but it could go both ways. Some people were sensitive to her presence and power, and its touch could suddenly, inadvertently, open them up to forces for which they were unprepared.

"I thought," said Bourland, "that it might be me. I've been told my job is not exactly low stress. My first instinct was that I was having a problem and saw something that wasn't there. The brain can be quite disturbing when it comes to manufacturing fantasies. I thought I'd experienced some kind of mental glitch—except for Michael phasing out like that."

"Does he remember what he's seen?"

"He says not, but I don't believe him. I didn't want to press things and make too much of it. For what it's worth I was going to phone Sabra today and sort it all out. Then we had that dream. Both of us. Three of us . . . ?"

Richard finally nodded. "Four, actually. Another reason why Sabra's coming in."

"Oh, my God."

"What else is there?" Richard asked.

"How do you know th—" he cut off, frowning.

"Just go with me on this."

Bourland sighed. "In for a penny, in for the whole bloody national debt. All right. I think he's able to project these . . . images . . . not only to a screen, but into other people's heads besides my own and he has no control over it."

Richard nodded, encouraging him to continue.

"On Wednesday one of the day maids quit. Michael was after a pre-dinner snack in the kitchen, and she was there. He must have phased out then. She ran screaming from the house. After what I've seen, I don't blame her."

"Is she all right?"

"I think so. She insisted the house was haunted and refused to come back. Stood in the street crying. My housekeeper had to take the girl's coat and purse out and drive her home. I didn't make a fuss with the agency, gave her a nice reference, but it was a damned awkward bit of business. I still don't know what she might have seen. Michael couldn't or wouldn't say. I don't think he means to, it just takes him over. He's broadcasting like a radio tower, isn't he?"

He recalled the vivid images projected into his mind by a much younger Michael, showing in too-graphic detail the murder of his mother and sisters. Even second-hand they carried power and still sometimes troubled Richard's sleep with nightmares.

"What I want to know—among other things—is where are these images coming from? They're . . . unworldly. I know he's not seen anything like this in a film or television, there *are* limits. He's allowed a certain amount of rubbish to watch if he wants, but not that kind of rubbish."

"His imagination, perhaps."

"Then the boy needs more therapy than he's getting."

"Can you describe what you've seen?" Richard's instinct told him there was more to this than Chichén Itzá.

"Better. Or worse. I can show you."

Anachronistically taking up space on the polished top of Bourland's Edwardian desk was another state-of-the-art computer system. He roused it from hibernation, got it fully awake, and entered a password. Then he opened a program and put in a CD. His hand rested on the trackball, preparatory to clicking the "play" icon.

"Here it is: after school yesterday Michael came in to ask me about something, then while he was standing exactly where you are now, he phased out. At the same time the images began to flash into my mind; I also saw them on my computer screen. Weirdest damned stuff I'd ever—I was set up to do some video copying and had just enough wit to try recording. It worked. I wanted to call Sabra then, but didn't know how I could possibly describe it. She's usually the one to call here, always knows when something's off, but she didn't. This is scaring the hell out of me, Richard. First, that Michael is subject to these fits, second, that *I'm* seeing such visions, and third, that they could even be recorded. I wish the latter at least was untrue."

"Why is that?"

"Because then I could put this off to shared insanity and check the lot of us into a psychiatric ward. But this is solid evidence. I can't ignore its reality. I'd hoped it would go away, but the dream last night and what happened upstairs just now . . . it's only escalating. What's to be done?"

"Let's see what you recorded first."

The show was as promised. It was a smaller version of the catastrophe at El Castillo, at another location. The image was less clear, but some parts were sufficient for recognition. "My God, that's Stonehenge." Richard's mouth went dry. The fragment of Sharon's message . . . but what did it mean? Was this what she'd seen there? And how had that sent her flying off to the Yucatán?

The oddly familiar storm faded, fuzzily replaced by—he couldn't quite make it out, like a badly managed handheld camera trying to focus on something too far in the distance. Unfortunately, the picture firmed up and became clear.

It was bad. Like a Hieronymus Bosch painting come to awful life.

Richard had known Bosch, had known the grotesque allegories in his nightmare paintings were based in truth. The artist had seen such horrors in his mind, God help him, interpreting and expressing them in his own way. They were enough to scare the hell out of anyone, which was the intention.

Things writhed on the screen, things with pale eyes and grasping claws, things made of darkness, possessing bottomless appetites, that delighted in making pain, things that had no business on this Side of Reality. These were not flat depictions on wood, not disturbing, but ultimately harmless renderings by a long-dead artist.

These *existed*.

And they were *aware*.

They seemed to look right at him. Hungry.

The image mercifully dissolved, went black.

"If," said Bourland, the color gone from his face, "if *that* is what got broadcasted into the poor maid's mind, then I don't blame her for running away screaming. I was rather tempted myself."

"But you didn't." Richard hadn't meant to say that aloud.

"How could I when Michael's in—what *is* going on here?"

This was definitely Sabra's pigeon, though he would help if he could. Somehow or other they'd have to try explaining to Bourland and hope he would prove open-minded enough to accept. He was well aware of Sabra's strong psychic connection to the boy, but overlooked it or perhaps rationalized it away as feminine intuition. He'd never interfered with her talks with Michael, evidently trusting her completely. She was a most dazzling woman, and he cared for her, but would that be enough?

"Richard?" Bourland had gotten no answer. "Thinking of Sabra? Oh, don't be surprised. You always look like that when she's on your mind. What about her, then?"

"Only that she'll talk to you about this."

"It's related to her?"

"In a way. I think. I'm as puzzled as you are."

"But you have more pieces, else you'd be sleeping in like anyone with sense instead of coming over here at this hour of the morning. You had that dream, too. The one that frightened Michael so. The one that frightened me."

"You—"

"Yes, I admit it. Like nothing I've ever in my whole life had before, and God spare me from another. Woke me up in a cold sweat, then I heard Michael crying down the hall—"

"He didn't say he'd been that frightened."

"Oh, come on. What thirteen-year-old is going to admit to his macho uncle that he cried because of a nightmare?"

Richard stared. "'Macho uncle'? Really, Philip, what in God's name are you telling that boy?"

"Not me, it's all him. He worships you. Of course he'd never let on, that wouldn't be the done thing for him, but it's there. I suppose he could have a *worse* role model in his life, but I can't think of anyone."

A look between them, then an abrupt breakdown to a soft chuckle. Brief, but enough to break the tension.

Then Bourland fixed him with a much too neutral eye. "Who's Richard d'Orleans?"

It had been a long time, a *very* long time since Richard had last been caught off guard like this. He didn't even try to cover and lie. Not much point to it, really. "Someone I used to be. He no longer exists."

"And why is that?"

"You know the type of work I've done and can do. Sometimes it's necessary to drop one's past and begin again."

"I had you checked out. Thoroughly. Back when we first met."

"I wouldn't have expected you to have done otherwise."

"Yours is an interesting but not improbable background with impeccable, even enviable references. But not one mention of anyone named d'Orleans."

"Because of the nature of the work then. I . . . offended . . . the wrong types once upon a time, and the powers that be deemed it necessary to my survival that I should be someone else ever afterwards. It turned out for the best, though." Damn, would he have to hypnotize Bourland again? It was one thing to calm a friend down, quite another to rearrange his memories. Richard hated doing that.

"And in the fifteen years I've known you you never once cracked the least hint, yet for Michael you threw it out almost casually. More important, he *knew*."

"Philip . . . I can't explain Michael's knowledge. It surprised me, but after all this time, it seemed harmless. On the other hand, you're reminding me that perhaps it was unwise to have relaxed."

"Oh, don't worry, I'm not backing you into a corner about it. Your secret's safe. God knows fifteen years ago I was a different man as well. My concern's for Michael. I don't want him ending up in some crackpot mind-reading or remote-viewing program for a bunch of soulless black-ops types."

Richard's jaw momentarily dropped. "Just what sort of rubbish have *you* been watching?"

"Never mind. Blame it on lack of sleep. I'm usually much more rational than this."

But your fear for Michael's future is real enough. Which was at the bottom of it for both of them. All of them.

His cell trilled. He checked the incoming number. "Sabra," he said to Bourland, hitting the button. "Yes? You all right?" Why had he asked that first thing?

"Not really." She spoke loudly, as people do when surrounded by noise. There was some kind of row going on. "The snow's gotten worse."

"You can't dig out?"

"I did that ages ago. I'm on my way in but there's a hell of a snow storm on 400."

"Where are you?"

"I'm coming up on the exit to 401. It's not that far ahead, but I'm having a hard time staying on the road. The wind's very bad."

"Then pull over. There's nothing here that can't wait."

"Yes. I called to let you know."

She sounded breathless and busy. In the background Richard heard the fast thump of her windshield wipers and on top of that an unpleasant howling. "Sounds like a hurricane from this end. Find a petrol station or something and stay there until it's blown over."

"I'll do that . . ."

"What's wrong?" Bourland asked.

"She's driven into a storm near 401." His alarms were blaring, full volume. *This is not right. Not at all right.*

Bourland turned, looking out the broad window behind his desk.

The view was that of a tranquil winter day, very overcast, but last night's wind was quite gone. "Richard . . . she's not that far north . . ."

But he'd already gotten it. "Sabra, wherever you are pull over now. You hear? Right *now*."

Her voice, garbled by static. Nothing intelligible came through. It was too much like Sharon's message for his peace of mind.

"Uncle Richard?" Michael was at the door, still in his pajama pants and hockey shirt, hair tousled, his expression somber. Had he grown a bit since Sunday? He looked so young. Vulnerable.

"Just a minute . . . Sabra, you there? Say again."

Tears on Michael's face. Tears streaming down.

Richard's guts swooped, and he pressed the earpiece hard against his skull, vainly trying to hear better. He thought she was shouting, but the static worsened between them. Please God, just let it be a signal fade out.

"Uncle Richard, you have to—"

"Sabra? Hello? Answer!" He struggled to keep his voice calm. It was just a strong wind. Nothing more than that.

"You have to call for her. She's in trouble."

"Sabra! Say that again."

"Dad, call an ambulance." Michael went to Bourland. "It's important. She's—"

Her voice. Shouting now, but Richard still couldn't understand the words. He looked at Bourland, who was staring at his computer screen. "What is it?"

Neither of them answered. Michael had gone still.

Richard came around the desk to see.

The computer screen showed gray and black movement. Snow and shadows? Bulky shapes emerging and retreating, a smear of white as they passed. Cars. Headlights.

Then he was there, pulled into the vision, standing on the side of a snow-crusted highway. Heavy flakes churned around him in the tearing wind, thicker than fog. Richard could *feel* them going right through his body, yet he saw himself as solid.

Cars, lots of them. The morning rush in full swing, even here, even in this weather, everyone driving far too fast, or so it seemed to one held stationary. Their tires hissed on wet pavement, hummed on the icy patches. A straight stretch of flat road was behind him, ahead, an overpass.

He saw her. Her car approaching. She was on the phone, her other hand on the wheel, fighting it as the wind buffeted the sides of her vehicle. She seemed unaware of him.

He spoke her name into his cell phone. Dead air.

The snow seemed to laze down now, everything slowing like a film running at the wrong speed.

She flashed by in increments. He saw her through clear patches on the car's side windows. In stages she spoke into her phone, scowled, and discarded it, gripping the wheel with both hands. She pressed back in the seat the way one does when slamming hard on the brakes, her lips parted, eyes wide with fear.

Then normal time kicked in.

The backwash of her passing vehicle hit him, along with the stink of exhaust. He blinked against it, arm instinctively up to protect his face from debris.

Snow whirled madly about her car, as though possessed of its own cyclone. The brake lights flared and died, flared again as she fishtailed all over the road. Other commuters hit their horns in protest, getting out of the way. Sabra sped up.

With the brakelights *still on*.

No.

She rocketed forward, faster, faster.

The wind screamed around her, a miniature blizzard.

Ahead, a patch of ice showing like a black lake across the width of the road.

Her front tires hit it at an angle. She made a long, agonizing spin, skidding sideways . . .

Hitting something. He couldn't see what. At that speed her car simply flipped right over.

And kept going. It seemed to fly, carried by the wind—

To smash into the unforgiving concrete of an overpass.

Chapter Five

Normandy, the Past

"If that's how he swings a blade, then it's just as well he's destined to take orders."

Richard's face burned, but he was turned away from Dear Brother Ambert and pretended not to hear the jibe. He struck extra hard at the straw-padded practice post with his wooden sword and felt the impact jolt up his arm with numbing force.

Too much. It knocked the sword from his hand.

Ambert doubled over, hooting.

Richard fought down a burst of rage mixed with red-faced humiliation. He knew a direct challenge to Ambert would only lead to a beating. His oldest brother had four more years of skill and fighting experience over him. And taunts. He was very good with those.

"Pick up your weapon," ordered the fight-master, who was working with Edward, Richard's next eldest brother. "Ignore him and do your drills."

The practice area within the curtain wall of Castle d'Orleans was muddy from last night's rain. A layer of straw had been thrown down, but was uneven in patches. Richard's sword lay in one of the bare spots. Just his bad luck. He cleaned off the grip as best he could and went back to work on the post, striking it again and again to strengthen his arm. At fourteen, he was as tall as his brothers, but lean as string. The fight-master said he'd not yet reached his full growth and muscle, but constant practice would fill him out.

Richard wanted that more than anything and pushed himself hard, but some days absolutely nothing seemed to work. It was as though his own body was at war with him, and all he could do was trip or knock things over, or both. In the last six months he'd shot up over a handspan in height. He was misplaced elbows and knees, overlarge hands and feet, awkward lengths of shin and arm and always hungry. When not on the field, he haunted the kitchens, charming the cooks out of extra food between the usual meals.

He grinned as the sweat began to run on him, pretending the post was Ambert.

Something wet slammed into the side of his face with bruising force. He lost balance, sliced downward, missing the post, and staggered like a drunk. A sizable dollop of mud clung to him and dribbled cold down his neck.

Ambert burst into laughter again. He'd thrown the missile. Quick as spite, he stooped and grabbed up another handful and cast with deadly accuracy. He caught Richard square in the chest and it hurt. There'd been a large stone in that one. He grunted, losing the sword again, and abruptly sat down in the mud.

"*There* he is, champion to the swine! All hail!" Ambert executed a mock bow and erupted into laughter again.

Before he could make a third strike Richard was on him. His aim was also good; he bodily tackled his brother, and they rolled and splashed messily into the broad puddle from which Ambert had supplied himself. He kicked and punched full force, but Richard was too angry to feel it, busy delivering as much damage as he could in the brief time he had before they'd be pulled apart.

Around them the younger pages yelled encouragement, the older ones made quick wagers, and the armsmen hesitated between laughter and interference. If two of the Duke of Normandy's sons chose to fight each other, then let them be. Taking sides now could prove dangerous later on. Ambert was touchy about being helped unless he called for it. He always won, anyway.

Richard's fists seemed to be working together for a change, though, and as quickly as things were going he became aware of their adverse effect on Ambert. His brother grunted and cursed, and when he did hit, it wasn't with his usual vindictive strength.

A third party entered the fray, shouting and trying to grab hold of Richard. Without thinking he lashed out and clouted Edward solidly in the belly, toppling him. Then there were three angry brothers rolling in the mud trying to commit bloody fratricide.

As if by magic Richard discovered his speed and used his training. For every blow he got, he delivered two more in return, and he didn't care who he hit so long as flesh gave way and pain resulted. He was like a hammer in the smith's hand, force and mastery and direction, and having a decided effect on what had once been unyielding iron.

He was dimly aware of commotion around them and of a sudden slackening in the fight.

Then he was on top, straddling . . . Ambert . . . and pulping his face. Edward . . . was lying over there, moving slowly, favoring his sides.

The first, the very first, thrill of true exhilaration ran through Richard's young body, his heart pounding so heavily he thought he might die from it.

I won! I beat them!

Then the fight-master waded in and dragged him off. He gave Richard a shake and growled his name, but it was not necessary. Richard was in control of himself, gulping in the giddy air of victory. He'd never felt this way before, almost burning from the triumph. Did anyone else see it?

Apparently not. They were busy looking after Ambert and Edward. As with other rare successes in his life, Richard would have to savor this one on his own.

Perhaps not entirely. Once his brothers were on their feet again they each shot him a look. Ambert's was suffused with hate and an implied promise of revenge later on; Edward's was . . . surprise. That was different. In the past those two more or less worked together. He limped over.

Richard braced for further assault, but none came.

Edward merely smiled, a grim smile, but unexpected. "So, the babe of the family's become a man at last."

Had that been said by Ambert it would have dripped with venom, but there was nothing malicious here.

"You fought well, Dickon." Edward glanced over his shoulder to Ambert, who was vainly trying to swipe mud from his clothes. "Don't turn your back on him. He doesn't forget insults."

A look between them. Abrupt understanding on Richard's part. He had acceptance. A very small portion of it to be sure, but still . . .

"Come and wash that muck off before you *are* declared champion of the swine."

He should talk. They were both filthy.

Edward led the way to a long trough by the smithy, dipped a bucket in, and poured water over his head, scrubbing the worst from his face. He had an eye swelling and going dark, but grinned through it. "Your turn."

Richard half expected to be hit with the bucket. But that did not happen. He was thoroughly doused with a full measure of water and then another. After all the exertion in the summer heat it felt delicious.

"This will do. We'll swim in the lake later to get it all off. Come on, then." He trudged back to the practice field.

"You hurt?" Richard ventured to ask.

"Not much, but from now on I'll leave it to others to keep you two apart. I've had my fill."

"Didn't mean to hit you."

"I know. This was Ambert's doing."

Ambert still bled from his nose, which looked to be broken. He threw down the rag he held to his face and charged Richard.

Who braced, fists ready to beat him again.

But Edward stepped between, catching another clout to his ribs as he caught Ambert. He took it and did not release his hold.

"I'll kill the little bastard!" Ambert shrieked, trying to struggle free.

Edward swung him around and threw him against the practice post, knocking him breathless.

Ambert stared with baffled shock. "You dare?"

"You're not lord of the castle yet," said Edward. "So, yes. You deserved what you got, leave it at that."

"You—"

"Look at him, brother, and use your wits. He's no bastard, and he's not little anymore. He took us both down without even trying."

Richard felt his jaw drop.

"So think twice before you go after him. Next time someone might not pull him off you."

Ambert's eyes blazed, but he made no move against either of them. After a moment he lifted his chin and smiled. Not a pleasant sight through the blood and filth. "Next time *will* come. Be sure of it."

He sauntered toward the trough. None too steadily, though he seemed to be trying to hide it.

"Back to practice," said the fight-master to his remaining students. "No food till you've sweated again."

Richard went through his drills and sparred with some of the taller pages. He had bruises and a cut inside his lip, but nothing that couldn't be ignored. What did unsettle his concentration was wondering about Edward. Sometimes he'd get between Ambert and Richard, attempting to head off Ambert's worst excesses, usually with a joke or insult, always at Richard's expense. He always made Richard their common enemy, but not to the point of encouraging an attack.

Until now Richard thought it had been only for their mutual advantage for Edward's main argument against the bullying was that they should avoid attracting their father's notice. If Richard got hurt too badly, even old Montague would step in to mete out punishment to all. It tended to be brutal, more harsh than anything Ambert could inflict or was willing to endure.

Until today that had been the extent of Edward's protection, such as it was. Had something changed? Richard found it hard to believe this acceptance was based solely on his one victory.

He got an answer at evening prayers. The brothers kept themselves widely separated in the chapel, an intuitive stratagem they'd adopted long ago to prevent clashes. The chapel became neutral ground for them, allowing them the freedom not to fight. It had less to do with the damnation of their immortal souls and more to do with the priest, for apart from the fight-master and their father, he was the only other man with any kind of authority over them and didn't put up with their quarrels. He had a heavy whip close to hand to enforce the dignity of his church, but rarely used it. Once was usually enough to put the fear of God into the most rambunctious worshipers, and witnesses to such demonstrations were subject to immediate conversion to respectful behavior.

They got through the ritual, and Ambert left for evening meal. Richard hung back, though, hungry for knowledge, not bread. Edward had taken to standing in front for prayers and to hear the mass. He'd done so again, then lingered to talk with the priest after everyone else had gone. They each noticed Richard standing by the door. Edward nodded, but only to acknowledge his presence, not invite him over, being more interested in what the priest was saying. It looked like they'd be there for a while.

Perhaps Edward's conscience had grown somewhat more sensitive of late from these talks. That would explain his help. Richard had heard of such things happening. He was himself destined to serve in the church when the time came, which would be soon, in the next year or so, and often brooded over the pending change with mixed feelings. It would liberate him from the discord and violence of his home, but also remove him from the wide world in general, which he was eager to explore. There wouldn't be much of that once he was within a monastery, not unless they went on a pilgrimage to some distant land. But instead of being a strong warrior on a fine horse leading the way, he'd be one of the robed and anonymous brothers walking barefoot in the general procession behind the guardsmen.

The priest had assured him that God called many, and they willingly followed, for the spiritual rewards were greater than anything this world offered. Richard did his best to listen, but so far had yet to hear the Voice that would instantly convince him to forsake the life he knew for protective walls and a calm routine of devotions and tilling crops.

Well, no one on earth or from heaven was calling him just now.

He shrugged at Edward's curious display of piety and hurried away to the main hall before the food was all eaten.

They were up at dawn, blinking in the new light, rousing for another day's lesson learning their warcraft. Ambert's face was swollen, mottled red and blue, especially his nose. Because of the gaudy damage he tried to escape practice, but the fight-master wouldn't let him.

"Think your enemy will feel sorry for you if you're wounded? Get at it or I'll give you something to really regret."

Ambert snarled and muttered, but took a wooden sword and drilled with the rest. When he chanced to groan, he got a switch across the backside from the fight-master for being soft.

Richard tried not to show amusement, but it was hard going. He kept his distance, though, knowing Ambert would blame him for every pain. The switchings put him into a truly foul mood, and he took it out on anyone within reach.

If Edward hurt from yesterday's scrap, he made no complaint and did as he was told, keeping up with the rest.

An hour of this, an hour of that, then it was time to use real swords. They were much heavier than war blades, their edges well blunted, and tended to clank rather than ring when struck, but the metallic sound still awoke an excited enthusiasm in everyone. If they mastered these clumsy tools, then might they be allowed to have something better later on, earning the right to wield a true weapon.

Richard pulled on a much-battered helmet that more or less fit. He had to wrap cloth around his head to get the thing to stay in place. The others were no better, except for Ambert, who had one of Montague's castoffs that served him well enough.

Their body protection was bulky padding, some with thick leather attached, all of it hot. No one complained. This was like real soldiering.

They were paired off and drilled over and over until their sweat ran in rivers and they were red and puffing fit to drop.

Ambert was merciless on his opponents, but drew no rebuke from the fight-master. That's why they were here, after all, to learn how to win. Those who were unlucky enough to match him used their best defensive skills and backed out of range when they could. Eventually, even he ran out of fight, and retired to the side. He peeled out of his leather armor and swilled down water mixed with wine to keep his blood going.

Richard was paired with an older page for shield and sword work; Edward was set against one of the armsmen. The sun was almost overhead. Another few bouts and they could break off for midday meal.

At a signal, they began free drills, which was Richard's favorite part of practice. It was very close to real fighting since you could choose your moves rather than going through the same ones in the same order. His winning yesterday gave him confidence, but his body wasn't cooperating as well as it had then. He felt awkward again, as though everything was back to being the wrong size, particularly himself. Besides, the page was ready with his own surprises. Richard missed some opportunities, but made up for the lack with his height and reach, and tried hard to regain the control he'd possessed. He knew fighting wasn't always about force, but in choosing how and when to use it wisely. The shorter page seemed to have that lesson down and was putting it to test.

Edward favored one of his legs, apparently still aching from his involvement in the brotherly brawl, and the armsman attacked on that side, forcing Edward to put more strain on the limb. The ploy worked, and Edward lost his footing and fell. Twice.

Ambert enjoyed both events, jeering each time. "See the great champion, crippled by a beardless boy."

Richard bit back reminding Ambert that he had also been bested the same way. There was clearly more wine than water in Dear Brother's cup, so he would be immune to good sense for the time being. Aware of this, the fight-master did not rebuke him or force him back to the field to sweat it out. Time enough for that after midday when food would sober him.

Not one to be ignored, Ambert continued his insults. Usually he held back from attacking Edward, since they were both of a size and age to match each other. There was also the easier target, Richard, who had ever been their common enemy. That was changed, but Ambert seemed quite willing to persist inflicting abuse on his own. He found much to criticize; Edward's every move was subject to unsympathetic judgment, and it had a worsening effect on his actions. Clumsy and panting, with every pass he grew redder of face and struck harder and with less discipline.

The fight-master told Ambert to stop, but got the argument that enemy soldiers were just as likely to fling taunts as spears and arrows.

Then the armsman who opposed Edward gave a brief guttural cry, staggered, and dropped, twisting to one side. He'd been hit in such a way as to draw blood. A normal occurrence during practice even with blunted weapons, Richard was used to seeing and hearing men in pain.

Breathless, Edward pulled off his helm to stare down at the damage he'd caused. He stood confused and suddenly pale for a moment, then in a strained voice called the fight-master over. Others also stopped their free drill and crowded close. Richard did the same.

The armsman was bleeding from the inside of his upper leg, and trying to staunch it with his hands. The only other time Richard saw such a flow was when the castle butchers were at work. If the animal wasn't yet dead from a knock between the eyes the blood would pulse from its cut throat just like that. The fight-master knelt next to the man and dug deep into the muscle with both thumbs, and yelled to the boys to go fetch a healer. Three of them hared off.

"You'll want the priest for this one," observed Ambert, who had joined the gathering. "Congratulations, Edward, you've made your first kill on the field of battle. Father will be very proud."

Even the grim fight-master, busy as he was, looked aghast. There was a moment of absolute silence as Edward's white face flushed crimson, then he whirled and fell on Ambert like a roaring storm. But Ambert was prepared and, grinning, threw his drink into Edward's eyes. It was one of his favorite ploys to immobilize an attacker.

Only this time it didn't work, not for a man already in a blind fury.

There was a near-inhuman roar of fury and pain, such a sound as Richard had never heard from anyone before, much less Edward. He slammed bodily into Ambert and both went rolling.

Richard was aware of shouts and hoots, of the fight-master's bellow, of pages and armsmen milling about, and all he could see was Edward trying his best to murder Ambert. There was no mistaking this for an ordinary fight. He just *knew*.

No one else seemed to, though.

He hesitated. Certainly he held no love for Ambert, who deserved every crack and clout he got, but Edward . . . he didn't need the mark of Cain on his soul.

So for Edward's sake Richard waded in and grabbed him, a strange reversal on yesterday's actions. He pulled hard on his brother's legs, dragging him clear. Edward was cursing and weeping at the same time, in full frenzy. Richard called for help and got it. Three of the armsmen had to hold Edward down while Richard went to check on Ambert.

His face was bloodied—his nose again—and he gasped like a dying fish, feeble hands to his throat. After pummeling him senseless, Edward had tried to strangle him. Ambert seemed out of danger for the moment, but he'd likely emerge from his stunned state himself ready to kill. Richard, in a rare moment of authority, ordered men to carry him back to the castle.

That still left the wounded armsman to deal with . . .

Resolved now. The fight-master was on his feet, shaking his head at the very, very still figure on the ground. Several of the men crossed themselves and began prayers.

A healer arrived moments later, but pronounced that nothing could have been done to save the man. One of the boys was sent to find the priest, making truth of Ambert's callous prediction. The fight-master found the cause of the man's death quick enough. The tip of Edward's otherwise blunted sword had broken off, leaving a ragged and wickedly sharp edge. It had cut through padding and flesh like a reaper's scythe and tapped one of the courses through which the lifeblood ran. Once severed there was no way to stitch it up again.

Edward now sat exhausted on the churned ground and gaped stupidly at the corpse, eyes dull, his battered face slack with shock. Richard stood close to him for want of a better place. He'd done what needed to be done, and wasn't sure what would come next.

The fight-master crouched next to Edward. "There will be no trouble for you on this, Lord Edward. Accidents on the field happen all the time. We lost two last year, remember? 'Twas but practice then, as well. If he had family you might have to pay recompense, but that will be up to your father."

Edward seemed not to hear. Eventually the fight-master gave up and left to see to duties concerning the situation.

Richard knelt by his brother, thinking he should say something, but no words came to him. Theirs was not a family to share thoughts or offer solace to one another. He felt an unfamiliar twinge in his heart. *I hurt because he's hurting.* It was awful, truly, truly awful, and it couldn't have been nearly as bad as what Edward must be feeling. He wanted to help him, but didn't know how.

The priest finally arrived and ordered the man carried to the chapel. Seemingly appearing from the empty air, Holy Sisters from the nearby nunnery clustered around the fallen. They also crossed themselves and prayed. Their chosen lot was to care for the sick and injured and, when needed, to wash and dress the dead for burial. They would shortly be at their task.

A slow procession made its way to the chapel. Edward painfully got to his feet. He tagged along in their wake, looking like a forlorn and beaten dog searching for a scrap. Not for food, but comfort, Richard thought. He knew what that was like.

None came.

Edward stood without the chapel door, staring inside as though waiting to be granted permission to enter.

None came. No one paid him any mind.

Richard drew near. Out of nowhere he suddenly realized he stood eye to eye with his brother. When had that happened? *Have I grown or has he gotten smaller?*

"It's not your fault," he said. He spoke clearly to be certain he was heard.

Edward blinked at him. His pale blue eyes were immeasurably sad, so much so that Richard felt like crying himself. "It *is* my fault, Dickon. I let Ambert anger me, else I'd have noticed the break on my sword. Instead I kept fighting as though that man was . . . was . . . *oh, God forgive me.*"

The last came out as a rushed whisper, and Edward turned and fled. He was across the yard and out the great gate before Richard could think to follow. He started tardily after, but the fight-master called him back.

"Leave him be, Lord Richard. He'll have to deal with this by himself. Whether by accident or in real battle, the first kill is always the hardest. You'll learn that . . . when it's your time."

Richard didn't see either of his brothers for several days afterward. Edward was not to be found, and Ambert was simply to be avoided. Easily done, for he was confined to his bed like a woman in labor. Several of his ribs were broken or cracked, and he couldn't move without screaming curses. The healer kept him well supplied with wine. A drunken stupor was better than listening to the howls.

Their father, Montague, was not unduly concerned by the incident. He grunted and laughed once, then dismissed it. Men fought and men died, that was the way of life. Get the praying and burying done and move on with things.

Training continued as usual. The castle swordsmith took the broken practice blade and blunted it down again. Though slightly shorter than the others, no one thought anything of it. Only Richard avoided using it, as though some remnant of ill fortune and death might be clinging to the metal.

Then at evening prayers Richard spotted Edward in the chapel in his usual spot at the front. He continued kneeling after everyone else departed. Richard went over, reluctant to interrupt, but Edward looked up and gave him a wan smile.

"Where have you been?" Richard asked.

"Walking."

"Where?"

"To the monastery."

"That's over a day's journey. On horseback."

"Our Lord walked everywhere except into Jerusalem, and I'm not worthy enough or humble enough to ride an ass, so I walked."

"Alone?" All roads were dangerous, even the ones in Duke Montague's rigorously patrolled lands.

"Not alone."

"Who was with you?"

Edward smiled again and pointedly glanced around them to indicate their surroundings. Richard saw only the castle chapel, a cold place within the thick stone walls, but with a very nice fresco of the holy baptism above the altar. His gaze rested on the central figure of the Christ, head bowed as His cousin John poured water over Him. Above them hovered a white dove, and what seemed to be rays like the sun shone from its milk-white breast. Richard knew the story well and thought the painting very pretty. Sometimes he wondered if Jesus had gone properly swimming after His baptism. It didn't seem the right sort of question to put to the priest, though, so he never asked.

"God was with you?" Richard wavered between doubt and the desire to hear something remarkable. There were many wonderful stories told about visitations and miracles, but they were also always in some other land happening to some other people. It would be nice to have such an event here at Orleans.

"He's always with me. Us. All of us."

Now he sounded like the priest. "Did you see Him?"

"Each time I look into another man's face."

Richard felt disappointment. "You learned that at the monastery."

"No. During my walk. I never went in. Just watched outside."

"Then why go there?"

"I wondered that myself."

Edward looked quite gaunt. He was also very dirty. Richard frowned, recalling stories of men who lost their wits and went wild, living as animals in the woods like King Nebuchadnezzar. Is that what happened to his brother? "Have you had aught to eat?"

"Not since I ran away. I've been fasting."

"Are you done, then? Evening meat is—"

"I'm *fine*, Dickon, and I need you to listen to me. I've things to say and no one else to say them to who might understand. It affects you, and I hope . . . well, I don't *think* you'll mind very much."

"Mind what?"

"You're supposed to be the one to take orders, and I'm to be the family champion."

"Yes . . ."

"That's not going to happen now. I'm taking your place. You will—"

"What?" That was impossible. Their fates had been planned since before birth. You didn't just *change* things.

"Be still and listen. I've prayed much and thought much, and it finally burst on my mind like a great light in a long darkness. I don't belong here. I've not been fighting for the family, I've been fighting God's will for me. I never was and never will be a champion."

"But you're strong, you can fight. You're good."

"Yes, I manage well enough, but there is no heart behind it. And after what I did there never will be. I have innocent blood on my soul, caused by an anger that nearly drove me to kill my own brother. I need to be elsewhere, in another place where anger like that will never overcome me again."

"The monastery."

"Yes. Or another like it."

"What about just staying away from Ambert?"

"I thought that through as well. It still comes out the same. I am the one who's been called."

"Father will be angry," Richard pointed out.

"When is he not?"

True.

"It won't be easy, but I know he will grant me leave to go."

Richard doubted that. Their father was infamously, often capriciously stubborn. That he would accept this change—even if it was argued to be God's will—seemed impossible On the other hand, if this was what God truly wanted for Edward there was little the Duke d'Orleans would be able to do against it. "You'll need the priest to help you."

"I've spoken to him. He will choose the right time, and then we shall speak to Father."

He took that to mean Edward and the priest, not himself and Edward. Richard thought he'd like to listen in, though. It might be very interesting to see the duke backing down before anyone, particularly to God Himself.

Outside, night had gently settled over the castle, and the chapel was quite dim. The altar candles still burned. The priest was diligent about that. They burned day and night, and when there was a death and a watch to be kept, more were lighted. Just a few evenings ago Richard had himself stood vigil over the dead armsman when it was his turn. He'd drawn the latest—or earliest—time and shivered in the pre-dawn chill until the next man took his place at sunrise.

That had been a long watch, his first acting as Lord Richard d'Orleans. He was old enough now for such duties. Just. Not that it had been his idea. The fight-master put him forward since Ambert was abed and Edward gone. After the novelty of wearing a special tunic and holding a real sword wore off it got boring. He had no fear of standing alone in the near dark with the dead man so close, only worried that the priest might catch him wavering. The sword, which had to be held respectfully upright, grew very heavy over the next few hours. It was hard to do that and remember to pray at the same time.

"I'm told that Ambert isn't well," said Edward.

Nudged back into the present, Richard shook his head. "He's drunk. They'll keep him that way 'til he's mended because of how he carries on. I've seen wounded pigs cornered by the dogs making less noise. The fight-master wants him on the field again before the moon turns, but that will be too soon for Ambert."

"He's that badly hurt?"

"He's that badly lazy. You know how he is."

"And I will be leaving you to his mercy."

Richard shrugged. "I'll get on all right. Won't care much that you'll be gone, though. I'm just starting to like you."

Edward suddenly laughed. Unlike Ambert's bursts of mirth, there was no derision behind it. "I deserved that. You're the only honest one in the family. Don't lose your honesty, Richard. It's important."

It must be to prompt Edward into using his given name. No one else did. Father and Ambert always called him "you, boy" or worse. "If you're going to the priesthood, then I'm to be the champion? For real?"

"God willing and if you're spared to grow into it. You won't have far to go the way you're shooting up like a spring weed."

His heart beat a lot faster than before. Lord Richard, Champion d'Orleans. That's what they'd call him. It was almost too large for his brain to hold. "There's so much to learn . . ."

"If anyone was born to the sword, it's you. You're already better than me and Ambert together. And doesn't Ambert know it. That's why he taunts you so."

"I thought it was because he has a foul heart."

"There's that, too. He has a darkness in him he got from Father, God help us. But men *can* change. Certainly I've found the truth of it. I will pray for them. And you as well. But until and unless that darkness lifts . . . Ambert will eventually come to fear you, Dickon. Beware of him."

"Fear me?" Richard couldn't see that ever happening.

"And what a man fears he will try to destroy. Never give him a reason to do so. He will likely provide his own, he always has."

He nodded agreement. Ambert was ever quick with excuses and explanations to show himself to be the injured party in any altercation. But he often had help. "If you're all changed, will you tell me why you used to take his side against me?" It was a risky question. Had he asked it a week ago, he'd have gotten a thump between the ears.

But Edward only sagged, looking ashamed. "Because I was a fool and afraid."

"You. Afraid?"

"Oh, yes, and very good at concealing it under the cruelty. But that part of me's gone. For good, I hope. It used to matter that I hide behind such a mask. Once it was very important that no one know my real face, especially my family. To show anything of myself was to be seen as weak, and here weakness is always attacked or at the very least mocked. But heaven help me, it took my killing of that poor wretch to see the wrongness, to know just how empty it makes the heart and soul. A few days ago I'd have rather died than show . . . but when he died instead . . . because I wasn't letting go of the fear . . . the anger . . ."

Tears? Edward weeping?

Yes. Even in the dimness Richard could see the shining tracks on Edward's face. He made no effort to hide them, or wipe them away. Were he here Ambert would have pounced with boundless glee until another fight broke out. When he was prepared for it, there were few things that gave Ambert as much pleasure as beating someone.

" . . . Perhaps one day you'll be able to forgive me."

This was indeed a new brother before him. The old Edward would never have spoken so. Maybe he had been touched by God, and with that thought came a sudden insight. Richard wasn't at ease with thinking this way, but there'd been something the priest once said . . . "Edward—are you able to forgive yourself?"

The question caught Edward by surprise. He was a time answering. "One day, but not now."

"Why not? If I forgive you then you have to forgive yourself."

Edward looked at him most strangely. "Maybe *both* of us should go into the priesthood."

Richard felt himself turn pale. The prospect of being champion had taken hold of his heart with eerie strength, and he did not want to give it up now that it was a likelihood rather than a hopelessly remote chance. "One priest's enough for this family."

"More than enough."

At that moment, Richard's belly gave vent to a very loud and unexpected growl, and, most shocking in a church, Edward abruptly doubled over with laughter. Before, Richard might have burned with mortification but it was all different now. He fell in with Edward's humor, the first time that had ever happened. Neither of them seemed able to stop.

The noise drew the priest in to see the source of such an unseemly disturbance in God's house. His reaction was not one of sympathy, and for their impudence he threw them out, slamming the thick oaken doors behind them.

This was also uncommonly funny, and they staggered like drunks toward the courtyard. Eventually, they settled down, catching their breath.

Edward seemed to notice his disheveled state for the first time. "Look at me. I can't go into meat like this, they'll mistake me for a pig and roast me on a spit."

"The lake then? The water will still be warm from the day."

"The lake it is. But let's not race. I'm tired."

They walked to the castle gate, nodding to the guards on duty there who cracked it open, allowing them to slip out. As they trudged on, Richard looked at his brother in the starlight and knew he didn't want him to go. "Do you *have* to leave?"

"Yes. But not tonight, nor tomorrow. Soon, though."

Well. That would just have to do. Edward wouldn't be too far away. Perhaps later on Richard could ride over to the monastery and they could laugh in *its* chapel. "You're sure about this?"

"We all have different roads, Dickon. This one is mine. And it's all right. Truly it is."

It must have been, for on Edward's young and weary face there was a measure of peace that Richard had never seen before. How strange that it should come to him only after he'd killed a man.

Chapter Six

Toronto, the Present

Several witnesses to the southbound accident on Highway 400 used their cell phones, reporting it almost in the same moment it happened. People stopped to help, emergency vehicles arrived, evaluations were made, and Sabra was transported by care flight to St. Michael's hospital downtown. By the time Richard arrived with Bourland and Michael she'd been whisked off to emergency surgery.

The nurses and the EMTs could not provide Richard much in the way of detail and nothing at all about Sabra's prognosis, only that she was concussed, with broken bones and possible internal injuries; it would be up to the doctor to give him full information. They did express amazement that she was still alive, so that was a good sign, where there's life there's hope and all that. Apparently her car had been thoroughly mangled. One of those who'd pulled her free called her survival a miracle.

Richard attributed this to the protection of Sabra's Goddess, but why not have spared her priestess from injury in the first place? He couldn't understand. Was the instigator—and Richard had no doubt the man he'd seen on the pyramid was responsible—*that* powerful?

Perhaps so.

Then why was Sabra a target? Because she'd been in the vision? Richard had been present as well, right in front, picked out for special attention from the great snake until it was drawn away toward Sharon. Surely that had been noticed by the shadowy figure who had thrown her from the top.

Of course, Sabra might have looked to be the stronger threat to the Otherside man. The rules were different there. Richard's unique strengths might count for nothing compared to her Gifts.

I must know more.

Sabra was his only source for an explanation, and she'd been— *not* cut down—made neutral. He winced at the euphemism. It was a cowardly retreat from reality. But he used it all the same. He wasn't ready for reality, not that kind. He never would be. She *had* to survive. Recover. Return.

Anything else . . .

He teetered on the edge of falling into a black, black pit, and willed himself away from it.

Focus on what's at hand. On what you CAN *do.*

All right. Sabra perhaps wasn't the only source for help, if Richard wanted to include Michael, which he certainly would not. The boy was frightened and confused enough, he didn't need to be dealing with questions about his visions. He was yet in shock about the accident. White-faced with his lips firmly shut, he couldn't help but be remembering his mother and sisters' deaths.

Thank God Bourland seemed aware of that and kept himself close, talking to him. They sat side by side on a waiting room bench, Bourland still in his day-off clothes, including the now inappropriate slippers. Michael had hastily pulled on jeans and track shoes with no socks for the drive to the hospital. They could thank Bourland for knowing which one; he'd managed to trace Sabra's destination. Even as he comforted Michael, he made phone calls. Before long a sober-faced man with the look of a bureaucrat turned up in the waiting room. He held a brief whispered conference with Bourland, then proceeded to run interference between them and anyone approaching with a clipboard and papers to sign. When one of the hospital officials questioned his authority, he flashed some sort of identification that made the potential difficulty magically vanish.

His shielding efforts left them free to wait and worry and hope.

Richard, though, was frozen to all feelings except that of absolute helplessness. The woman he loved more than life could be dying only yards away.

It was impossible.

Unthinkable.

If they would just *tell* him something.

More than anything he feared the approach of a very sympathetic sad-faced doctor come to break the news that the worst had happened.

My blood can spare her from death.

Maybe. His heart raced at the prospect. He wanted it to be so.

The only thing that prevented him from bursting into the operating room was a conversation he'd had with Sabra on that very subject. He'd not thought it fair that she was fully human again. It put her desperately at risk and sooner or later she would die. For all her joy at being able to walk freely in the day again, it seemed an uneven trade. What were a few decades in the sun compared to centuries more of life?

But Sabra said the magic wouldn't work twice. "We can exchange blood as we did before, and though there would be mutual pleasure in the act, it won't change me."

"Why not?" he wanted to know.

She shrugged. "It could be magic or biochemistry or something to do with immunity factors. I'm not a scientist. Suffice that the Goddess's gift was given once and once only. She's passed this other gift to me to use, and that is how it must be."

He knew better than to voice his opinion that the so-called advantages of being human were hardly comparable.

Sabra must have read his heart, but did not rebuke him for it. "That chapter of my life is past," she said with cheerful conviction. "This is how I can best serve her purpose, and it's ever been well for us, has it not? I must go forward, never back, forward to wherever I'm supposed to be and do."

But she couldn't have anticipated this.

And seemingly, neither had the Goddess.

Another impossibility.

The man-thing on that pile of stones, a shadow shape, outlined in sickly green light . . . Sabra said he'd had protections. Had they concealed him *that* well? Even from a deity?

"Richard." Bourland's voice.

He snapped back to the drab waiting room, coming instantly alert. As if in fulfillment of his fear a tired-looking doctor was at the door talking to Bourland's watchdog, who let the man pass.

The news wasn't good, but neither was it the worst.

He also spoke of internal injuries, crushed limbs, concussion, the car's airbags had done only so much. Richard couldn't take in the technical details or terms; his mind could only cope with the basics. She was out of surgery, still in critical condition, but stabilized. He liked that word, so far as it went.

The doctor added that she was better off than they'd expected, given the damage. She'd survived this long, now they had to wait and see.

"But there's nothing any of you can do here. She's unconscious and there's no telling when she'll wake up. If there's a change of any kind, the nurse will call you."

Richard let Bourland ask all the questions, but the answers were never any different. She was alive, barely, and had a small chance. That she'd gotten this far was a good sign, but wait and see, wait and see . . .

When it came down to it, medicine used the same language as faith and magic.

"I want to see her," said Richard. His voice sounded strange. He was prepared to be refused, but the doctor nodded and passed them off to a nurse, who guided them to the intensive care unit.

They were only allowed to look through the glass inset of a door. The ward beyond was festooned with functional-looking medical equipment and several beds. Three had occupants. With the obstruction of the in-place paraphernalia it took him a moment to sort Sabra from the others. That wasn't right. He should have spotted her instantly. He could always sense where she was when nearby.

"Is she dying?" asked Michael.

"No," Bourland and Richard chorused together.

Richard's tone was denial; Bourland's was reassurance.

Richard could pick out the sting of disinfectant they'd used on her from here. And the scent of her blood. It was so faint, all but overwhelmed by necessary intrusions of her meds. There was a mask on her face, probably for oxygen, needles taped to the back of her hands and tubes attached to the needles snaked up to bags on pole stands. Her head and shoulders were immobilized, and leads to monitors were connected to her pale, pale skin. A nurse was checking something or other, the routine of her movements encouraging. So long as she continued calm with no undue worry . . . yes, that was good.

Bourland kept his hands on Michael's shoulders as they stared with him through the glass barrier. "I know it's very frightening, but all the things they have in there are to help her get better. Her body's been through a bad shock, and it will be a while before she can talk to us again. Remember when you slipped during hockey practice and landed so hard on your back?"

"I couldn't breathe."

"Knocked the breath right out of you. That's pretty much what's happened to Sabra."

"Only worse."

"Yes," he admitted. "But you were able to get up after a bit. Give her some time and she'll come around, too."

Is that for me as well as Michael? This man, who was but a fraction of Richard's age and experience, was working to reassure them all. And to some degree succeeding.

"How long?" asked Michael.

"I don't know, but they'll tell us." Bourland pulled out a business card and gave it to the nurse. "My private cell number, for *any* change. Richard."

With much effort he dragged his gaze from the small sheeted figure on the stainless-steel bed. Only sheets? Wouldn't she be cold? "W-what?"

"Michael and I are going home—"

"But I don't want to, Dad."

"It's just for a little bit, then we'll come back."

"I can stay here with Uncle Richard."

"No doubt, but we're ill prepared for a long wait, and I rather think that's what this might be. Richard will hold the fort. You and I have things to do, then we'll relieve him."

A spark of rebellion crossed Michael's face, but he nodded. "We'll come right back?"

"Yes. I want to be here for her, too."

Richard felt selfishly glad it was Bourland's chosen lot to look after Michael. He would not have been able to do so, not with that level of confidence. He shot Bourland a look and was shaken by a flash of intense agony in his friend's eyes that had somehow not affected his calm, in-charge tone of voice. How was he able to hide *that* from the boy?

"You'll be all right?" Bourland asked.

Richard knew his reply had damned well better be a yes. He managed a nod and fished out his keys. "Use the Rover. I'll phone you every thirty minutes until you're back."

"Well, in that case, I'll want an assistant to take on the extra load." Bourland gave his cell to Michael. "That's your job."

"For real?" He clutched the phone. He had his own, of course, regulated to his backpack and used primarily for keeping track of his after-school whereabouts, but this was a step up from it. His father routinely got calls from people like the prime minister.

"Don't go all heady from the power. Come on, then. Let's see if Richard's in a no-parking area."

"Will you fix the ticket if he is?"

"Certainly not. Do him some good to go to court." He herded the distracted Michael toward the hall and elevators. The watchdog reappeared there, listened to Bourland, then moved purposely off, apparently with an errand to do.

Richard continued to look through the glass until a nurse—he wasn't sure if she was the same one—got his attention and suggested he might be more comfortable in the nearby waiting room. An impossibility, but he was blocking traffic, so he retreated to a dull chamber with muted lighting and old magazines. There were Bibles on a table in French and English and a bin loaded with bright plastic toys. Thankfully there was no television. He'd have smashed it.

After two minutes of silence broken by people whisking back and forth in the hall, their rubber soles squeaking on the polished floor, he quit his corner chair and went to the ICU entry to peer again.

Nothing had changed since his last look. That was good. If she was quiet, she was healing.

He couldn't bring himself to return to the waiting room and paced down the long hall, past the nurse's station to the end. Bright lights, mysterious voices paging names over the loudspeakers, the smell of illness overlaid with the scent of cut flowers, centrally heated desert-dry air—how on earth could people work here? This was hell to him.

He pushed through the exit doors and took the stairs on the other side, not clear about reaching any particular place, just needing to keep on the move. Eventually he emerged, wandered, oriented, and either by chance or guided by an invisible influence found himself in the hospital's chapel. From the activity by the altar they were holding mass.

Richard stood at the back, listening without really hearing. This was a matter of feelings, not words. The atmosphere, whether here or places like Chartres or under the open sky, was always the same for him. The smell of candle wax and incense were instantly comforting, inducing a strange hush within him, reviving a frequently dormant, but ever-present connection to something larger than himself.

He slipped quietly into one of the pews, bowed his head, and sought to find what he needed in that vastness.

Bourland's man proved himself uncommonly useful and inconspicuously, if not supernaturally, efficient. When Richard returned to the ICU area, he found that Sabra had been moved to a special glass-windowed room at the far end. This alarmed him until the man explained that it was Bourland's doing. Strings had been pulled. Because of this change Richard would be allowed to sit with her so long as he was quiet and kept out of the way of the staff.

He could do that. Anything to be closer. He humbly thanked the man and went in.

She looked so small and frail. Where was the strength that made her seem so much greater than the limits of her form?

Very carefully, as though it might add to her injuries if he moved too fast, he gently took one of her hands. Her fingers were so cold and inert he had to look to make sure he was holding them.

He bent low, lips to her ear, murmuring just loud enough to be heard over the beep of the monitors. "I'm here, Sabra. You were in an accident, but everything's going to be all right. You rest and get better and I'll watch over you."

He waited, but there was no sign that she'd heard, no flutter of eyelids or movement from her hand, no variation of her heartbeat. Well, he'd not really expected . . . but it would have been encouraging if . . .

I'll be right here. I promise, he repeated. Since it was a thought, he could speak in his mind as loud as he liked. He practically bellowed it.

Still no reaction. But he felt an odd certainty that he'd been heard. He kissed her cold fingers, backed away, and sat in the room's only chair which was against the far wall a few feet from the foot of the bed. He watched her steadily, unblinking for a few moments, then pulled out his cell to make his first call to Bourland.

Bourland and Michael returned as promised. They'd kitted themselves out with proper clothes and seemed prepared to settle in for the duration. Michael insisted on sitting with Sabra, promising to be *very* quiet and still. Children were not supposed to be in the ICU, but there was no way they could deny him. Richard spoke with someone in charge and an exception was made.

"Any more phase outs?" he asked as he and Bourland retired to the outer waiting room.

"No, thank God."

"Did he say anything about the last one?"

"Hardly says anything at all. He was remarkably cooperative, though, about getting ready to return here. I'd say he's worried, but not in such a way as we need worry about him. It's like he's getting down to business, where other children might panic and go weepy."

"Startled?"

Bourland shook his head. "He's strong. Let's hope he won't have to draw on that strength. How are you?"

"Bloody awful, but it's easier to be able to sit near her. Thanks for that."

"If not me, then you'd have done it. This is how I deal with frustration." He had a laptop case with him and a phone, evidence that he would continue his work.

Several hours of turn-on-turn with no worsening of Sabra's condition seemed to bolster Michael's shaken confidence. Richard watched over him at a distance, on guard for problems, but the boy was the picture of self-possession, showing a depth of maturity that should have been beyond his years. On the other hand he'd been in various stages of therapy since the catastrophe with his family, so he must have had a wealth of psychological tools to help him contend with this crisis.

Bourland continued to deal with it via his mysterious labors. He took and made phone calls, and employed his assistant to make more. Richard got the impression that many things were being caused to happen elsewhere and on several levels, but checked his curiosity. When Bourland was ready to talk, he'd convey in detail what was going on.

Richard's own internal defenses were the result of considerable experience. He'd been in such situations before; he knew how to wait and the futility of fretting. But this was *Sabra's* life, which made the ordeal rawly new to him. When it came down to it, he was wholly terrified.

Not a damned thing he could do about it either.

He'd put his cell alarm on quiet mode. The silent jolt when it buzzed shouldn't have been a surprise, but it did make him twitch.

It was his Scotland Yard friend, with nothing too enlightening to report. He'd put the fear of God into the woman at Lloyd's, who again confirmed (more politely and with more details) what'd she'd said earlier about Sharon Geary. He then traced Sharon's movements as far as Heathrow. Her car was in one of their long-term lots, and she'd taken a flight to the Yucatán, buying the ticket direct from the airline's counter. Apparently her decision to take a trip had been a sudden and last-minute thing. Like other world travelers she carried her passport as a matter of course.

At a question from Richard, the man replied, "No, we found nothing unusual at either Stonehenge or Woodhenge . . . well, a few of those potty New Age types were upset about something or other at Stone. Said the place was ruined, but our man there couldn't make any sense of what had them so stirred up. One of the women was in moaning hysterics, had to be taken away by her friends. They told him the place had been bombed. He conducted a thorough look 'round with the staff, but they didn't spot any damage or ticking packages, that sort of thing."

Richard would have given a lot to have interviewed the New Agers. Obviously someone gifted with Sight had seen whatever had happened on Otherside. "What about the staff? Did they see or hear anything odd in the last few days?"

"Nothing like that. A few tourists fainted there today, I'm told, which certainly is not part of the normal run. They complained of headaches and keeled right over. The staff's in a dither worrying about lawsuits, but everyone recovered and went on their way. Put the blame on everything from jet lag to low blood sugar. There's one man who said the 'feel' of the place was off, but that's the limit. What's this about? Should we expect another rash of crop circles?"

"I think not."

"Good, because the farmers here are getting rather fed up about people sneaking into their fields and trampling over everything in the dead of night in the name of art. I know of one fellow threatening to electrify his fences if he could afford the rates."

"That won't keep out aliens."

"He's not worried about *them*, just losing his harvest to thrill seekers and tourists. I've told him to charge a fee every time one of them raises a camera."

Richard thanked his friend sincerely and rang off, wishing he had that frustrated farmer's problems instead of his own.

Around six o'clock Bourland persuaded Michael that it would be all right to go home for dinner, which would be better than the hospital food they'd snacked on throughout the day. Regardless of that and the situation, Michael had packed away an amazing amount of it. Richard was invited, but said he'd stay on. It was lonely after they left, but he was used to it.

He eased into the chair, his arms stiffly resting exactly along the line of its arms, hands bunched into fists until he forced them to hang loose. He watched the monitors, and speculated long and hard about attempting a blood exchange. It was impossible for Sabra to partake directly from him, but he could easily accomplish what was necessary with a syringe. God knows this place had enough of them lying about; he'd already nicked a couple without getting caught. But would it do more harm than good?

Or would it, as she said, make no matter at all?

He rather thought it would not, but perhaps . . . just to be *sure*, it mightn't hurt to at least try. Then he would know that he'd done everything within his power for her.

He was forced to wait. This was a 24/7 place, though he'd already picked up on the general rhythms around him. Sooner or later there would come an interval where he could make his move. To prepare for that he got the staff used to seeing him getting up and standing by her bedside, his head bowed, his back to the glass partition. No one looked twice that he could determine. In this facility they were accustomed to people openly praying, and there was a kind of selective blindness in effect that allowed privacy for spiritual matters. He would naturally take advantage of it and had only to bide his time for his best opportunity.

If Sabra had the time, if she remained stable. Should that change, then all cautions were off.

Sitting so still in the chair, Richard out of the blue fell asleep, snapped awake, was bewildered for a tenth of a second, relaxed as he recognized where he was, then tensed again. His neck and shoulders ached from being held in place. How long had he been out? It seemed only a moment.

His single clue that whole hours had fled and late afternoon had come was what his watch told him, and then he wasn't sure that it might be lying. There was no day or night in this part of the hospital; his body clock had its own unique process for marking time and for now was not to be trusted.

He checked the monitors. No change in the displays. They beeped on solemnly but held steady. So long as they continued smooth, all was—almost—well. To keep from jumping up every few minutes he'd earlier asked the nurse on duty a few quiet questions, and she gave him a briefing on how to read them, what was normal, what was not. He was a long way from her expertise, but the additional knowledge made him feel like he had a tiny measure of control over the situation, that perhaps he was more useful than before. He very much needed that.

The nurse came in, on schedule, checked Sabra's blood pressure and other stats, made notations on a clipboard, and asked Richard if he needed anything. He said not.

"You don't have to be here, you know," she said. "It's very exhausting to sit and do nothing."

"I'll be fine."

Apparently she'd seen the syndrome in many others and knew better than to disagree. She nodded sympathetically and left.

He had thirty minutes at least. She was busy with one of the other patients, and would next go to her desk station.

He rose to put his back to the window as he'd been doing throughout the day, effectively blocking all view of his actions. Not making untoward moves or looking in any way different, he drew the hypo from his pocket and quietly peeled off the plastic wrapping, removing the protective casing from the sharp end.

Having watched the nurse draw off samples from Sabra, he knew which catheter implanted in her arm to use to do the same. It had been a bit of a struggle to stand and coldly observe, but he got through it and now repeated those same steps.

Damned if it didn't work.

Hopefully Sabra wouldn't suffer from the minute loss.

Returning to the chair, he sat as before, throwing a casual look toward the next room. Business as usual. No one taking the least notice of him.

He inspected the hypo reservoir to see if there was a top he could pull off. No, the unit was sealed. Breaking it open would make a mess. Have to do it *this* way, then.

Gingerly resting the needle between his lips almost like a cigarette, his tongue tucked well back out of danger, he tried the plunger.

The sudden stream of her blood, still warm, startled him. He swallowed.

The taste . . . chemicals . . . lots of those. Unidentifiable drugs, maybe antibiotics. Nothing that would affect him, but they were unsettling. He tried to discern some suggestion of her emotions, but it was as sterile as the out-of-date stuff he kept in his refrigerator. That was it, then, she was completely unconscious. Whether that was a good thing or not remained to be seen.

He waited, watching the monitors, listening to the sounds of the ward, and feeling—or imagining that he felt—Sabra's blood working through his system. So small an amount would have no physical effect on him, it was strictly in his head. His mind alone supplied an image of its journey as it flowed to his belly, was absorbed, and eventually dispersed through his body. It needed time to mingle with his own unique blood.

The nurse came again, made her notations, and departed.

He'd been successful at not thinking about what came next. No putting it off now. He freed the second syringe from its plastic, took off the cap. My, but that end of it looked to be very shiny and sharp.

Grimace.

Richard hated, really, really *hated* the things. It was utterly absurd. He'd withstood sword gashes, arrow wounds, crossbow bolts, spears, bullets, bombs—name most of the weapons used in the last fifteen centuries and he'd likely been a target ten times over for all of them, but for some reason an inch-long hollow needle little thicker than thin wire absolutely put him in knots.

He could almost hear Sabra giggling at him.

Hypodermic, meaning "below skin"—derived from the Greek—*syringe*, descended from what they now called Middle Latin . . .

Stop stalling, old lad. Just get on with it.

Oh, yes. Somewhere she was definitely laughing.

How did one do this, anyway? Jab it into a vein? Where? The inside of his left arm he supposed. Those bloodlines were clearly visible, threading just beneath the surface.

Oh, God. Oh, Goddess.

He held the needle above his wrist. Hesitating.

He winced. Practicing, really. It wouldn't hurt. Not much. Not compared to other things he'd been through. It was just the *idea* that pitched him into such a state. Good grief, teenaged girls and younger got their ears pierced all the time. Diabetics stabbed themselves with these things as a matter of routine. The lot of them miles braver than himself, apparently.

Well, come on, before you're spotted by the nurse.

Bloody hell. Literally.

He pushed it inexpertly into his skin. Ow. Ouch. It took more force than he'd imagined. Was that far enough? Had he hit the vein? Sweat flared on his body. His hand trembled, and his head went light. This was ridiculous . . .

I am not going to faint.

. . . Completely ridiculous . . .

Not.

Cold all over, then hot. He gulped air and held it.

Not. I really mean it. Not.

Gradual release of breath. Take another. Deep and even. Let it out. There. Not too horribly bad.

He didn't care to look, but had to in order to reverse the plunger or whatever the thing was. He suspected he'd taken the wrong sort for drawing blood. He thought they used something different on television shows—if they got that right.

But slowly, slowly, the plastic cylinder filled up with a bounty of red fluid. When he'd retracted it as far as it would go, he pulled the thing free and held his wrist to his mouth to sweep away any seepage until the minuscule injury closed.

Should have used my teeth to make the damned hole, he thought sulkily. He'd done that before and with much less mental fuss. But he'd have still felt the same about dipping the needle into any wound. Ugh.

He crushed the bout of squeamishness. Sabra had any number of the damned things stuck in her. Hopefully he could alleviate that necessity.

Again, Richard stood at her bedside, in the same place.

An injection would be the wrong way to go, no telling what his blood would do to her system if introduced so directly. By mouth, as always. That's how it worked.

He parted her lips, pressed the plunger with his thumb, and hoped the tiny stream wouldn't choke her. He put in only a few drops, waited, then a few more, taking his time. Whatever power lay within would work its magic however large or small the amount.

Richard's own change had been brought about by a massive draining on her part, taking from him, and then she'd shared it back again, though his memory was less clear on that part of things. It had been as much for lust and ceremony as anything else. In the times that came afterward she told him even a taste was enough to bring about the dark rebirth. Not as pleasurable, but sufficient.

If it would just work again.

He gently took her cold hand, shut his eyes, and silently *prayed*.

"Richard?"

He gave a great start at the sound of Bourland's voice. Richard had been so involved with his internal concentration he'd not heard anyone approach.

His friend, standing in the doorway, coat still on, looking diffident about his intrusion. "Hallo. Sorry. How are things?"

That was indeed the question. Richard checked the monitors. "The same, it would seem." Good or bad or too soon to tell?

Bourland came in. He had a modest vase of fresh flowers in hand. Miniature pink roses, expensive at this time of year. He shrugged a little when Richard glanced at them. "Silly of me, but I saw them in the flower shop downstairs and . . . they probably won't allow it here. In case she's allergic. There's no place to put them."

"On the floor by the chair should be fine. Out of the way. She's not allergic to them."

He accepted the suggestion with relief, placing the flowers between the chair and the wall. Their sweet scent began to war with the medicinal air of the room.

"Michael's at home?"

"Yes. I managed to talk him into it. My housekeeper's staying over to keep an eye on him. She's to call me if she notices any problems. There've been no more phase outs, thank God."

Could that mean Michael's episodes had somehow been connected to Sabra? It seemed likely, except that before ever meeting her he'd projected visions. It had been his only way of communicating through his trauma. Perhaps he was simply too distracted now for such activity.

Bourland came around the other side of the bed to look down at Sabra. "She's so impossibly young," he whispered, brushing back a stray tendril of her hair that was outside the bandaging. It was an unexpectedly intimate, tender gesture, and he was likely unaware of how much it revealed about their relationship.

A nurse newly come on shift and clearly unbriefed about the exceptions being made for this patient, appeared at the door. "I'm sorry, but visiting hour is over."

An hour? More like five minutes. Richard fixed her with his gaze and softly recommended she find something else to do, they were allowed to be there. Her face blanked for a second, then she smiled amiably and went away. Bourland noticed, but Richard didn't care.

"I'll be outside," he said, wanting to talk with Bourland, but reluctant to impose on his time with Sabra.

He went to the waiting room near the ICU ward. There was a different governmental type in a plain dark suit hanging about playing watchdog. He didn't seem armed, but Richard got the distinct impression the man might be RCMP. The man nodded to him and went to stand in the hall, looking cordial of all things. Ah—there they were, regulation boots under the suit. Dead giveaway.

Well . . . good. Nice to have a guardian angel standing ready.

Richard stretched out on the padded bench seating along one wall. He'd known harder beds; this one was only worse because of its hospital location. Still, he could get a bit of a nap in.

Only Bourland didn't let him. He came in a few minutes later. "I seem to be making a habit of—no, please, stay as you are. Grab sleep when you can. That's what they tell soldiers, isn't it?"

"So I've heard." Some rules remained ever constant. "What's up?" He continued flat on his back, glad for the change in posture from the chair.

Bourland sat opposite, leaning forward, elbows on his knees, hands clasped. "I'll wager you've been beating yourself about the *why* of the accident as much as I've done. Michael wanted to know why, too, and there's never any answer, so I shifted over to the *how* of it."

"Go on." This must have been what had kept him so busy earlier.

"I had her car taken to a place I know," he said. "A place full of experts. I got them to fine tooth comb it for anything unusual, and set people to interviewing witnesses to the accident. So far nothing untoward has surfaced. It was just as we saw, she lost control on the ice when a freak wind—"

Richard shook his head. "It's more than that, and you know it."

"Yes," Bourland agreed in a carefully even tone. "We both know it. At this point we're the only ones who do. What I'm seeking is any kind of proof of whatever else was involved that caused it. You saw the brake lights when she passed? She was trying so hard to stop that thing and it just . . ." He shut his eyes a moment. "My God. I even felt the snow . . . Richard, this is so bloody impossible."

"I know it is. Can you get past that?"

"To what? Telepathy? Ghosts? UFOs?"

"To being there for Michael, whatever happens."

"Of course I will." Bourland snorted. "You do know how to go for the throat, don't you?"

"No comment. In the meantime, yes, there is a strangeness going on. Michael's projecting visions, and we all had the same dream. Nightmare."

"But why? How?"

"I was hoping Sabra would be able to explain. You may have noticed her insight to . . . spiritual matters; very unique, very strong. She's always used that to help Michael."

"It's hard not to notice their connection. Sometimes when they're together it's like two people with one mind. But it seems to work. She's a bit eccentric on some things, but I know she loves him, and would never harm him."

This was promising, but it was yet a long way from acceptance on the level that might be required. It would be easier to just hypnotize Bourland, give him a basic download of Otherside facts, and tell him not to panic. Not yet, anyway.

"You said Sabra might explain. But you know things also, don't you?"

No escape. Richard sat up to face him. The bitch of it was that he knew so damned little himself. He could clarify some aspects of the shared nightmare, not much more.

Bourland gave him a long look. "Richard, this isn't the time."

"What?"

"I know the signs. It's clear you're steeling yourself up for something unpleasant and this is just not the time. Anyway, I might be ahead of you for once."

Richard was at sea. Had someone kidnapped the Bourland he knew and replaced him with a mind-reading clone?

"I think we can agree on the fact that there is a paranormal aspect to this business. There, the word's on the floor for all to trip over."

"Philip . . . really now . . ."

Bourland raised a hand. "An important part of maintaining intelligent pragmatism is being able to recognize when one is out of one's depth. When you've eliminated all other possibilities, then whatever remains, however bizarre, is probably worth looking into. I've contacted some different experts to look into things. They've sent a team to look over the crash site, take measurements and such; the car's going to one of their labs for more work—"

"What do you mean by 'different experts'?"

"I know of a group that investigates the paranormal, not with ouija boards but with science. One of their senior men is an old school chum of mine, so I rang him up and asked for an assist. As it happens, they were already prepping to send a team off to the Yucatán to look into some odd reports from there."

Richard came fully awake. "Such as . . . ?"

"Don't know yet, that's why they're sending a team. Whether what's drawn their attention has to do with that shared vision remains to be discovered. They've got people operating in London who are checking out similar reports concerning Stonehenge. Of course, my friend was highly curious about my interest and the car and the rest. I said I'd explain later. If I can't then I'll have to buy him one hell of an excellent bottle of scotch to—Matt?"

Bourland's attention snapped toward the doorway, where stood a very tall, lean, bordering-on-the-gaunt, man wearing a black ski cap and sardonic expression. Next to him was a slim woman with honey-blond hair, her cool eyes set in a resolute, beautifully sculpted face.

The man said, "Should my ears be burning?"

"Almost." Bourland got up and went over to shake hands. "What are you doing here?"

"Frank told us to stop and see you before our flight to fun-in-the-sun Meh-hee-co." His gaze settled on Richard a moment, friendly, but oddly analytic. Piercing without being offensive. Richard got the impression his face had just been filed into a highly efficient memory for later retrieval if required. Behind them stood the watchdog fellow, still looking cordial, but observant. The couple had passed inspection and were allowed to invade.

"Excuse us," Bourland shot to Richard, then smoothly herded them from the room without seeming to do so. A very seamless technique of compartmentalizing everyone, if that was his aim. With his position in the government, it must have been second nature to him. "My God, I thought you'd have been kidnapped by space aliens by this time."

"Well, now that you mention it . . ." The rest of the man's reply was obscured by a hospital page.

Richard assumed the couple were the team sent by whatever agency had involved themselves. Apparently they had begun checking things independently prior to Bourland's involvement, and that was perfectly fine; there was no way in hell that Richard would leave Sabra and go haring off to the Yucatán at this point.

He hoped they'd be safe. The man-thing on the pyramid . . . what he'd done . . . he was likely long gone by now, but on his way where? Off to destroy another ancient sacred site? Which? There were thousands. And toward what purpose? What was to be gained by ravaging such places?

"Mr. Dun?"

God, he'd gone sleepy again. He sluggishly realized he'd stretched out as before, and the charming young woman was bending over him with an apologetic smile. Given any other circumstance the view would be exceedingly welcome. He boosted up, rubbing his face as she introduced herself. He didn't snag the name long enough to hold, only that she was a researcher. Didn't seem the type to be burrowing through library stacks, but she had the polish of a confident professional about her.

"Yes? What is it?"

"Philip said you had a dream or vision?" she prompted. "It might help our investigation if you could tell me what you saw."

He glanced at the card she gave him along with her self-introduction and recognized the emblem next to her name. "Oh, you're *that* lot."

She must have been accustomed to the response and smiled. "You've heard of us."

"Yes. I catch things on the television now and then about your doings."

"You can't believe everything that goes on the air. They generally regulate us to Halloween shows or an exaggerated and garbled documentary."

What a pleasing voice she had, very soft, almost liquid. "Well, you're not running about in tinfoil hats, which puts you ahead of other groups with which I've dealt, but I prefer to keep my name out of any records if you don't mind."

"Not a problem. On request we assign a pseudonym or a letter designation—if we bother. I'm told that this is an informal and off-the-record sidebar to the official investigation. Consider it a private one-on-one."

He decided he liked her. "Thank you."

"Your dream?" She drew out a small tape recorder said the date and time into it and identified him as "Mr. B." He assumed Bourland would be "Mr. A."

Without embellishment or emotional coloring, he described exactly what he'd seen, and after a moment's consideration gave Sharon Geary's name to her.

"This was definitely someone you know?"

"Yes. We were very close once. If you can shed any light on what happened—on where she might be, I would very much like to be informed. Immediately."

"Then you believe you saw and perhaps interacted with an event that actually took place, *as* it took place."

"I know it did. Just not in this Reality."

She did not inquire what he meant by that, and his respect for her group rose a bit more. "Shared dreams are not unheard of, but the ones I've investigated were not quite so detailed as yours. They more commonly occur between close family members like twins or a parent and child. You and Philip aren't related, are you?"

"I'd say we're brothers under the skin," he said without thinking.

"Well, there is something of a physical resemblance."

"Nonsense."

"Has anyone else had this same experience?"

"My"—he almost said "godson" and changed at the last second— "Our friend in there, in the ICU. She was on her way in to talk with us this morning about it when she had her accident."

"I'm sorry."

"She called me last night, rather early this morning. She'd had an identical vision that woke her. We all saw each other in it, along with many other people we didn't know. It had us rather upset."

"And you couldn't identify the man in it?"

He shook his head. "I wish I could. I saw only his outline in light. The rest was darkness. Sharon was . . . glowing brightly. Very symbolic, I'm sure."

"Philip has suggested that there might have been a paranormal factor to the car crash."

"I would take that seriously, yes."

"We have people checking it out."

"So I've gathered. One thing . . ."

Perfect eyebrows raised with inquiry. "Yes?"

"Please do be very careful while down there, use extreme caution. I did not see the man—or whatever he was—clearly, but my every instinct tells me he's extraordinarily dangerous. If the vision was pure imagination combined with coincidence, then you've nothing to fear. But if not . . ."

"I understand, Mr. Dun."

He put her card in his wallet and passed over one of his own. "If you find out anything about Sharon please don't hesitate to call my cell at *any* hour no matter how late or early. Consider it urgent. I must know what—what's become of her." He pressed the point home with a firm hypnotic nudge. She blinked and swayed as though he'd done it physically.

"Of course." Her eyes cleared, she favored him with a kind smile, shook his hand, and left.

Oh, God. Sharon.

He rubbed his face again and suppressed a groan. How long since she'd been taken away? He stared at his watch. Over twenty hours. If she was lost in the Otherside she wouldn't have lasted ten minutes with the creatures there. But that snake . . . or god, as Sabra had called it. The young woman had suggested it might be Kukulcan. That couldn't be good. The ancient natives had done blood sacrifice to him. Richard could still call back from memory the smell of it soaked deep into the stones of the pyramid. So much death . . .

He put an arm over his eyes and tried to will himself unconscious but the dreadful thoughts and worries kept coming like legions.

Sharon Geary drifted in darkness, struggling mightily against mind-numbing, heart-stopping terror and mostly succeeding. Wild animals were like that when trapped in a cage. After a few moments of blind panic and beating against the bars they go very still, either conserving effort or fallen into shock. If they didn't get past the shock they died.

She told herself she was conserving effort.

But where . . . ? The last thing she remembered before the dark sealed around her was Richard. He'd just stood there not doing a bloody thing. Then again, what *could* he be expected to do? Fly up and attack the serpent with his bare hands? That was a bit much to ask, though Rivers had had no trouble doing the latter, it seemed. By God, if she ever got her own hands around his throat . . .

Oh, yes, anger was a great way to keep the fear down to manageable levels.

Where the hell was she?

She felt along one leg of her BDU pants and the cargo pocket there. Her torch was still inside. Brilliant. Pun intended. She pulled it out, holding it away from her, and switched it on.

Not what she expected, though she could never have said what that might have been.

Hand-sized scales, glittering like jewels set in polished steel, completely surrounded her. It was like she was inside a gigantic ball some dozen feet across made from . . .

Mother of God, the sna—serpent—bloody big monster. It was wrapped all around her. A living cage made from its enormous body.

Bad enough, but she was *floating* in it.

She'd seen films of astronauts training. They achieved a state similar to the microgravity of orbit by going up in a plane and waiting for it to go into a dive, then they seemed to float about the compartment. It looked like great fun until you remembered it lasted only a few moments, then the plane had to come out of its controlled dive and climb again.

Sharon knew she'd been here for much longer than that. Where was "here"? And were they falling? Falling a long, long way?

Think, girl. She wasn't in outer space. What other options were available where gravity was scarce?

Otherside? That didn't seem right. She'd been halfway in it when Rivers threw her from the—*by God I'm going kill that bastard!*—pyramid. Then the serpent, Kukulcan, had reached her, wrapped around her . . . and it felt like something had seized them both. What could be out there big enough to pull this size of creature off course?

There's always a bigger fish, it seemed, wherever you found yourself.

Cheering thought. Sort of.

Relatively calmer, she drifted close to one of the living walls. Each round of its body was as large across as the biggest oak tree she'd ever seen, and she'd seen some that—*my God, it's breathing.* Very slow, but constant, she watched in awe the massive expanding and contracting of her prison.

How about that? They had air.

For some reason, she'd not been too very certain about it. She could—rotten thought—be dead, after all. It wasn't likely. She had firm ideas about the afterlife and this wasn't even close.

She studied the structure, such as it was, and made a rough guess on just how large her reptile friend might be to create this size of a hollow space around her with its body.

Oh, yeah. Big. Really, really big.

Relative to its length and girth, this substantial space was rather small. The thing must be wrapped around her in a very tight, tight knot and likely had yards and yards of itself left over fore and aft.

What, if anything, would happen if she touched it? Would the serpent even notice her? And react? Adversely?

One way to find out.

She touched the scales. Lightly. It'd be just her bad luck if the god was ticklish and crushed her by accident, but nothing happened.

She ran her hand along the curve of flesh, registering the texture, smooth one way, rough in the other as she'd observed on some types of lizards. So the head would be wound in *that* direction, likely on the outside of the ball it had made of itself. What a relief not to be able to see it. Size factors, scary features, and big teeth aside, she had a gut feeling that it was just not the done thing to look a god in the eye unless one was invited. This god wasn't of a religion she was particularly familiar with, but that didn't matter. It was a respect thing.

"Hallo? Anyone out there?"

Why in hell had she said anything? Well, there were no "keep silent" signs up. Might as well have been. The walls threw her voice back, flat, as though no one wanted to hear her little troubles.

Sod that.

"Hallo? I'm up now. Want to tell me what's going on?"

Uh-oh, that's torn it. She saw and felt a vast shifting all around. Her cage was on the move all right, thankfully not inward. That was good. Don't crush your redheaded date, all right?

Two rounded sections parted lengthwise in a body-long curve. She steadied herself against the opposite wall and shone her torch into the dark opening. It was a good foot wide. Enough for her to squeeze through, but instinct told her that might be a bad idea. Air swept in, indication of wind activity. Until now she'd been unaware of the stuffiness of her confines. It smelled strongly—no surprise there—of snake. They did have a distinctive scent. She knew a man who could smell them. He didn't like them much, either, which might have had to do with his sensitivity to the odor. This place would have given him a heart attack.

Her light caught on a black yet glittering surface. Large. Everything here was large except herself.

Sharon gulped. It was an eye. Kukulcan was looking at *her*.

Bloody hell, what was the polite thing to do for that? In just about every mythology and religion she'd read up on it was usually a bad moment for the mere mortal who caught the attention of a god.

"Hallo. I'm Sharon."

It didn't blink or move, just kept staring. Snakes didn't have eyelids, did they? Some kind of inner membrane or the like. It threw mammals off-kilter concerning their body language, which they didn't care for, probably why people made such an issue about killing snakes. Even a lion chasing you down on the veldt for its supper can blink. You could understand that, guess what was on its hungry little mind by the smallest facial signals.

No such signals of similarity here. The mind here was as alien as it could get and still be on earth.

Maybe not on earth. Not the world or Reality she knew.

"See here, things were pretty bad back there, an' I'm thinking that you helped me. If that's so, then I thank you."

Holy Mother, *what* was she *doing*, chatting up a god?

On the other hand, her gran always said good manners cost nothing and were usually appreciated.

"I'm very glad you came along. But you're probably a bit busy . . . so if the storm's over could you drop me off where I belong? I wouldn't want to put you to any trouble. Any old place will do for me."

The eye withdrew out of range of her light.

After a few moments' wait, she grew curious enough to push over to investigate. It was amazing how quickly she'd gotten used to floating like this, almost like swimming, but you didn't have to worry about drowning.

Or not . . . there's different ways of going without air. She hoped her hollow wasn't completely air tight. Otherwise she'd have to depend on the big fellow outside to remember to let in fresh air when she needed it. Like now.

Peering through the long opening, she played the torch beam around. It ran out of light before the ambient area ran out of darkness. She squirmed partially over the bulk of one coil, trusting the creature would hold itself steady and not squeeze her in two. There, torso out, arse in, like hanging from a Dutch door. Up, down, in, out with the beam. No end to the dark, no structures, no ground, this must be what they mean by infinite . . . wait—a glimmer of something there, far, far above. It was big, ocean big, filled all that part of the sky. If that was sky.

If that was ocean. Maybe, but it was either way over her head, or she was suspended upside down, which did not mean very much here. So if there was no gravity, how was it the water stayed in place? How was it *they* stayed in place?

"This is very interesting, but I'm not sure what I'm seeing. You trying to tell me there's no landing pads about?"

Sharon sensed rather than saw the great head looming next to her. Hesitantly, she spared it a sideways glance. Yes, very big. Might have even grown some since the brawl with Rivers. She could stand upright in its yawning mouth, stretch high, and still not touch the top of it.

Oh, what a remarkably *bad* mental picture to conjure up.

For all that, she was almost getting used to its presence. Make that Presence. She'd met a few film stars who had it going for them. Theirs was nothing compared to this fellow's impact. No wonder he had the ancient natives building bloody great temples to him in the heat and humidity.

Bloody. All those poor bastards with their hearts cut out jolly with a knife. Another bad mental picture. She had to stop doing that.

Something flashed past the torch beam, positively rocketing by, with an aggressive organic hum. It provoked a reaction from Kukulcan, who swung his heavy head in that direction, the jaws going wide.

She played the beam all over, trying to see what it was, then it occurred to her, as a seeming earthquake—snakequake?—shuddered through the god's body, that she would be safer inside than out. Hastily, she wriggled back, retreating as best she could. Hard to find purchase, and it was too easy to catch a scrape if she rubbed the wrong way against the scales.

There, ouch, nothing too painful—

Then something *slammed* noisily against the serpent, and her hollow ball chamber lurched in reaction. She got the barest, fastest glimpse of wings, massive sectional body, claws, eye clusters, and insectoid mandibles. Her mind translated it as a cross between a spider and wasp, bigger than an elephant, which was the only reason it hadn't achieved an entry. The mouth part extended outward, snapping, a long thin tongue shot clear, whipping rapidly all over, seeking. It flicked past her arm and a stray drop of clear fluid flew off, landing on the back of her wrist. Sticky, it was sticky as—God, if that thing touched her and got a good grip . . . *no* place to hide, no cover, no weapons . . .

She hadn't the breath to summon a scream, and by the time she did, the being vanished. Not as in going invisible, but as in being yanked suddenly away.

Outside there was considerable violent movement and commotion along with a nasty hissing sound like a very large tire venting an air leak. Heart beating fit to burst, she went low toward the opening, aiming her light with a shaking hand.

She definitely had the catbird seat for the battle, such as it was. Kukulcan had the—well, call it a bug for want of anything better— headfirst in his mouth. The evolution-gone-right-out-the-window thing was making a mighty struggle: clawing, hissing, and probably biting, but the serpent's inwardly curved fangs prevented it from escape. The only way out was through, which was via a gigantic digestive tract.

It was strangely fascinating, like watching a train wreck. Come to think of it, the sizes were on the same scale.

Down the bug went, flailing all the way. One of its wings snapped off and floated into the darkness, spinning slowly, streaming black fluid. Very educational, in fact, that was much more information than she ever wanted to know about the workings of its anatomy.

Kukulcan finished the last of it, and she followed the progress of the elephant-sized bulge as it advanced past the feathered crest on its trip down the long gullet.

After-dinner mint, anyone?

She hoped that wouldn't be herself.

The serpent god stared long at her, then the head swung away toward the seeming water above. She followed its gaze.

"Ah—I get you now," she whispered. "I'll just wait inside out of the way, all right? Thanks for the peek. Look after yourself."

She slid quickly in and the long opening sealed tight shut again, enclosing her. She was ready to kiss the scales in gratitude and relief. Good thing she was floating because her knees would have buckled. Was it possible to faint in zero-gravity? She might be the first to find out.

The "water" above them, all that movement, large as an ocean, was composed of a *swarm* of those overgrown bugs. One of them must have noticed her light and come diving in to investigate. Lucky her, bad luck for it.

Time to sit tight and try to work up some way out for them both, because Sharon didn't think even Kukulcan could eat that many of them in a sitting.

Chapter Seven

Toronto, the Present

Bourland concluded his interview with the tall, angular man, shook hands, and bent to peck the woman affectionately on one cheek. From his vantage by the waiting room, Richard read his lips: "Good luck and take care." They moved off toward the elevators.

He hoped they'd take care, that the woman paid attention to his warning, remembered it if they—

Bourland paused on his way back to look through the glass inset on the ICU doors and remained there. Richard joined him. There was activity by Sabra's bed, a doctor and nurse, studying the clipboard, not the patient.

"It's all right," Richard said. "Routine check. I've seen them do it a dozen times over."

Bourland relaxed, but not by much. "I wish . . ." But he didn't finish.

"I know you do. Come and tell me the latest. Let them get on with their job."

He sighed and followed Richard to the room, where they resumed their chosen seats. This time Richard sat rather than reclined to keep himself awake.

"About that psychic group . . . ?"

Bourland raised a brief smile. "They're off to whatever. I doubt anything will come of it, but I want to cover everything."

"Will they be talking to Michael?"

"Absolutely not."

"Good, because I didn't mention him."

"Neither did I. Nothing on his phasing out, either. That lot would have him in a lab with wires stuck to his head; no, I'm not putting the boy through such nonsense. They can bumble along without his participation."

"You don't seem to have much confidence in them."

"Actually I do so far as the scientific aspect is concerned. But when the hard edge of the universe I know blurs and drifts sideways into the paranormal stuff . . ." Bourland shrugged. "It's rather removed from my usual round. They're all top-notch scientists and researchers, with more PhDs than MIT, but running about with magnetometers trying to find ghosts and decode crop circles? On the other hand one can't expect much, considering the subject matter."

"Too elusive?"

"Yes. But I can't ignore this. Not with what's going on with Michael."

"There's something else you can look into, if possible." Richard said. "And it's concrete, in the hard edge."

"Name it. Please."

"Find out what flights left from the Yucatán today. There must be videos of everyone who passed through customs, there and overseas. I want a look at all the departing and arriving male passengers." That man-thing might have a presence on this Side, and if so, then he was traceable. Of course, there was no guarantee Richard would recognize his human form, but he possessed a better insight than most for it.

Bourland's eyes went wide at the enormity of the task. "*All* the flights?"

"Connecting ones as well. Whoever was in Chichén Itzá last night and left today, I want to know who it is. You can narrow things down to cross-referencing the names with arriving Toronto flights at first, give them priority. After what happened here, I was thinking . . ."

"A connection to the accident?"

"Maybe." Sabra said that distance meant nothing in Otherside matters, but the force that caused the storm might well be in the area. That's why he'd been at watch over her. In case it returned. That Michael hadn't had any visions since was very reassuring though. "And see if you can track Sharon Geary from there, too."

"Sharon? What's she to do with this?"

He'd forgotten that Bourland might not have recognized her in the vision, having only met her once, way back when. He explained she'd been the one thrown from the pyramid and taken in midair by the flying serpent.

"You're sure it was Sharon?"

"I'm sure. Already gave the name to that young woman who left. Sharon was at Stonehenge the day before, and Michael had his episode then, the one you recorded. Sharon must have seen something there because the next thing she's suddenly on a flight to Cancún."

"How'd you get that?"

"I've a friend at Scotland Yard who owed me a favor. I'm thinking that she saw something, or particularly someone, and followed him. If you can find out what she did and where she went once she arrived in Cancún—I don't know how helpful it might be, but—"

"Right. That kind of intel-gathering is outside my department, but I know some specialists with the resources to crunch massive amounts of data very fast."

Richard rather thought he would.

"Tracing people is their bread and butter, but this won't be easy." Bourland got on his cell phone. The call took some time, first to get through and then to explain the urgency. Next he stared at his phone as though it had just made an insulting noise. He closed it, snorting. "They'll call me back once they've set up a secure whatever-it-is."

"Who are they?"

He looked uncomfortable. "I'm not allowed to say. Part of my work. Official secrets business."

"Oh. That lot." There was one in every country, each with varying degrees of competency.

"Yes, they don't exist."

"Even to each other."

"Especially each other. Seriously, they're a scary bunch, very full of themselves, but damned efficient when they have to be. I'll make sure they have to be. I'll probably catch hell for using them, but bugger that. Who's to say this isn't an international terrorist plot?"

"Whatever it is." Richard rubbed his face again. It was still there, along with the start of a beard. His eyes felt gritty, the lids puffed. If he'd been human he rather thought he'd have a bomb of a headache by now.

Bourland saw and went sympathetic. "Listen, you've been here all day and need a break."

"But I—"

"No. Not an option. I don't care where you go, sleep in the car park downstairs if you like, but get out of here for a few hours. For your own good. And hers."

Richard had accomplished the blood exchange. It would work or not, so there was no reason he couldn't leave for a little while.

"I've exhausted all my distractions," said Bourland. "I need to be here. Besides, that party I called won't show themselves until you've gone."

"Skittish are they?"

He nodded. "Paranoid as hell."

"I'll pick up some things and go over to your place, keep an eye on Michael."

"And rest."

"All right if I borrow your computer?"

"That's not resting."

"Ten minutes. Research."

"Right, I know how that goes, follow one thread and before you know it the whole night's gone by. You'll want the password to open the desktop, but after that the Internet access is open, anything in the files requires more passwords."

"Canadian state secrets are safe from me. The recording you made is all I need. I'd like to see that again."

"Brave man. It's not locked up, just hit 'play' on the DVD; the disk is still inside. Hold out your hand." Bourland wrote down a series of nonsequential letters and numbers on Richard's left palm with a felt tip. "Wash that off when you've learned it."

"What? You've not picked the name or birth date of a loved one?"

"I'm not an idiot. This is harder to memorize but more secure." He gave back the Land Rover keys. "Michael wants to be here first thing in the morning, but see to it he eats. Don't overlook yourself for that, either. I think you've been living on air all day."

They left the room together, Bourland going into the ICU to sit with Sabra, Richard continuing to the elevators. He checked his coat pocket for his cell, though he knew it would be there. Nerves showing. It was a wrench leaving her, but she was being watched over, and at any given time he'd be only a quarter hour away.

Bourland had parked within a few places of where they'd screamed in that morning. It felt like days had passed since then. Richard gulped down cold outside air, grateful for the change. He'd be back before dawn, though.

He slipped into the seat, his body adjusting better to its more comfortable confines than the hospital chair, and went through the routine of starting the vehicle and driving off. St. Michael's stood right on Queen Street; he turned left and sped away as fast as the lights would allow. The streets were still wet, but a full day's worth of traffic had cleared away much of the slick ice.

Another hour or even half hour, and that wide patch of ice across the highway might have been broken down. Would it have made any difference to Sabra if she'd waited? Probably not. That wind. That bloody Otherside wind had been the culprit. Who had sent it? Why?

He tried—again—to block out the memory of her panicked face as she'd passed him, fighting the wheel, slamming the brakes . . .

He was forced to hit his own as some fool darted in front of him and revved away, leaving blue exhaust behind like a parting taunt. He let the annoyance distract him until he reached Neville Park and went right.

End of the block, pull into the drive, park, cut the motor. The house looked different from when he'd left that morning, but he knew the difference was within himself. Catastrophe had turned the familiar alien, showing him once again that he lived in a safe, friendly, sheltered world with no more substance to it than tissue and just as easily ripped.

He went inside, this time to the answering machine first. More ads. He ought to disconnect the ridiculous thing. When the last one played out, he hit the erase and moved glumly to the kitchen.

The blood which he'd taken from Mercedes White would hold him through tomorrow, but he didn't know what to expect over the next few days. From one of the lower vegetable drawers where it was hidden under a still airtight package of three-year-old turkey bacon he drew out a bag of blood. It was also beyond its usable date, but only for medical purposes. It suited him just fine for his singular requirements. He cut a small hole in one corner, poured the lot into an outsized plastic commuter's mug with a sealable top against spillage, and dropped the exhausted bag in the trash compactor. Very tidy. He loved this century.

While gradually drinking his meal, he made quick use of the shower to wake up, shaved, and donned fresh clothes, throwing plenty more into a travel bag. Richard knew the guest room of the faux-Tudor house was open to him for as long as he liked.

He finished the blood, ran water to thoroughly rinse the mug, and shrugged on his long leather overcoat. He loaded the Rover, then went back to set the house alarm and lock up. It was so damned quiet, even the lake. He went out to the end of the street, where the old concrete stairs led down to the beach. The vast plain of water was perfectly still, almost as though it had iced over. That kind of calm didn't happen often. He hoped it wasn't a bad sign, but then he always hoped certain things he noticed weren't a bad sign. Usually as soon as the thought came, it departed, and he forgot it. This one stayed longer than it should. Was that a bad sign?

God, no wonder people fell into superstition.

As he walked around to the driver's side one of his boots trod on a patch of ice the wrong way and that was all it took. He pitched violently forward, hitting the truck and just managing to twist, palms out and arms bent to absorb the shock, a reflex action. That's what kept him from breaking both wrists when he landed on the driveway, but it was a nasty jolt all the same, and set his adrenaline buzzing.

He got up after a minute, grumbling, dusted snow and wet from his front, and slid gingerly into the Rover, favoring new bruises. It took two tries to slot the key, his hand shook so much. When he'd bashed against the Rover's body he'd banged his shoulder rather hard. It wasn't dislocated, but there was a hell of a bruise forming already.

Unsettled by the fall and disgusted for letting it get to him, he shifted gears, backed out, and left, roaring up the street.

What in hell was *wrong* with the world? He did not *need* that little surprise.

Fifty yards away, Charon was also disgusted. He'd waited for hours in this exterior deep freeze for his moment and all for *nothing*. The damn jock's luck had saved him.

Charon dismantled his long rifle with the huge silencer, carefully returning them to their special case. It was hardly worth hauling the thing out of storage if this was to be his only chance. Queered, totally queered, not even one shot. He'd set too narrow a window, gauging the sights and the rest for just this precise distance. Should have bagged Dun when he was at the end of the street looking at the pretty water, aw. But Charon's hand-eye coordination wasn't what it used to be since his change back to human, and the medications were way too good at ballsing them up even more. What should have been an easy-peasy-in-the-barrel snuffing had become a thorny challenge because of his limits.

He didn't dare try after Dun took that fall and dropped behind a row of scraggly bushes. Another hesitation when he stood up and wobbled. Too easy to screw up. Had there been a miss he'd have seen the bullet's impact against the body of his truck and come hunting. Charon was in no shape for any one-on-one dancing with that dude. A couple years ago, perhaps, when he used to swig down the red fire himself, but not now while he was human-weak, not even with the razor-edged bowie knife he'd purchased that afternoon at a sporting goods chain store. Dammit to hell, but he'd had a clear line of sight right to the bloodsucker's chest. It wouldn't have killed him, but certainly have taken him out long enough to move in and cut his head off. Instead, the son of a bitch had been oh-so-conveniently swept from his feet by . . . what?

There'd been no way to get a good look at it, like trying to see wind, but Charon caught an impression, a shimmering flash of silver light zipping along the ground. There was force to it, enough to pitch old Lance right over. What a look on his face. He'd had no clue that something had done him a favor.

Something powerful.

Charon—minus his eye patch now—squinted, frowning, trying to see what was not normally visible. His Sight was usually pretty good, but he was aware of his blind spots, and the stuff eating him alive from the inside out didn't help. Even if he'd been at two hundred percent it might not have served here. That was the problem with the opposition; most of the time they're invisible until it's too late to dodge them. And, for some reason, they often remained so even to their *own* people.

Damned cagey flakers.

He sensed plenty of energies in this place, some of it natural interference from the nearby water, but there was a decided protective glow hovering around the house, Dun, and his vehicle. He thought about draining it off the property for a recharge, but better not. Fang-boy might be tuned in enough to notice and call his old lady over to play bloodhound. She'd be able to track quick enough. Better to wait until the jock was toast.

There he goes, driving cluelessly toward Queen Street.

Too late to follow, but from the look of the bag Dun carried, he might be away for a few days. No telling where. Off on one of his little quests, tally-ho and rooty-toot-toot, damn him to Hell. The real one.

Charon emerged stiffly from his makeshift hunting blind in the snow-crusted bushes of a side yard. The other houses along the street were occupied. He'd picked this one for the dark windows and snow-drift drive. The occupants, if they had any sense, were in a place where winter was something you only saw in calendar photos. His shiny new arctic gear had served to keep him from freezing during his stakeout, but now he wanted to get truly warm—

A sudden, intense spasm of pain and a wash of weakness, of

gut-twisting nausea, halted him in his tracks. It crashed home hard
and went on for several minutes, with him fighting it every inch,
until he staggered against the house wall and puked his last meal.
Then he moved off and dropped to his knees, panting until the
booming in his ears subsided. He was covered with a sweat that
raised more of a chill in him than the goddamned weather.

Damn. *That* was starting up again. He hoped he'd left it behind
at Chichén Itzá. Great. He fumbled at a pocket and one of the
containers tucked inside. Pulling a glove off with his teeth, he
wrestled with the child-proof cap and shook out a pill, swallowing it dry. The bitter taste clung to the back of his throat.

That decided him. It would be safer, better to strike Lance down
from cover, but Charon couldn't afford to hang here indefinitely
hoping for his return. Time was getting short, and he was losing
ground.

He didn't want show his presence, though. No sense letting Dun
know who he was dealing with until the last possible moment. With
any luck, it *would* be Dun's last possible moment.

Charon wondered what had become of the witchy girl friend.
He kept tabs on his enemies, but sometimes it was impossible to
find out the why behind their actions. She'd left her Vancouver
hermitage and moved here for *some* reason. Maybe to do with
the Grail or so she and Lancelot could start banging each other
regularly again. With her turned human too, she couldn't have
many years left for it.

Fine with me. Either way, she was conveniently close to a
bullet.

She'd not been at home when he phoned. That had been taking a chance, but he figured she'd not be able to identify him if
he hung up just as she said 'hello.' But all day long it'd been the
freaking answering machine, so there'd been no reason to go driving
up to her wilderness hut to whack her.

If he could arrange things just right, make a feint or, if possible,
a solid hit at her from a distance, it would bring Dun in roaring,
perfectly primed to be chopped.

Which would take some setting up. Might as well plan it in a
nice warm hotel room and give the pill a chance to work.

❖   ❖   ❖

All was quiet at Bourland's house, except for the ubiquitous television noise. Richard was not immune to watching hours of it himself when the mood was on him, but he never left his own set running just for the sake of having it on.

Not so for Michael, who had taken up residence in the TV room. On his way to the office Richard looked in. His godson was sprawled on one of the long sofas there, his socked feet up on its arm. He stared at the screen as though phased out, but was methodically clicking the remote through the satellite channels several times in a row. He finally settled on a hockey game, but pressed the mute button, watching the players gliding on the ice in a silent, near-hypnotic dance.

"Wanna watch?" he asked, barely glancing up.

"Shortly. I've some things to do first."

"You staying over?"

"Your very kind housekeeper's prepping the guest room now."

"Good."

"Are you all right?"

Michael rolled his eyes, exaggerating. "Between her and you and Dad and my therapist . . . I'm fine."

"Your therapist?"

"Dad called her, and we talked on the phone. I'm *fine*. It's not like I'm made of glass and gonna break, okay?"

"Okay. Then I won't ask if you've eaten anything."

Michael's head lifted and swiveled his way. "There's this pizza place that delivers late . . ."

Richard delved into his wallet and pulled out money. "Get whatever you want, no caffeine in the soda. Don't forget to tip the driver. He'll expect something decent from this neighborhood."

"Deal!" Michael launched up and rolled over the top of the sofa like a commando, just missing a lamp with one of his feet. He tore off to the kitchen where presumably the pizza number would be magnetically clinging to the refrigerator. Richard's was similarly adorned, for his guests' convenience, when he had any. All the food he kept on hand was for show and usually expired. There was a fifteen-year-old can of peas on one pantry shelf that had to be a biohazard by now. Or a collectable ready for an on-line auction.

He moved on to the office to fire up the computer and when it asked, entered the password Bourland supplied. It opened to the desktop without hitch, which was well, since he'd washed the letters and numbers off in the shower.

The DVD player program was on top. He clicked it awake and once more wondered how in hell it had been able to record Michael's vision. Richard had heard of electronic voice phenomenon, where ghostly voices could be recorded on magnetic tape, but this was several light-years beyond that. The mixing of Otherside powers and Realside technology was very unsettling. Especially when they worked.

However it happened, the images on the disk had not lost their ability to disturb. He played the glimpse into this apparent Otherside hell again and again, freezing it for study, hoping for recognizable clues. He felt out of his depth and missed Sabra desperately.

There was only one other who could help them, and she was the breadth of a continent away in an isolated corner of Vancouver. Certainly she would have sensed this calamity, and might be able to help, to explain the signs, but how to contact her . . . ?

"That's the bad stuff, isn't it?" asked Michael, standing in the doorway.

He was too tired to jump. "Yes. It is."

"Dad wouldn't let me look, but I've already seen them in my head."

"You remember them?"

"Yeah, it's like watching a movie trailer. Real fast, so it blurs, but some pictures stay. Can I look at these?"

Richard debated inwardly. Bourland's hesitation must have been based on trying to protect Michael, but the boy seemed unafraid. "All right."

Coming over, Michael studied the screen, frowning. "What do they mean?"

"I was rather hoping you might have an insight."

He shrugged. "Aunt Sabra was going to tell us."

"Wasn't she helping you interpret dreams for yourself?"

"Yeah, sort of, but this is way farther along than we ever got. The one last night with the pyramid and the snake and the rest . . . but that was a vision, not a dream. It just happened to come when I was sleeping."

"It frightened you?"

He moved off to collapse untidily on the tufted leather couch. Didn't boys sit at all? "Yeah. She'd tell me not to be afraid, though, wouldn't she?"

"I'm sure she would."

"You're not afraid, are you, Uncle Richard?"

"Not of a dream, no."

"But that *wasn't* a dream. It's something that really happened."

"I think so, yes. But none of it was your doing."

Michael's shrugged, quite a feat, given his horizontal position. "I feel like I could have done something to help, but I didn't. All I did was stand there and watch like everyone else. If I'd known more maybe I could have stopped things, but I kinda thought *you* were supposed to do something."

"Any idea what that might have been?"

"No. I wish I did."

And be careful what you wish for, he automatically thought. "Did you see anything else? I was rather busy looking at the snake."

"Uh-uh. Just that man and woman fighting and the pyramid and the storm . . ." Michael squirmed around until he sat up. "Aunt Sabra told me that sometimes what I see is like that." He pointed to a small TV stuffed into a bookshelf. "When the news is on and they show a story about something awful, you see it, but there's nothing you can do because it's already happened. It's okay to feel bad, but it's not your fault, and it's not the TV's fault for showing you. It just *is*. And it's going to go on whether you watch or not. When a tree falls in the woods it *does* make a noise."

Richard agreed.

"Like what happened to me when I was little. Aunt Sabra always says it's not my fault. You all do."

"We're quite right, too."

"I know." But Michael sighed. "I know it up here"—he mashed a palm against his forehead— "but sometimes not here." He thumped his chest over his heart. "That's when it hurts here, too. She says everything's connected. Is what happened in Texas connected to what happened in the vision?"

The only connection Richard knew was Michael himself, but saw no help to the boy in saying it. "I don't know. We'll ask her when she's better." He said this quite on purpose, looking at Michael for a reaction, conscious or not, in case he knew what was to happen. There was none. Sabra was the one with the Sight, for not only seeing the future, but the possibilities of multiple futures. It was just as well Michael did not possess that particular facet of the Gift.

"Is Aunt Sabra dying?" Michael asked.

Richard smiled. "Of course not." And he hoped to God and Goddess that was true.

The doorbell rang. The chimes of Big Ben, of a lesser volume than the original in London, notified the house of a visitor.

"Pizza!" Michael again launched out. It was as though he had two speeds: complete stop and Mach 1, with nothing in between.

He trailed Michael to the front entry, hanging back to allow the boy freedom to enjoy firsthand the pleasure of participating in the wonders of commerce. Still, he kept an eye out for trouble. Some force had made a try at killing Sabra, there was no reason to think Michael might be immune. Richard thought it most unlikely, though. No visions since this morning. Though they were powerful, the boy was yet a novice, not worthy of notice yet from anyone or anything bad. Sabra was the more dangerous foe on that Side.

Michael swept his steaming prize off to the TV room, laying the flat box out on the coffee table and calling for company to come share before he ate it all. The housekeeper, used to the ritual, disappeared and reappeared with paper plates, a wad of paper napkins, glasses, and a bucket of ice for the soda. She took one slice and announced that if Mr. Dun planned to remain, then she'd prefer to go to her own home if that was all right. Richard said it was perfectly fine, thanked her, and off she went. He was invited to dig into the feast, but begged off, claiming he'd eaten earlier. Which was true.

The TV still played the apparently prerecorded hockey game; Michael set the sound to low so small voices droned in undercurrent to his meal.

"Those commentators are so boring," he said. "I mean, we can *see* what's going on. Do they think we're blind or something?"

"Sometimes they catch things we miss. The cameras aren't always fast enough to follow the action, but the babble can be annoying."

"That's the word. I wish they'd just shut up and let us hear the crowd instead. It'd be more like being there."

The food, such as it was, heavy on pepperoni, peameal bacon, and God knows what else, served to fill up even Michael's usually bottomless stomach. After finishing nearly the whole thing he fell into a doze.

Richard had stretched out on the other sofa to keep him company and found himself drifting off as well. A stray thought, some idea he was sure he should have come up with before, floated toward him, hanging out of reach. He'd forgotten something. No matter. His mind was good at throwing out the right idea given the chance.

Damn, but his shoulder *ached* from that fall. No matter. It would mend in a few hours, good as new . . .

Normandy, the Past

Richard cracked his heavy eyelids and stifled a grunt of pain. Someone was doing terrible things to his shoulder.

"I'm sorry, Lord Richard. I did not mean to wake you." The Holy Sister tending him looked stricken.

"What . . . ?"

"I was just bathing it clean."

"Is the tourney over?"

"Yes, your lordship. Two days now."

Two? "Impossible, I was there only this morning."

"And wounded by that afternoon. We brought you here for healing."

"Wounded?" He dimly recalled besting one of the other champions, then in a fit of spite the man on the ground slammed upward with his blade and got under Richard's armor. No one on that side of the field claimed to have seen the dishonorable blow, of course, they were all angered at losing. Richard recalled cursing him and staggering off, and then two squires rushed over to help him back to his pavilion. He'd bled like a pig at the butcher's, and that's where things went thick as fog. "The reckoning—how did it fall?"

"You are still the Champion d'Orleans, your lordship."

He lay back, relieved, then grunted again at the sudden pain of the movement. How his shoulder throbbed. It was as though the sword blade was still in him. He couldn't see much of the wound, just a little of the stitching from the corner of his eye; it was too much work to twist his head to look. He felt hot all over and even his bones seemed bruised.

With a murmured apology for the hurt she must bring, the Holy Sister continued to bathe his wound as gently as possible. He tried not to let his discomfort show, knowing that she and the other women here had been uncommonly kind to him. They always were when he got injured fighting.

"I've slept two days?" he asked, trying to remember.

"And just as well. You would not have liked what we had to do to stop the bleeding."

From the color of the water in her bucket there was still flow from his wound, unless that was from some other hapless warrior under their care. He seemed to have a room to himself, though. Being a duke's son, albeit the third one, had its advantages, though he knew they would have looked after him well whatever his station.

He was wakeful yet lethargic, and too weak to get up. A page sent from the castle to watch his progress was brought in to hold the slop bucket so he could pass water lying sideways on the bed. Richard went dizzy after that. Someone brought him wine mixed with cold broth, but he could only manage the smallest sip, refusing the rest. His belly wouldn't stand it. The fever in his shoulder seemed to be spreading, and no amount of cool, wet cloths on his brow eased it.

In turns Richard shivered and sweated and cursed and whimpered, but nothing curbed the growing pain. He thought another night passed, but could not be sure. The chamber had but a small window, high up, and no real light came through. He was told it had been raining since the tourney, all the time raining, the summer days gone ominously dark . . .

❖　　❖　　❖

"Not dead yet?"

He didn't bother to open his eyes, recognizing the comfortless voice of Dear Brother Ambert.

"You, there. You hear me?" Richard felt something prod him in the side. A sword or cudgel, it made no difference; he simply didn't care, giving no protest. Thirst tormented him far more than ever Ambert could. Dear Brother sounded drunk. That was normal.

"Lord Ambert, your brother is sorely stricken and needs your prayers lest he die." A woman's voice. The eldest Sister, who was in charge of the place, no less. She sounded severe and reproving. Wasted on Ambert. He had too much of old Montague in him.

"Heaven will get my prayer of thanks when they put him in the ground and good riddance to him."

A gasp of shock. He liked doing that to people. Fortunately, the Sister was canny enough not to respond. Ambert was not above striking a woman, any woman, who annoyed him. By God if he dared, Richard would rise and kill him, wound or no wound.

"See to it I'm told when he's *dead*, not dying. Until then keep your damned messengers to yourselves. I've more important things to worry about."

Richard looked in time to see Ambert's departing back. The Sister crossed herself, shaking her head.

"I'm sorry . . ." he whispered. He was ashamed to share blood with the man.

She heard and came over. An older woman, thirty at least, she spared him a kindly smile. "Your brother is not your keeper, it seems."

He tried to nod and smile back, but couldn't manage. His lips were so dry and cracked they hurt.

She dipped her fingers in a cup and dripped water into his mouth until he had enough, then smoothed an oil on the chapping. "There, now. Rest. We will pray for your recovery."

But he gave a sudden shiver from cold and stifled a cry of pain. When the tremor passed he knew her prayers would be for nothing. He'd caught a whiff of his own stink; a foulness was coming from his shoulder. Soon it would spread to his blood and that would be the end of him. He had seen enough men fall to it before; now it was his turn.

Oddly, he felt no panic, no regret. He'd done well in his twenty years, and would always be remembered as the undefeated Champion d'Orleans. Life was harsh and laborious and heaven would be all the better after his earthly sufferings. He'd seen worse deaths. All he had to do was go to sleep and wait. He knew how to do that.

The Sister departed as he sank into slumber.

It was uneasy, though. Fever kept him from fully passing out, which was all he wanted. When he was unconscious, he had no pain, and at this point the agony thundering in time to his beating heart was such that dying promised to be his best and only release. He lay in his sweat and panted and prayed for it to come lift him free of his infected and exhausted body. Slow hours passed, and he thought with relief that things were at last fading away as his chamber got darker.

Then one of the Sisters came in with a candle, making a lie of his expectations. He could not see her face, the soft white mantle covering her head came down almost to her lips. The veil was so delicate it seemed to float with her smallest movement. Perhaps she was one of the great and wealthy ladies who took orders to escape their husbands or who had been sent away by a family not wanting an unmarried female in the house. Each of the women here had her own secret story, but all were made alike by their simple robes. For the most part. Sometimes the robes were of fine weave or the woman carried a cross made of gold not wood.

This Sister wore no cross, but she knelt by him and seemed to pray. She seemed very young, a tiny little bird of a woman, with a voice as gentle as mist. She pulled off the wrappings on his wound and clucked over it. The skin on his arm was hot and tight from the swelling.

"Drink," she whispered, lifting his head.

He didn't think he could, but from the cup she held came the clearest, coldest water he'd ever tasted. There was a hint of crushed flowers in it, as though she'd distilled the air of springtime itself. Finally, at last, his awful thirst eased.

"Your pain is no more," she told him decisively after lifting her veil to look hard at him.

She had the most amazing eyes; their light seeming to sweetly pierce him right to his soul. His pain fled. Even when she poured the water over his hot and festering wound he felt nothing of it. Dimly, he noticed when she produced a knife, heating it in the candle flame. It caused him no alarm, not even when she cut into his corrupted flesh, removed the stitches, and laid her hands on to squeeze out the poison.

As though from a distance he heard himself groan piteously in response, but she told him all was well and painless. He utterly believed her. There seemed to be a glow about her form; his eyes playing tricks perhaps.

It entered Richard's head that he was having a vision of the Holy Mother Herself, though why She would be concerned for him in particular was beyond his ken.

She paused in her work, giving in to a shudder and catching her breath. It was an altogether human reaction, but he could still not shed the impression of an unworldly presence.

Washing the wound again in the cold, cold water, she stitched him back up and lay a fragrant poultice on it, pressing it down firmly against the outraged flesh and holding it hard in place. He should have been screaming, but as she told him, he felt nothing.

"Lady . . ."

"Hush, all is well."

Then she sang to him, very softly so only he could hear. He didn't know the words, but there was no need; he understood them from a place outside his mind. They went straight to his heart, kindling feelings he never knew existed. She soothed him without and lightened him within.

This is how safe and loved a child feels when his mother sings him to sleep.

No one had ever done that for Richard. His mother had died birthing him long ago.

What a lovely, lovely voice this woman had. He wanted to tell her so, tell her quite a lot, but one mustn't say such things to a Sister.

As he began to finally drift away, she leaned close to kiss his brow. "Live and thrive, my Richard," she whispered and turned to leave.

He raised one hand toward her, wanting her to stay. "Wait . . . please . . ." He forced his eyes open . . .

. . . and looked on the face of his brother Edward looming over him.

It was no mistake. Strong daylight poured into the room from the high window.

"How, now, Dickon? Are you going to stay with us after all?" Edward gently asked.

"Where is the Holy Sister?"

"Here, Lord Richard."

But the woman who replied was the eldest Sister who had dealt with Ambert. She seemed pleased.

"The other one," he said. "The one who cared for me last night."

She gave him a puzzled smile. "We were here for you, we only."

"The other one," he insisted. "She sang."

She and Edward exchanged a glance, then she left. He found a low stool and sat next to the bed. "You worried everyone, Dickon."

"All but two," he said without bitterness. Ambert had appeared once to sneer, and Montague had simply not come. But for Edward to have traveled so far for a visit . . . Richard was deeply glad of that. "Water . . . please."

Edward dipped a cup into a bucket by a small table. He carefully held Richard's head, tilting the vessel so it would not spill. One would think he tended the sick every day. His hands were so much larger than hers had been . . . but the water was the same.

"Drink, you must try some," said Richard.

Shrugging, he took a sip.

"Is it not good water?"

"Very good."

"Don't you taste it?"

"What?"

"Sweet, like flowers."

Edward made naught of the miracle. "I suppose the Sisters flavor it. They know much of herbs."

"But that one who came, she tended me all night, took away my fever. I must thank her."

"What did she look like?"

As best he could Richard described her and what she'd done, especially how she'd freed him from pain through what should have been the worst torment.

"I've seen none here like that," said Edward. "And they all turned out for my arrival."

They would, since he was a bishop now. As a scion of the d'Orlean's house of course he would rise quickly within the church no matter what, but it didn't hurt that he could also read and write. He was very good at it, too.

"When did you get here?" asked Richard.

"Three days ago they sent for me. I was told that if God was merciful I might arrive in time to deliver the last prayers to speed you to heaven. It would seem He is being most kindly to spare me from the work."

Edward's humor had ever a backward slant, but Richard found he could smile. "I've slept long, then."

"You've barely slept at all, Dickon. I was sitting right here for the better part of two days, you just didn't know it. We kept praying for the fever to leave you. Only last night did it finally break."

"But she was here. She came at sunset and cared for and sang to me for hours."

Edward pursed his lips, looking solemn beyond his years.

Richard, cast about for some other proof besides the water, and touched the poultice. His wound was still tender, but like a bruise, not a raging fire. "She put this on me after cleaning out the rot."

"Ah—yes—well . . ."

"Was it one of the others?" Richard desperately wanted that not to be true.

"Actually, it's a bit of a mystery to us."

"How so?"

"You say this was last night?"

"It must be, for I was like to die from the fever, and she took it away. You said it broke last night."

"There were several of us sitting vigil here then. Through the whole of the night. No Sister tended you in the way that you said. When light came one of them noticed your dressings and stitches were different, and the poultice was in place."

Richard's heart pounded. "What does it mean?"

"That . . . we all must have fallen asleep."

He couldn't believe it. "Everyone?"

"So it would seem. And while we slept, this unknown Sister came and tended you."

"Without waking anybody? How did she get in? The gates are always locked."

Edward spread his hands. "I was here. I saw no such woman. Not *here*, anyway."

"You know her."

"I can't be certain if she was the same one, but a veiled Sister came to the monastery insisting I hasten to see my wounded brother. I knew there was a tourney on, but Ambert had sent no word that you'd been hurt."

"He wouldn't."

"She arrived at the monastery gate on horseback—a very fine animal it was, too—with no escort. What Sister would travel such a distance alone and that way? And at night in the rain? None that I know. She was as you said: a tiny little bird of a woman, young. I cannot be sure of her voice being beautiful since she was shouting, not singing. Once she gave her message to me, she kicked the animal and took off. Never saw a woman ride a horse so well. Held on like she was part of its own skin then vanished into the darkness."

"But you saw her."

"I saw *that* woman." Edward liked to be precise. "If both are the same, then yes, she is real."

"How can she not be?"

"Well, you said you thought she might be a vision of the Holy Mother. What if she was? The one here, that is."

Richard deliberated for some while. He was tired, very weak, but his mind had cleared, and his memory was fresh. "No, she could not have been."

"You're so certain?"

"Had she been the Holy Mother, then . . . I would have not felt as I did toward her."

"And how is that?"

Richard frowned. The eldest Sister stood just beyond the doorway, her clasped hands hidden by her robe sleeves, her head respectfully bowed, pretending not to listen. "Closer."

Edward obliged, leaning in.

"I'm speaking to you brother to brother, not brother to bishop."

"Speak on then."

He did, in his lowest voice. "I felt toward her as a man feels toward a woman. If that was the Holy Mother, then . . ."

Edward straightened, smiling. "Yes. Quite blasphemous, I'm sure. So this woman could not have possibly been a Vision. The Holy Mother inspires devotion, but not that kind."

"I'm glad you agree. Very glad." Despite his conviction, Richard had been sincerely worried for a moment. He now felt exceedingly heavy, especially at the eyelids. Couldn't seem to keep them raised for some reason. "Find her, will you? I want to thank . . ."

When he dreamed, he heard her singing.

Despite Edward's official dismissal of the event, or perhaps because of it, the story got out, and seemingly in an instant the puzzling mystery bloomed into a major miracle. Whenever Edward came to visit during the early days of Richard's recovery he brought a new version to tell.

The best was that the Holy Mother had appeared at the altar in the hospice hall in a blaze of light that rivaled the sun. All the warriors who happened to be touched by that glow were immediately healed of their wounds and told to never fight again. This was widely believed despite the fact that many of the men being cared for in the hall remained in their beds, either healing or dying.

"I don't remember that taking place," Richard said, almost chuckling. It hurt to laugh, but he was able to sit up today, and had begun eating more strengthening food than wine and broth. He'd just experimented with bread dipped in warm honey, and it seemed to want to stay down.

"Neither does anyone else, but the villagers are passing it about as fact. I shall have to speak about it at the Sabbath mass. I'll tell them exactly what happened as we know it and let them walk through the hospice to see for themselves. Doubtless they will make a tale of it, but at least I'll have done the right thing."

"You're staying that long?" Edward's visits were rare and usually brief in duration.

"The good Sisters here are expecting it. Mustn't disappoint them. They seem to like hearing me say mass."

"Do *you* like what you do?" To Richard, his brother's isolated life behind protected walls dealing with spiritual matters was at best, bizarre, and worst, a living hell. He counted himself most fortunate to have escaped such a fate.

"Yes, very much. Of course, it's not nearly as rousing as getting your arm half lopped off in tourney battles, but has its rewards. I'm also a very busy man, so you keep yourself out of trouble from now on. Can't expect me to drop the whole lot and leave just to look in on you every time you're like to die."

"Then I'll to come by and visit you instead. My last winnings included a fine mount."

"I saw him. You've finally got yourself a horse to suit your size. He's not gelded, either. You'd best find a mare sturdy enough to handle him and breed more of the same."

"I plan to."

"Good. I wouldn't count on continuing with tourneys to support you in your old age."

"If I live to see it."

Edward looked at him a moment with an odd, amused expression. "I think of all of us, you're the one who will. The chances are against it with what you do, but I've a feeling—"

"What?" An abrasive voice interrupted him. "Prophesy from the priest? You get above yourself, Brother."

Ambert stood in the doorway, one hand on his sword belt, the other holding a riding whip.

Edward stiffened slightly, then abruptly relaxed. Smiling and kind, he turned. "Hallo, Ambert. Good to see you engaged in charitable works. I've been told the depth of concern you showed to Richard on his sickbed."

"Faugh." Ambert was impervious to sarcasm, even when he wasn't too drunk to understand it. He seemed clear on the meaning today. He swung his attention on Richard. "So—the pup's to live after all."

"Indeed. This evening we hold a special mass of thanksgiving for his recovery. You'll come of course. My son."

The last was proof that Edward still had some devilry in him. There were few other things that set Ambert off than the reminder his younger brother was in a position of power over him. In spiritual matters. Though not a very secure place—for Ambert was loath to pay much mind to the nurturing of his soul—it was sufficient to infuriate him. He turned a dark, murderous eye on Edward, who continued to inoffensively smile. "I'll be there—and see to it you regret the invitation."

"You will behave yourself, Ambert. God's house is no place for drunken riot and disruption."

"Or what, you'll damn me to Hell? I can find a dozen other priests to pray me out again."

Edward stood. "Yes, as a priest I can damn you to Hell, but as your brother I can send you there myself. Don't forget what I used to be before I took orders. It was a rare day when I couldn't best you when I chose, remember?"

Ambert rumbled under his breath, apparently remembering his broken ribs. "You'd fight me in the church?"

"And win. I'd do penance, but it'd be worth it for the story to follow. Lord Ambert d'Orleans, beaten to a pulp before the whole congregation by a lowly monk. Think of the bread your enemies will make of that grain. Before the story gets too far they'll have you being worsted by one of the younger *castrati*. I think you'd rather not have that put abroad."

Red faced, Ambert lashed out with the riding whip, cutting right at Edward's eyes with the handle, but his brother's arm came up fast, blocking the blow. He got a grip and pulled, twisting, yanking the whip clear. In a second Ambert was on him, and it was pummeling fists and roars as they thrashed about the chamber. Richard watched unmoved and unalarmed from his bed, thinking that it was just as it was when they were growing boys.

With a difference, now.

Edward was not as tall as Ambert, but more robust. The monastic life toughened a man. Ambert's nightly devotions took him to the wine cask, not an altar, and it was clear which was better for the health of one's mortal body. He was soon stretched on his back, puffing greedily for air, while Edward stood over him, rubbing his barked knuckles, looking satisfied.

"I always enjoy your visits, Ambert. You've a way of making the dullest day interesting, but we mustn't overexcite Richard. You should be off now." He hauled Ambert from the floor, and shoved him staggering away. "See you at mass, my son." He slammed the door shut, and put his back against it to prevent a return attack. One of the seams in the front of his robe had parted wide in the set-to, and he noticed. "Dear me. Have to sew that up, won't I?"

Oh, God, it hurt to laugh, yet Richard couldn't help himself. He held his sore shoulder, trying to keep from pulling the stitches. "You are a wicked, wicked man, Brother Bishop."

Edward had better success reining in his humor, dusting his robes and straightening them out. He sighed, wearing a face of dignified long-suffering. "Yes, after each visit home I spend more and more time in the confessional reciting my most recent sins. Ambert makes it too easy for me to wander astray."

"You're not angry, though. You used to get so incensed with him all the time."

"And one time too many." He sighed as he always did for that grim memory, then glanced wryly at Richard. "See, I have grown like a tree, with a much thicker skin than a few years ago. Once one of his axe-blows would have cut me down. Now I feel I could dull the edge, if not shatter it."

"This is what doing God's work has done for you?" Richard felt a small pang of envy for his brother's self-control, his apparent immunity to Ambert.

"In part, along with travel and learning to see the truth about people." He came and sat next to the bed again. "It will do you well to come along with me the next time I make a long journey. You've not seen much of the world yet. There are places behind the horizon you can't begin to imagine."

"When I'm better." Richard wanted to do that. "Just send word. Father will give me leave to go if you ask it."

Edward snorted. "Make that 'request and require as my office demands.' He still has some respect for the Church. It is my title, not me, he listens to for such matters."

"But he *does* listen."

"There's more to it. My life is no longer hostage to him. I have no more need of his good will for my meat, drink, and bed. Once I took orders his hold over me ceased. He'd never admit it, but he understands that if he is less than civil I will leave him entirely, never to return. His pride won't stand for that. Ours is an ugly give-and-take dance at times, but he does know when to back down, and I know how far not to push him. That's how we're able to get along. You need to do the same for yourself."

"Take orders?"

"If you're called, but in the meantime work to get yourself free of him. Build up your tourney winnings, breed horses and sell them, see to it he never knows what's in your purse. Make yourself independent."

It sounded wonderful, but Richard knew that could never be, and said as much. "I've already sworn fealty. He'll never release me from that. Even if you speak to him, he won't."

"He could change. I did. He might. Ambert, too. Any man can change if—"

"Edward, there are too few good hearts like you and too many of them."

"All right, then here's something more reasonable to think on. Father won't live forever. When he dies, what will happen to you, the Champion d'Orleans, with Ambert as the duke? Life is uncertain, Father could pass ten years from now or in the next hour."

"I've not thought of that."

"You haven't wanted to."

"No, but I expect I can find a place in one of the other households. Far from here, so Ambert can't order them to turn me away. And if worse came to worst . . ." He trailed off, and felt some nonfeverish heat in his face for what he almost said.

Edward grinned and finished for him. "You'd take orders. *You* in a monastery. There's a laugh. It sits well with me, but *you*, Dickon?" He shook his head and chuckled.

"I'll find something. I will. It's just hard to work anything out. Ambert's got a sharp eye for what he calls mischief, and that's whatever I do that benefits me. Whenever I get any gold to call my own he sees to it I turn it over to Father. For 'safekeeping' he calls it. I never see any afterward, though."

"Then I think you would be well advised to become more pious than you've been. This wounding of yours can account for the change of manner. Donate your winnings to the Church before Father gets them."

"But I—oh. You'd look after them for me?"

"Of course. Your coinage will be safer in the monastery than your room in the castle with Ambert roaming about. If you've any from this last contest, I can carry it along when I return."

Richard had trouble taking it in. Not so many years ago, he'd have never trusted Edward with any small possession he might have hoarded for his own. Now he was turning his future over to him. And it was all right. He knew in his heart his brother would truly watch out for him. "Thank you."

"Bless you, my son." Edward raised his right hand, making their pact a sacred responsibility, but given and accepted with a fond smile.

Richard laughed, but kept it subdued to spare his shoulder.

Then Edward went serious. "Mark this, Richard: you and Ambert are each dangerous, and in some ways you're both fools, but his words and acts are inspired by fear, yours inspired by honor. That's why you will always be the stronger, and well does he know it. For all that, beware of him."

"I always am."

"I mean especially now, while you are in a weak position." He bent and picked up the fallen whip, giving it to Richard.

He took it with his working hand. The thing was uncommonly heavy, the bulb-shaped end weighted. Pushing aside the leather braiding revealed the dull gray of poured lead. It made a fearsome weapon without looking like one. "You think he—"

"I think nothing. But we both know him well. He may not have

come here with the intent to use that on you, but with his temper and you all but helpless . . ."

"One thing leads to another."

"He's a bully, and they ever single out the weak, and this is
as weak as I've seen you since before the day you beat him into
the mud."

"Even he can't still remember that or hold it against me. Too
much wine."

"Can't he? When was the last time he ever forgot an insult, real
or fancied? Beware of him, always."

Richard nodded, solemn.

"I'll stay until you're on your feet, that should be enough, though
I'm thinking you have a far stronger protection over you than I
can provide."

"The Lady?" The thought of her warmed him inside.

"Whether she was real or a dream, she would seem to be
looking out for you."

"Were that so, then she might have turned aside the other man's
blade and spared me a bleeding in the first place."

"I was told what happened by the squires who saw. It was an
evil thing he did. Sometimes good is unable to see what evil is up
to, and despite our best efforts terrible things come to pass. She
did mend you afterwards, though."

"Saved my life, you mean."

"Indeed. No doubt for some good purpose, so don't waste it.
Hm?"

Toronto, the Present

Richard's cell phone trilled, jerking him abruptly from what had
been a deep, satisfying sleep. Where the hell was he? Bourland's TV
room, the hockey game replaced by a tennis match, the sound low
and droning, with Michael on the other couch, twisted around like
a pretzel and thoroughly unconscious. Only children ever seemed
able to reach that depth of sodden slumber. Memory reasserted itself
as Richard noted the late hour on the clock above the television.
He hurriedly checked his cell's caller ID. Not Bourland's number,

so no problem at the hospital. An unknown in fact. Who'd be phoning him this late?

One way to find out. "Hallo?"

"Mr. Dun?" The voice seemed distant, but was recognizable: the lovely lady who had interviewed him so much earlier that evening.

"Yes?"

"I'm sorry to wake you. The time zones are the same, but it's still late."

"Not at all. How's Cancún?"

"Not a clue. We've been on the run since landing. We only just got back from the ruins. We're staying in Merida."

The name meant nothing to him; he assumed it was close to their investigation area. "Have you news of Sharon Geary?"

"Sort of. It's not much, but I thought you'd want a report."

Well, he'd primed her for exactly this. "What's going on?"

"Nothing at the moment, we didn't expect to start until tomorrow, but were told there was some ceremony on tonight, so we got fast transportation out to Chichén Itzá to catch it."

"Ceremony?"

"It was a kind of summoning to bring back the spirit of their old god. According to one of the elders here, the god was stolen from them, and their holy man murdered by the thief. That's as much as we could get being outsiders. They wouldn't let us talk to the shaman—I mean—*ahkin*. He was busy and still new at the job. His old teacher died early this morning. At the airport."

"Died? How?"

"The authorities aren't sure yet. There's some to-do about the body. His people—the ones claiming he was murdered—want him back, but the doctors want to perform an autopsy. What with the world situation they're very hyper about biological weapons, and an old peasant man who's never been more than a mile from his forest village suddenly dying at the airport is suspicious. So far as I can see from a report made at the scene by the ambulance people there was no sign of obvious foul play. The man just collapsed, with bleeding from his nose, eyes, and ears. There are some perfectly normal disorders to account for those symptoms, but combined with other things like your vision, it works out to be odd."

"Why was he at the airport?"

"According to the elder, he was chasing down the thief. He fought with him and lost. But airport security maintains all was quiet, business as usual when it happened. In fact, the only disturbance was him dropping dead."

"Could his people describe this thief?"

"Not in concrete terms. Emotional, yes, but nothing the police could track. If I had to make a guess—and this goes against the scientist in me—I might think he was the one you saw in the vision. Others here—the locals—claimed to have had a similar dream last night."

"Really?" All those other lights. People standing there . . .

"They said they saw a spirit of darkness fighting a spirit of light on top of the god's temple. The darkness threw down the light, but their god rushed in to catch it. That's when he disappeared into a larger darkness, taking the light with him."

"That sounds familiar." The sparse information was full of meaning for him.

"Your story, but in more symbolic terms."

"About the light—if that was Sharon Geary—have they any idea where she is?"

"It's a fuzzy area. We're having translation problems but should have them sorted by tomorrow. We've got a meeting set up with the *ahkin* if he's rested enough to talk. The ceremony took a lot out of him, though all I saw was him sitting there in front of the Temple of Kukulcan. He might have been doing his version of a spirit walk, and I've heard those can be very exhausting."

"Did it work? The ceremony."

"From everyone's reaction, I don't think so. They all looked disappointed.

"And no word of where Sharon might be?"

"We've started an ordinary inquiry with the police. She took a hotel room, but hasn't been seen since she checked in. They're supposed to go through her things, see if there's any clue of her whereabouts or where she's been. If we're lucky they might let us have a turn in the morning. I'm sorry there's not more."

"I'm sure you're doing your best. You sound all in, though."

"Still in my city clothes and asleep on my feet," she confessed.

"Then get to bed. Thank you for calling."

"My pleasure, Mr. Dun," she warmly assured him, and she sounded wholly sincere.

They rang off. He reflected there was a peril to hypnotizing women, even briefly, even for a purpose other than acquiring nourishment. It made for a hell of a strong connection to him. Fortunately the effect faded with time, but in the interim . . . well . . . there it was, a one-to-one fan club between them.

Sharon. His mind snapped back to the larger peril for her. The police there had not, apparently, found a body, but then they wouldn't be able to if she'd been pulled into the same place with the great snake god.

Which was where? Richard couldn't begin to speculate, for then he ran though the same futile thoughts and worries and resentments that had tumbled through his mind since the accident. This was when Sabra was needed the most and her Goddess had let *that* happen? Why? *Why her?*

Despair flooded him for a moment. He bowed his head, fighting it.

The Grail, you fool.

He came up, fully alert, his heart pounding with excitement and hope. Dear God, but he should have thought of it before, first thing in fact, even before exchanging blood. *Why* had he not? No matter. It had healed her before, it would again. He'd run up to her house, grab it—

The tennis game on the television screen seemed to ripple. It did not look like a normal kind of service disruption, not with those colors. The image twisted and danced, ceasing to be players on a clay court and becoming something . . . else.

He caught his breath and glanced at Michael. There was no outward sign from him of anything being amiss except for the quick darting movements of his eyes beneath their lids. He was dreaming again.

Forms flowed over the screen like fish shadows in a fast-running stream. Bits began to coalesce, hold in place, making blurred letters.

They eventually spelled out "*protect*."

A frisson of chill went through him. He frowned. What the hell did that mean? "Protect from what? Protect who?" Was this a warning or an instruction?

Eventually: "S 2 prtct her."

Then the screen popped back to normal again, players lobbing a ball over a net and back again. Michael had not stirred, was even snoring softly.

But he was *smiling*.

It was such a sweet, ingenuous expression, and so unexpected that Richard felt a strange lifting in his heart.

His cell phone trilled.

"Get down here," said Bourland, and his voice was dreadful.

Chapter Eight

The room heat on high, Charon was thoroughly kicked back in one of the penthouse suites at the Cambridge Hotel. Unable to sleep for the pain, he'd ordered some good booze from room service, lined up his pill collection, and popped the ones that might help him get through the next few hours until he came up with Plan B. It didn't used to be like that for him. He always had a Plan B, with C, D, E, and F if needed, but these days it was harder and harder to focus on more than one thing at a time. Like the rush he'd gotten on the pyramid. No distractions from that gleeful joy. The downside being no way around the misery he was going through now. His body was giving him royal rotten hell as the disease worked to reassert itself for the setback he'd handed it.

Waiting for the meds to kick in, he distracted himself from the stubborn pain and the frustration of his failed hit on Dun by flipping through his complimentary copy of the *Toronto Times*.

It had all the usual Strum und Drang side by side with the repetitive daily-living crap. That was the way of things: total disasters are fine so long as they don't happen to you, isn't it a pity, but all's well *here*. You'd think seeing the global body count piling up and having each catastrophe presented in graphic detail over their dinner, not to mention forty-eight times a day on the boob tube, would wise people up about the world being a Nasty

Place to Live. Yet—and this was the knee-cracking kicker—there was always an undercurrent of shocked surprise in the reporting. Was it an act put on for the masses, or what? He was still trying to figure that one.

Huh. They should live a stretch of *his* life, see the things he'd seen—and done. That'd turn them inside out. Literally.

"And, man-oh-man, you ain't seen nothing, yet," he chuckled, then paused and winced, his breath short again. Things were getting worse, more painful than before. He took a different pill, chugging it down with the whiskey. You weren't *supposed* to do that, but Jesus palomino, he was *dying*, what's the worst that could happen now?

He gave it ten, then popped an extra. The edge slowly softened and withdrew for the time being. That had been a bad one. He'd have to wind things up here quick while he could still function.

So, how to take out fang-boy and his doll of delights . . . hello . . . ?

Drawn by the headline, he fastened on a short inside piece below the fold about the bizarre accident on 401 that morning, a car going out of control on ice, a freak gust of wind slamming it into—he grinned at the name of the woman driving: Sabra du Lac. It just *had* to be witchy-girl. Who else could have a moniker like that? Jeez, they didn't even try to get her a decent cover name when she relocated here from the other coast. Must have cost a fortune to forge the paperwork. Where did they take her . . . ?

He laughed. Oh, man, they were making it just *too* easy. St. Michael's Hospital was just around the block. Even in his shape he could walk it.

What the hell, why not? The pills were starting to kick in. He'd have a one-hour window before they knocked him into tomorrow. Plenty of time to suss out the lay of the land, figure a possible ambush. If Dun was there . . . assume he was, since that would explain his overnight bag and hurry to get moving. One thing you could count on was the way he hung on to that little piece of ass. With her being human again he'd probably be freaked out of his mind about her. Off guard.

Oh, hell-*yeah*, baby.

But even with that possibility, Charon would have avoid him, avoid a physical confrontation, but still . . . it couldn't hurt to be prepared to improvise. Just in case an opportunity popped up. Cripes, it was a *hospital*; the place was set up for taking people apart and putting them together. All he had to do was make sure the pieces were too completely scrambled for reassembly.

Charon pulled on his heavy overcoat, gloves, and wrapped a thick muffler around his face. The cold hit him harder than it used to, like everything else. After a moment's thought, he found the eye patch and put it on as well. There'd be security cameras all over that place. Might as well give them something memorable to focus on. The same principal worked for people, too. Most tended to remember the patch, not the man wearing it. Damn, he should have thought of using the scam centuries ago.

It was well after 4:00 A.M. One of the night nurses came to check on Sabra. Philip Bourland roused enough to watch, then couldn't sink back to his doze again. He'd been told—with considerable sympathy, for the staff was excellent—his presence wasn't necessary, that they'd call him if Sabra woke, but he'd be damned before he budged just yet.

If she woke. The way the nurse said it gave him hope that Sabra would come around. Thousands of people came into their care here every year, with such experience they had to get a feel for each patient and know who would make it, who would not, if only on a subconscious level. Had she said *if there's a change* which was more ambiguous, he might have been more pessimistic.

He still wouldn't have left, though.

Philip stood and stretched, stiff and sore from being propped in the chair for much of the night, but didn't care. Aspirin would take care of it easily enough. He wished it was that simple for Sabra.

As Richard had done before him, Philip went to stand by her bedside. He wanted more than anything to feed some of his own strength into her, keep her going, bring her back. If there was a way of doing it he'd have made it happen. Seeing her so still and helpless against his memory of her normal boundless vitality, it wasn't fair or right. She was a good woman, not deserving of such a turn.

He wondered if Richard knew just how much he loved her.

You try not to show it, to spare the other man's feelings.

Of course he'd known from the first she and Richard were involved with each other and had been for a long time, but Sabra said it wasn't exclusive, that Richard wouldn't mind.

Philip minded. He had too much respect for Richard to do him an ill turn. "I'm old-fashioned that way," he told her.

"So am I," she said, smiling. "You've no idea."

It was the summer he'd adopted Michael, and not long after she'd moved to Toronto. He and the boy were still devastated from the loss of Stephanie, Elena, and Seraphina. Had his own daughter and grandchildren been murdered it couldn't have hurt more. Sabra couldn't take away the pain, but she had a way of making it easier to bear just by being around, and she was over at the house often, looking out for Michael, helping him.

Helping me as well, Philip admitted, noticing her a lot more than he thought he should.

She, being perceptive, also turned out to be receptive, but did not resort to any obvious flirting. A look combined with a warm smile here and there were enough to set his heart racing into overdrive. Then one night, while Michael was asleep in his room, she stayed on later than usual, and they got to talking in Philip's office. First it was about schools, private versus public for Michael, then on to other subjects.

Philip had no memory of the conversation, yet Sabra's eyes and voice held his whole attention. In a "what the hell" moment, he'd opened a bottle of wine. That loosened him up a bit, but not to the point of pressing things even though they'd moved from chairs to the big leather sofa. They were chuckling over some point or other, one of Richard's eccentricities, perhaps, then Sabra was somehow very close. It seemed the most natural thing in the world for her to be kissing him like that. He started to kiss back, then remembered Richard and eased away.

She's so damned young, she has no idea what she's about on this.

Which turned out to be completely wrong. She knew exactly what she was doing and what she wanted, but she also eased away to hear him out. Then she shook her head over Philip's diplomatically worded qualms.

"Richard and I have always been like this. When we want to be together, we are, and when we're apart . . ."

"How could he not want you all to himself? And you him?"

"He does. He has. I do and have. Philip, it's all right. He knows."

"Oh, my God."

Sabra laughed at his chagrin. "He has no objections whatsoever."

"How can he not?"

"Richard and I are each free to go our own way. It's always worked for us."

He didn't know what to say to that, except for holding a secret relief that they'd not picked him out for some exotic threesome activity. His dignity wouldn't have stood for it. "It's brilliant, but absurd. You're utterly wonderful, but I'm much too old for you."

There it was, his greatest apprehension and also his last, best line of defense. He'd said it just right: resolutely, but without self-pity or giving offense, just a statement of irrefutable fact, allowing her a graceful exit.

It should have worked, too.

Sabra only burst into laughter.

After a moment, he began to laugh, too. He blamed the wine.

After another moment she was back in his arms giving and receiving a second kiss. This time when he pulled away it was to allow himself to look at her anew. She was absolutely "breath taking," in the literal two-word sense. He'd not been this stirred up by a woman in years.

That smile of hers—was "bewitching" also too old-fashioned a term? Whatever, it worked. With surprising, insistent strength, still laughing a little, Sabra pulled him on top of her, and they were thrashing about on the sofa like couple of sex-starved teenagers. Dear God, but the energy of it, where the hell had he been keeping it all these years? She seemed to bring it right out of him, in more ways than one. He'd never been so focused, hardly noticing when they rolled in seeming slow motion from the sofa to the more spacious floor. Kissing and fondling in their heat, exploring and tearing off clothes all at once, how had they managed?

And then it came down to that most intimate part of the exchange, and for him it was not only about flesh into flesh but soul meeting soul. It's one thing to shed clothes and share bodies, it's quite another to summon the courage to allow your soul to be seen by another. Everything was there in the eyes . . . or not. Adults often had trouble holding a steady gaze with each other, even when they were in love. It could be too personal an invasion, taken as a challenge or judgmental, all the wrong things, so most never tried for very long.

When you looked into your partner's eyes and saw . . . what? Each and every time it was different, even with the same partner. As they lived and grew, so changed that soul behind their eyes, revealed, if one dared to trust, dared to be seen.

Philip dared while looking at Sabra's soul and . . .

. . . saw himself through *her* eyes.

That couldn't have been right, but the longer he looked in wonder as he pushed into her, bringing her nearer to her peak, the more it became a certainty. She looked right back, exultant, wholly centered on him.

He suddenly knew he was loved, without restraint, without conditions, with all her heart, here and now.

He couldn't help but return it.

She called out *his* name in her crisis, her open gaze still locked on his face as he rode through it with her. She understood what this meant to him. He'd *never* before had that with any woman. She let him *see*.

And in that moment, he experienced her climax as well as his own. Until now he'd never known that half of it. Sabra took him there.

Good God.

Was "devastating" the word? Close. As close as one could get.

The French had gotten it so right, the *petite mort*, because afterward he simply lay like a dead thing, unable to move because his overloaded senses were still trying to catch up with and process what had just happened to them.

All he could do was continue to look into her eyes and hold her until sleep seized him away.

They were still close when he woke a bit later. Naked, on his side, the carpeted floor hard, but with her soft, warm little body tucked firmly against his, her back to him.

She sighed, then giggled.

"What?" he whispered, his lips right by her ear. Her hair smelled of flowers. Real ones.

"Just something Richard told me right after he noticed that I liked you."

Philip wasn't sure he wanted to know, but went with it. "Which was . . . ?

"He said, 'Please don't break him.' "

"Oh, really?" Now that was funny.

"He should have said it to you instead, about me." Another giggle that went all through her, transmitting to him via her flesh where they touched. A lot of that. They were like two spoons, with her delightfully bare ass right against his . . . *oh, my, this is very nice.* It got better when she responded to his questing caress.

No need to look into her eyes this time.

And now her lovely clear eyes were shut, with tubes and wires attached to her fragile flesh, her battered body shielded by a thin sheet and bandaging, and only the beep of a monitor to tell him she still lived.

When he wept, it was with his hand before his face so she didn't have to see what turmoil and terror for her had done to his soul.

He brushed his fingers against the one wisp of her hair that had escaped the gauze dressings, then went back to sit and wait and pray.

Damn. She's so young, a sweet, caring woman not at all deserving of such a cruel turn. Why her? Why . . .

The regular slow beep of the monitor lulled him. So long as it continued all was well . . .

Philip let his head droop. The scent of the roses he'd brought floated up to him. That helped. She *had* to wake and see them. And smile. All really would be well once she opened her eyes and smiled again.

So powerful was his confidence in that, he actually saw it take place in his mind. Sometime tomorrow she would come awake. She likely wouldn't remember the accident, but she would be back with them. That's all that mattered.

His waking dream shifted to reality a moment, and he seemed to be just slightly outside himself, seeing his big form slumped in the chair, his long legs stretched toward the wall so as not to trip the staff when they came in. He listened on one level to the routine of the ICU ward going on outside the glassed-in room, taking comfort from its calm. He'd barely noticed the other patients, but they also had people, families waiting on them, hoping, praying for a recovery. The poor young man over there, body alive, but his head turned to pulp when his cycle went out from under him on road ice. No helmet. An older woman on that side, brought in when her heart kept stopping during surgery.

Then out in the hall was the special guard he'd arranged for and got. A tall man with the rare ability to make himself unobtrusive despite his severe dark suit and multiple concealed weapons.

Philip had also reluctantly accepted the oddness surrounding Sabra's accident and done what he could toward that end by bringing in the paranormal group to investigate. For whatever else—just in case there was a more corporeal threat afoot—that's why the guard was there.

Now, if Richard would just open up and say what *he* knew about it.

Pressing him would do no good. Whoever he'd worked for and whatever he'd been involved in before taking on the identity of one Richard Dun, security specialist, he must have been damned good at it. It wasn't hard to believe that he'd been involved in some type of black ops training and projects. Maybe when this was all over he'd let slip a little more information. But Philip had a name: Richard d'Orleans. Couldn't be many like that about. Easy to trace with the right contacts, and he had plenty of those here and abroad . . .

Philip's waking dream was gradually taken over by the sleeping kind, where he had no control over what crossed his mind's eye. Those were not always pleasant. This time he dreamed of something black flowing into the ICU ward, rising up like a walking cloud.

Only no one else saw it. They went about their business unaware. How could they possibly miss the damn thing?

It drifted purposely toward him, filling the glassed-in room with itself.

Solid. The thing was solid. It fell on him, dragging his sleeping form from the chair with iron-hard strength. He crashed hard on his back. It knelt heavily on his chest. He punched and clawed and thought he connected, but the pressure was crushing, crushing, crushing; he couldn't breathe.

He fought until his air ran out. The thing utterly obliterated him.

Puffing hard with the sweat running free from the exertion, Charon stood away from the big man's body where it lay on the polished floor. For a bare, hopeful moment he thought the pale-haired dude might be Richard Dun, but no such luck. Bagging two in one would have been great, but go with what's handed you and all that. Charon could have fed off the man's energy, but he didn't have enough of the right kind to do any good. It took energy to take in energy. You could be surrounded by food and not have enough strength to lift it to your mouth. That was his situation. *I got only enough juice for one shot. Priming for the pump.*

Lancelot could walk in any second, too, better hurry—life was short in more ways than one.

So always have dessert first.

Charon flipped up the eye patch and with his fading Sight concentrated hard on the frail, tiny woman on the bed. No contest, even in a coma she was still one hell of a heavy hitter. The protections surrounding her threatened to sear his skin like the sun. It would be much safer to take her out from six feet away with one of the wadcutters in the pistol he'd smuggled in. That's what he'd intended on doing given the chance.

Except for the stuff inside eating him alive. The way it was growing now, in another day he'd be in a bed just like that with the best modern meds dripping into one arm, keeping his body going, and in the other hand a button leading to a pump so he could dose himself with painkillers, and they never gave you enough of those. Damn, he could have learned a lot from this bunch in his early days when he was still refining his torture technique.

He reached forward and tasted ever so cautiously of the protective energies. Oh, yeah, *that's* the real hooch. And just under them was the *good* kind. What she was using to make herself better. Strong.

Healing. Wouldn't want to overdo it, but he desperately needed the time that fix could buy him.

Charon moved next to the high bed, his open hand hovering over her face. There was no outward reaction from her, but he saw and felt the enveloping protections going wild. One freaking powerful hurricane-level wind swept out of the Otherside and tried to haul him away from her. It bit at him like the biggest damn dog ever, roaring around the room, flinging things about as he drained strength from her.

Oh, yeah, that IS *the good stuff!*

The force of the fresh energy slammed into the top of his skull and down to his feet. He swayed and staggered, but kept feeding. This was even better than Snaky's blood, there was more of it, and he didn't have to fight as hard for a drink. Full-bodied, baby, and then some. He felt it rushing through every part of him, meeting the out-of-control cancer cells and blasting them to screaming bits. Yeah, that'll teach 'em, mess with me, huh? Take that, why don'tcha?

But maybe—as fresh sweat broke out on him—too strong, like switching to bourbon after a lifetime of water. There was such a thing as alcohol poisoning. In the Yucatán he'd had his shields to hide him and time to prepare and maintain control over the flow; the old snake god hadn't been expecting trouble. This babe had all the doors bolted, with psychic razor wire surrounding her like a cocoon. Her energy was working in him, though, making the gains worth the pain-price.

He bared his teeth at her defenses, braced against the wind, and continued to feed, but people were beginning to notice. Someone in the nurses' station, maybe sensitive to Otherside matters, looked up and saw the stranger in the special room. Never mind that he was in doctor's scrubs, he wasn't supposed to *be* there.

Instead of coming to check herself, she made a detour to the doors opening on the hall. Through the whirling Otherside debris, Charon saw her bring in a new player, that security type in the suit who'd been cooling his heels ever so quietly. Feeding time was almost up, dammit.

The man directed the nurse to one side and approached with

caution. Sensible fellow. She got on a phone, probably calling for reinforcements.

He spotted the big guy on the floor and pulled a gun.

Charon grinned. This could get interesting.

"Move away from her," the man said, aiming the weapon, textbook pose. "Hands up and move away."

Charon raised one hand, palm out, holding the other over the woman. Just a little redirection of the power and a mental nudge—

The security guy went flying backward too fast to register surprise. He whammed against the wall behind him, making a hell of a noisy landing and did not get up again.

Wow. That was impressive.

The nurse gaped and dove behind her desk, dragging the phone along. The cavalry had to be on the way by now. Charon was reasonably sure he could fight off them and all their cousins, but that would only be channeling the energy, not storing it, not using it to heal himself. Wasteful. A hell of a lot of fun, but not too smart.

He went all out now. Both hands over the bitch, and take all he could while he could. This was prime feeding, too bad he had to hurry.

The rush made him dizzy-giddy in a good way, not the weakness kind when his pills were screwing with his brain chemistry, but the sort you get on a really fast plane ride with a wildman pilot. This one was all climb, no drop.

Of course, it couldn't last forever. The first jolt out of his fun was when she went into arrest. Major dip in the graph, but she still had plenty of juice left. He sucked it in . . .

Until something *hit* him.

He couldn't see it. Must be the opposition. Pissed, too.

Charon felt it first as a firm punch in the shoulder, which he ignored. The second strike had more meat to it. He was knocked straight back, struck the wall, cracking his head. He slid down, fast.

Ow. Not fun now.

Dizzy, no giddy. Man, someone was *really* pissed. What a howling in the wind.

He pushed partway from the floor and considered having a quick second helping, but the brouhaha had attracted too much attention. The nurse was emerging from behind the desk as other people crowded through the door, trying to assess what was going on. Several went to check on the security type, who was groggily stirring.

The energy high went to Charon's head like sucking beer through a straw. He could knock them all over and no problem, but . . . wasteful. No point. There wasn't anyone in that pack he couldn't take out the ordinary way in his sleep. Better to get out, digest the feast, and make good use of the high while he still had it.

Standing, he prepared to bull his way through the medical version of the Keystone Kops, but paused.

He grinned down at Sabra, shoving his black patch back in place. "Hey, baby, was it good for you, too?"

Blood streamed from her ears and closed eyes.

Bourland gave a violent start and tried to shove the overwhelming blackness away. Stubborn stuff, and he was so weak. No air for a while, now it was back in force and tasted odd. Then the restraining darkness evolved into a nurse struggling to keep an oxygen mask over his face. He still fought, but she won. Giving up, he let her do her job, and tried to sort out what had brought him to this confusion. He gradually regained full consciousness to a thunderous headache, and became aware of activity around him.

No longer in Sabra's room, he was outside on the floor, and there was all sorts of hell going on. Doctors and nurses were hustling, alarms buzzed, beeped, and shrilled. Strong enough now to fend off help, he lurched to his feet, horribly sick and wobbly-weak, and stared through the glass at the frenzy around Sabra. So many staff, security guards, and noise in this otherwise quiet place . . . what the hell happened? What was going on? He fumbled out his cell phone, and clumsily hit the autodial for Richard's number.

"Get down here," he said.

With a satisfied grunt, Charon eased deep into the broken-in backseat of the cab he waved down near the hospital. What a party. He should have fun like that every night. His body felt light for a change, the way it was supposed to feel, all parts in working order, *sir*. He figured he'd bought well over an hour of battery power, which should be enough.

That was a job well done, minimum of fuss, and even the security cameras turned out to be a snap. On his way out he'd cupped a hand over the front of one like muzzling a dog and, with the feedback cracking along the wires in ways that it shouldn't, given Realside physics, had shut down the whole system. Any recordings made prior to that would be unaffected, but so what? He'd be just another out-of-focus shape in an overcoat, the eye patch obscuring his face. There'd been no camera in the small room where he'd slipped the medical scrubs on over his street clothes and clipped on a stolen badge. *Security, my ass.* Hell, he could have walked in there wearing a clown suit and gone anywhere he liked.

Well, he was out now and on his way.

"Where to?" the driver asked.

"North to 401 until I say different."

"Sounds like a long trip. You sure?"

Charon put three hundred in U.S. bills over the seat top. Ben Franklin had fans on this side of the border. "I'm sure. Move it, I'm in a hurry."

Swallowing further questions, the driver sought out Yonge Street, going north to 401, then headed west, the first leg of the trip. Witchy babe lived—make that used to live—out in the boonies. Charon had scoped the place via maps and aerial photos, so it was almost like he'd been there earlier. Man, weren't computers a gas?

Despite the energy rush, he felt the pills he'd taken earlier trying to make him sleepy. Well, he could fight that off easy enough now. The pain had dulled down to almost nothing. If he could hold it off just a little longer . . .

The taxi's suspension swooped as they hit some change in the highway grading. God, but Canada was just the living end about road repair. Never finished, year after year, how did fang-boy put up with it? Well, too bad, soon none of that crap would matter. People would have other things to worry about than resurfacing the damn highways. Woozy in the gut, Charon rolled down a window and let the cold night air work on him. Too freaking hot in here, but he could deal. Every click of the meter took him closer to the brass ring.

Where had Lance gotten himself to, anyway? He was still tight with his old lady, so he should have been with her, not the other guy, whoever the hell he was. Put up a good fight, just lucky for him he didn't have the right kind of wattage or that would have been too bad, that's all she wrote.

The driver made the exit and they were barreling north, tires hissing loud on the wet road. Snowy fields and black fences sped past. Charon felt every bump and dip, but so long as the heap got them there he could hang on. They were in the home stretch. He gave secondary directions. The man said he knew the area and made the correct turns when they came.

Charon had no need to count down the minutes to their destination, he could feel things slowing inside of him. The power hit had helped a lot, but was not going to last. The one at Stonehenge had been good, Chichén Itzá the best, draining off the old *ahkin* had been a taste-treat sensation, but this must be the downside of the bell curve. He suspected the boosts would continue to shorten in duration until . . .

Hey, belt it, already. I'm almost there.

He held things in, conserving himself until the driver slowed, checking mailboxes along a narrow road. When had they turned off here?

"This it?" The headlights fell on a new mailbox with the name 'DU LAC' on it in reflective letters.

"You got it, pal. I need you to wait." Charon dropped another c-note over the seat.

The driver still had change left above the meter charge from his original retainer. "Sure."

"Won't be long, but you can cut the motor."

The man did so, and Charon let himself out.

He trudged up a driveway cleared of snow along two narrow strips, just wide enough for car tires. There'd been a hell of a fall here recently, which was a good reason to live in the Caribbean. Maybe he'd go there afterward. Or not.

The house—more of a cottage, really—looked to be World War II vintage. With all her money you'd think she'd have done better for herself than a dump like this, but her choice probably had to do with the local energy lines or some crap like that. Lots of trees, you almost couldn't see the house for them. Evergreens and oaks. Very symbolic. Ho-hum predictable.

Lights showed behind the windows, but they were only part of the security system. Lance would have insisted she have one, probably installed it himself just to be *sure*. Yup, nothing was too good for his old lady.

Charon got past it in a very few minutes, but then he was an old hand at getting around such snags. He let himself inside by the front door and turned on more lights as though he owned the place.

Comfy living room, all the usual stuff, nothing too ancient or too new to give away the truth about her background. He knew one of them had a da Vinci or a Botticelli hanging on a wall like a magazine pinup. Well, it wasn't here. He was after something way more valuable, anyway.

Oh, hell.

It struck fast, felt like a killing constriction around his chest. For an instant he feared Snaky had invisibly returned somehow and was doing his crushing thing. Be just like him to change his size and come slithering up from Nowhere for a surprise ambush. Charon hastily backed out of the house, and the tightening abruptly eased.

Heart attack? No way. The pain was different from that or the cancer. It had nothing to do with his human-weak bod or his disease; witchy girl had some less prosaic protections set up in the place. He backed off more and used his Sight.

Holy moly, what a light show. Millennium bash in Times Square.

He wanted sunglasses. The babe knew her noodles. That kind of barrier was into overkill, and it was just the defense. She could have death traps rigged all through the place.

Hm. Maybe not. Her type had a thing against using that kind of power. They really should get over themselves and grow some sense.

Invasion was going to be a hell of a strain on his dwindling energy, so he'd have to hurry. Plan it out, then. Where would she keep the thing? Near an altar? Nah, her type was so far up the corporate ladder as to not really need one. Still, she might have something set up as kind of a respect thing. Look for one of those first. Besides, she wasn't the sort to shove her treasures under a mattress. He would guess it would be . . . ah, screw it, just go for the money and make it *fast*.

He took a deep breath and dove inside. The pressure wound tight around him again as invisible forces tried to expel his unwelcome presence, but he endured them. Sweat broke on his body. He tripped on things that weren't there, stumbled from one room to another, trying to sense his target while the pressure threatened to squeeze him in two.

Finally. In a back room that was chock-full of plants and grow-lights, he found it. She didn't even try to hide the thing. Good grief, it was right *there*, sitting like a decorating statement on its own table near one of those New Age style mini-fountains. You'd think she'd show it more reverence as hot as she and her boy-toy were to get hold of it in the first place.

Charon whipped off the piece of white gauzy silk covering and picked up the small cup. The pressure on him suddenly ceased. Okay, that was good. Made it, but jeeze, he was pooped. No reserves left. If he had to go through the gauntlet again . . . nah, break a window out for an exit. Keep it simple.

The trophy itself was not much to look at, being a kind of half-sphere less than a handspan across and made of humble brass not gold, but a mile away you could see it was the real magilla, the one and only, accept no substitutes, one hundred percent gen-u-ine Holy Grail.

Sweet.

So, how about a test drive?

He put the bowl, cup, whatever in one hand, held the other over it, took another deep breath . . . and oh-so-gently touched on the power. Had to be careful, this was like trying to hand-dip a thimble of water from Niagara at full rush. Lose your balance and you were in, over the edge, and bye-bye.

His hands shook. This was no place for amateurs.

Here it was: *The* moment of truth or consequences . . .

Pale light seemed to leap from the cup to his outstretched fingers like soft lighting. Warm tinglies traveled up his hand, wrist, up and up, the light fading the higher it went. His shoulder, yeah, something was working there, a decided warmth as it seeped into his chest, a definite heat when it hit his lymph glands.

Freaking hell, talk to me, baby!

Free air, singing with the living energy of the plants, whooshed right to the bottom of his lungs, cleaning them out. He exhaled and his Sight picked out the microscopic particles of his disease hanging before him like black vapor.

Ohhh, yeaaah. This will do. Once he got it to the right place and could make a proper job of it. This would serve as a fine pick-me-up in the interim.

Then the air seemed to congeal. Shit, too much of a good thing. All the difference between getting a little sun tan and facing down a flamethrower. He fell away, knocking over the fountain. Crash, bang. Bull in a china shop interlude as he struggled to keep his feet. Water splashed everywhere, the pump whirring loudly with nothing to drive. Burn-out soon. For them both.

He hastily withdrew from the cleansing while his head was still on the end of his neck. The house's protections abruptly kicked in again, trying to get rid of him. Fine, he had the brass ring, time to exit, stage left; he was strong enough to deal with them now. He wrapped the little cup in the silk, slipped it in his coat pocket, and got the flock outta Dodge.

Hustling into the cab, he told the driver to take him back to Toronto. The meter was higher than Everest; the man cheerful, totally clueless about what going to happen at the end of the ride. He didn't have the kind of spiritual energy of the old *ahkin* or witchy girl, but now Charon had the means to change that. With the Grail and a little Otherside switcheroo he could order up room service whenever he needed from anyone at hand. By the time they got back to the city a light snack would hit the spot. He could get his cash back and remove a witness. Neat.

Charon hugged the precious Grail to himself, the anticipation making his heart thrum.

Not long after Bourland's call Richard arrived at the hospital with Michael, the two of them tearing up to the ICU ward. The news was what he feared most. The attack on Sabra had her on the edge. If not for the machines, she'd have slipped away already.

Bourland was in the hall outside, relegated there by a preoccupied and hyperbusy staff. He looked awful, ghastly pale and stinking of chloroform. Hospital security was all over, along with the police, and a couple more of the dark-suited security types he'd brought in. The ant nest was thoroughly stirred.

"What happened?" Richard demanded after he showed ID for the umpteenth time. They'd almost not allowed Michael in for not having one, but Richard fixed things with a single piercing look and an inarguable order to butt out. The cop had rocked back on his heels and let them pass.

Bourland had trouble finding the words; he looked to be in shock. Richard leaned close. "You're scaring Michael. Get a grip."

Visibly pulling himself together, he set his teeth, nodding once. "Sorry. I don't know much, just what they've told me. Some man in medical scrubs and an eye patch got in. They saw him standing over Sabra. The security man tried to stop him and got thrown across the room for his trouble. They're treating him. Concussion."

"What happened to you?"

"Not sure. I was asleep in the chair." Bourland's face went scarlet. "They think he put me out with chloroform, something like that, then went after Sabra. Her life support alarms went off. The doctors should have gotten to her in time, but they can't figure out what's been done. Then they threw me out."

Richard looked through the glass inset on the door. Everyone was still working, still rushing about, focused on her. So long as they didn't stop . . .

Michael had not said a word since Richard roused him from sleep and told him they were leaving. "Uncle Richard? Dad . . . ?"

Bourland went to him. "It'll be all right."

The boy's head drooped. "Tell them it's like an aneurysm." He stumbled over the word as though he'd never said it before.

Bourland didn't pause to ask *how* Michael knew that; he bulled into the ICU and got someone to pay attention. Only after one of the doctors heard and took him seriously did he allow himself to be guided out of their way.

Richard fought off his own personal meltdown, holding everything at a distance. All he wanted was to rip the world apart at the seams. He managed not to for Michael's sake. And Bourland's. They did not need to see that side of him, ever.

Why hadn't his blood helped her? There should have been an improvement, or at least a strengthening. It would have begun working in her from the first, changing things, returning her to life and health.

Unless she'd been right. The dark Gift given once could not be given again.

The sheer helplessness surged over Richard, but he cast that to one side as well. There was only one way he could save her.

The Grail.

If he had the time to get to Sabra's house and back.

They had life-support machines. If they could keep her body going until his return . . . and then he'd hypnotize the whole damned hospital into forgetting if need be.

"Michael—I've got to go fetch something. Tell your father not to give up, have them put her on a machine if they must, but don't give up on her. I'm going to her house and back." He started for the exit.

But Michael seized his hand. Strongly, dragging him to a halt. "That is not for her."

He paused, resisting the reaction to shake clear. Michael held fast. "W-what?"

"That's not her road." The boy was very intense, very certain, not to be ignored.

How did he *know*? "It will make her well."

Michael streamed tears and shook his head. "That's not your road, either. You must take another."

The voice was Michael's, but the words were his *own*, from a long-ago time . . .

Chapter Nine

Britain, the Past

Richard boosted Galahad up into the saddle as he'd done over a thousand times before since the day the lad was big enough to ride a horse by himself.

"You'll take care," he said, making it an order, not an admonition. He didn't like sending his foster son off on his own, but there were too few of them and too many of Mordred's forces, at least in this part of the land. Sabra said the boy would be fine, though, so . . .

"I'll meet you at the river ford in two days, sir," Galahad promised. "With more support for the king. I swear by St. Michael and St. George."

"Support or no, bring yourself back or your mother will do away with me." He made light of it, but in truth he'd never be able to face Elaine if anything happened to her son.

Galahad shot him a grin. "God be with you, sir, and mother, too." Then he kicked his horse and joined up with the dozen mounted men who would ride with him. Off to another keep to give the king's word to the lord there and hopefully hold him to their side.

It was so damned frustrating.

Arthur still ruled, but only just, for his court had been poisoned by dissension and betrayal. It had been years in the making, but

189

his bastard son Mordred had finally pulled together enough malcontent lords to make a challenge to take the throne. All that had been so perfect and stable was being torn apart by one man's foolish greed. All that Richard and Sabra helped to build was crumbling.

It was a hard blow for them both, harder still for the kingdom, which would fracture into smaller holds easily conquered unless they moved fast to stop it. Like Galahad they were also on a journey to summon together allies for the king, to keep them heartened. Richard would have gone with the boy—a man, now, by God, for he'd lately turned fifteen—but knew he would not be welcomed by that particular noble. Too much history and bad blood were in their past, and the man was petty enough to let it influence his duty to his liege.

Galahad, though, was a great favorite with most of the lords of the land, admired for his courage and piety. He'd proven himself as a warrior, and his devotion to God seemed to make him more than half priest, yet he had a good-humored humility that somehow touched hearts. Rough rogues who only went to church to nap would smile when they saw the lad. It was because of his buoyant, confident spirit that loyalty to the king remained strong in some.

These days Richard was rather less admired than he had once been, those rumors about himself and the queen being at the core. All distorted out of hand with telling and retelling, but the damage was done. Yes, he *had* been with her, but not in the way others thought, and certainly not in the times or places they'd given in their accusations. That's how he knew Mordred and his followers had been spreading lies. They didn't know the *truth*, else they'd have seized on it instead, and Richard would have been hounded away or destroyed by now.

According to the stories that were abroad Lord Lancelot had committed adultery with the queen every time the king chanced to nap on his side of the royal bed. One had their fornication concealed only by the tapestry hanging behind the throne itself while the king obliviously held court. Never mind that the thing cleared the floor by a good twenty feet and was backed by a solid wall, people actually believed the ridiculous lie—even the ones who had *seen* the throne room and knew better.

It did not help that the queen had made Lancelot her favorite above all the other lords. He really should have talked with her about that, but any pass between them created more rumors. Ignoring the situation made it worse. By the time Sabra had a chance to influence her to temper her conduct it was too late and the lies were rooted and growing quick as weeds.

No help for it now. It was their lot to keep things going. Richard took a lesser seat to Galahad, providing him with advice and escort as needed on his rounds. He was content with that role, for he loved his foster son well, proud that one so young was accomplishing so much. There was hope yet for saving the kingdom from Mordred.

This day had been muggy and dark, threatening rain, which had been a relief to Richard and Sabra both, for they'd been exceptionally busy. The rain never fell, though, and they were thankful for that as well. The roads they traveled had not been made by the Romans, and consequently became mud wallows when it got wet, slowing them.

They'd avoided an encounter with Mordred's people only the day before. Sabra's Sight proved very helpful, but of course they had to pretend it did not exist. There were quite enough rumors about the queen using witchcraft, no one needed to think any of her ladies were practicing as well. It was up to Richard to think up a good reason to keep his party camped one more day on this side of the forest until the enemy force moved elsewhere. Not hard, there was always something to do or repair when on the move, and the horses as well as the people needed the rest.

Though Richard was absolutely certain of the loyalty of every man under his command, he was less sure of the camp followers. One couldn't sit down and influence them all. Not quickly, anyway. Besides, if they were spies, they could report little to help the enemy; as though this was a tourney, everyone was in good spirits and full of cheer.

Most of which departed with Galahad.

Those who remained were uneasy and trying not to show it. Richard understood it was because of the division of their forces, with the greater number of them gone off. Sabra assured him there was no danger from Mordred's men while they remained in place. He would have given much to be able to pass that on to the others.

They would leave in the morning for the ford, and preparations were going on, saddles and tack repaired or oiled, traveling food cooked. Richard made the rounds of the now much smaller camp himself, debating on whether to send the followers away yet. There was fighting ahead. He didn't have Sabra's Sight, but felt it in his belly. The others seemed to think this would be like a tourney, where yielding if outmatched meant only the loss of your gear or the payment of a ransom. Mordred and his men had no such honorable notions; they were warring for booty, property, and power, and you didn't acquire those by a fair contest.

Richard told his people again and again that real battles meant ugly death, and though they nodded somber agreement, he could see they didn't believe him. The peace in the land had been so strong during Arthur's long reign that this new crop of warriors did not know what war was like.

Their first real fight would be the only cure for that innocence, and he prayed they would live through it. He'd trained them hard enough, but training was never truly the same thing.

As evening came on he sensed the sun's departure with his skin, not his eyes, for the dull gray sky showed no change. The thick air turned chill, and fog gathered in low areas and began to fill the surrounding woods like lost spirits. A long way off, but still too close for those nervous of heart, a wolf howled at a moon it could not possibly see.

Across the camp, Sabra paused in her task of rubbing down her horse, and glanced toward Richard, not smiling. After a moment, she continued her work. There were pages for such jobs, but she liked tending her own animal, saying it eased her heart. The wolf howled again, and the horse stirred, restless. She whispered, and it calmed down. If there was a pack of wolves in the area, they'd not come near, Sabra would see to that, but there was little she could do to stop their song of hunger.

So long as it's not Annwyn's hounds a-howling, he thought. That never boded well.

"Riders, my lord!" One of the pages came pelting up to him out of the dark, red of face and excited.

"How far?"

"A quarter mile," he puffed. "Walking, not running. All armed. There's a priest with them, armed, too."

Which meant nothing. Priests were everywhere, with the king's men and the traitors alike, and everyone went armed these days. "How many?"

"Fifteen, my lord. They look foreign."

"How so?"

"Their banner colors. I never saw the like before."

"Describe them."

The page did, with great accuracy, rattling off every detail he'd seen from his hiding place near the main road.

Richard searched his memory, but there were no lords in Britain with such a banner, nor in Wales for that matter, only across— oh, good God, it couldn't be . . .

Sabra left off work and came over. "We have visitors."

"A ghost from my past, I think." Richard's heart felt ready to burst, it beat so hard and quick. If what he thought was true . . .

She put an hand on his. "Don't worry, all will be well."

"But the last time anyone came here from Normandy—" It still hurt to think of that awful day; it would always hurt.

"All will be well."

One of his warriors came up, having heard. "Shall we arm, my lord?"

"Yes. Prepare, but make no move unless I order it. Let's see them first. They could be friends."

Sabra, apparently unconcerned, went back to her horse. Some of the more perceptive women in the camp took that to mean no trouble was afoot. Had she gone to put on her sword, they'd have been scrambling like the men.

Strangely, there was not a lot of noise from their stir. It was as though they were quiet to catch the first sign of the horsemen's approach. There was no point to it, though. In a very short time the fog had turned thick as porridge, muffling and distorting sound. Even Richard had trouble discerning anything until the traveling party was quite close, the thud of hooves, the jingling of a bit.

Challenge was issued and answered, the reply in a familiar accent, a familiar, but long-unheard voice. Richard stepped eagerly forward, then halted suddenly as speaker—who was the priest— pushed back his cowl and revealed his face.

My God, he's an old man. Richard's heart swooped, freezing him in place as he recognized his brother Edward.

"I seek Lancelot du Lac," he said, looking right at Richard.

Does he not know me? "You've found him, good father," he whispered.

Edward's blue eyes flashed. His face was ancient, he must have been close to fifty by now, but his eyes were sharp and knowing. "Glad I am to have found thee. May we stay here for the night?"

"You are right welcome if you are friends of the king."

"We are friends of all good men, which includes the king."

"Then rest and break bread with us."

At a sign from Richard a page came forward to hold Edward's horse while he stiffly dismounted. He and his men were muddy from long traveling, but looked alert. They had a modest pack train with them, their two-wheeled carts filled with gear, but able to roll along fast if need be.

"May I speak with you apart, Lord Lancelot?"

"This way." Richard led off to his pavilion, and they ducked inside. He let down the flap, allowing them privacy. When he turned it was to be swept up in Edward's overpowering bear hug.

There were tears in his voice. "Dear God, I hardly dared hope you were to be found."

Laughing, Richard returned the embrace, thumping his brother on the back and was himself unable to speak for a few moments. When they broke apart, Richard lighted candles from the flame of a small oil lamp on a table and they were able to get a good look at each other.

"Life with the Britons agrees with you," said Edward. "You don't look a day older than when I saw you last."

"There's no sun in this land of rain to bake the skin to a crust," he said, shrugging dismissively.

Edward snorted. "I must be overdone, then."

Richard made no reply. This was hard, bitter hard. Sabra had warned him he would outlive everyone he knew, and the harshness of that truth was very visible on Edward's seamed face. The last time Richard saw his brother had been soon after the defeat at that last tourney at castle d'Orleans. He'd been thirty-five then, Edward just a few years older. Now Richard had the eerie feeling he was seeing his own face as it might have been had he not taken the path Sabra had offered him.

"What brings you so far from home?" he asked.

Edward found a cushioned stool and eased down onto it with a pleasurable groan, shifting his sword belt around out of the way. "You call this summer? Ohhh, my bones think it's winter already."

Remembering his manners, Richard found a skin of wine hanging from the central tent pole and handed it over. "Warm them with this, then. I'm sorry there's no cup, but—"

Edward waved off the apology and took a swig, grunting his approval. "We both know what the road is like. Except for one night under a roof, I've been eating my bread in the saddle for I don't know how long. Before that I ate none at all because I was hanging over the side of a ship while we made the crossing from Normandy. The next time you decide to lose yourself could you do it on the same side of the sea that I'm on?"

He smiled and promised he would, then went to the flap and ordered meat and bread brought to his guest. The cook fires had been going all day, so food was ready. In a gratifyingly short time Edward had a special folding table in front of him along with a roasted fowl and a flat, weighty loaf with a bowl of hot drippings to dip it in.

"You won't partake?" Edward asked.

"I've eaten. Please, fill yourself." Richard burned with questions, but forced himself to polite patience, sitting on another low stool while his brother happily gorged like a field peasant at harvest.

"By God, that was good," he said, giving a well-mannered belch. "I've not had better for a very long time." He sucked the last grease from his fingers and wiped them on the hem of his traveling robe. He looked to be only a priest, but Richard knew he'd risen to archbishop, perhaps higher. "You've done well for yourself, Dickon."

"Would that we were at my keep and I could show you better."

"In truth, I went there first to look for Lord Lancelot. Your lady Elaine was exceedingly kind in her courtesy. By the way, she is in good health and sends you her love and instruction to look most carefully after yourself and your son."

"Thank you. How recent is the news?"

"Two weeks and a day. You—a father." Edward looked pleased.

Richard was well practiced at hiding the ache that word sometimes caused him. "Foster-father. Galahad is not my son by blood, though he is in my heart. I've raised him as my own since he was so high—" He held his hand palm-down to indicate the height of a small child.

"Galahad." Edward smirked. "Better here than in Normandy."

The boy's name had ever been a sore point with Richard, but he'd learned to live with it. "His mother picked that one, not I."

"That goes without saying, but I've heard of him, of you both. The tales of the good you've done here under the name of Lancelot have traveled even to my humble monastery."

"And the bad, too, no doubt."

"'Let he who is without sin' and all the rest, brother. Aside from myself, you've been the only truly decent man in the whole of our family, and I know how enemies love hurtful gossip—and you've not asked about them, our family, that is."

"I thought you'd get 'round to it in your own time."

"Yes, and me with little time to spare."

"What do you mean?" He sharply looked Edward over for signs of ill health. Although old, he seemed hearty enough, his movements quick and decisive, his eyes and speech clear. Certainly his perpetual dry humor was yet firmly in place, along with his appetite.

"I've come to fetch you home—for a visit only," he added after seeing Richard's horrified reaction.

"Why?"

He grimaced. "Because our father is dying."

Though Richard kept himself apprised of second-, even third-hand news of Edward, he had little interest in the doings of the d'Orleans court. He'd rather thought old Montague had already passed away years ago. "That is nothing to me. You know how we parted." Not the whole story, but enough of the truth to satisfy Edward at the time.

"That is why he wishes to see you. He wants to make amends."

Richard was not successful at stifling his bark of laughter. "Toward what end? To finish what he tried to do? Murder me? Has he become addled and forgot the night he tried to gut me with his knife?"

"No, he is not addled, and yes, that was a terrible thing he tried to do."

Achieved. Had Sabra's gift not changed him, Richard would have died at his father's hand. Had he not stayed his own rage, he'd have drained the wretched man of all his blood, and have that murder forever on his soul. With Richard's agelessness and long memory, forever could be a merciless torment.

"But he is dying and would see us one more time," said Edward. "For his soul's peace."

"No. I bade him good-bye those years ago and closed that door. I will not see him on this side ever again. I'll light a candle toward his soul's peace, but that's all I can bring myself to do." Richard knew he'd have no heart behind the prayer, either. For his own peace he always tried not to think about his father at all. Edward coming in like this revived pain he thought to be dead.

"Do you think I've forgotten the evils he's done? Or that I'll ask you to forgive him for all that he's done to you?"

"Edward, you're too wise to ask that of me knowing I could end up lying to you or lying to God, or worse, to Father. My lack of sympathy is as close as I can come to forgiveness. I've worked very hard to bring myself this far."

"He's a dying man with a last request. I know you—you'd give as much comfort to a beggar wretch fallen on the side of the road. Father's committed many sins, but your being there will lift some of that weight from his—"

"That's what *your* place is about. *Ego te absolvo*, brother, and that's as easy as you can make the passing for him, and it's better than he deserves."

"Now you sound like Ambert."

Richard took no offense. "We are as Father made us. And as he made us, so now does he come to appreciate the kind of work he's done."

"At least think about it."

"I have. I can't leave, anyway, not with this war brewing. I won't leave my king."

"Your king will grant you a release from your obligations for this. You've but to ask."

"You overestimate my influence in court. Some of them barely tolerate me."

"The king's will is all that matters."

"And you overestimate that power as well. He may release me to go, but still needs me. If the others see the king's own keeper seeming to desert him when he's most needed at his side . . ."

"You can explain—"

"It's *not* to happen. Even if we were at peace with no Mordred to trouble the land I would not leave."

"That's a hard thing, Dickon. You'll have to live with it all your life, and then endure it when you yourself pass the veil and are judged."

"I will have to live with it, yes." He'd gotten very good at ignoring certain aspects of the future.

"Very well, then. If you won't go for Father's sake, then go for your own. Do that which is right, you always have."

Richard clapped both hands to his forehead, near-exasperated. "I *am*! My duty is here, and *it* is more important than anything, including Father dying, including my soul's rest in the next life. God's merciful, or so I'm told, and I think He will forgive me if I'm here trying my best to keep His anointed king on his throne."

Edward held silent, his jaw working, his eyes grown hot. For a moment he seemed to verge on giving in to anger, but it gradually passed. "All right," he finally said in a quiet voice. "I've done *my* duty, and can see it would be a sin to press you to go against your conscience on this. It *is* your conscience, isn't it?"

"Yes. Take me back there, and I'd be on my knees for the rest of the year confessing the lies I'd have to speak to get through it. But, Edward, please know that I am sorry you must bear this alone."

He chuckled. "I, of all people, am not alone. Hm?" He flicked his gaze briefly toward the tent ceiling.

"Sometimes I forget who and what you are."

"Well, that's good. There are days when I get so full of the bowing and respect and the blessing and all the rest I could just rip at the seams."

Richard blinked. "Really?"

Edward cocked his head. "Actually, no, I quite love it."

They stared at each other a moment, then erupted into laughter. It didn't have the same light-heartedness of their long lost youth, but was richer for their mutual understanding.

"I've missed you, Dickon. I'd hoped that on the journey back we would have time to talk, but it's not to be. I must leave at first light and pray I'm not too late on my return."

"What ails him?"

He shrugged. "Age. He has a sense this is his last summer. I've seen the same with others. Some just know their time has come, and they prepare. I'll tell him your duty holds you here. Which is the truth."

"What about Ambert?"

"He's mostly the same, more girth, not nearly as loud as he was, saves his strength that way. He doesn't snarl at me as he once did, and he gave up trying to hit me years ago. Might even be mellowing."

"That *would* be a miracle."

"So, all those prayers of mine have wrought some good." He smiled, but it faded. "When this is over . . . will you come and visit me? A real visit. You need never see Castle d'Orleans."

He solemnly took Edward's hand. "I swear I will do that."

"God will that you be spared."

Richard murmured agreement. "You need rest, I think. This tent's yours for the night, it has the best bed. I'll have someone bring coals for the brazier, warm it up a bit. Our summer nights can get cold. Ask and they'll bring you anything you want."

"Where will you sleep?"

"I've another place. Don't have much need of sleep lately. Generally I keep watch with the men."

"I better tell mine what's going on while I still can."

They emerged to find Edward's escort had been looked after as honored guests. Fed and bedded down, Edward sought out their captain and gave him the news of their morning departure.

"Will Lord Richard not be coming with us?" The captain shot Richard a look of unabashed curiosity. A young man, he might well have grown up on tales of the one-time undefeated Champion d'Orleans. They'd have to be whispered, too. Richard heard Ambert loathed any reminder of having a youngest brother and had been known to flog people who accidentally mentioned the fact.

Edward glanced around, apparently mindful of other ears who did not need to know of Richard's past. "He will remain. While we're here, always call him Lord Lancelot, hm?"

"Yes, my lord bishop."

"No need to set up my tent. His lordship is kindly loaning me his for the night. Sleep while you can, we leave for the coast at dawn. If there's any way of telling when the sun's up."

"I'll let you know," said Richard.

"Did I make the right choice?" he asked Sabra later. They walked slowly on the edge of the camp, making round after slow round, keeping watch in the night that was their day. He'd already told her of his conversation with Edward. Sometimes she answered such questions, but others she did not, seeing a multiplicity of futures, often not knowing which was the one that would be. Much of the future—and one never knew which parts of it most of the time— was ever and always in change.

"You are the best judge of that," she said. "You know the truth of what's best for you in your heart."

"Well, then, I feel better. My heart has been heavy."

"And now it's lighter?"

"Yes. Had I made the wrong decision, you'd have let me know with a different answer. Anyway, I told Edward if there was no war coming still I'd remain here. Why did you not come to meet him?"

"It isn't time yet. Besides, he only knows of you and the Lady

Elaine. I think he'd be more comfortable not knowing about my presence in your life. It's bad enough with the rumors about you and the queen."

"Best not to add others about me and one of my pages?"

It was an old joke between them, still able to bring a smile. Everyone in the camp knew the Lady Sabra, but turned a blind eye to her preference for a page's clothes. Though considered immodest, they were much more practical for traveling than her court gowns, and not one of their party ever cast forth a disparaging comment. Even if Richard could not influence them all, she was herself very thorough. Sabra also saw to it their people did not notice many other oddities as well.

"Yes. The king's enemies have enough false grain for their lie-mills. Let's not give them anything real."

"Then I will try hard not to kiss you in front of them." He paused, bent low, and caught her squarely on the lips. "There, no one saw that one, I'm sure of it."

"They'll see less if we're deeper under the trees . . ." She took his hand and led him into thicker shadows within the fog.

"We're supposed to be on watch," he said.

"There's no one within two miles of our camp. None are abroad in this murk. And if they were, we'd hear them before the horses did."

He could trust the truth of her otherwise unconfirmed information "Let's be quiet, then."

She found a place for them, a moss-cushioned depression beneath an oak as wide as Richard was tall. Its black roots, as big around as his body, thrust high from the soil as though reaching for something. "There's power here," she whispered. "From him." She nodded respectfully at the oak.

"You're sure he won't mind?" Richard was still sometimes taken off balance by some of the things she said, particularly when she ascribed awareness to objects like trees.

"He'll enjoy the company."

Another advantage to her page's clothes: they were considerably easier to remove than her elegant gowns. Grass and mud stains were normal as well. An excellent arrangement for them both.

That in mind, they both arranged themselves in the makeshift bed. Strangely, there was much more privacy here than they had in his pavilion, surrounded as it was by the camp, certainly better than Sabra's tent, which was full of her female servants with only a drape of linen to separate them from view. Richard liked the change.

The air was chill on his bare skin, but he had no mind for it, only Sabra. Perhaps she was right about there being power in this spot; he thought he sensed it as a heady rich scent coming from the soil beneath the moss.

"Were you here earlier?" he asked.

"How did you know?" There was a smile in her voice.

"Because of the singular lack of fallen leaves, bark, and twigs. No acorn shells, either." They'd made love in several other forests over the years, and such debris could be very distracting.

"Silly, it's a male tree."

He knew better than that. "Oaks put out male and female flowers. You told me yourself."

"Then this one must be more male than female," she insisted, giggling.

"I'll show you male," he rumbled.

She put a hand over her mouth to smother a small laughing shriek as he fulfilled his threat. Her humor turned to long sighs as his lips roamed over her breasts and flat belly, questing ever lower until reaching her treasure. With a great deal of satisfaction for her response, he lingered long there, growing hard himself, anticipating what was to come. She was the best, the most beautiful, and absolutely unique.

"Soon now, my love," she murmured.

Indeed, yes.

Skin on skin, he moved up again, tasting every part of her. His beast within was quiet this night, strangely peaceful, as was hers, for there was no change in her eyes. There would be no sharing of blood, but this was enough, more than enough.

Kissing and loving, breathless, yet silent, she let him know she was ready and twisted around so she was facedown on the ground. She spread her arms wide as he rode her, and knew she was embracing the earth itself. Her hands clutched convulsively on the oak's roots when she climaxed, and in his own fever Richard imagined there were three presences there, man, woman, and the unseen, benign spirit of the ancient tree sharing its vast strength with them.

Hours later, the fog vanished and the night sky cleared. Moon and stars shone down coldly on them. The morning would be cloudless and bright. Richard almost cursed. He'd have to spend the day beneath a thick, tightly woven cloak, hood pulled well down, his gauntlets on the whole time to avoid burning. Sabra would have it no better, either.

For now they continued their slow walk around the camp. The fires gone low, they stopped to add more wood. Sometimes people would wake just enough to notice and nod off again, sometimes not.

In a way they were still alone and together. Richard longed for a time when they could truly go off by themselves and not have the responsibility of so many others to look after. Perhaps by the fall Mordred's rebellion would be broken, and they'd be free to cross to Normandy. It might be a good thing to maintain the name of Lancelot—he still had fame and respect over there—then Ambert need never know. How amusing it would be, though, if Ambert sent an invitation of hospitality to Arthur's greatest champion only to discover . . .

It would be worth it for the look on his face. Oh, yes.

"What makes you smile, my Richard?" Sabra asked. She'd been on the other side of camp and now returned, slipping her arm in his.

"Something that's likely not to come to pass. You aren't the only one who sees futures that never happen."

"What did you see?"

A lift in her tone caused him to glance at her. Her eyes were flushed bloodred from a recent feeding. It made him want her again.

As she had time and again, she knew his thoughts. "I took enough for us both."

"Oh?"

"I fed from two, not one. It would please me to share with you."

"It would delight me to please you," he returned. They'd often done this for each other. He wasn't hungry, but to have her once more . . . "The oak again?"

"Just out of the firelight will do. I'll *try* to be quiet." Hand in hand, she led the way again.

He could smell the fresh infusion of new bloods rising from her now-rosy skin. This time they stood, she bracing her back against another tree, her feet on its roots, lifting her tall so they were on a level with each other. Their love-play was brief, but intense, for she was eager again for him as well. No need to shed clothes, for the effect when he bit into her soft throat was the same as if they'd been joined in a more traditional manner. She tried to muffle her gasps as he fed from her and didn't quite succeed. No matter. None would pay them notice.

She held tight to him, urging him to take his fill. He made it last. This was no serving wench to be influenced into forgetting the familiarity, this was *Sabra*. Her blood-heat ran through his own body, as intense as any climax, touching different areas, fulfilling, nourishing flesh and spirit alike.

And it was all the more terrible when he chanced to look up and saw Edward's face, ghost-pale in the moonlight. He was only a few yards away, and it was clear from his stunned expression he'd seen everything he shouldn't. Frozen for the span of five heartbeats, he quickly retreated from sight.

No!

Sabra's drowsy eyes opened wide. "What is it?"

"My brother saw us. He knows what I am." Richard was shaking, shot through and through with fear. He broke from her and went seeking.

He caught up with Edward just on the edge of the camp, dropping a hand on his shoulder and turning him about. Edward whirled, his cross in one hand, a sword in another.

"Touch me not!" he snapped.

Richard fell back as though struck. "Wait—please—"

"Away from me!"

"Let me explain."

"There is none for this."

"I am the same man, your brother. Edward, hear me!"

Edward paused, his heart's turmoil showing on his face: panic, horror, fear, and infinite, ghastly sorrow. "I see now why you appear so youthful, but God, Richard—why? How could you allow . . . it—it's unclean . . . *oh, God* . . ." He shot away toward his tent. Richard tried to follow, but Sabra, suddenly catching up, stepped between and stayed him.

"Let him be," she said.

"I must go, try to tell him."

"It won't work. Your brother is unable to hear you now. In the morning."

"When he can see us cower from the light? *That* will reassure him."

"Let him bide alone, he's afraid and must see his own way past it. Let him pray and think and remember who you are." Sabra left, going toward her own tent.

Richard held off, still disturbed, fearful, still wanting to talk. God, if he lost Edward because of this . . .

He hated what thoughts his brother must be thinking, what alarms and apprehensions were nesting in his mind.

I'm not a monster.

But why should Edward believe him? So many years apart, they were near-strangers, their worlds impossibly different.

Richard paced, knowing he was too stirred up to wait until dawn, but seeing the wisdom of allowing Edward at least a little time to get over the first shock. If once he was calm enough he would have to listen.

And if not . . . then Richard would *make* him listen.

It was an action that smacked of dishonor, but shameful as it would be to force his own brother's mind to accept a truth, like it or not, better that than lose him to fear and ignorance.

So be it, but he hoped it would not become necessary.

Having thought that through, Richard swiped at his mouth, wiping away any lingering blood. His eyes should be normal by now, and Edward— What the devil was that . . . ?

Richard came alert at activity near Edward's pavilion. Men were moving about in the shadows, their movements furtive. These were not sleepy soldiers scratching themselves early-awake, nothing sluggish about this lot . . .

And their swords were out.

He silently drew his own weapon and moved in.

Sabra! He hoped she would hear and know the meaning of his urgent thought.

Two men were just entering Edward's tent. Richard grabbed one by the scruff and plucked him from his feet, throwing him well away. The other man completed his rush inside, raised his sword, and struck at the fur-wrapped figure in the bed. The blade bit down swift and hard.

Roaring, Richard dragged him around. He was the captain of Edward's escort. He slammed his sword pommel against Richard's skull with vicious, killing force, broke clear, and darted from the tent, yelling.

Shouts and screams ran through the camp, and two more of the escort came at Richard. One of them managed to get a single strike, his sword cutting into Richard's shoulder, but it served only to anger, not fell him. Their deaths were brutal and quick. He saw the captain rushing away, urging the rest of his well-armed company to take them all, take them all.

Richard's uncanny speed put a halt to that. He was before the man in less than an instant, full of fury. The captain had time to blink once—after his head was off. His body dropped like a stone. Another man bent on avenging his commander hurtled forward, shrieking. He seemed to move ridiculously slow to Richard's heightened perception. He died fast enough, though.

A dozen yards away . . . fighting by another tent . . . women screaming. Sabra was there.

Yet another warrior got in Richard's way and was cut nearly in two by his passage, almost an afterthought. More of the escort men, instinctively seeking to take out the greatest threat, mobbed him.

They were nothing, less than children playing at soldiers, slow and clumsy, and also soon dead. He gave them no mercy, striking them down with the chill efficiency of a butcher at his trade.

Then they were gone, and he pressed toward Sabra where he'd glimpsed her fighting by the red light of one of the fires. She seemed aflame herself, but that was from splashed blood. Four men lay at her feet, her blade smoking in the cold air from their gore.

"See to Edward!" she shouted at him.

He hurtled back, fearing the worst.

No others came at him, they were either killed or running. His own people had realized the tumult for a traitorous attack, fought back, and were in pursuit.

Richard tore into the tent, his heart in his mouth as he knelt by the bed. No movement, no heart-sound.

"Dear, God—Edward . . . ?"

He choked as he pulled back the coverings. The huddled form beneath had been shaped by Edward's saddle and wadded-up blankets.

"I've not forgotten all there was to being a soldier," Edward said from the tent opening.

Richard sagged with boundless relief and came out, but Edward backed from him, cross and sword still before him.

"You've naught to fear from me, brother." To prove it, he reached and took the cross from him and kissed it. "And I thank our Lord that you are unharmed."

Edward let out a shaky breath, staring. "Which is more than may be said about you."

Now that he had time for it, Richard noticed the wound on his shoulder. It was in the same spot as the one that nearly killed him all those years ago, and looked to be as serious. Blood yet flowed, soaking his tunic, blending with the blood of those he'd killed, but he could also feel the burning sensation that meant healing. "I will be well, soon enough."

"You should be flat and groaning as happened once before."

"Would you prefer that for me now?"

"If it meant you would die as a man with prayers to ease your soul's passage. But this . . ."

"Yes, this. Which has saved the lives of these good people. Were I a man such as you I'd have never bested these murderers. See me as I *am*, not as what you fear!"

But Edward couldn't seem to take his gaze from the wound and shook his head. " 'Tis not natural. It goes against God."

Richard held up the cross. "Were that true, then let Him strike me down." They each waited, but nothing happened. Richard stepped forward and pressed the cross into his brother's hand. There was blood on it. "See? We both abide under His sky. Guard you the day and I the night. There's room enough for us all."

Edward continued to shake his head. He was not in utter rejection, this was more like being overwhelmed and unable to take it in. "I must pray . . . and see to the fallen."

"Very well. This is an evil thing to come to us. You're needed here."

"And for some I've come too late." He seemed infinitely sad.

"No, think that not! What's happened to me has been a gift bestowed to help me better serve. Without it you and likely everyone in this camp would be dead instead of—by God, I never thought I'd have to raise my sword against the d'Orleans banner. Are these men of the house or did you hire them for your journey?"

"They are of the house. Ambert sent them to the monastery to be my esco—oh, St. Michael protect us." Edward bowed his head, crossing himself. "I had a suspicion, but no, he couldn't have. It's too iniquitous."

"Yet you set up that ruse in the tent. Is that why you were in the trees?"

"Yes, waiting there, watching. I had a feeling something was not right. And then I heard . . . I saw what you were doing to that girl . . ."

"She's all right."

"But—"

"See for yourself." Richard gestured off to the side where Sabra energetically directed a rough cleanup of what had become a battlefield. Their men were dragging bodies together in a row like logs, and a knot of the women saw to a wounded survivor. "Trust me on this, not for all the world would I see harm come to her or anyone else under my protection—which includes you. I have pledged my life to that."

"But the means you've used . . ."

He held up his sword. "This is the means. The change in me makes me stronger and quicker—"

Edward backed away, one hand waving, palm out. "No, this is too much. I can't . . ." He did not finish, but turned and left.

Richard almost started after him, but caught Sabra looking his way and forced himself to stillness. Sudden, leadlike weariness settled on him. He would need some hours of rest to fully heal and to take more blood. There were plenty of dead to serve for that. He would feed from them, but not just yet.

He called for servants to come and deal with the bodies here, to carry them over with the others, then fled into his tent, out of sight of the coming sun.

From the thick shade of the woods Richard and Sabra watched as graves were dug in the noontime glare. Edward occupied himself giving the dead of both sides the proper rites. He moved from one to the next, the cowl of his black robe pushed back, his head bowed, lips moving from prayers he'd said a thousand times and more. Richard, his shoulder still aching, was rather less charitable concerning the fate of some of those souls.

"They'd have murdered a holy man as he slept," he said to Sabra. "My brother is old now, what harm could he possibly be to anyone?"

"You know the answer. So does he. Neither of you like it."

"I can believe it. He doesn't want to."

"He is a good man and would prefer to see only the best in others. When they don't live up to that it makes the truth a difficult thing for him to accept. He's been disappointed many times, but still he hopes."

There, the last one blessed and prayed over, the last spade of earth in place to cover his corruption.

"My lord bishop!" Richard called.

Edward heard, and after a moment trudged over, standing away from them in the now hot sun, sweat running down his face, his hands dirty from the fresh-turned earth. He was so weary, so old in the harsh light. Every seam on his skin was cut deeper than before, his fair hair gone silver, the look in his eyes heartbreaking. He spared one curious glance at Sabra, who was still in her bloodstained page clothes, partly covered by a winter-heavy cloak. "Yes?"

"Tell me one thing: did you go to d'Orleans and see Father yourself?"

Clearly this was not the question he expected. "No. I got a letter from Ambert. He pleaded with me to hurry. The men he sent carried supplies and coin to speed us to look for you."

That alone was cause for suspicion. Ambert never did a charitable deed unless he got something in return for it. Edward must have thought the calamity of a dying father had softened him. "Ambert knew you and I have been in contact over the years. Knew you would be the only one able to find me."

"And I came too late. My poor brother Richard died years ago. I will pray for his soul. And I won't trouble Ambert with this."

Richard sneered. "Ambert? You *know* he was behind this! Those were his men instructed to kill us both when the time was right." He gestured at the graves and waited.

Edward only crossed himself.

"The other certainty is our father is already dead. Ambert brought this about to make sure neither of us made any demand for our share of the inheritance. Ambert is not the taunting boy we sparred with; he's darker and more deadly than ever Father was, and was ever greedy. It's no one's fault, just what is."

"But from our own brother, our own blood . . ." He swiped a dirty hand over his eyes, leaving tear streaks in the sweat, then looked at Richard. "All men change, not always for the good. No one is the same as before, none of us, and some are worse and some are lost. I am alone now, but for God." He turned away.

Once more Richard perceived that same terrible sadness from the day of their last practice, when Edward accidentally killed the armsman. Edward's walk was the same, consumed with defeat and despair.

Sabra, thickly hooded against the sun and silent until now, broke from Richard and went to Edward. He halted to look at her.

"You know me," she said, with certainty.

"And you, too, are the same as you were from that time so long ago. I'm sorry, but I cannot—"

"What did I do?"

"You came dressed as a Holy Sister to bring me to see . . ." He cast a helpless eye toward Richard.

"Because you needed to be with him," she said. "And he with you."

"But you're . . ." he could not speak the words.

"Charity, good father. Judge us by our *deeds*, not by your fears."

"I've tried, but—"

"See me as I *am*," she whispered.

The change was subtle, but even in the daylight Richard saw a glow about her that had nothing to do with the sun. She put a hand on Edward's arm and looked deeply into his eyes for a very long time. Whatever he saw there must have spoken to him, for he finally nodded, the stiffness in his shoulders easing.

"Be at peace, my brother," she told him.

For all that, he still looked troubled.

Quick preparations were made for everyone's departure. The last of Ambert's murderous escort had been caught and would be taken north to Joyeuse Garde, Richard's stronghold. Elaine would look after them until there was time to spare to render a verdict on them for the attempted murder of an archbishop.

The whole camp gathered itself and pulled out, heading for the main road. When they reached the juncture of the lanes, Richard nudged his horse over to stand next to Edward's mount.

Edward gave him a polite farewell, speaking the expected words, but did not quite meet his eye. Perhaps Sabra had imparted some peace to him, but it was that of a forced truce; there was no true healing between them.

Richard thought this would be the last time they would ever see each other and the grief of it tore at his heart. He looked at Sabra. She smiled and shook her head and pointed up the road, not down, which was the way Edward originally came, the way he would have take to return to Normandy.

"You're sure?" he asked.

She nodded.

"Sure of what?" asked Edward, thinking he'd been addressed.

Richard gestured. "This isn't your road. You must take another."

"But it's my way back."

"Not anymore. You cannot return there. Not for a while, yet."

"What are you saying? I don't care if Ambert has a hundred deaths for me. I am needed home. They await me at the monastery—"

"You are needed here, now. There's an abbey not too far from this spot in Glastonbury. Our people will see you safely there. Shelter with the monks, speak to the abbot. Let him tell you what your dead brother has been doing all these years, and *then* decide whether you still think me Godless and cursed."

Edward had no response for that. But perhaps, just perhaps, there was an awakening glimmer in his eyes. What it meant remained to be discovered.

"Safe journey, brother. Pray for our father for the both of us."

Letting himself be led the other way, Edward rode off, casting one unreadable glance back at them, then pressing on.

"When will I see him again?" Richard well knew the perils of asking about the future, but couldn't help himself.

"When next you are needed," said Sabra. "He will be healthier there than anyplace else."

"What of the path he would have taken?"

"Ours now, along with the danger it holds. We shall deal well with it, my Richard." She rode with a sword the same as the men and checked to see that it was loose in its scabbard. "Let's not keep the traitors waiting."

She kicked her horse up, and they cantered to meet the threat lying ahead.

Chapter Ten

Toronto, the Present

"What do you mean?" Richard demanded. Time was short; the delay angered him. "What other road is there?"

Michael shook his head. "I don't know, but this is to protect her."

He remembered the cryptic words on the computer screen. "How will her dying protect her? There's no sense to it."

"It just will, that's all I know."

"I won't let her go like this. Not when I can—"

"But it's only a *change*. She told me I've been through it hundreds of times. It can't be so bad."

Richard gaped at him, mouth dry, mind reeling. Surely not. The Goddess would do something, make things different, and save her. She wouldn't do this to *Sabra*, not to her. If she did . . . no. No matter what, he wouldn't let that happen. He'd do whatever was necessary to keep her alive.

But he'd defied the Goddess once before. Or tried to.

He looked at Michael, a young boy who understood too much. "I won't let her die."

It's not your choice.

He shivered as an instantly familiar voice whispered in his mind. "Sabra?" He stared around, knowing it was futile.

All will be well. Bear this, my love. You have strength to . . .

"I will *not* bear this!"

You will! For Michael! You WILL! And then the precious voice ceased. He waited, holding his breath for another word until his chest ached.

"Sabra . . . ?"

No reply.

It was the worst, most absolute silence Richard had ever known, as though he'd been struck deaf.

Michael let out a keening whimper and shuddered. Tears ran free down his face. Richard knew what happened and it hit like a sword thrust. He staggered; his insides felt ripped out, and he gave a soft cry, his soul's denial.

Bourland slowly pushed through the door. His face told all. He couldn't speak, only bow his head. He sat heavily on a waiting room chair. Michael went to him, hand on his shoulder. Without looking up, he wrapped his arms around the weeping boy and held him close.

Paralysis crept over Richard and took solid hold, trapping him in sheer, yawning emptiness. He wanted the earth to open up and swallow him. This was beyond endurance, beyond his strength; she was gone, yet he remained. That could *not* be. It was others whose lives came and went, flourished and faded, but they were *always* together. That never changed.

Alone.

Truly alone. Never to see her again. It was too much.

No, I cannot, will not go on . . .

He stared down the long vanishing length of the hospital corridor. It stretched to infinity, full of harsh light, hard corners, and busy, unconcerned strangers.

"For all the good it will do, there's a full investigation on," Bourland tiredly said.

"All right," Richard acknowledged in a hollow voice so soft as to almost go unheard. He was yet in shock, he thought. He found himself reacting to things people said, but was strangely insulated from them. There was considerable sympathy floating about and some fear; quite a number of the staff had been very shaken by the incident in the ICU. Bourland's plans promised to shake things even more.

The police had come and gone, leaving behind patrolmen. Reassuring, but only to civilians. After that, some of the internal excitement diminished and routine reasserted itself to some extent. Of course, everyone knew something of what had happened, and they all knew Richard, Bourland, and Michael were closely involved. Professionalism prevented the hospital staff from asking direct questions, which was a blessing.

Midmorning had come and gone, but one could only tell by looking at a clock. They were still in a place where losing track of time was an ongoing hazard, and it was a very dark day outside.

Richard felt cold, unable to warm up at all, though there was plenty of heat in the room, and he kept his coat on. Bouts of shivering swept over him at unexpected times, and he desperately wanted to sleep, but couldn't seem to close his eyes. Whenever he did it was like turning up the volume on the ambient sounds of the place. Sitting made him restless, but he was too weary to pace. Once he left for the mens' room and for the first time in years doubled over as his belly tried to turn itself inside out. Nothing came forth, only retching misery, followed by icy sweats. He went through that drill for nearly an hour before the fit passed.

Exhausted, he crept back to be with Bourland and sat on the floor, his bowed spine pressed to a wall because he couldn't trust himself to not fall out of a chair. He turned away offers of help and suggestions to have a sedative.

Bourland understood and got people to leave him alone.

The worst, most damnable part of it was Richard could not weep.

For those raised under certain social rules, it wasn't the done thing for a man to cry, but even Bourland, grown up in that generation, had broken down for a time.

Richard tried. Nothing came forth. He rubbed his eyes to see if they were working and raised a sting of watering, but no tears.

Shock. That's all it is.

When his gut settled and some strength returned, he crept into a chair by a small conference table and sat for a time, trying to notice other people besides himself. Bourland looked haggard, but functioning; Michael was off in a nearby hospital room, asleep, thankfully, after that first storm of reaction. A policeman stood outside, alert for one-eyed strangers.

Richard longed for the luxury of oblivion, but he would put it off; he would ignore the blackness. He had but one reason to keep moving: to find Sabra's killer . . . and deal with him.

Bourland channeled his own postponed grief in compulsive activity, doing what he did best, setting wheels in motion. He'd spoken to the top people of the hospital's administration, talked to their security, talked to the cops, talked to God knows who else, and managed to commandeer someone's office. He made a call to the special outfit that was so secret, bulled through to their director and damnation to their security protocols. He made demands and got someone to listen.

He filled Richard in. "Two of their best people are on the way to look after us, but their prime concern will be to bodyguard Michael; they're also bringing photos. They have shots of arrivals from the Yucatán. Too bad the hospital's surveillance tapes were buggered. There's some techs looking into the problem. The whole damned system . . ."

Richard nodded bleakly.

"Coffee? You look as though you could use some."

"No, thank you. I still feel woozy." Richard had no idea how coffee could possibly help.

"Richard?"

"Yes, what?" He jolted from wherever he'd gone, startled by what a wall clock told him. Apparently an hour had slipped by unnoticed while he stared into space. *Focus. Wake the hell up and focus.* He pulled himself together by remembering what it felt like to be that way. *Fake it 'til you make it.*

"They're here."

Through the office window he observed a man and woman approaching, each in black leather coats, wearing designer sunglasses on a sunless day. They were of a kind, and Richard recognized the genus.

"What lovely people you know," he murmured to Bourland.

"Hm?"

"Those two killers." He saw that much in their body language, the way they held their heads. The man in particular, moving like a panther. The woman was better at blending, her walk influenced by her heeled boots, but still unmistakable to anyone who knew the signals. Or lack thereof.

"It's a nasty world, isn't it? But they're on our side for the time being."

Richard noted the qualifier. "Are they from . . . ?"

"Yes. For your own well-being pretend you don't know that particular department exists. They're rather appalling about keeping their security intact."

Bourland *had* called in serious firepower. This was a few steps beyond the guards ordered up to keep watch.

The couple simply came in; neither identified themselves. The man was lean and dark, in need of a shave and haircut. He handed over a flat, padded envelope without preamble. He didn't remove his sunglasses, but Richard knew he was being closely examined and memorized, the information to be added to whatever dossier they kept on him. He didn't give a damn.

The woman was more accessible, pushing her shades up on her forehead to hold back her straight blond bangs. She gave Richard a small, neutral smile. A lithe and lovely blue-eyed charmer, evidently trained in seduction, keeping it dampened down until needed. That was likely one of their ploys when working. One for distraction, the other for destruction, switching roles as needed for any given situation. Richard nodded once at her, to be polite, then shifted his attention to Bourland's envelope.

The man said, "Your target has been narrowed to twenty possibles." His voice was low; he barely moved his lips. Slight French accent. "They've been initially cleared by background checks, but each fitted the profile you supplied. A single man, traveling alone, possibly on a British or American passport, but we checked many others. At this point all of those who traveled to this city from the Yucatán or the rest of Mexico are accounted for and were elsewhere when the attack here was made."

Richard looked at various still shots taken from an airport security camera, obviously set up at customs. None of the men or the names on the pages attached to the photos meant anything to him. The thumbnails of each of their lives tripped no alarms.

Bourland didn't recognize any of them either, but admitted he'd never gotten a look at the invader. "Did you show these to the other witnesses yet?"

"Yes. They were unable to identify their attacker. Most remembered a beard and an eye patch. Recollections of height and weight differ among them. Such variations are to be expected from witnesses under extreme stress. One of them said there was no beard at all. Our best description came from the one we sent over as guard."

"Yet he could not pick anybody from your collection."

"No."

"Only twenty?" asked Richard.

"Yes."

"Unacceptable. We'll have to widen the profi ... wait. What about this?" Richard pointed to the upper corner of one shot that showed part of a convex mirror. There was a blurred male form in it, the curved reflection misshapen, but there was enough to show he just might have a beard and eye patch. "Who's he?"

"We can find out." The man gave nothing away, though he should have been chagrinned that something as obvious as that had been overlooked by his people.

"Do so. Did you bring a copy of the videos made?"

"Of course."

The girl pulled an unlabeled CD case and a notebook computer from her shoulder bag. "When we digitized the recordings, we cleaned the images up. All the other passengers cleared our check, though." She had a pleasant, husky voice.

She put the disk in the computer's DVD player and activated it, speeding through the shifting images until Richard told her to stop. The scene matched the one in the top photo, but as it played out, the picture suddenly deteriorated and ceased. The recording kicked in again, but by then the suspect was gone. Whoever was reflected in the mirror got through without leaving a clearer shot of himself behind.

There's no such thing as coincidence.

"Does this machine have a screen-capture program?" he asked her.

"Yes, along with photography software."

"Good. Freeze on that image in the mirror, copy it to the program and let's see what it looks like."

She seemed to understand exactly what was wanted and manipulated the process with a swift, deft touch. A few minutes' work and the screen had a larger version of the mirror on it, the pixels just starting to show. She refined, sharpened, drew out more information, then removed the distortion caused by the curvature. Even her aloof partner with the pale, narrow face came around to look over her shoulder as she progressed from one improvement to the next.

Richard snorted at the final result. If this outfit was so deadly efficient, they should have spotted him. "You'll need to upgrade for your background check procedures, I think," he said. He glared at the freeze-framed stocky man, his skin reddened by the tropical sun, his face partly obscured by an eye patch.

"Who is he, Richard?" Bourland asked, leaning in.

"It's Charon."

Bourland was silent a moment. Staring. "You're sure?"

"Absolutely."

"Who's Charon?" the woman wanted to know.

"A legend," replied her partner. "Professional assassin. A very good one."

Richard glanced at them. "And quite out of your league. I'll take it from here."

The man went still, his version of saying "oh, really?" and the woman lifted her chin seeming ready to argue, but didn't. They were probably too used to being at the top of the food chain and not pleased at the reminder that even nastier predators existed.

The man looked at Bourland. "We can locate and remove the target, if that is what you require."

"What I require is a bodyguard for my son until Mr. Dun gives the all-clear. *He* will deal with Charon."

"We are aware of Mr. Dun's credentials and mean no disrespect to his abilities, but our resources are considerably greater than his. We are better prepared to deal with this level of threat."

"You have no idea what the true level is." Richard was in no mood to engage in a pissing contest.

Bourland didn't hide his flare of anger, though. "Obviously not, since you let Charon breeze past your security check. That bastard could be anywhere by now."

"He'll still be in Toronto, Philip," said Richard. "He has one more target to take out. Me."

"You're not going underground to avoid him, are you?"

"No. Quite the opposite."

"That would be ill advised," said the man.

"It's the only way to find him."

"You'll want an invisible perimeter around you. We can arrange—"

"No, I won't, and you won't. Your lot is to watch the Bourlands. Don't argue, Philip. If he figures out your connection to me you'll be in the line of fire, too. I have to be Charon's only focus. If he succeeds, you should be safe enough, though I wouldn't trust that. But it's a moot point. I'll see to it he fails."

"How?"

"He won't expect me to be functioning after what's happened here. He is presently unaware we know about him. I'll use that. The tricky bit will be making sure no one else gets hurt."

"Again, how?"

"I'm working on it. In the meantime, we behave as close to normal as possible, given the circumstances. Go through the expected motions."

Bourland shook his head. "I'd rather not."

"I know, but assume we're being watched."

Richard looked at the couple. "Mr. Bourland will show you where his son is; make sure the policeman on duty there sees the right credentials from you."

"We have them," the woman assured, showing him a plastic card with her picture on it. It was an excellent forgery, proclaiming her to be an employee of his own security firm. Though one division of it dealt with the hire and employment of guards, they were of the more ordinary unarmed variety. It nettled him that such things could be so perfectly duplicated so quickly, but their organization had a reputation for frightening efficiency.

"You're the only two on this, anyone else turning up you will consider suspicious. Should that happen, use your best judgment on how to neutralize them, but keep it discreet."

"None of that collateral damage idiocy," Bourland put in. "Paul may not mind, but *I* do."

The girl's eyes flickered. She liked him.

Richard added, "And lose those damned sunglasses. You two look like Boris and Natasha on a bad day."

She suppressed a twitch of her pink lips and started for the door, pausing for her partner. He stared down at Richard, who was not the least bit interested in the young man's issues. The man removed his sunglasses, revealing the soulless, dead eyes of a killer. No surprises there. Richard stared right back, unimpressed.

"Hey," said the woman, breaking their lock. Evidently she was the balancing factor for the duo, keeping the guy in line when needed.

He finally followed her out the door, putting his shades back on.

"There's a bomb waiting to go off," Bourland muttered.

"And you want *them* around Michael?"

"No, but they're the best. They don't have to be likeable so long as they do the job, which they will do or die trying. But if Charon's the one behind this . . ."

"Then you're damned lucky you're still alive."

"And you. If I hadn't taken the night shift—"

"This place would be full of bodies. Had I been there Charon would have tried to kill me, then God knows what would have happened." *Sabra might still be alive.* "You know, you've not mentioned bringing the regular law into this, Philip. That's unusual for you."

"The police are out of their depth with someone like Charon."

"It's more than that."

"I know how these games are played; we're on a different kind of field with him."

"This was before we knew he was involved. You've played it close with them."

Bourland rubbed the back of his neck. "Yes, but it's all very simple. You kill Charon—or whoever—and I bury him, with no one the wiser. If you want to go vigilante, it will be with my full backing, cooperation, and a quiet cleanup to follow. A coverup if necessary. Just don't ask for anything in writing."

Richard managed a wan smile. "Your word's always been good enough for me."

"What now?"

Richard blanked for a second, then the ugliness of mundane practicality kicked in. "When the coroner is finished with his post-mortem, we should . . . make arrangements."

Bourland's face clouded. He turned away, hand over his eyes.

Charon's murderous foray in the hospital took less than fifteen minutes; that was how much time was missing from the hospital videotapes. The police did not know how he'd been able to sabo-tage all the cameras and tapes at once. Richard had an idea, but knew better than to share it with them.

Human or not, Charon was far too dangerous for ordinary law enforcement or even the extraordinary as represented by that couple. They were trained in every kind of conventional weapon and com-bat, but utterly unprepared for supernatural confrontations.

After Sabra drank from the Grail her healing changed her, turned her human again, but she still retained her Gifts. If anything she was stronger than ever before in them. Had the same happened to Charon? Did he even possess Gifts? *Assume so.* If not back then, then without doubt now.

He'd caused the Otherside disruption in Stonehenge, Chichén Itzá, and certainly must have conjured that freak wind on the highway. The alternative, that the Goddess had to do with it—had done it on purpose—Richard refused to consider. Her part in it could only have been damage control afterward.

Charon's motive was elusive, though. He had thoroughly dropped himself from sight for the last few years. Richard had patiently hunted for him, not liking to leave a job unfinished, but discov-ered no sign of him until now. Why had he so suddenly surfaced, and what the devil was he up to?

Sabra would have been able to figure it out.

He fought off a wave of darkness, of overwhelming grief. No tears, though, only a terrible sickness of heart.

No. I will not give in to you just yet. When it's done and that animal is dead, I will mourn.

Then he thought of the Grail again and went cold.

Sharon Geary stirred from her nap, feeling sluggish not from her unplanned slumber, but from lack of fresh air. She'd gotten—mostly—used to the strong smell of snake, but every few hours had to let her companion know when she needed a breather. Literally. He had her sealed in tight, which was both a good and bad thing.

She'd forced herself to deal with floating in the pitch blackness, wanting to conserve her torch batteries. Stretching out, she touched nothing with hands or feet, meaning she could be an inch away from any given side, or smack in the middle of the scale-lined sphere the serpent had made from his knotted body. He really had been *very* decent to her, but needed reminding about certain basics. So far, he didn't seem to object.

Swimming motions didn't cut it, but she had some success getting herself moving by blowing a stream of air as though trying to inflate a really large balloon. Though most of Newtonian physics must have been tossed from this corner of the universe, the action-reaction thing still worked, more or less, in here.

A few moments of huffing and puffing and she was able to reach a curved wall and touch it, hanging on precariously by means of the roughness of the scales. To protect her palms she'd put on some fingerless gloves stowed in one of her cargo pockets, the material acting like the soft side of fabric fastening tape.

One hand in place, she banged on the living wall with the other. "Hallo! Need some air in here again!"

She'd gotten used to dealing with the god in a very short time. Must have been from being Irish.

Kukulcan was evidently awake and still obliging. A vast shift took place as on the other times before, and a long opening appeared in the darkness. It was dark outside as well, but still lighter than her little sanctuary.

Fresh air blew in, cleaning out the stale. Must have been quite a wind out there. Cold, too. Until now she'd not noticed warmth or chill.

She ventured to take a peek, trusting her large friend would eat anything nasty before it ate her. And there he was, almost within touch, one of his great eyes looking at her.

"How's it goin' ?" she asked. "Any luck gettin' us back where I belong?"

Apparently not.

She got the impression that they were moving, though. Except for the influx of wind, no hint of it transferred to her in her shelter, but the feeling was there all the same.

She decided to try her Sight. At first she'd been too preoccupied, but now that she'd become more or less used to the situation it occurred to her she should explore other venues that might lead to an escape. Not that the company wasn't good, but in much of the mythology she'd read mortals who hung around with gods often came to a bad end, and she'd rather skip the honor, thank you very much.

Sharon wriggled partway out and focused quick, not knowing how long she might have.

Wow. A rainbow lightning storm. How about that?

The colors were considerably more intense than anything she'd seen on her side of Reality. Fireworks came the closest, but they were less bright and didn't last as long. The bolts of energy shooting around here went from one side of her wide view to another, slower than what was normal to her, lightning taking its own dear time. She was able to pick out every tiny little branch and fork. Now that was just amazing.

Silent, too. The place should have been roaring and booming like a battlefield. Very strange, but fortunate for her, considering how much noise might otherwise be slamming about. Wouldn't want to blow out her eardrums.

Kukulcan might be feeling it, though. Ordinary snakes were sensitive to heat and vibration. She noticed neither; in fact, the air was getting colder by the minute, if still fresh. Must be a ton of Otherside ozone about, but she hoped the chill wouldn't slow him down. Maybe that white blood of his kept him going.

"Where you takin' us, if you don't mind my askin'?"

No verbal reply came; she didn't expect one. However, she could see some kind of disturbance far, far ahead—or what would be ahead if that's where they were heading. She couldn't tell, distance was impossible to reckon, and as for time . . . well, she knew she'd been here for hours on end, more than a day at least if she could trust her watch, yet she felt no hunger or thirst. Or other bodily needs for that matter. Either the god or this place had something to do with it, which was very fortunate.

"Thanks for the peek. I'll let you get on with things."

She pushed back in, and the crack closed, but not completely. He'd left an inch-size opening, and she didn't think it was an oversight on his part. It gave her a constant supply of fresh air to breathe, and a narrow view of things, even a bit of light. She could deal with the darkness, but would rather not have to; perhaps they were clear of the area where the giant Sharon-eating bugs swarmed.

She found a way to hold on with her palms flat on the scales, resting her chin on the back of her hand, with her weightless body bobbing gently clear so she could watch the light show. It passed the time, however time was passed here.

The disturbance seemed very small, but then the noonday sun looked small given the gap between itself and the earth. It seemed just as intense, though moving, a tiny, twisting spiral with a brightness in the center. She wasn't sure if she liked it or not.

Hopefully, Kukulcan knew what he was about. In a place like this one needed friends.

Toronto, the Present

"Daniel Dean?" said Richard, looking at a fax of an American passport that had just come into the commandeered hospital office. The name and address were unknown to him, but the cheerful, beaming face—what was left of it with the scars under the patch on the right side—was Charon's.

Bourland grunted an affirmative. "His name when he landed at Pearson. He seems to have shed it the moment he left. There's an ongoing search of hotels in the area for one-eyed guests, but no luck so far. He could have shed the eye patch, too."

"In which case we are still looking for a one-eyed man, albeit with considerable facial scarring."

"Cosmetic restoration surgery? A glass eye?"

Richard remembered the damage Charon had taken that day when they'd fought over the Grail. "He could be in sunglasses, so I wouldn't put too much attention on that one feature."

"Then we'll only find him by luck or the next time he purposely shows himself."

"Or by taking note of oddities. Any more on that cab driver?"

Earlier in the morning a man had been found slumped behind the wheel of his cab, the motor still roughly chugging away, less than a block from St. Michael's. His fare records were gone, though his dispatcher had his call-in just minutes after Charon left the hospital. The destination address was the road where Sabra's cottage stood. The dead driver had bled heavily from his nose, ears, and eyes.

"The prelim postmortem indicates some kind of internal hemorrhage." Bourland slid a copy of a handwritten form across the conference table.

"Just like Sabra."

"They think he may have felt something was wrong and tried to drive himself in for help, but the violence of the bleeding..."

"He was murdered."

"I'd like to know how."

"No, you don't."

Bourland made no argument against that. "What about the break-in at her place?"

Richard had been on the phone with the police, having called in a possible burglary to them. Because of the special circumstances and Bourland's influence, he'd been able to listen in as two officers walked through her home, describing their progress into their radios. Richard might have gone up himself, but knew it was too soon. To see her things scattered just as she'd left them ... no, better to have someone else do that for him.

They reported the front door being open and the security alarms shut down. Nothing taken, apparently. He relayed instructions for them to check one of the back bedrooms. They found a mess, some overturned furniture, a table fountain upset and broken. A brass bowl some six inches across? No, nothing like that here. Why?

"They're looking for fingerprints," he said to Bourland. "Doubt if they'll find any."

"But why did he go there afterwards? What did he want?"

Richard shrugged.

"You know. What is it?"

"He was after a memento of hers." Richard gave a lean description of the Grail.

"All that for a brass bowl?"

"It's an antique. *Very* old. Priceless in some circles. His way of rubbing my nose in it."

"Has it worked?"

"No. I'll get it back for her."

Mortality sucked. That's it, that's all there was to it. It purely, grade-A homogenized, top to bottom, in your ear, out your ass *sucked*.

Charon felt the gradual loss of strength creeping over him already. Damn, you'd think the drain hole would be plugged up by now with all the juice he was pouring in. He didn't believe in things like Fate and that he was destined to die from the cancer and that would explain why it was using so much freaking effort to fight it and keep going.

The power he'd taken from the cab driver was slowly failing against the stuff eating him up from the inside. His sweet little brass prize was handy at translating other energies for his needs and could indefinitely sustain him, but it was like grease through a goose. He'd have to keep the feeding tap in the on position just to maintain himself. Not a problem if he had to, but the opposition was bound to notice a thing like that and come after him.

Just because he'd taken out one of them while she was flat on her assets didn't mean there weren't others around to fill her hobnailed boots. And chances were they'd be able to walk all over him once they figured out what was going down. Didn't she have eight sisters wandering around out there doing their Earth Mother scene and saving the rain forests and other crap? Whether they were on this Side or not, they would close in on him.

Then there was the other thing: there was *no* substitute for the rush that people-energy gave him. However, he'd have to go easy snacking on human targets. Fang-boy and his friends would just *love* following a trail of bodies to the Cambridge's penthouse suite. They were cruisin' to give a bruisin'.

Frying witchy-girl had made one hell of a royal stinkola, much more than Charon had reckoned on. His police-band radio sputtered all night and all day with reports and traffic on this and that. He'd been in the lobby when a couple of guys in plainclothes came in flashing their badges all over the place and waving a composite picture of himself.

Oh, yeah, keeping the eye patch on for his venture had been a very good ploy. They thought they'd gotten around it by having a second photo done without it. Part of his face in that one was puckered with lines of scar tissue, but still no good to them. Mr. Snaky's oh-so-sweet blood had fixed that. He should open himself a franchise offering face-lifts to aging actresses.

But the bottom line was this city was sealed up. Lance had some heavy guns on his side for some reason. He must have increased his level of influence over the local politicos in the last few years. That meant there'd be more cops at the airports, train, and bus stations than passengers, and not all could be counted on to screw up and miss a beauty like Charon. All they had to do was correctly identify the left side of his face, then the moose shit would hit the fan. Yes, he could probably drain a few dry, but he'd still be stuck here. They'd take away his toy, lob him in jail, and then the dickster knight would come in all full of righteous vengeance . . .

Nope-nope and nada. Had to take him out and get across the border, or the other way around. Whatever. Dickie's death would keep the hounds distracted, chasing their tails, especially if they had lots of false trails to play on. Those were easy enough to arrange. How the cops loved to backtrack the forensic evidence stuff, could keep 'em busy for months.

Dun was a tough bastard, though. Have to make sure he was gone, gone, gone and bye-bye three times over. Shouldn't be too hard.

Charon had had a lot of time in the last few years to work up several scenarios. Pick one.

Not standing up to his ass in snow-covered bushes, though. Charon scowled. What had he been thinking? Make that taking. Damn pills . . .

So . . . what was a good Plan B?

With the pain dulled down and some of the drugs out of his system he was able to think better. He still had hours to go yet before he'd need another refreshing hit, better make the most of them.

All Dun wanted was a push in the right direction, and he'd trip on his own feet running to his death. Push. Pushing was good. Yeah, that was a good one. Big distraction, too.

Charon worked out his deadline, measuring it against his declining strength and the tools he had at hand, deciding what he could set up the fastest with the least effort. A side trip to a special storage garage where he'd hidden some valuable professional toys a few years back was needed, but he could get the rest at Eaton Centre. Man, they had *everything*.

Wasn't modern living great?

In the late afternoon **Richard**'s cell phone trilled. His caller ID display blinked 'UNKNOWN'. Useless things. Maybe it was from that young woman in the Yucatán.

"Hallo?"

"Hey, this Richard Dun?"

He shot upright as though touched by a hot wire. The voice was electronically disguised, but there was only one man who would bother with such games. But why a direct call? The smart thing would be to lie in wait and pick him off with a long rifle, then move in and finish the job. *Play it carefully, old lad. Pretend you haven't a clue.* "Who is this?" He hit a button on some highly specialized hardware linked to all the phones in the room, including his own. It would both record and trace the call. The sudden motion attracted Bourland's notice; he came across to listen in.

"Never mind that," said the voice. "You wanna chance to get the guy who snuffed your girlfriend?"

"Who are you?" He raised his tone, injecting the right amount of rage and rising frustration, an edgy man barely in control. "What do you know about it? How in hell did you get this number?"

"Not gonna get that info, bud. Deal with me like this or don't deal at all, but I can give you the bad guy for some cash. You want him or not?"

"Of course I do."

The harsh, robotic voice buzzed on. "Then you know how these things run. This ain't amateur night, I'm a player and wanna keep my ass right where it is and not shot off or in jail."

"Keep talking."

"I want half a million in U.S. dollars. That's the bounty. Non-negotiable, cheap at the price."

It was nicely calculated. Enough to be worth someone's while, but not too much for a wealthy payer to lay out. "In cash?"

"Better believe it."

"Not until I have proof."

"The guy you want wears an eye patch."

"You've seen the police showing the photos around. You're just using the situation to cash in. No, thank you."

"Yo! Dun! Heads up or you'll lose your window from being too smart."

"Give me more proof, then."

"Okay-okay! This dude's got an attitude, makes pit bulls roll over and piss themselves, y'know?"

"Sorry, not enough."

"Okay-okay, the dude is called 'Charon.' Ring a bell?"

Richard held silent, as though stunned. "Are you certain?" he whispered.

"Yeah, I'm certain. Look, I'm the guy he came to to work up a new alias. I've worked for him before and got him set again, but he welshed. The thing is, he did it from a distance. He thinks he's killed me, but he shot another guy instead. A friend of mine. You pay, I tell you where Charon is, you do what you like to him, and we never see each other again. That's the best deal you're gonna get, so what d'ya say?"

"How do you even know about me?"

"Well, this was the weird part: he was talking to himself and your name came up. He seemed into nailing you flat. I've heard of you from my side of the street and knew who to call when the smoke cleared."

Richard snorted. "Oh, I'm sure."

"I *mean* it. The guy's gone loony. He always used to be edgy, but he's gone right over into the rapids. Creeped me out the way he was pacing around and arguing with himself. I figure that's why he wanted me offed, he knew I'd heard too much. He was like Hannibal Lector on crank, y'know? Hyper as hell and nuts. I figure he's into drugs, but his money was clean and then he dusted my pal and . . ."

"Right, and you want some pay out as well as payback."

"Hey—my life's on the line the first hint he gets that he missed me. I need money to scram myself off the map—in case you don't get him. No offence! I heard you were good, but this is *Charon* we're talking about."

"What's his new name and where is he?"

"You get his name and destination when I get my money. I'm square on that. I don't need the both of you chasing me. When it comes down to it I want you to win, 'cause I know you'll be square as well and let me go, y'know? If you don't like what I have to say, then you don't have to pay, y'know?"

"I know."

"We gotta deal, then?"

"Only if I like the information. I can confirm it within a few minutes of receipt, so you'll stick around that long."

"Nuh-uh, no way. I'm in, I'm out. Faster the better."

"You want your money?"

"Freakin' hell, yes, but—"

"Then that's how it's played. I've got other resources than you to find him, what I'm paying for is saved time."

"Well, okay, but you *promise* . . ."

"Yes. We'll meet at the CN Tower, that should be public enough."

"Can't, I'm not in town. I got a trip lined already. You come to me."

"Where?"

"Can you get to Niagara by six? With the cash?"

Richard checked a clock. "Barely. Between the bank and the evening rush hour—"

"If you leave now you got lots of time. You get on the Rainbow Bridge, you know where that is?"

"Of course I do."

"Great. I'll meet you there, halfway across on that sidewalk they got on the south side. You bring the money and your phone, and I tell you what you need. Don't be late cause I hate the cold. Brass monkeys gonna be dropping their balls right, left, 'n' center out there."

"Why not pick a warmer place?"

"'Cause on a bridge you can see who's coming at you, especially that one. Halfway across is too long a shot for a sniper."

Not a sniper like Charon, Richard thought, but agreed. *This is Charon's way of arranging things so I'll feel safe. Bollocks.*

"You get your info, and we don't see each other again, okay? Okay?"

"Very well. At six tonight." He rang off and looked at Bourland, his eyes blazing. The hunt was up.

Chapter Eleven

Charon's prediction about brass monkey genitalia was correct, though the source of the expression had nothing to do with primates. It *was* just that cold, more so.

Richard hated being on the Rainbow Bridge, but now that he was in place could agree about the difficulty of anyone achieving a long shot. The wind was high and even an expert like Charon would likely miss under these conditions. Still, Richard felt too much out in the open, with no place to put his back to a wall.

The sky was fortunately dim and gray, almost the same color as the roiling water below, plenty of insulation between himself and the dying sun. The constant roar of the American Falls ahead and to his right competed against the traffic noise on his left. Both were sufficient to get on his nerves; he liked to be able to hear when people came up behind him and kept turning about, using his eyes to compensate for the deficiency. Then again, he was supposed to be projecting unease.

Making a damned thorough job of it, too.

He paced up and down with a shiny new briefcase in his left hand. It was full of marked bills, minute tracking bugs attached to them and the case, along with sufficient explosive to blow his arm off. He carried one trigger, and Bourland had the other. The idea behind that was to take out Charon in the event he was successful in his hit and stupid enough to pick up the money. The infernal device had been prepared by Bourland's pet group as though they kept such items ready and waiting on a shelf for similar occasions. Hell's teeth, they probably did.

Richard had a good view of the more spectacular Horseshoe Falls, or would have were they not nearly obscured by the thick cloud of vapor rising from them. Both American and Canadian courses were framed by gigantic formations of icicles that covered the tumbled rocks on either side. The frosty layers from the constant spray must have been yards thick in some places. On occasion the river below the falls could freeze making an ice bridge, creating uneven mounds piling up to fifty feet thick. Not this year, though, not nearly cold enough yet. The river flowed endlessly under his feet, fast, gray, and perilous.

He scanned each of the pedestrians on the ten-foot-wide side-walk that ran along only the south face of the bridge. Apparently the northern view wasn't deemed interesting enough to warrant the expense of placing a walk there. In the warm months this place would be jammed with people. The few around now were only the most hardy tourist types, and they were on the move, taking their well-wrapped selves back to their hotels; the multicolored lights on the falls weren't enough to keep them out in this wind. Good, the fewer on the scene the better. Bourland was all for clearing the bridge entirely, but the group judged it would be too much of a tip-off to Charon. They did agree to prevent others from wandering on after Richard was in place, sending their own people in as substitutes. They were set dressing . . . in body armor with semiautomatic weapons.

Despite increased security by the border guards on both sides looking for the more ordinary—if there was such an animal—type of terrorist, plenty of car and truck traffic rolled past. He'd have to watch that. He was vulnerable to a drive-by, but did not think that was quite Charon's style. Risky, too, since the shooter could be stopped at the other end.

Besides, guns were notoriously hard to explain to the border guards, especially these days, so a shooter would have a hard time smuggling one through from either direction. Nonetheless, if

Richard fell, safeguards were in place to deal with aftermath and capture. Against that possibility Richard's torso was encased in plated Kevlar. He could survive getting shot, but it would be damned inconvenient waiting to heal, so he submitted. His body armor took him back to the days when he wore the articulated sort now displayed in museums. In a way it had been like suiting up again, but with fewer pieces. This weighed him down and was bulky, but his big leather coat covered it. He wished for a muffler and something more substantial for his head than a knitted ski hat, but that might have further restricted his movement; his face and neck burned in the wind.

"You all right?" Bourland's voice in his right ear. It came through clear, the receiver smaller than a hearing aid. Very sophisticated, very expensive.

Richard adjusted the front of the cap to indicate "yes." Had he touched the back it would have told them he wanted help. There'd been no chance to work out a signal that meant "I'm bloody cold and feel like hell, so stop bothering me."

Bourland was in a shelter on the Canadian side of the bridge, watching the target area as best he could in the waning light with field glasses. They'd grabbed another office to use as a field HQ for the operation, filling it with laptops, radios, small arms, and grim-looking people in sunglasses.

"Count your blessings," Bourland continued. "The Americans have gotten wind of this. They know something's up, but haven't any details. They want to swoop in and be helpful."

Richard made no signal back to that one. If things did not go right, then they just might want to invite over some well-armed and armored Yank troops to help with the mess. But God help them if Charon was already on their end of the bridge.

"We've got a man putting them off for the moment, though. The premise is it's a domestic criminal we're after. Thanks, chaps, but we can deal with it."

Richard touched his cap-front again, then turned away. He hoped Bourland would correctly read the body language signal as annoyed impatience and stop the chatter. He usually wasn't this nerved up. Likely impatient himself for things to come together.

The wind knifed right through Richard despite the lined leather, metal, and plastic; the cold penetrated his boots and worked up his legs. He was more immune to it than most, but could still freeze. Which might happen in the next few minutes if Charon didn't shift himself. Richard considered the possibility of a magical attack, of another freak wind. At this height, over two hundred feet above free-running water . . . yes, Charon knew exactly what he was doing when he picked this spot.

Past six, but Richard continued to loiter at the halfway point. It had taken a hell of a lot of fast and frantic behind-the-scenes work to bring him here, not the least of which was getting Bourland on his side for it.

"You're not going out there," he'd said.

"Oh, yes I am. Cooperate with me on this." And with no qualm or conscience for the attack Richard brusquely hammered the point home with a hypnotic clout that rocked the man back a step. There was no time to stand there and convince him. "Did we get a trace on Charon's phone call?"

Bourland was a moment answering, first shaking his head from the mental assault, then checking the communications hardware. "No, dammit. Too many protections. He could have phoned from the hospital lobby for all the good this junk is. You do understand it's a trap?"

"Yes, and before you ask, no, I've not the faintest idea why Charon's showing his hand."

"It is odd. He's prone to strike from cover. A clean kill and get away fast. He's got a good location in Niagara with access to the rest of Canada or the States. Unless that's what he wants us to think."

"Wants *me* to think. One of his weaknesses is he tends to underestimate me. He likes to imagine he's got more brains. Maybe he does, but I've played down to his expectations before and got the better of him. Very aggravating to him, I'm sure. We'll take his bait. It's all we've got."

"I'll have to do one hell of a lot of shifting to bring this together in time."

"Use Boris and Natasha's people. He may not know they're involved: It'll give us a hell of a technical edge."

"Plan to." Bourland looked doubtful, despite the clout.

"Philip, I'm no fool, I *want* full security on this, but it has to be done *my* way. Make that crystalline to them."

"No problem."

Over the phone and in clipped, precise language Bourland told someone what was required and how fast it had to be in place, and they made it happen. Richard got the feeling his friend had ceased to call in favors and was now putting himself in debt to many, many others.

In a spookily short time a nonmedical type of helicopter touched down on St. Michael's roof landing. Richard and Bourland climbed in, and the pilot shot them off south over Lake Ontario, taking a direct route toward the falls. Bourland put on a headset and continued to work out details with nameless people. Richard submitted specific input through his own headset, outlining what was wanted against what was possible. By the time they reached the landing pad at Niagara—the same one used by civilian 'copters to take tourists on aerial trips—many things were in place or getting there.

Richard fully cooperated with them about some security matters, hence the Kevlar. He had people staked out at both ends of the Rainbow Bridge and on every tall building within a most generous shooting distance. The hard part was having enough eyes on the look-out, but not so many as to attract notice. It was impossible to cover every window within view of the bridge, though he understood that there was an army of research techs hacking their way into hotel computers looking for anyone of interest.

They were primarily thinking of long rifles, but other weapons were considered, even the prospect of anti-tank missiles. They were expensive and the launching gear hard to conceal while walking along the street, but the possibility was not to be excluded. Teams disguised variously as maintenance workers, police, and tourists had been dispatched to go over the bridge, looking for in-place explosives.

There truly was no way to predict what method Charon would use. He'd broken from his normal pattern of operation and turned it into a game of assumptions. Charon assumed that Richard would be onto the phony drop scenario, Richard would assume Charon would try for a hit, Charon would in turn—ad infinitum; it was a case of just how far one wished to carry it.

Richard could count on the high probability that Charon wanted to shut him down fast and with absolute certainty. That's all that any of them knew for sure.

"But he'll get his chance at you and then escape," Bourland argued.

"Not if we have enough surveillance up. If that lot you brought in can keep their act together they can trace Charon the instant he makes his move. He's not one to hang about, so they better be prepared for anything."

"You're still the bait. How will you get out alive?"

"I have a plan," Richard assured.

"Would you care to share it?"

"That would be telling."

Bourland quietly fumed, but was too busy to press. The truth was Richard had no plan of escape. He would rely on the other professionals and his own best instincts for survival. Those, and the Goddess's protection, which was not something Bourland would understand.

I'm not sure I do, either, but deep inside Richard was convinced he would be able to take out Charon. Though he had no gift of seeing the future, he was as certain of it as Sabra ever was about her Sight. There would be a reckoning.

And if I'm wrong, then so be it. I'll be with her. So long as Charon was killed, too.

Perhaps Richard was to be met by a passing car, which would either have a shooter inside or be rigged with a bomb. The easy counter-measure: don't get into the car. Better to drag the driver out and dangle him off the bridge to scare information from him. If the driver turned out to be Charon himself . . . not likely, but—

Richard's cell phone rang. He put it to his right ear so Bourland and the others could hear everything. It was the disguised voice again.

"Cold enough for you yet?"

"I'm where you want me, Charon. Now let's settle this."

Charon chuckled but continued to use the voice device. "I

knew even you would figure it out sooner or later. You got people recording this?"

"Of course."

"And the area is crawling with troops. I've been watching them hanging around getting frostbite. You and your bunch of clowns are a bundle of laughs, Lance-baby."

Richard hoped the tech people could somehow trace the call this time. "Come on out, I'll buy you a drink."

"Yeah, right. I know you're pissed off about your girl, but it had to be done. Nothing personal, but it had to be done."

This was meant to provoke him. Given the chance, Charon liked to torment his victims. "And here I thought it might be a little revenge thing on your part, for that time we pulled your teeth."

"Well, sure, there's that, can't deny it. But it's just a change in diet. You think I don't have any fucking *power*?"

"Yes. Else you'd be down here to enjoy a face-to-face."

"Only 'cause I'm not as dumb as you. Got a news flash for you: single combat on the field of honor is long-gone with the wind. I've moved with the times, you're still stuck in the dark ages—which were fun, don't get me wrong—but there's better ways to snuff people."

"Just what did you do to Sabra?"

"Heh—wouldn't you like to find out?"

"Then why have you got me out here? You must want something or you'd have dropped me before this."

"Whoa, pard, you developing some brain cells in your old age? If that don't beat all." He fell to chuckling, an ugly, sobbing sound with the sound distortion. "Weeeell, as a matter of fact I do have a tiny little problem. Seems I moved too fast on your old lady. I should have picked up the magic muffin first, *then* thought about doing her. As it is, I could do with her help about now. Instead, I'm forced to talk turkey with *you*. If it makes you feel better it sticks in my craw like a fishbone. You remember eating fish, don't you?"

"What do you want?"

"For you to be dead, of course."

"Any special reason?"

"*Love* your sense of humor. Your girlfriend might have been able to explain, but tough nuts and all that. This has to do with the dingus I lifted from her place. The damned thing's attracting the wrong kind of attention to me. Screwing things up like you wouldn't believe."

"What things?"

"The stuff she was into, stuff I can't describe. It's messing with my head—making me see things, *feel* things, fer Chrissake. It wants to go *back* to where I found it, if you know what I mean."

Richard could believe that, but not quite. Charon was lying, but only because his lips were moving. "So?"

"So I'm giving it back. It wants to be with *you* for crying out loud. The fucking thing's *screaming* at me. Has been since I grabbed it. Making me nuts, y'know? Check out the cab coming your way. The driver has it."

A yellow cab approached, slowing. The driver peered at Richard, who braced. The man was either a dupe or an agent. Charon was known to subcontract scut-work jobs. The cab pulled over and stopped, motor running. The driver leaned across and opened the passenger door. He looked perfectly ordinary.

"You the guy?" he asked. "I got a delivery for a man using a cell phone. You him?"

"Yes."

On the seat next to him was a thick briefcase similar to the one Richard carried, shiny-new. "This dude told me to give this to you."

Richard stepped back, his instincts buzzing into overdrive. He dropped his own case. That was the signal for everyone to run clear. Grab any civilians and *run*. He hesitated in place, hoping to stall things a few more seconds. Yes . . . people were moving . . .

"Hey, dude, *are* you the one? I'm gonna have to cross and return and go through that customs crap—"

"Get out of there and run. Now!" he told the driver, knowing it would be futile.

"Huh?"

"You've got a bomb in the car." Richard repeated his order, louder, but the man wasn't getting it.

"You kiddin' me? Hey—?"

Backing off, the phone still to his ear, Richard heard Charon's warped voice. "Well, I got things to be and places to do. Hasta la Winnebago, asshole."

This was *it* . . . and Richard couldn't move fast enough. He sprinted for all he was worth, but couldn't outrun the speed of light. He felt an almighty wallop against his whole body, a blinding flash of red and yellow, and went hurtling over the shattering guardrail as it blew outward. There was no up or down for an endless moment, then gravity seized him. He had only a second to see the steel gray water of the river rushing up.

He spun, trying to hit feet-first—

Charon watched from his hotel window on the Canadian side of the river. He pressed the autodial on a second cell phone in his left hand. A third cell, carefully wired in the briefcase, got the signal . . .

"Hasta la Winnebago, asshole."

. . . Got the signal and detonated, neat as neat.

Kaah-boom—or so it looked from here. Big noise. A second later and the windows rattled.

"God, I *love* it when tech works!"

He had a powerful telescope set up on the balcony, focused on a man's black-clad figure on the bridge. Well, he used to be on the bridge. The flames, dust, and smoke didn't quite conceal his long, swift fall. He turned once, frantically trying to right himself. An instinct thing. Hopeless, of course. If the five pounds of C-4 Charon rigged in the case didn't blow Dun to ribbons, the drop and running water would finish him for sure. Of course, all three combined made the ideal scenario.

Lots of smoke. In almost the same instant as the first, was the secondary *boom* that would be the car's gas tank going up. Nasty. There wouldn't be enough of the driver left to fill a shot glass, but they didn't need much for DNA identification. He'd get his spot on CNN in due course if not the balance of payment for his one-way errand.

As for Lance . . .

Let's see, just over three seconds of free fall for a two-hundred-foot drop, he'd get up to at least sixty miles an hour, and at that speed the water would be like concrete . . . talk about pulverized.

It hurt like hell to laugh, but Charon couldn't help himself. *Damn, I'm good!*

There was no sign of a body in the water; the splash and any resulting blood would be quickly swallowed up by the river's violent flow.

He clinically observed the gradual response to the disaster. Yeah, first the boom, taking a short second for the sound to travel to every building in the radius of effect and do its window-rattle thing. Then the shocked silence as everyone wondered "what the hell was that?" Heads turning to find the source, then spotting and beginning to move toward it. There would be some major freaking out over whether or not the steel arch bridge would collapse . . .

In another minute the sirens would start up, people would jam the 911 board, trying to be helpful, and so on and so forth, but it was all waaay too late for old Lance.

"He's Dun for," Charon said to them, smirking. He washed down a few pain pills with some celebratory Jack Daniel's, then picked up his carry-on bag with the Grail and walked out of the unoccupied room he'd broken into, leaving the telescope as a parting gift to the hotel.

Philip Bourland's gut twisted in sharp agony as he watched Richard's sickening plummet into the river.

No!

His friend's black figure, still alive, turned once in the fall and then was gone, swallowed by the water so fast the splash was lost. One of the people who'd helped set up the surveillance cursed; others, whose jobs were to react to worst-case situations, did just that. Cell phones were opened, babble commenced, things shot into motion. No one tried the radio link to Richard's receiver. What would be the point?

Philip was on his own phone, running to a waiting car. It was too late to help, far too late, but he called for the 'copter to be ready to lift the moment he was inside.

To lose them both, so close together. Dear God, what will I tell Michael?

He snapped out orders, people scrambled. Another helicopter was already in the air racing toward the bridge and the smoke; he urged his driver to more speed to get to the pad.

Richard never should have done it, never, never, never . . .

The car skidded to a stop. Philip sprinted out and hoisted into the warmed-up machine; it leaped into the thick gray air, roaring angrily. He belted in, was passed headphones against the noise, and put them on.

As they approached the bridge it was evident that their prep work was in place and running as well as could be expected. Traffic from both ends was shut down. A few straggler vehicles hurried to get clear and were directed to holding areas for search. Ambulances appeared, nosing their way against the current.

Swinging around, his pilot carefully avoided the other machine. They were busy getting pictures.

In the exact center of the Rainbow Bridge black smoke rose from the southern side. Little was left of the burning cab. He thankfully could not make out any remains of the poor driver. Some people had caught the shock wave of the blast, maybe struck by shrapnel and other hurtling debris. A few were down, others moved toward them, helped the walking wounded away.

It looked like some unseen creature had taken a bite from the metal and concrete of the bridge, but Philip's focus was the water below, searching vainly for any sign of Richard. The Kevlar and body plating might have protected him from the blast, but the fall . . . *no, don't think that, don't.*

Philip wrestled with his earphones and headset, then motioned for the pilot to dip low. They cruised back and forth just above the water, churning the restless dull surface to froth. Even if Richard was there, how could they see him in that mess?

A third helicopter appeared, bearing the logo of a TV news station. They made a pass by the bridge, then sped away, apparently warned off by the police. His machine swept wide, its searchlight spearing at the water.

His headset crackled, making him jump. He adjusted something and suddenly heard the pilot.

"—won't be here anymore, I'm sorry, sir."

"What?"

"The river flow will have carried him away by now. Our best bet is to have people on watch at Niagara Gorge. That's where the bodies always turn up, sooner or later."

Bodies. Body. A quarter hour ago Richard Dun had a name, a life, friends, family. Now he was flotsam.

His only awareness was of infinite burning pain through his entire being.

Water. Deadly, free-flowing water. Ever his enemy.

The stuff festered in his mouth and nose, scorched his lungs from the inside.

His clothes dragged at him, pulling him heavily downward to dark death.

Had to fight it. He'd always fought it. Had always won.

Instinct moved his sluggish limbs, but he had little control. It hurt, *Godithurthurthurt . . .*

Awakening. His Beast. Last resort. The thing that served him for so long, and now here was a threat to its survival, a cessation to feeding its hunger. No. That *must* continue. It roared awake, but too late, had to be too late. But still—

He struggled with coat buttons, clawing them off, shrugging himself free in the blind, spinning dark. Boots, they weighed tons, he got rid of them.

What else? What held him back? The armor. The fasteners were unfamiliar. Never mind, tear them off. Tough stuff, doesn't want to come loose.

There, one of them snapped, another . . .

So dark, so heavy, too much pain, but he was growing strangely numb. Overload on the nerve endings, the boiling acid he drifted in was quickly destroying them, eating them away one layer at a time.

Ripped another fastening, fingers numbed, desperate, twist out of it, *ohgodthathurtsnopleasemakeitstop.*

Too tired to move. Even his beast slowed and succumbed, not knowing up from down.

Relax, relax and float up . . . but he couldn't, the pain was worse than fire. The awful, deadly water filled his lungs, burning. It hurt, but brought oblivion after the first shock. That was best, go back to what came before, back to when he breathed water in the womb . . .

Dim perception of light. No, it wouldn't be here, not in this safe place. This was the one haven where darkness was good and light meant the assumption of troubles. Light was life, and he didn't want that anymore. *Gobackgobackgoback.*

His arms thrashed, feebly. Sudden sting of cold air on his face. *No, not ready for this. Leave me here in the sweet dark.*

But his muscles contracted, and he gave a violent cough, spewing fluids. He coughed and choked and tried to breathe, tried to keep his head above water . . . water?

What's happened? Where was he . . . ?

He glimpsed high rocky bluffs coated with snow looming around him, speeding by. A swift, freezing stream tossed him this way and that, carrying him helplessly along. The air he gasped was made thick by intense cold, and there's death . . . hovering close, just above the surface, over there. Trying to hold it in sight, he reached out, but it backed shyly away. He wanted to die; Sabra was waiting for him on that Side. He had to get to her.

He'd done this before, swimming in blackness, in a watery hell, the burning cold on his flesh, but for a good reason: to keep the Grail from that bastard. Fight and swallow water and spit it out and keep going because Sharon was at the other end of the stream, only he'd not known that, but he hadn't dared stop.

Sharon, taken by blackness herself. Was she lost in an Otherside hell or dead? He'd failed her; he should have tried to help in that vision. She'd helped him, hauled him from the well, loved him, left him, but called to him at the end, and he'd done *nothing.*

Too late now. The Goddess would forgive. She would know this had been too much. He'd reached his limit. She would look after Sharon. Have to . . . have to . . . keep . . . going . . . get to . . . death, touch death . . .

He heard Sabra singing—encouragement to him—but she was yet far in the distance. He *had* to reach her and made a frenzied effort to swim toward her clear voice. She was the siren who would bring him release from the pain, not continuance. His legs dragged, no feeling in them, couldn't move them, might be just as well, might be a good sign, death creeping up slow and easy so as not to frighten him. No need, he *wanted* it.

Come on, dammit. Take me!

His body fetched up hard against ice-coated rocks, and he seized them, with his last strength pulling out of the deadly current to get to her. She was just that way, just a little more. *Good, good, but how the wind bites.* He would freeze to death here. An easy enough way to go. Just fall asleep. He knew how to do that.

But he was hungry. Too hungry to sleep. Of all the rotten times for his Beast to make demands.

Slowly a bit of unpleasant, unwanted life came back to him. He was desperately hungry, but too weak to hunt. If he rested, just for a minute . . . the icy water lapped at him.

It was the black of deep night, the sky still clouded, yet perversely the stars and moon were out, dancing like fairy lights under its canopy. They wafted close and swerved away, shifting erratically. He thought one of the lights might be Sabra, coming closer, closer. He wanted to properly greet her, but was not ready yet. Too injured to move, too weak to rise, too anchored to this broken vessel of flesh to soar free. He was still trapped in a harsh world of pain; until he could let that go, she'd always be beyond his reach.

"He's here!" a man bellowed, intruding on his death. Shining dazzling light into his eyes.

More shouting. Interlopers flooded into his dream of easy release. What were they on about? They must leave him alone so he could . . .

Not Sabra, but Bourland came into blurred view, his face pinched-white and incredulous.

"My God, get a medic down here! He's still alive!"

Chapter Twelve

Dreamtime.

He was aware of others moving around him, but they were like phantoms. They called his name but it held no meaning for him. The only reality was cold agony. They were so careful with him, but their least touch only made it worse.

An airlift out, strapped to a board swinging suspended under a 'copter, flurries of activity when he was returned to earth. Roadside triage. People and more people. Phantoms.

Needles, tubes, a blessed rush of sustenance into his starved veins. Not his preferred method of feeding, nor his food, but the liquid would do to stave off the hunger. Drugs, a special blanket. He began to warm. What a lovely, comforting thing that warmth was . . .

Richard awoke slowly, at night; he felt that much of the world outside. Day had a specific kind of pressure, easily ignored with practice. For a moment he thought he was on watch in Sabra's intensive care room and had just dozed off, for he heard an identical beep of monitors nearby. But that couldn't be right, she was . . .

He groaned a little, eyelids fluttering, finally staying cracked open enough for him to look around. Hospital room, yes, only now he was the patient. He wasn't quite up to moving anything else yet. Much better to lie very still.

Bourland, seated next to the bed, leaned into view.

"Well, now, Richard. Are you going to stay with us after all?" he gently asked.

"Where is she?"

"Who?"

"Sabra. I heard her singing."

Bourland looked at a loss for a moment. "She's . . . she's not here, Richard."

Oh. Of course. Dream. Muddled delirium. Desperation. Desire. Not to be. Not yet. "She's gone."

"Yes, she is." He swallowed. "Do you remember what happened to you?"

A normal human would have quite sensibly blotted out the whole horror. "Yes. The bridge. Bomb. Fall." God, he was tired, but apparently he'd slept enough and his body insisted on waking up more and more. "St. Mike's?"

"This is a different place. More secure."

No doubt. Bourland would be paranoid about preserving security after what had happened to Sabra. Not his fault. No one's fault but Charon's. Got to kill that animal . . . "Charon? Did we—?"

"We're looking for him. Don't worry, he left a trail a mile wide."

A false one. Richard knew they'd never find him. Not now.

It was all for nothing.

"Richard, that fall you took . . ."

Here it comes. He really didn't want it. "How bad off am I?"

Bourland visibly considered the question. "They wouldn't tell me everything. Probably thought I'd not be able to handle it, but I know how to read a chart, and I've overheard things."

It was quite an impressive list. Both legs shattered to pulp, ribs, arms, his back, skull fractures, nerve and soft tissue damage . . . if anything could be broken it was broken.

"They said you're stabilized, but you should be dead. No one could have survived such a fall. But you're healing, at an amazing speed. That's what's flummoxed everyone. And me."

Them? Oh. Doctors. A nice army of them and likely to bring in reinforcements to have a look at the curiosity for themselves. This was too much to deal with, and they wouldn't leave him alone, ever.

"The insides of your arm should be pocked from the shots and from when they drew blood. I sat here and *watched* the holes vanish. Why is that?" Bourland's voice dropped to a whisper.

This was bad. Richard always feared someone in this modern age would discover his edge and put him under a microscope, but after all he'd been through, still sick with grief for Sabra, he just could not bring himself to give a damn.

He shut his eyes, hoping Bourland would take it for sleep. There was a shifting, a creak, soft footsteps, a door opened, shut. Silence. The only heart beating in the room was his own.

Sweet Goddess, why did you spare me?

He'd been so close.

Richard napped lightly, never quite going fully out, his mind drifting, but not to anything important or traumatic. He wouldn't allow it. Battered inside and out, he needed the downtime. He tried moving once, a finger, then a toe, but nothing happened. Best to give it a while.

He thought a doctor came several times to check on him. He was fairly sure of hearing low voices discussing him. Some people were very astonished. They asked him if he could feel this or that. Ignorable.

They were feeding who knows what directly to his veins to judge by the plastic bags just within view. It tamed his hunger for the time being. Good. Now if it would just take away the dizziness. That twist before he'd hit the . . . no. No memories allowed, remember? He shut down again to drift some more.

When next he bothered to surface he noticed the camera up in one corner of the ceiling. He was familiar with the type of installation. It wasn't a retro-fit, but part of the planned construction, meaning this room had been originally designed with the intent to observe whoever was in it. Assume there were listening devices as well.

Was this place to do with the Boris and Natasha couple? If so, then this could prove very bad indeed. Bourland's influence with that group might be insufficient protection to keep off the vivisectionists.

Why do I even care?

Because he still had to go after Charon. He'd murdered Sabra, stolen something precious and holy, and the bastard had to be stopped. Richard had no idea what else, if anything, was afoot, but it wouldn't be anything good.

Bourland returned. Perhaps he'd been in a booth or type of nurse's station with monitors to show when the special patient was awake for longer than a minute. There seemed little point pretending to drop off again. Richard had questions.

So did Bourland. "How are you?"

"Read the charts." He was sure he was hooked to a number of sophisticated data-collecting devices.

"You know what I mean. Are you up to talking?"

"If it's short. Isn't a doctor supposed to nag you about keeping visits brief?"

"He's outside looking after things, and I know when it's time to leave. Has to do with the way your eyes suddenly roll up into your skull. Are you in much pain?

"Like a migraine all over."

"They have an automatic dosage thing set up . . . the button's in your hand." He pointed. "Want me to press for you?"

Richard thought the offer might also be a test. Could he move his fingers or not? He didn't want to know just yet and hedged. "Where's Michael?"

"In a safe place close by. Well guarded."

"Any more phasing out, visions?"

"No, thank God. He's been normal, but quiet. Because of Sabra. He's still . . ." But he did not finish.

"I know. We all are." Richard understood Bourland's pain and grief down to his core and beyond. "I'll find Charon. I swear it."

Bourland was good. He managed to conceal his pity. So far as he knew Richard was going to be confined to hospital beds, dependant on machines and gentle, helping hands for the rest of his life.

"How long have I been out?"

"A day."

"That long?"

Incredulous stare time. "Listen, my lad, we didn't think you were going to wake at all the way you were knocked about. I am still dealing with the impossible: that you survived. How is it that—"

"Tell me what's happened. Please."

He got a headline report of the bridge aftermath. News of it had gone around the world a few dozen times since Richard's fall and was likely to stay the top story before the insatiable TV cameras until the next disaster shifted the media's short attention span elsewhere.

"The official account is that it was a freak motor accident involving the gas tank, but there's a large number of outsiders supporting the failed terrorist bombing and cover-up theory. Every law enforcement agency you can think of is all over this one, but I've had a talk with the people who matter, and they'll see that certain aspects of it are buried. They're nettled we weren't up front from the start about Charon."

"The Americans?"

"Of course. I rather like them, but they do love to be the star players in every game."

"Let them. They've a vested interest in the bridge, and they've a right to look after themselves. In this case it won't be a problem because the ones in charge know where to rein in their people."

"As long as no terrorist group decides to take credit for it. I'd hate to be responsible for the repercussions from that."

"So what if they do and get slapped down? Fewer bad guys in the world."

"Well, you've every right to be bloody-minded after—"

"And you need to read more Winston Churchill."

"I have, and things are considerably more complicated than when—"

"No they're not."

"Now, just a damned—" Bourland caught himself, gaped, and shook his head. "You son of a bitch. Lying on what should be your deathbed, yet throwing out smoke and mirror distractions."

Richard couldn't laugh, but his lips twitched. "Guilty, m'lud."

He shut down again.

It seemed only a few moments. When he woke, his head was more clear, but so was the pain. His extremities ceased to be so wonderfully numb. Pins and needles darted through the layers of his bodywide migraine, white hot. Bourland was in view, sitting in a chair, just as he'd done for Sabra.

"Philip."

He was up and there in an instant.

"Press that button for me, would you?"

"You're feeling things, hm?"

"God, yes. Please."

Bourland did so, and in a few moments the torture eased back to its bad, but still tolerable levels.

"What's happening out there? How long's it been?"

"Still the same. You slept for an hour. Sleep some more."

"Soon. Get my mind off this. Talk to me."

"They're still looking for him. That group guarding Michael thinks they found where Charon staged his operation. Unoccupied hotel room, telescope, electronic equipment modified. Still had the Eaton Centre sales receipts. Left a mess."

"That's our boy." Though personally neat, Charon was not one to keep a tidy environment around him.

"Specialists are going through it. They think he set the bomb off using a cell phone as a long distance trigger. C-4, they're estimating how much."

"The driver?"

"Dead."

"I tried to tell him . . ."

"Not your fault. Charon's. The man was dead the moment Charon picked him as his mule. His name's not been released yet. Nor yours."

"Good."

"Not released as in we let on to the media you were killed."

"Good. "

"I must say you're taking it well. Being dead."

I've had practice.

He continued. "Seemed the best way to give Charon what he wanted."

The door opened and a white-coated doctor came in, smiling. He was a very dignified, kindly type, bald with a carefully tended white beard. "Hello, Richard. We've been looking after you. So far you've been our most remarkable patient."

No doubt.

The doctor examined, made notations, shone a light in Richard's eyes, and asked banal things like his street address and what year he'd been born. Richard cooperated, thinking that would get rid of him faster.

"I've some questions if you're up to them . . ."

But he would get no answers. Richard fixed him with a look. "Later, please. Philip and I must talk."

The doctor, still wearing his kindly smile, went on his way, no arguments.

Bourland saw. "What the devil is it you *do* to people?"

"He knows I'm on the thin edge. Whatever he wants can wait."

"But you just—"

Another man poked his head in, very tall, with piercing blue eyes, frowning. "Everything all right?"

Bourland twitched annoyance at the further interruption. "We're fine, Frank, but could you keep your people out for the time being? He's not up to being put under a microscope just yet."

Oh, my prophetic soul, Richard thought.

Frank nodded, gave Richard an intent stare, then withdrew, snicking the door shut. It had a substantial lock on it. On the outside.

"This isn't a regular hospital, is it?" Richard asked.

"It's more of a research lab. Private funding, but we keep our eye on them when necessary. They're another branch to do with that paranormal crew I brought in."

"Not the sunglasses-in-the-rain crowd?"

"Heavens, no. That lot's specialty is deconstruction, not repair."

What a relief. Sort of. This bunch could prove just as harmful, like a curious baby elephant, and as hard to divert.

"They're very interested in you, my friend. Tell me why."

Richard would have shaken his head, but realized with a shock it was held immobile in some spiderlike contraption that harkened back to the days of the Inquisition. This thing was stainless steel, shiny and efficient. And bloody uncomfortable. He shut his eyes.

"I rather thought that'd be your answer," said Bourland. "Whatever it is has them stirred up, but they won't bother you. Frank will see to that."

"Good for Frank." Whoever the hell he was. Bureaucrat, perhaps. He had the look of a long-term player. Nice suit. "Charon? Progress?"

"We're assuming he's slipped out of the country, but so far no clue by what means—air, train, bus, car, on foot, or hang glider— they're checking every possibility. It might help if we had a clue as to his destination."

This wasn't what Richard wanted to hear, but there was little he could do about it. Charon must have been up to something big . . . and it could involve another holy site, but where . . . oh, God. "Glastonbury," he whispered.

"What?"

"Have people on watch in Glastonbury. In the U.K. Armed."

Bourland gave him a narrow look, then pulled out his cell, hitting a quick-dial number. He relayed the information. "No, I can't tell you why, just see it through. Standing orders on Charon are still in effect."

"What are those?" Richard asked.

He closed the phone. "To kill him. I think we're both agreed he's a cancer in the gene pool, and the sunglasses crowd has no problem with removing him. They got a bloody nose the other day by failing to get him. Why Glastonbury?"

"A hunch. That's all I can say. Really. It just came to me. How's Michael?"

"He's fine so far as it goes. He knows you were hurt and about the cover story of your death. He wants to see you, but I thought later would be better. When you're awake for longer than a few minutes at a stretch."

And also to prepare the boy for the shock. It would be wholly frightening for him to see another of the adults he loved and relied on flat on the back held immobile by such scary, painful-looking bracing. Hell, Richard was having trouble coping with it himself.

A soft double-knock on the door as it opened. Frank pushed in, shot a brief, cool, apologetic glance to Richard. "Philip, that report you wanted from Chichén Itzá—we've the hard copy now."

"Right. Thank you."

"Report on what?" Richard asked.

Bourland hesitated. "How awake are you?"

"Enough. If it's short."

"It is," said Frank. "I can paraphrase."

"Please."

He read from a folder in one hand. "Our team in place has been interviewing people, one of them a very respected local healer and spiritual leader. He said through a translator that their god had been taken from them by a man who—this is what he said exactly—'caused the great snake to be swallowed up by the darkness. The man then fought with and murdered our village elder, a holy one. The man is very dangerous. He's eating the light to keep himself alive.'"

"'Eating the light'? What the hell does that mean?" asked Bourland.

"Perhaps it's a translation problem," Frank suggested. "I'll get a follow-up. But the team earlier reported that an old native man did collapse and die in the local air terminal a few days ago. The cause seems to have been a brain hemorrhage. The medicals are still trying to get a final determination."

Richard and Bourland exchanged looks. Brain hemorrhage, hell.

Frank continued skimming the report. "There's going to be another ceremony to try to bring their god back; they'll be staging it a few days from now. They're delaying until there's a larger crowd. The team says more and more people are coming out of the forest, converging on Chichén Itzá."

The report again made sense to Richard and Bourland. All those other lights that had been in Michael's vision . . .

"Stonehenge," said Richard.

"What about it?" asked Frank.

"Anything similar happening there?"

Frank apparently wasn't the sort to share information, even when cross-connections were going on. "Oddly enough, yes. We've a team in place watching things. There's a troop of New Age types gathering. They're going to hold what they call a 'healing ceremony.' Hundreds have shown up already. Not the usual publicity seekers, either. Ordinary types. The local media is on them, but they're not getting much. No one's in a mood to talk, even to our people."

"Timing?"

"What do you mean?"

"Find out when each ceremony is to take place. I'll wager that though both are an ocean apart geographically, they will take place at the exact same time."

Frank's eyes didn't give anything away, but did flicker once. "Well-well. Wouldn't that be an interesting coincidence?"

"You think? Especially if the organizers on each side are unaware of the other group's plans."

"I'll look into it." He left.

"What do you know?" Bourland demanded.

Richard sagged, or would have if he'd not been immobilized. "Damn little. It just seemed a logical thing to check. I've heard of this outfit. More often than not their investigations have no satisfying conclusion."

"So does life in general, and you're trying to distract me again. Do these ceremonies have to do with Charon?"

"He left another mess; they're only trying to clean it up."

"And Glastonbury?"

"A mess about to happen, I think. You could see about notifying the Stonehenge gathering that something might happen there next . . . maybe not. Don't want to put civilians in the line of fire."

"What's there to draw him?"

Richard tried the shake his head again, forgetting the bracing. He felt a sharp heat prickling along the nerves in his neck and spine. Not pleasant, though it meant progress. "It's an ancient holy site, like Henge and the other."

"He's eating light to keep alive? Is that symbolism or an actuality? Could he be ill?"

"That . . . I find very interesting. I've heard of people drawing on place energies to heal themselves."

"Tree-hugging?"

"Don't knock it until you've tried it."

Bourland opened his mouth to reply, then seemed to think better of it. "I just might. Is that your secret?"

"Yes. You've found me out. Bring an oak in here and I will give it a manly embrace . . . oh . . . oh, God . . ."

"What?"

"Hurts." Too much too soon, now he had to pay for it. His nerves were waking up all over, all at once, screaming. It took his breath away.

His friend pressed the dosage button again, waiting. "It's a timed thing so you don't overmedicate yourself. Damn, nothing's happ—there, it's coming through now. You'll be all right."

Balm for his nerves as the inflowing meds adjusted his brain chemistry and prevented horrific messages of pain from being delivered. But he wanted recovery, full restoration. Only one thing could give him that.

"You may need a higher dose than an average man. I'll fetch the doctor."

Richard was asleep by the time the door closed . . .

And alone the next time he woke.

Except for his Beast, who was hungry now. Richard's throat hurt from the thirst. That's what dragged him from his oblivion. Need.

It was yet night, but very late. A dim, windowless room, no clock in view, but he could tell. Whether it was the same night or the next he did not know.

He could move his fingers, could discern by touch again. There was some object in his right hand, probably that dosage thing. No need for it, he thought, experimentally flexing his limbs. Some residual ache and stiffness, like an all-over bruise, but the worst of the healing process must be over, thank heaven.

So far as he could tell, not being able to move his head, they'd opted for some kind of shaped plastic forms and bandaging instead of plaster casts to encase his shattered limbs. Plaster was better protection, but only for a man expected to get up from his sick-bed. It was better at sparing the broken bones from knocks. So far as they knew Richard was quadriplegic and like to remain that way. This lighter stuff was more comfortable for him and easier for them to conduct routine maintenance and cleaning.

We'll see about that.

"Doctor? Anyone there?" Someone must be listening.

Sure enough. The white-bearded doctor came in, light from the hall falling over Richard's sheeted form. The doctor's eyes were puffy and red. Must have been pulling a long shift because of his special patient. He turned the room lighting up.

"Yes, Richard, what is it? More pain?"

None today, thank you.

"It's silly," said Richard. "But my damned nose itches. It's driving me mad."

The man smiled and came in close to help. There was more than sufficient light. Richard had him frozen in mid-reach.

"Who else is watching this room through the camera?" Richard whispered, hoping the microphone would not pick up.

"I'm the only one for now," the doctor readily answered in a normal voice.

Very good. "I want you to shut it off, stop all further recording, then come back here with some clothes for me."

"Clothes?"

Richard knew he'd better be specific or his hypnotized ally might leave in search of a tailor shop. "Have you any spare scrubs? Extra large?"

The doctor returned some moments later with an armful of clean, pastel blue cottons: a loose V-necked top, drawstring pants, and what looked like thick paper shower caps, which turned out to be shoe protectors.

"Right," said Richard. "Camera off? Good. Now get me out of this."

"You're still hurt."

"I'm fine, you must help me. Quickly please." He nudged things a bit to encourage cooperation and asked to be freed of the head brace first. "Who else is here?"

"The director, Mr. Bourland, security people downstairs, a few techs."

"Anyone likely to walk in here soon?"

"They're busy. Your friend's asleep in one of the other patient rooms. He was all in."

"What about your director?"

"Feet up in his office on the other side of the building."

"Fine, if you see any of them, head them off, all right?"

"All right."

With the doctor's expert help Richard was gradually released from his high-tech bindings. The most unexpected—and unpleasant— surprise turned out to be a catheter. *Ye gods.* That thing made a slop bucket much more appealing than he'd ever thought possible. Scowling and wincing and moving *most* gingerly under the doctor's guidance, he removed that horror with a minimum of discomfort. He let the doctor take out the drip needle catheter they'd planted in his shoulder. Somehow finding the first one made the other almost tolerable.

He was able to stand, able to walk, but still weak and desperately hungry. The drugs they'd pumped into him had dulled his appetite as well as the pain, and it was roaring fully awake. "Does this place keep any whole blood on hand?" Upon getting an affirmative, he sent the man on another errand. Richard made his unsteady way to the room's small bath and ran a very hot shower to massage circulation back to his newly mended limbs. This kind of running water was much more preferable to the river. He wanted to shave, but found no razors handy.

"Richard?"

He almost jumped, mistaking the voice for Bourland, but it was the doctor back with another delivery. Two pints of group O-positive. He watched impassively as Richard drank them straight down, one after the other.

"You're not to remember any of this," he said, after his last shuddering reaction passed and his Beast went back to sleep.

"Of course not."

Would that everyone he met was this agreeable. Richard dried off, pulled on the make-shift clothes. "Are all the records you have on me in one place?"

"The hard copies, yes. The computer records are in the database, the biological samples are in the lab, the videotapes are—"

"Fine. I want you to destroy or erase all of them, *every* scrap that has to do with me. Do you know how to delete computer files down to the hard-drive level? Delete my records, however many backups, then go into the delete program and lose those, too. You have to be thorough, as though I'd never been here. It's important, very important you do this. Everyone's safety depends upon you thinking of everything."

That impressed itself as nothing else could, for protecting others would better overcome any subconscious blocks the scientist in him would have against destroying data. He sent the man off, confident that he would be thorough.

Now Richard had to get out of here. He'd find Bourland, persuade him to drive them away and leave this lot with another mystifying event to go unsolved while he disappeared himself.

He saw to the med charts in his room, tearing the records small and flushing them away, then emerged into the hall for the first time. It stretched long both ways equally, modern, clean, and too easy to get lost. He should have had the doctor draw a map, but he'd no idea the place would turn out to be quite this big. Privately funded projects usually tended to be smaller in scale.

Richard went right, passing doors with identifying signs like 'XENOPATHOLOGY' and 'CRYPTOZOOLOGICAL LAB'. He didn't think the latter had to do with canine retrievers. Maybe it did, only here the animal might have three heads and radar-dish ears.

Distraction. He was good at that, at throwing it out, even for himself. He felt cold again and shaky despite the blood. It was still doing its job of healing, but wasn't enough. He wanted—needed— more than mere food.

He paused to listen. Close by, someone moving about. That door, light showing under it. Someone pulling an all-nighter? It seemed too late for any janitorial staff to be working.

Knocking politely, he pushed the door open a crack. "Hallo?"

A stunner of a young woman, petite in her lab smock, and evidently startled. She relaxed a trifle at the sight of his blue scrubs, since they indicated he might have a valid reason to be wandering the halls. "Can I help you?"

He put on a confused face, looking around to see if she had company and only poked in with his head and shoulders, keeping his bare feet out of sight. "Oh, yes, please, I hope so. I was looking for the director, and I am hopelessly lost. The doctor with the white beard said he was in his office?"

The references reassured her. "Administration's in the other wing. You've got a walk. Go back down until you reach the elevator hub and turn left. There's a map up. His office is on the ground floor. Just follow the coffee smell. I think he lives on it."

The wide room had several computer stations, tables with acid-proof tops, gas connections, and apparently a number of works in progress at the various stations. No one else. "You must too, I think." He smiled and nodded at a machine with a steaming carafe on one of the tables. Pleasant odor, that stuff.

She responded with her own smile. "Have to when it gets busy."

"You've a project on?"

"Several. Yourself?" She seemed glad to have company.

"I'm working on that basket case they brought in the other night. The fellow who was so banged up."

"Yes, I helped on some of his blood samples. Strange stuff."

"Really? Anything I could have a peek at?"

"Oh, everything's been and gone. I put the data in and went back to my other work. Interesting protein markers, possibly unique. I've never seen anything like them before, even in this place." She seemed disarmed enough for him to venture in. When possible, he preferred to avoid frightening his ladies. No fear here, she stared at his feet. "Have an accident?"

He made a deprecating gesture. "You must be a mind reader."

"They're in the basement. What happened to your shoes?"

"That's what I need to talk to the director about."

"Where's your ID badge?"

He picked up the tiniest change in her voice, a tightening that would turn to alarm given the time, but he was close enough to gaze into her smoky brown eyes and make everything so much better for her.

"Will you please show me the data you entered about the strange blood?"

She obliged, walking to a station, going into the computer, and calling up the most recent file. The computer emitted a flat-toned beep and told them the file was not available. That was a relief. Apparently his good friend the doctor had gotten there first by another machine, efficiently deleting things.

Richard had some deleting himself to accomplish and instructed her to forget everything about the odd blood samples and their unique protein markers, whatever those were.

Then he suddenly felt tired. There was a stool next to the computer. He slipped onto it. His legs were whole again, yes, but subject to wobble. He smiled at the woman, holding his hand out, extending his will toward her as well. "Over here. Please."

He could have simply ordered her, and she'd have been just as happily obedient. Her mind was under his control, and she was mostly unaware of things, but there was no need to be uncivilized about it. She could have a trace memory of an agreeable dream or an ugly nightmare. He'd had too many of the latter himself to inflict more upon his partners.

With a soft word, a guiding gesture, he drew her close so her back was to him and pulled the shoulder of her coat partway off. A nice, easy, button-down blouse was under it. She undid the buttons herself and leaned back against him, very close, very comfortable, as though they were long-time lovers. Between the height of the stool and her own diminutive size, they were on a perfect level with each other. She stood between his knees and he wrapped his arms bearlike around her, his face buried in the crook of her shoulder, and gratefully breathed in her scent.

Beneath the powders and fragrances and artificialities of modern hygiene he found it, that basic wonderful difference that made her female, that made her and her many sisters so desirable to him. It was with substantial relief that he felt himself stir and grow hard. No such invasion of her on that level would take place, he'd not been invited, but he was glad enough to satisfy his need in another manner.

He gently tilted her head to the left, making taut her skin under his lips. He ran his tongue over the spot where the heat was greatest, delighting in the foretaste and her reaction to it. Were things different he might have lingered there long to see just what she liked, but didn't dare. Though one advantage to hunting in such a warren of identical halls and doors was being able to achieve— for a few necessary moments—a degree of privacy, he couldn't push it. Someone might take it into their heads to look in his room and send up the alarm.

But this was so nice, holding her, soaking in warmth and touch and comfort. He needed that contact as much as the blood.

He picked up the change in her, the scent of arousal. Oh, good for her. He nuzzled deep into her neck and bit down on the stretched skin, knowing it would now cause her pleasure, not pain. The same happened for him when her blood flowed into his mouth. Much, much better to take it fresh from a living vein, to taste her climax in it, to hear her long sighs as he held her, her body trembling against his.

She shivered, her breath coming faster, more rough, growing more vocal. It took some of them that way. He soothed her down, continuing to drink. Couldn't have a row.

Let's have a lovely, drawn out peak, intense and quiet . . . that's my sweet, beautiful darling . . .

The last healing suffused heat through him. He felt complete, made whole again, full strength returned, and it was as much from the purely animal contact as from her blood, a psychic as well as a physical connection.

He ceased to take from her, kissed her skin clean, and that should have been it, but he continued to hold on, not wanting to relinquish the solace she unknowingly brought him. She was tiny, like Sabra, and though much else was quite different, there was enough similarity for him to hang on just a little longer, rocking gently back and forth. He'd never had the chance to hold Sabra, to say good-bye. She'd once taught him how important good-byes were . . .

Richard felt a sting in his eyes, and thought that now, finally, he would break down and weep for her. He choked twice, but nothing more happened. Forcing it was no good. There was *nothing* inside. What was wrong with him? The one woman he loved beyond measure and he couldn't shed a tear for her?

After a moment he pulled himself together and kissed his innocent surrogate on her temple. "Thank you. You're not to remember any of this, but thank you all the same."

"All right," she lightly agreed and moved clear, adjusting her clothes back to the way they were. She glanced at him, smiling, then went on to whatever she'd been doing before his arrival.

He took in a cleansing breath, straightening up, and with his eyes still flushed bloodred found himself looking right at his friend Bourland, who'd seen everything he shouldn't.

Chapter Thirteen

A black moment for them both.

Bourland shrank from the doorway where he'd apparently been standing quiet for some time. His expression . . . shattered.

"Philip—"

He turned and kept going. Richard rushed after, his heart in his throat.

Bourland did not run, but walked very quickly, coming to an abrupt stop outside the open door of Richard's empty room. When he turned again . . . there was a Walther in his hand; he smoothly racked the slide to chamber a round, but did not bring it up to shoot. Instead he let his arm hang straight down, the pistol pointed at the floor. But he had a finger on the trigger.

They regarded each other for a long, long time. Richard heard his friend's heartbeat loud in the silence between them. It hammered swiftly and hard for a time, then gradually slowed, but not by much.

Richard finally worked up to say something to break the unnerving stretch, but Bourland beat him to it.

"So . . . now I know," he whispered.

"Yes. You do."

"That story about porphyria you handed me back when we met . . ."

"A necessary cover." Richard's standard one to explain his aversion to daylight and other quirks.

"I can understand why. Is this also why you've not changed in all this time? You still look to be in your thirties, and how long have I known you? Fifteen years. Until now I never noticed . . ."

Richard gestured toward the room. "Let's go in, sit down."

"No, they've a camera there. They monitor everything in this place."

That was good, that Bourland was mindful of such things. But was it to preserve Richard's secret or to leave no record of a shooting? "I shut it off. It's safe enough."

Neither man moved.

"Are you going to use that?" Richard indicated the Walther. It was a P-99 with a full sixteen-round magazine, and Bourland would know well how to use it.

He seemed to realize it was in his hand. He puffed a laugh at it. "My God, after what you've been through, what you've survived, this would hardly make a dent, would it?"

Richard was pleased to hear that line of reasoning. "Let's not find out, if you don't mind."

Bourland put the safety on and slipped the pistol into the shoulder holster under his arm. "I came back to see if you might be awake. My cell phone woke me. There's another brain hemorrhage case, this one on a plane that just landed in Heathrow. Charon must have been on it. They were still screening off-loaded passengers. I came back here and saw the impossible: you on your feet and walking down the hall. I couldn't believe it. Then you went in that lab, the young woman, what you *did* to her . . ."

"She's unharmed."

"You drank her blood," he stated. He was frightened and angry and disgusted.

"She's unharmed, Philip. Doesn't remember a thing."

"To hell with that, you *drank* her *blood*!"

"I had to," he said softly. "And she *is* unharmed. I swear that on Michael's life."

This put him off a little, but he was clearly still unnerved. "Sabra—she knew about you?"

"Yes. Everything."

"Does Michael?"

What? "Why should he?"

"That's no answer."

"The truth is I'm not sure. Michael knows many things beyond his years. He just . . . knows, like how he got my real name out of thin air. If my . . . my condition is part of that knowledge, then he's never seen fit to mention it, nor did I ever raise the topic with him. I doubt Sabra did, either."

Apparently Bourland was doing some fast thinking, but this bombshell was a lot for him to process. "You and Stephanie."

Richard bowed his head at her name. So much pain there. His lover. Michael's mother. A second daughter to Bourland. "I *loved* her, Philip. Loved and lost."

"Is this why you never married her?"

Not what he expected. He'd thought Bourland would go on about the blood-drinking, demand to know if she'd been touched in that way, had been harmed by it, revolted. But this . . . ?

"She wanted children. I'm . . . not fertile."

"You think that would have mattered to her?"

More surprise. "I was certain I could never give her the life she wanted. It seemed better for her to move on."

"Yet for all that you are, she might be alive today if you'd—"

"Please, Philip, don't go down that road. I've been there a thousand times, and there's no answer, only pain. What we have, the things that happen that are out of our control, for good or ill, is what *is*, not what might have been. That's what we all live with, and we either accept it or not. We deal with it or let it crush us. What do you think *she* would say to you?"

That hit home. Harder than Richard had ever intended. Bourland's body jerked as though he had been struck, and his eyelids blinked rapidly, but he mastered himself, lifting his chin. "You can make me forget the last few minutes, can't you? I've seen you work whatever it is on others. Certainly with that woman back there."

"I could. But I'd rather not."

"Why? It's safer for you. God knows it'd be easier on me."

He shrugged, discomfited. "I think this was meant to happen. That you were supposed to find out."

"Why only now? You've had years to decide whether or not I could be trusted."

"This isn't about trusting. I said nothing because it was always for the best. But Sabra taught me that things happen for a reason. I'm thinking that now *is* the time you need to hear everything."

"Why?"

I've lost so much, please, don't let me lose you, too. "Because you're my only friend . . . and we both loved her."

Bourland caught his breath, his face twisting as he fought his emotions. His eyes glittered a moment with unshed tears. He looked away a moment, then back, his shoulders slumping. "Look, there's a break room up the hall. Perhaps . . . perhaps I can deal better with this with some coffee in me."

They talked into the early hours. Even when Richard touched only on the barest essentials it took a very long while. The story of one's days is never a quick or easy tale to impart, even for a man with an ordinary span of years.

He told of his life as the Champion d'Orleans, of Sabra saving him from death by handing him defeat, and how she'd delivered death to him after all, and with it, a dark rebirth, the Goddess's Gift.

"Sabra was like you?" Incredulity now.

"Older than me. I never knew how much older, but sometimes she talked about the Romans in Britain. Not kindly."

"My God. No wonder she laughed at me."

"About what?"

"Never mind. Go on. She became human again. How?"

At first Bourland sputtered with questions, but they ceased, and he listened. He managed one cup of coffee, then stared at the table as he heard the truth about the Grail. Richard was finally able to give him the backstory of what was really going on with Charon. In this bright and sterile place, rife with the most sophisticated scientific gadgetry outside of NASA, Bourland was able to hear and accept legend, superstition, and the mystical without demur.

"Of course I may wake in a few hours and with great relief know it was all just a dream," he pointed out.

"You won't."

"I suppose not. It certainly explains why Charon kept calling you 'Lance.' I thought it might have been one of your cover names from whatever you did before you came to Toronto. The sunglasses crowd are still looking into it."

"Do they know the d'Orleans name?"

"No."

"Then nothing will come of it."

"I'll see to that."

"Thanks."

And just then she walked in. The woman Richard had fed from. She moved slowly, her eyes dull.

Bourland froze.

She didn't notice, continuing on toward a wall of cupboards above a sink.

"Excuse me," he said.

She paused to glance at Bourland. "Hm?"

"Are you all right?" He got up to look at her.

That action earned him an odd look in return, then she snorted. "Only asleep on my feet. I'm out of my gourmet blend, now I get to try the company-bought battery acid." She pulled a red plastic packet of pre-measured commercial coffee from the cupboard, then went to a coin-operated dispensing machine. After consideration, she picked a candy bar. "You guys up late or in early?"

"Up late."

"My sympathy. All-night rush jobs are the downside of salaried pay, I tell you. I've been getting one a week for the past month. I should form a union and go on strike."

On her way out, she glanced at them, staring puzzled at Richard's still bare feet, but making no comment.

Bourland was also silent. Then: "She *seems* all right. Didn't seem to recognize you at all."

"As I said."

"Indeed. No huge damage, just two small holes and a lot of beard-burn."

Richard suddenly felt himself coloring. "Philip, the new hemorrhage case . . . ?"

"God. I'd forgotten. That's all I know at the moment. This morning in London—their time—a trans-Atlantic flight landed with a dead man aboard, the investigation's ongoing, they'll let me know if and when."

"I doubt they'll be able to get Charon."

"Oh, come, he's not superhuman."

"Don't be too certain, and he has help. The Grail. And whatever powers he's learned to use since our last run-in."

"I thought the Grail was only meant for good."

"So's electricity." He let the inference sink in. "Intent and use are all."

"To think she had that thing sitting in her back room. I thought it was just some curiosity she'd found antiquing or something. Clueless, that's me."

"Safe. Come on."

"Where?"

"You're all in, as am I. Rest while you can. Tomorrow could be busy."

Bourland grunted, but allowed himself to be guided out. "Dear God. All this time. You." He shook his head, then fixed on Richard. "So . . . what was King Arthur really like?"

He gaped, but his friend was utterly serious. "Well, he sure as hell didn't look like Sean Connery."

Richard went back to his room. For the time being he had no other place to go, might as well sleep while he could.

If he could.

He lay in the dimness, waiting for the morning to bring fresh news, and humbly thanking the Goddess for Bourland's acceptance. It was good to have an ally on that level, one who knew everything.

Richard had few left with Sabra gone.

He touched on that raw and bleeding wound. He wanted to scream. Howling out one's grief was allowed, and he drew breath for it, but none came forth. Richard struggled again to let go, to

cry; he *wanted* to break down and let it out here in this impersonal space where it would be safe, but nothing happened. No tears.
He'd been ripped in two, the better part of him taken forever, and
still he could not weep.

If he could just hear Sabra's voice again in his mind as he
always had before and know she was all right wherever she might
be, then he wouldn't feel so empty and lost and afraid. But the
silence within was absolute and final. She was gone. All trace of
her had departed but for fragile memories. One small inadequate
tear did finally trickle from his right eye, past his temple to his pillow, but it had nothing to do with release so much as reflex from
staring at the ceiling.

Eventually sleep settled lightly on him, and with it came dreams.
He'd had none during his healing, now they poured through his
mind, one after the other. Only flashes, not solid as the visions, but
still vivid. He glimpsed the great snake god, coiled into a knot,
seeming to float in space. It noticed him, shifting. Within the vast
loops of its long body Richard thought he saw something . . .
someone . . . Sharon?

Just as he tried to get closer he was pulled away, flying toward
the sun. It didn't burn, though the brightness made him wince. A
green, flat land stretched below, very familiar. Its fields were criss-
crossed by glowing lines of power, many intersecting. Where there
was an intersection was a marker, either a man-built hill or a stone
circle. Strangely, some of the intersection points were darkened, as
though blasted by the heat of a fire, or as though a bomb had gone
off. The stones were shattered, their power gone.

He almost had the meaning . . .

Then he was wide awake. Someone was in his room, moving
stealthily close.

Frank the bureaucrat was at the side of the bed, his great eyes
startled, quite startled, to see the change in Richard. "What th—"

To spare both of them future bother, Richard had to move fast.
The door was shut, there wasn't enough light to hypnotize. He rolled
from the bed, caught Frank by his perfect suit coat and slammed
him against the near side wall. That knocked the wind from
him, but not the fight. He'd gotten training from someplace,

and Richard had to block two powerful moves that might have hurt had they landed. He struck three nerve points himself in speedy succession that paralyzed, but did not knock the man out, then reached to flip on the overhead light.

Puffing and face to face, Richard put him under quick. Damnation, why hadn't he knocked first? Richard could then have put on a light and taken care of this with much less exertion. Why was it when you were in a hospital situation people took it as their right to simply barge in on the sick?

"Why are you here?" he demanded.

Frank gazed calmly past him now, unseeing. "Looking for Philip. Something's wrong. Our computer files on you are gone. They've been tampered with."

"Oh. Not at all, *you* ordered it. You were under orders yourself to do it, and you and any others involved with my care will never speak of it or me again. Mr. Bourland and I are only special guests here for the time being, and in need of your full cooperation and resources. Isn't that right?"

"Of course."

"But before we leave, let's make sure all the little loose ends concerning me have been snipped . . ."

As the day waxed in Canada and waned in the United Kingdom no news came of finding Charon. By inference, the hemorrhage case on the trans-Atlantic flight meant that he was in the country. Via Bourland, Richard had people on that side checking airport arrivals video.

"*All* of them," he insisted. "And remember he may no longer be wearing an eye patch."

Copies were digitized and sent across so he could comb through them himself. He parked at a computer and worked with a graphics expert updating a composite of Charon's face, removing the facial scarring. Several versions were now on the same sheet, with and without the patch, scars, add a beard, leave it out, short and long hair, wig, hat, sunglasses. They used the distorted image captured from the curved mirror, cleaning it up even more, refining. It was all they had so far that could be considered a current picture.

But he felt it was wasted effort. If they'd not caught Charon at the airport, then he was elsewhere and well hidden. Richard was certain Charon had thrown up some kind of shielding to get himself past the thicket of security. Of course, he couldn't actually make himself invisible, but he could arrange to simply not be noticed. A subtle difference, but just as effective. It might have been such an effort that had buggered all the cameras in the other airports and at the hospital.

Also, Frank's people in the field did confirm Richard's guess about the timing of their ceremonies. The ones at Stonehenge were preparing for theirs to commence at moonrise. Since it would be a full moon, that would put it just at sunset. The people at Chichén Itzá would conduct their ceremony in the full light of day—but the same moment. Neither knowing about the other, they had arrived at the times independently.

Afternoon in Toronto passed with nothing else coming in from nightside Britain. Thankfully no further odd deaths were reported, though Charon was certainly capable of hiding a body if necessary.

When it was sufficiently dark, Bourland and Richard left in the back of an anonymous white van for a safe house Bourland had set up. By now Richard was in more substantial clothing than the borrowed scrubs, all of it new, since it would be a breach of security to go to his house to pick up anything of his own. The stuff fit, even the hiking boots. Some very meticulous people were looking after things.

The house was in one of the newer Toronto suburbs, and had an attached garage. The van went in, the garage door went down, and they got out, entering through the kitchen. Once inside, the door went up and the driver departed. Richard judged they would be safe enough with himself in shape to guard again.

He never got a look at the exterior of the place. The curtains and shades in every room were drawn, only to be expected, but it was comfortable. There were several bedrooms, kitted with two and three beds each, allowing not only for the people needing to drop from sight but space for those assigned to protect them. The furnishings were inoffensive and impersonal as a hotel suite but comfortable, and some very wise person had invested in a largescreen

TV with a satellite hookup in the fight against cabin fever. Current magazines were neatly lined up on tables, and in one corner was a shelf stacked with a surprisingly large collection of well-thumbed comic books. Escapism at its finest.

Michael was overjoyed to see Richard, though he wasn't his normal ebullient self. The safe house was strange territory and the abrupt changes left him very subdued. A retreat to the familiar for comfort was impossible. Bourland had done the best he could to bridge things, and an importation of books, movies, CDs, and video games served to keep the boy diverted.

Excused for the time being from school because of the family emergency Michael still had homework. He had no heart for it, though, and no one pressed him. Understandable.

Improbably, the two specialist bodyguards turned out to be excellent sitters. The cold man played vid games with the same deadly focus and speed as Michael, and the woman taught him how to partner-dance.

Richard raised an eyebrow at that one, curious as to how the subject had ever come up, but whatever filled the time and distracted. Apparently Michael knew his adored foster uncle was a good dancer, but was too shy to ask to go to an instructor to learn for himself. Being taught by a pretty woman with time on her hands was an ingenious compromise.

With Bourland and Richard's return, the bodyguards were no longer needed, their murderous talents fortunately unused and required elsewhere. Richard could not admit any regret at losing them, though Michael had developed quite a crush on the lovely blond woman and couldn't stop talking about her. Also understandable.

It was a bleak evening as Bourland and Michael ate microwaved frozen dinners in the kitchen while Richard sat at the table to share company. None of them were able to speak about Sabra. Now and then Richard was aware of Bourland looking at him, but he let it pass without comment or question. His friend was simply curious, and needing to get used to his new knowledge. Bourland would be matching the long and ancient background history up to the man he knew and trying to merge the two. Not easy. He must have still been bursting with questions, but those could wait.

Bourland had been in and out of the paranormal center through-out the day, seeing to other errands that could not be accomplished by phone or computer, and right after his meal dozed off on one of the living room couches.

"Shouldn't he go up to his room?" Michael whispered, troubled. He was sensitive to adults behaving out of character, and watched Bourland from the couch opposite.

Richard said no, and came over to sit next to him. "He'll get a better sleep there than he will in a bed. I don't know why, but sometimes that's how it works out for grown-ups. Just keep the TV volume steady and it'll be fine."

"He told me you were dead."

That change of topic drew his sharp attention. If Michael had taken the information the wrong way... "When?"

"Not like *that*. Dad said you'd only been hurt, but everyone's supposed to *think* you were dead so they could do stuff to catch that guy. Real spy stuff. Dad told me not to, but I watched the news. Was that really you going off the bridge?"

Richard had also seen the bouncing, fuzzy amateur video taken by a tourist who happened to have his camera in the right place at the right time. After a distant pan of both falls from the Cana-dian side, the view swept jerkily along the gray river to the bridge, where a puff of smoke and fire suddenly erupted, and a black flailing figure shot clear of the explosion and fell, turning once before hitting the water. It amazed Richard how quick it had been in actuality compared to his nightmare memory of the experience. Seconds. There and gone.

His identity was yet to be revealed, for which he was grateful, but there was no doubt in his mind that Charon would have seen the circus many times by now. Probably having a good gloat.

"Yes, that was me."

"You don't look hurt."

"In truth, I'm sure I broke every bone in my body. I just heal fast."

Michael grunted, noncommittally. "Did you have to have shots?"

"Don't remember."

"Did you have a nurse?"

"Sort of, and she was very pretty." Richard wondered again how much Michael knew, but not to the point of asking. When it came down to it, his condition and outré diet weren't all that important to their relationship.

"I miss Aunt Sabra." Michael leaned over against Richard as he used to when he was much smaller. He put his arm around the boy, knowing the contact would reassure.

"So do I."

"She didn't hurt, did she?"

"The doctor said she was completely unconscious. She wouldn't have felt anything."

"I miss her . . ." Michael's voice went up and then the tears came. His sobs were quiet, but enough to wake Bourland. His eyelids cracked open, a questioning expression.

Richard put a finger to his lips and opened his palm outward to sign that he'd look after things. "It's all right," he whispered, holding his godson.

He waited for his own tears to come. One would have to have a heart of stone to listen to such crying and be unaffected.

And apparently his had turned to granite.

Nothing.

Richard dozed himself, only dimly aware when Michael got up, sniffling, to turn off the TV and wander into the kitchen. Domestic noises as the boy made a snack. Mourning or not, he was growing, packing food away like a starved squirrel. Bourland snored on the other couch. Good, he needed the rest.

Sabra's memorial service was tomorrow.

Bourland had managed to keep a low profile for Sabra despite her being the victim in the much publicized hospital invasion. Interest in the incident had been thoroughly knocked aside by the bridge explosion, so the media was likely to be busy elsewhere. Her family could grieve for her in private. Richard could not be there, though, since he was dead himself. In case Charon had agents on the watch.

Bloody bastard.

Michael finished in the kitchen and returned to the living room.

Richard opened his eyes enough to see the boy gather a pile of pillows into the corner by the bookshelf, turn on a handy light, and pull the entire stack of comic books onto the floor with him. He liked to read himself to sleep. With a large bowl of popcorn and a canned soda for company he settled in for a marathon session. Richard eased back, dozing again. In between Bourland's snores he could hear the solid thump of their heartbeats. So long as they continued, all was—almost—well.

He *ached* for her . . .

"My lord, you must come now." The Abbot of Glastonbury himself shook Richard awake. Knowing what it meant and hating, *hating* it, he roused from his bed in one of the dim cells and followed.

It was just coming to sunset. Richard felt the pressure of the day's eye on him like a great searing weight. Soon it would lift. Too soon.

The chamber to which the abbot led him was clean and comfortable as could be made. In one corner three monks murmured soft prayers. Candles burned against the approach of night. There was a tall window in the west wall that looked out on green flat fields. The sun stared through like a curious pilgrim. On a low bed facing the window, well padded with many coverlets, lay a very old, old man. He wore a simple dark robe like the others, but on one finger was a gold ring proclaiming his rank in the Church. His white hair had been carefully combed, spread evenly on the pillow. Snow in the summer.

Tears welled so in Richard's eyes he could barely see. The abbot seemed to understand, took his arm, and led him over. Ignoring the harsh orange orb of the sun, Richard knelt on the stone floor by the bed and wiped his sight clear.

"How now, Dickon?" whispered the old man, blue eyes staring up. He'd gone blind in the last months and raised a gaunt, questing hand.

Richard took it, too conscious of the brittle bones beneath the thin skin. He pressed his lips to his brother's fingers. "I am well, Edward."

Edward made no further speech for some while, his breast rising and falling under the wheat-colored linen sheet. With each fall, it seemed to take longer and longer to rise again. Richard willed him to continue.

The fading sun was fever-hot on one side of Richard's face. He leaned close to murmur to his brother. "There is yet time. I can help you."

Unexpectedly, Edward puffed a very quiet laugh.

"I *can*. Please. Let me spare you."

"Spare me from heaven? No, thank you, Dickon. I look forward to it. This life hurts too much."

"That will vanish. You will be restored. I promise."

"We've had this talk before. You know how it ends. I always win." He hummed another laugh.

"You love the Church so much, think of the good you can do by sustaining your life. You can be young again."

"I've a perfect body waiting for me already." Edward's sightless gaze drifted toward him, a flash of sorrow in their blue. "You only hurt yourself by clinging so hard to this flesh, and that comforts me not. I'm ready to let it go. It is my time, and it is all right. Ask your lady. She agrees with me."

"Edward, I need you. You're my only family."

"I am not, just the only family you like."

"Please . . ."

"Richard, *listen*. This is what is to be. Accept it and know I am happy. I will not turn my path this time. You've chosen yours and I mine. I love the light too much to give it up for more life on this side. My Lord calls me, let me pass to Him with a joyful heart."

Richard could stand it no longer and bowed his head and wept hard, his own heart breaking.

"There now, Dickon, there now . . ." He reached across with his other hand and stroked Richard's hair until the storm eased. "I feel the sun going. Would you lift me? I want that warmth on my face."

As gently as he could, his eyes streaming, Richard gathered Edward up as though to look on the sunset. His brother's once strong body was as light as a child's. He eased the white head against his shoulder, and settled in, arms protectively around him.

"That's better," said Edward, his voice barely up to a whisper. "This is good. You know, I have a very dim memory of . . . I think Mother held me like this . . . I was so little, though. It might have been a dream . . ."

Richard held him and watched the sun for them both.

"Richard?"

"I'm here, Edward. Right here."

"Richard, it's getting late." Bourland shook his shoulder.

He blinked at the unfamiliar room, the frail-looking furniture, the stranger in the odd clothes bending over him. The past and present slewed chaotically over one another in his mind, until things sorted themselves into their proper place. Fifteen centuries slid away in seconds. By the time Richard sat up the safe house looked normal to him again.

"The services are at nine," Bourland reminded. "I know you can't be there, but—"

"I'll manage." He rubbed wearily at his growing beard and wondered if he should shave.

Why was his face wet?

Richard stood solitary in a snow-covered cemetery, a black-clad figure blending with the tree trunks and ornate tombstones. He watched the quaint little nineteenth-century chapel from a distance, waiting for the service within to end. The only attendees in the family's pew that morning were Bourland and Michael. Nearby would be Bourland's school chum Frank, and standing back by the door the Boris and Natasha couple. To anyone else so small a gathering might have seemed pitiful and sad, but Richard knew Sabra would have preferred it that way. She'd looked on death as a passage to something better, and he believed that himself, but it was hard, cruel hard on those left behind.

The silence in his mind was the worst. How he missed her voice. In the past it now and then had annoyed him when she'd disrupt his thoughts with a comment or say something that would set him off into laughter at an inappropriate time. He'd give anything, go through anything, to bring her voice back again. A few words, a moment to tell her he loved her, to say good-bye. If she could only tell him she was all right, that all was well.

He'd once been on a tour of a cave in the Ozarks, and to make a point about the place, his guide had shut off his flashlight. The dark was so profound, even Richard's eyes perceived nothing, only phantom afterimages of light, which soon faded. The place was as quiet as it was black, and he was aware of the hundreds of feet of rock between himself and the surface. Without that light he would wander and perish—eventually—trying to find his way out.

Sabra's voice and spirit were gone from his soul the way the light was gone from that cave.

Only a matter of time, he thought, looking at the surrounding graves in the soft snow.

By listening hard he could just hear recorded music coming from the little gray stone building. He managed a tiny twitch of a smile, catching the faint strains of "In My Life." Sabra had loved that song. Lennon and McCartney's words and music pierced him through and through with their simple truth.

The sky was heavy and grayer than lead. It began snowing again, though the fall was soft, the flakes coming straight down in the thick, windless air. Richard was glad to be out here. Better to be under the sky in the cold than in the chapel, haunted as it must be by the spirits of the dead along with those who sorrowed after them. Thousands of others had passed through before him, and he would have felt, or imagined he felt, their combined presences. He couldn't bear the idea of sitting quietly, listening to the priest uttering the same terrible words yet again.

It had been nearly impossible the last time, when he sat in there for Stephanie and her little girls, Elena and Seraphina. He'd held together for Michael's sake, and because Sabra had been with them. Richard had buried and mourned for hundreds he'd dearly loved and lost, but he would go mad if he had to do the same for Sabra. Not her, never for her. He'd thought of another way to deal with her loss. All he had to do was hang on long enough. See to it that Charon was shot screaming into hell, and then . . .

A rush of dry flakes swept around him, a random breeze stirring them up . . . but not quite. Otherside wind. He turned, bracing, expecting an attack.

Instead of his enemy, a tall woman strode toward him out of the flurry, hands in the pockets of her long coat. Her strong, sturdy figure seemed to coalesce from the flying snow and the black trunks, growing more solid the nearer she got. She was wrapped in many layers of protective clothing. Some of it looked very new. Her western-style boots were well-worn, though.

She came close, pulled off the knitted muffler that covered her brown face, and smiled up at him.

He caught his breath, recognizing She-Who-Walks.

He'd not seen her for a couple of years, but she'd never been far from his thoughts. His lover, his sister, his brown-eyed daughter in blood, chosen for him by Sabra to share their dark Gift. Of all the people on the planet, only *she* truly understood the depth of his grief. He embraced her hard, and she murmured to him in her own language. He did not know the meaning, but recognized words of comfort and love.

They clung to each other, standing like stones themselves among the graves and silence, and something within him suddenly cracked and shattered under her gentle touch and voice.

He felt it like a physical blow. His knees gave way. She-Who-Walks held him tight, kneeling, too, in the snow. Finally, agonizingly, his tears came. His pent-up grief flooded forth.

He clung to her and sobbed, sobbed like a child.

"While I'm away from Kingcome Inlet, you should call me Iona," said She-Who-Walks. "I travel light. It's easier to carry."

"Is that your name rendered in your language?" Richard asked. Though intimate on many levels, he yet knew little about her. She struck him as being decades more mature than when he'd last seen her. Something to do with her serenity. She wore it like a warm blanket.

She chuckled. "It's Celtic, Greek, or Welsh—depends on what you want. I like the Celtic. It means 'from the king's island.' Fits well. The Dark Mother suggested it for me before she left to live here."

They sat side-by-side on a wooden bench off one of the winding paths. The chapel was behind them; only grave markers were within view. An appropriate place for the dead to talk.

She-Who-Walks (he strove hard to say *Iona* in his mind) also possessed the gift of Sight. She'd seen the visions that Michael had been projecting.

"There have been no others since the Dark Mother's death?" she asked.

"None. Did they come from Sabra?"

"No. They were from the Goddess. Warnings."

"What are we to do?"

"Our best."

"That's not what I meant."

She gave him one of her little smiles, the kind that made her eyes dance. "I know. It's better not to ask what to do until the time is ready. That will be soon. Today."

He waited for her to continue, but she looked out over the stones. The snow still fell, and flakes stuck in her lashes. How he'd missed her. "I hoped you would come," he said.

"How could I not?"

"If I'd been able to phone you . . ."

"Not in that place." The idea amused her. Her home was one of the spots for which the word "isolated" had been invented. "I knew I would be needed when the vision with the stone house and the snake came to me. That's when I left home. Took a long time to get here. Sure like your weather." She meant it. The Vancouver area was very wet. Snow was a delight to her.

"Michael had visions before that."

"Yes. Not as strong as that one. The Dark Mother was looking after those lesser ones for him."

"I didn't know. She should have told Philip. He's been troubled that they were hurting Michael."

"She was looking after those on *Otherside*. He wouldn't have understood."

"He does now. I've told Philip everything, my history, everything."

"About me, too?"

"Oh, yes."

"Good. We need him."

Again he waited for more information, but none came. She seemed content to enjoy the gray, dark day, like him, ignoring the cold.

"Why is Charon doing this?" he asked. "Do you know?"

"He's dying. He's doing all he can to stop it."

"Dying?"

"Cancer. He should have died weeks ago. It's his path, but he wouldn't take it and began fighting it. He's eating power and souls to put it off. He shouldn't do that. Big mistake."

"Dear God. Now it makes sense. It's funny, but Philip said he was a cancer in the gene pool. . . . If we'd only known sooner. Sabra said his protections had been broken by the fight with Sharon Geary."

"That's what I felt, too. It left him vulnerable to the Dark Mother's Sight and she to him."

"But he acted first. The car crash. Where was Charon when he caused it?"

Iona looked at him. "He didn't cause it. That was the Goddess."

Richard went very still. Shock. He couldn't have heard right. "No. it couldn't possibly . . . no."

"It was—"

"Did you have the vision of Sabra's accident?"

"Yes. And it was bad to see, but I knew it was to protect her." Iona continued to look, the appalling truth in her dark eyes, until he had to turn away.

"*Why?*" He wanted to roar his fury, but held himself to a whisper. Shaking.

"You know why. To protect her. The crash was meant to happen. Charon had nothing to do with it. Otherwise the Dark Mother would have gone after him. Tried to stop him."

Richard choked on suppressed rage. "The Goddess did that? Hurt her own priestess? And her death? Why did the Goddess allow her to die?"

He got another long look. "You know there are some things even the Goddess has no influence over."

"My bitterest lesson," he snarled.

Iona did not offer comfort or distraction. "If she had not been in the crash, she would have gone after Charon and lost. The Goddess would not have been able to save her from him. He'd have fed from her soul until it was gone. Some things are worse than dying; having your soul eaten is one of them."

"She could have sent me in to stop him. I'm the warrior."

"Then you'd have both been lost, then Michael, then others. This was the only path that had life, not death for them on it. And her soul is safe, now."

"I wouldn't know that. Her voice is gone from my heart."

"You will hear it again, Dark Father."

Not on this Side, he thought.

"What is, is," she stated with a shrug. "We may not like it, but there's always a reason."

Nearly his own words to Bourland. Why was it that teaching a truth to another was so much easier than learning it for oneself?

"What about Sharon Geary?" He told her of his dream. "I thought she was with the great snake, but before I could be sure, I was taken to that green land. I think it's Glastonbury."

"Then it must be. The snake god could be protecting her."

"From what?"

"Many things. They're in a bad place, but even drained or hurt by the soul eater man, the god has certain untouchable powers. He will use them to bring himself back if he can. Maybe bring her along."

"That or the dreams are my own wishful thinking. Wherever she is . . . can we help her?" He was afraid to hope for Sharon's safe return, but if her soul could be set free . . . that would be something salvaged.

"We will try. Soon. There are very big powers involved, and they're being disrupted. Charon is eating them, upsetting the balance. He is like a bucket with a hole that grows. The more he pours into himself, the faster he empties. Soon there will be nothing but the hole itself. He will turn everything inside out, and that will turn the whole world mad."

"How?"

"Dark Father, you don't want to know. But we must stop Charon before he works his power again. Another rip between the Sides will be . . . bad."

He remembered the hellish creatures from the image captured by Bourland's computer and stopped his imagination from going any further with the thought. "How do we stop him?"

"When we're together. You, Michael, Michael's other father. I will show you—but it must be on the Dark Mother's special ground."

Chapter Fourteen

Charon reached beautiful, not-quite downtown Glastonbury in his anonymous rental, pulling into an empty car park and killing the lights. The sky had been clear all day, and it promised to continue through the night, which was just beginning to descend. Few lights showed in the town, which like many in the countryside, really did roll up the sidewalks after dark, much to the annoyance of the American tourists. Well, too bad for them.

He wanted to rest before taking on the last leg of his trip, which would indeed be on his legs, unfortunately. God, he was tired. It had been one hell of a long haul from leaky Niagara, first by train, then that snail-paced bus trip, the other train south to Atlanta, an endless parade of paranoid security people looking for terrorists—and himself, of course—then the flight across the Pond.

The plane trip to get to London damn-near killed him, even in first class. All that sitting in place and the brainless in-flight movie and nauseating food. He'd all but taken up residence in the forward crapper, dropping his cookies in the stainless-steel well, flushing it away with the chemically hygienic blue water, the astringent, overly sweet smell of which only encouraged him to repeat the performance.

The flight attendants became aware of his illness, and he was hard pressed to stave off their well-intentioned offers to help until they finally noticed the bastard in the row ahead of him. When the man keeled over bleeding that got them nicely freaked. That admittedly risky feeding plus their combined tension, horror, and sick worry kept Charon sustained for the rest of the flight. Nice floor show, too. They'd pulled a doctor out of coach to look after things.

Imagine! A doctor flying coach. After the mint they charged me and for nothing, the damned quacks. One idiotic test after another just to tell me I'm gonna die. Well, screw that, them, and all their cousins.

Man, if the flight crew knew the truth of what he was planning they'd have gutted him with their pre-packaged plastic forks, then cracked open the rest of the plane's mini-bottles of tasteless champagne to celebrate. Too late for them, now.

After that, Charon was forced to have a full collapse in a London hotel under his latest and possibly last necessary alias. It had proved a good cover, slicking him past customs and all those watchful cops easily enough when combined with his metaphysical camouflage. Even his case full of pills was no problem, though of course anybody could see he was sick. But he was well aware that he was being hunted by a specialized bunch that made the CIA look like a knitting guild. Can't have them putting a foot into things at this stage.

His illness was taking a visible toll on him, even with the near-constant feeding by using the Grail to channel the resident psychic energies. In the hotel's bathroom mirror he noticed his ribs showing. Not something he'd seen since he was a scrawny teen centuries ago. His face flesh hung loose on emerging cheekbones and what a terrible color his skin was under the tropical tan. No real color at all, just veins showing through the thinning skin. Have to do something about that. Tonight. While he was still able.

He slumped in the car seat, hugging the Grail close, using it to funnel in random energy to keep him going. Not too much to get himself noticed, just enough for a nice buzz and to build up reserves. Save the Spielberg effects for later when they were needed.

There was a good old full moon coming tonight. That additional energy oughta put a corncob up the Goddess's ass. Once he was done, she wouldn't know what hit her.

He'd wait an hour past sunset, then start up the tor.

✧   ✧   ✧

Driving the unmarked white van, Bourland, Iona, Richard, and Michael arrived at Sabra's wilderness cottage well before noon. Strictly, it was not in a true wilderness, but distant enough from neighbors for Sabra to enjoy the isolation. There were several acres to the property, very private. Iona walked around to the backyard, which was profuse with large trees and virgin snow. The trees formed a circular clearing some ten yards across; in its center was a stone construction that more mundane eyes might take for a homemade barbeque. It was cone-shaped, made of concrete and native stone, about waist-high, and a yard across at the base. Sabra had built it herself soon after she'd moved in. Its bowl-shaped crown was blackened from past fires. There was no sign of a cooking grill.

"It's good," said Iona. "Let's go in."

The police had shut things up, and Bourland sent people from Richard's security company out to repair the damage to the alarm system. He used his own key to let them in, entering the code into the wall unit before it went off.

Richard feared this moment, but decided it was easier to look at Sabra's things with the others along, easier to think that she was just in the next room. Everything was as she'd left it when she'd bolted out the morning of the shared vision, a few unwashed dishes in the sink, a book she'd been reading open across the arm of a chair.

Michael was hungry. He and Iona poked around the kitchen. She found eggs and still-fresh peameal bacon and asked if he wanted scrambled or over-easy.

"Both," he said, taking his usual chair at the kitchen table.

Bourland touched Richard's elbow, and they went to the small living room. The place had central heating, but that had been turned down. He went to adjust the thermostat and the room began to warm. Bourland uncharacteristically fidgeted, pulling his gloves off, shoving both in the same pocket, taking them out for a look, then shoving them in again.

Richard had confidence in Iona and Michael, but how would Bourland handle this? His inexperience in Otherside matters would work against him; it might overwhelm him. Richard wanted to leave him out. Iona insisted, though. She'd first met him when he,

Richard, and Sabra had taken Michael on a visit to Kingcome Inlet. They'd found common ground teaching Michael to night fish.

"What's this about, Richard?" Bourland asked. "She didn't explain much of anything."

A damned good question. "It's a way to perhaps stop Charon."

Bourland held to a straight face, but his heart began to drum loud enough to be audible to human ears. Was it terror or anticipation? "How?"

"The ceremony will cause us to travel in spirit to where he is."

"In spirit?" His tone lowered. Skepticism. "What will that be like?"

"Unsettling," said Richard. "But you get used to it. Just accept what you see and feel as reality and respect it."

"And if I don't?"

"It can kill you. There . . . and here."

"I see. You've done this before?"

"Yes. The last time was to help Michael."

"I don't know as I'm quite the right man for this. What am I supposed to do?"

"Be there," said Iona cryptically, looking in from the kitchen.

"For what?"

She shrugged and went back to frying eggs. Somehow, that had been a very significant-seeming shrug.

Bourland looked at Richard, who also shrugged. "There is no answer since the future is in flux. More so now because of what Charon's been doing. He's upset balances, God knows why, because he must be aware there are always consequences when you muck about with such forces."

"'Eating the light'? Feeding off psychic energies and such to fight his cancer?"

"To fight off death. He should have been gone by now. Once he missed his sell-by date . . ."

Bourland snorted. "I'm not sure if any of this even exists, but if you're all taking it seriously, then I shall, too. At least for today. By tomorrow I want everything sane and plodding along as usual in the normal sort of madness. But until then I'll do whatever it takes to kill the bastard."

On that, Richard knew, Bourland could be entirely relied upon.

✧   ✧   ✧

Michael must have looked on Iona as a surrogate for Sabra, for they spent the time over his lunch talking. Richard wanted to listen in, but intuition told him to keep clear. He wanted to speak with her, too, perhaps to find some ease for his own inner pain, but there would be no chance. Iona said they would have to take action this day, while the moon rose over distant Glastonbury.

"The time difference can be confusing," she said. "It's a big world, but we have friends." She knew about the Stonehenge group's healing ceremony and the villagers convergence at Chichén Itzá. He'd not told her about either of them. For all they knew similar ceremonies might be going on in other places as well.

"Will time as we reckon it really matter?" asked Michael.

"It will where he is, and that's where we must be."

Iona was serene, Bourland restive and worried, Richard determined, and Michael . . . sad.

"Why?" Richard asked.

The boy shrugged, the gesture must have been contagious. "Change is coming. I like things just as they are—were—anyway, it's all going to be different. Me and Dad, me and you. With Aunt Sabra not being here . . ."

"Have you dreamed of her?" Sometimes Michael dreamed of his mother and sisters. It was a source of comfort for him, had helped much in his healing. Richard wanted some crumb of that for himself.

"Not that I remember." He saw Richard's disappointment. "I'm sorry."

"It's all right."

"I know you want to talk with her."

"We all do." The silence in his mind was still terrible. For nearly all his long life she had *always* been there. While the brief lives around him flourished and swiftly died Sabra continued on. With him. She was his one constant in an existence rife with disappointments, betrayals, joys, and disasters. He could bear anything, survive anything so long as she was breathing the same air. Half his soul had been ripped from him, and unlike a physical wound he would never quite bleed to death from it.

That would be a happy release.

✧   ✧   ✧

Sharon Geary jerked awake when her drifting body thumped up against the side of her snaky protector.

Newton's whatever-the-number Law: a body in motion stays in motion until acted upon by . . .

Or something like that. The short version being that Kukulcan was slowing down, while she in her hollow space continued forward. She was very glad he'd not slammed hard on the brakes or there might have been a nasty collision for her.

She pushed off and sought out her long, thin peephole to the outside. Very bright there, now. She'd fallen asleep—hard to fathom—watching the rainbow lightning ripping across infinity.

"How goes it for ye, sir?" she called, expecting him to widen the opening so she could have a better look. She could just see his massive head in its usual place, above and to the left of her. How long had he held himself so carefully still in this position? Did gods get muscle cramps? She checked her watch and noticed the second hand wasn't moving.

Uh-oh. Was that a bad thing? She shook it. The battery was no more than a month old. Maybe the lightning had buggered it; lots of energy playing about out there, might have been like being next to a magnet. She had a friend at school who killed watches if she wore them for more than a few days. "Magnetic personality" they'd teased and always knew what to buy her for birthdays and Christmas. None of the teachers said it was possible, but the watches, electronic and mechanical alike, died all the same.

Sharon peered through the opening, wary for giant bugs, but seeing bright light. That distant spiral he'd been heading toward . . . was this what it might look like close up? She determinedly did not think about black holes, maelstroms, or even bathtub drains.

Kukulcan seemed to be too occupied to pay her any attention, and anything that got such a level of focus from him was likely to be important.

She resumed her place, anchoring as best she could to observe, her heart speeding up. *Something* was going to happen, or so her gut told her, not her Sight, not her reason.

"Tick, tick, tick, tick," she muttered, green eyes wide.

Toronto, the Present

Richard brought kindling and shavings from the woodshed, arranged them in the bowl-shaped depression in the top of the cone, and touched a firelighter with a match to get things going. It certainly beat striking a spark off flint. God, those days when after your sword a tinder box was your most important tool. He used to collect the things, acquiring a new one whenever someone made an improvement.

Once the kindling caught, he added several pieces of dry firewood. Oak, he absently noticed. They soon caught as well. The flames were very high and merry under the lowering sky, yet small against the forest darkness. The fire seemed to light only the immediate area; the surrounding trees pressed close, as though seeking warmth. Richard's shadow, made large, moved black against their trunks like an unfriendly spirit.

Iona threw on piles of sage and sweet grass and soon thick, fragrant smoke flooded the clearing.

Richard, Bourland, and Michael took their places two yards from the cone at three of the four compass points. Sabra had long marked them out with little stones, but those were hidden by the snow. Richard shivered in place, aware of a nervous nagging within. He felt naked. When his right hand twitched once across his body, an unconscious gesture, he realized he wanted a weapon. Club, sword, P-90, but he understood that such things on this Side would not carry over in the physical sense. If he had to fight it would have to be with whatever was available on Otherside. He'd been on such a journey before, and knew his mind could conjure him a tank if need be, but it took concentration. He'd just have to wait and see. The Goddess—hopefully—might have whatever he needed most already prepared.

But if not . . . why then his own bare hands would more than suffice, providing he got within reach of Charon.

I'll rip your heart out, if you have one.

Iona, finished with her prayers, backed away to her fourth point, chanting in her own tongue, her arms spread wide. Richard stood opposite, watching her through the yellow flames and pouring gray smoke. Her smooth, serene face calmed his heart for a few precious moments. Rage and hatred for an enemy, however deserving, would not help. Richard breathed deeply of the pungent sage smoke and cleared his mind. Listening to Iona's soft but powerful voice soothed his heart. He did not understand the words, but there was no need.

Bourland kept most of his attention on Michael but cast about, looking for some sign of what was to come. Richard had tried to explain this was a journey of the spirit, not the body, but didn't think it had fully sunk in. Well, they'd all know in a few more minutes.

The smoke suddenly billowed dense and swirled around the circle, seeming to have a guiding force directing it. Richard's eyes smarted as it enveloped him. He swiped at the sting, then no longer felt the same kind of winter cold. He smelled rain instead of wood smoke and snow. A chill *damp* wind breathed on his bare face.

When his sight cleared he was in Glastonbury, standing at the top of the great tor. St. Michael's Tower was gone, green winter grass covering the flat spot where it should have been. He truly was in another time and place.

The full moon was well risen. The ceremonies in the other sites must have been under way for some while now. The moonlight on the surrounding land was harsh and silvered, and showed damage to the countryside otherwise invisible to mundane eyes. The land below the tor was empty and blasted in places as it had been in his dream about a bombed landscape. Even the ancient bones of the once glorious abbey that had stood for long were gone. *Are we too late?*

He found himself outwardly changed, wearing clothing and battle gear from his youth. The sword on his hip was his own, given to him by Sabra to replace the one lost in his last tourney as a living man. It should have been in its glass case in his Neville Park house, not here. This weapon gleamed as though new, the blade sharp and flawless, and it felt *right* in his hand. Lying in the lush, wet grass was one of his old shields, also new again, which he took up. The weight was also right and solid, reassuringly familiar. When had he lost it? At Camlan field, hacked to splinters and gone to dust over the centuries.

Where were the others? He walked cautiously around the uneven edge of the summit, searching.

We were supposed to be together. What's gone wrong?

No sign of them and no sound but the wind sighing through the grass.

Clouds roiled on the western horizon, bloodred, lit from within by lightning, galloping toward him unnaturally fast. That couldn't be good.

The storm reached the tor in moments, filling the sky, blotting out the friendly moon; wind screamed around him, tearing and biting cold, but no rain fell. He could smell its hanging threat, but its promise of cleansing had been perverted. The air rushing down from the heavy clouds was tainted with burning and the stink of rotting flesh. Instead of thunder he heard screams and howls, nothing earthly in those sounds.

"Iona!"

He cast about, looking for her, for any of them, on one level glad they weren't here, on another worried about where they'd gone. He listened within, hoping to hear her voice as he'd so often heard Sabra's, but all that came was the pounding of his heart.

An aberration flickered in the corner of his eye but seemed to vanish when he looked directly. He only saw it by its absence, vaguely man-shaped, the edges blurred like fog, moving purposely along the tor's winding maze path to the top. It was fast and did not have far to come.

Richard checked for cover. None available with the tower gone. Too bad. A good old-fashioned bushwhacking would have taken care of things nicely. Fair play wasn't a factor in war. He was a soldier, and the job was to defeat the enemy decisively and quickly, then go home.

Have to make do with what was at hand.

He marked the progress of what he assumed was Charon, worked out what direction he would come from when he made it to the top, and slipped down on the hillside several yards distant. Richard lay flat in the clumps of grass, holding absolutely still, trying to listen in spite of the wind howl . . .

Until something dropped like an anvil across the back of his neck.

He tried to twist out of it, but the weight pressed him harder into the ground, almost to the snapping point for his bones. A thick-soled hiking boot was just within his view, wet, with bits of grass sticking to it, very effectively pinning him in place. His sword was plucked from his hand, his shield taken and tossed aside, and he anticipated the blow that would kill him to come next. Instead, he heard an incredulous, exasperated voice:

"Jesus Palomino, what does it *take* to *snuff* a bastard like you?"

The boot lifted, and he rolled quick to his feet. Charon had the sword in one hand and the Grail in the other, and stared at Richard with two healthy eyes. The damage he'd taken years back in their last confrontation was healed, but he was thin and wasted. His gray skin clung tight to his skull; his hands verged on the skeletal. He didn't look strong enough to stand much less fight, but Richard had felt preternatural strength holding him down.

"Or are you one of the guardians of this place?" Charon asked, cocking his head and squinting.

Richard made no reply. This was new. The man had ever been so sure of himself.

"What are you? Hm? You gotta answer, like it or not. Them's the rules. Who are you?" His eyes were fever bright, restless. "I said *answer me!*"

"Richard d'Orleans." Richard had intended to remain silent just to nettle him, but Charon's words drew the name out all the same. What the hell . . . ?

Charon snorted, not believing. "Yeah, right. Big fat hairy deal. Your goddess can't scare me that way. I know better. Whatever you are, you just *hold still* while I—"

He swung the blade faster than the lightning; it chopped deep into Richard's chest, and he fell with a grunt.

"—kill you. Again."

"What's happened?" Philip demanded. He strove to keep his voice under control, but it was bloody hard. Richard had been standing, eyes shut, and suddenly dropped like a stone. Philip had instinctively started toward him, but Iona sharply told him to stay in place.

"Otherside attack," Iona said. Her eyes were also shut.

"He's *bleeding*, dammit!" Philip stared, aghast at the flow. Dear God, it was *pulsing* out of him. There was too much of it. They'd never get him to a hospital in time.

"He'll be all right," she murmured.

But he could not believe her. Philip was now all too aware of what a precious necessity blood was to Richard. Tough as the man might be, he couldn't survive such a massive loss.

"Stay where you are!" Iona ordered an instant before he began to move.

He hesitated, fuming and fearful, and glanced across the fire at Michael.

"Chill out, Dad," said the boy. His eyes were also shut. "Call it a learning curve."

Richard hadn't even tried to dodge. Charon's words had utterly frozen him in place. He felt the heavy blow as a distant thing, seeming only to knock the breath from him and no more, but his blood gushed onto the grass. No real pain, though. It could be like that for dying men. He was ready to die, but to depart without finishing Charon? No, couldn't allow that. But how to fight a man who could control with his voice alone?

Oh. Of course. That'd be easy enough. Cut his throat so he can't speak. Now . . . how to get up and do it?

He pushed feebly against the earth; his limbs refused to cooperate. Mortal wounds were just too good at shutting things down.

But only for a mortal body. He wasn't sure how much of himself was on this Side, but knew his solid self was in a snowy clearing on the other Side of . . . of . . . fine. He'd only needed reminding. *That* was his Reality. Whatever happened to him here would echo there, but only if he allowed it. Charon wasn't the only one with influence.

Oh, damn. *Now* it began to hurt. The more real this Side became to him the more . . .

Shut it out, then. The sword doesn't really exist so it never caused any damage.

Easier thought of than carried out, especially when all his senses told him different, but he did his best. It helped to remember Iona's face, imagining her standing before the fire, arms raised. *She* was real, this wasn't. This was Otherside, a place of gods and demons, of spirits and forces. He was just a tourist.

The blood began to reverse back into Richard, his wound knitting at atypical speed, even for him. One just had to know to work with the rules of the place. He wasn't used to it, but could adjust. By the time he was on his feet again, he had another sword in hand, identical to the other.

Charon had moved off, apparently seeking a certain spot in the long oval that formed the summit of the tor. Richard thought he might be looking for the hidden opening that led inside the tor itself, though why he'd want to was beyond reckoning. They'd each taken that path once. Richard had barely survived. He'd often wondered how Charon had escaped from the shattered and crumbling earth, and if he was worried about guardians, there were the Hounds. Annwyn's cold pets resided in that secret place. He would think the Grail would protect him, and well it might. Richard did not know. The hounds could also be loose and flying in the storm; this was their season to hunt.

Softly, softly, he eased forward, though it was unlikely anything could be heard with the stormy row above.

Yet Charon was aware of him and turned. He laughed once, shaking his head, then looked at the sky. "Sweetheart-honey-baby, don't you know when to *quit*?"

Apparently he still thought Richard was some kind of simulacrum fashioned by the Goddess. Richard went into his guard position, sword at an angle, his other arm up to fend off blows.

"I said *hold still*." Charon glared, and Richard froze.

He couldn't help himself. *He only has as much power as I give to him.*

"That's better . . ." The sword in Charon's hand changed, metal shifted into wood, a sharp, barbed point formed on one end. When the transformation finished, Charon rammed the newly-made spear square into Richard's chest.

Tried, to, anyway. This time Richard ducked clear. Very fast.

"Oh, that's cool, you finally figured—whoa!" His turn to duck, as Richard waded in.

Sword against spear, reach against power and speed. Their pass was over in seconds, neither achieving an advantage.

"Sweet," said Charon, puffing. "Just try not to have too much fun."

Richard feinted quick to the right, cut left and across, and felt his blade slam hard into the wood staff of the spear. The impact went up his arm as it had a thousand times and more for him, from those summers sweating his youth away hacking at a practice post to his days of manhood fighting and killing to keep his king on the throne. Charon barely got his guard up in time to avoid losing his head.

Richard circled him, kept him turning, most of his focus on Charon, another part mindful of the storm and the creatures caught in its chaos. If any of them managed to break free and descend . . . best not to think about that lest it happen. Using his speed he got in under Charon's guard, knocking the spear to the side and hacking down decisively with the blade. It passed through air, not flesh, and he had to spin with the momentum to maintain his balance.

"Oh, very fancy move, I'm sure," said Charon. He looked more out of breath than he should have been for the effort made. Perhaps all that was needed was to wear him down. "But you're playing out of your league."

Richard went for a layered attack combination, swift, clean, but battering with its force. Charon barely kept up, unable to counter until the last second, when he managed to bang the dull end of the spear into Richard's shoulder. There was just enough force behind it to make him pause.

"You're not so bad for a puppet." Charon squinted, cocking his head. "Unless you're . . ."

Richard mirrored the head tilt. "The real deal? Wake up and smell the coffee."

Charon was baffled a moment. Good. "Oh, no. Nononono. No *way*."

Oh, yes, you bastard.

"Dickie-boy? That really you?"

No reply seemed required.

"Well, I'll be damned."

That's the idea.

Hastily, Charon shoved the Grail into his overcoat pocket and brought the spear to bear in both hands for a proper defense. The cut in it smoothed over, and the wood turned ebony dark. It likely was indeed ebony. More difficult to break. No matter. Richard's real target was soft enough.

Another pass, longer in duration, and Charon had to retreat to make use of the spear's length. It was too unwieldy for this kind of combat. Charon changed the spear back to a sword, something from a later time that was lighter and swifter than Richard's weapon, designed for stabbing as well as hacking. He knew how to use it, too.

Another pass. Richard felt like he was fighting his own distorted image. Neither made contact, neither advanced or retreated.

Charon grinned, pulling the Grail out once more and clutching it close to his chest. His face looked less skull-like than a moment ago. He was using it in some way to replenish himself even if he couldn't see the effect except by inference. Charon's form was filling out, getting stronger. Better shut that down before he got too robust.

Richard's own blade became lighter, turning into one he'd used in a much later century. Their fighting styles changed to suit the weapons and their next pass was considerably faster. Each took a nick, and each healed.

"Uh-oh. Looks like we're too evenly matched, Lance old boy. That won't last, though." Charon brought the Grail up, holding it before him. His form lit, briefly, white fire that turned an unhealthy green and seemed to sink into his flesh. When the glow faded he looked completely restored and far too happy about it.

At his feet, in a rough ten-foot circle, the grass had turned bone white, each blade desiccated and needle thin. Even the ground looked dead.

Richard held off from another attack, wary, alert.

He didn't see it. He felt it. Like an invisible wall smashing him all over. It slammed him right off his feet and seemed to fall on him to hold him in place.

Laughter. Not good. Charon loomed close. Without delay he put his sword point over Richard's heart and *pushed.*

That hurt. A lot. The breath rushed from him too fast to form a scream and refused to return.

Charon grinned, eyes dancing. "Face it, Dickie-boy, in this place my fu is better than your fu."

Pushed. Charon slammed downward until the hilt was against Richard's chest. The razoring blade stabbed through flesh, splintered bone . . . piercing through his body into the soil of the tor.

The earth screamed for him.

Philip, palms to his ears, bent almost double against the onslaught of noise. It was the insane shriek of a factory whistle, but much louder and strangely organic, as though from a living throat, not a machine, and it took the starch right out of his legs. He staggered, but struggled to stay in place. Richard had somehow recovered from that terrible wounding and gotten up—eyes still closed, dammit—but was now fallen again and worse off than before. He lay spread-eagled, obviously in great pain and unable to move.

Neither Iona nor Michael had budged, though they'd recoiled at the sound. What did they *see?*

He shut his eyes, but perceived only the dim red flicker of the firelight playing on his lids. Why was he here? He wasn't doing any of them a damned bit of good. He looked again to Iona. Despite the cold, her face was sheened with sweat, almost glowing from it. Her outspread arms shook as though barely supporting a great weight.

"Iona! Help him!" he bellowed.

She didn't seem to hear.

Michael's face also shone in the firelight, silver and gold with his fair hair and dark skin. Philip called to him, but got no response. His every instinct told him something had gone wrong, and he felt desperately ill-equipped to deal with it. Iona had only told him he was to "be there," whatever that meant. Here where he stood or "there," as in whatever place Richard had gone?

This time Iona snapped no objection when Philip darted over to check on him. He was bleeding out again, a fearful and clearly fatal chest wound but no sign of what caused it. His eyes were still fast shut, and he struggled desperately to breathe, blood bubbling from his lips and nose. Oh, God—another attack like the one that had taken Sabra?

Philip lay a hand on Richard's forehead—so cold, corpse cold. "Richard!"

His friend flinched at the touch and groaned. "Where are you?" he whispered.

"Right here, dammit. Open your eyes!"

"They are op . . . Philip?"

He sounded so lost. Philip shook Richard. "Wake up!"

The shrieking rose and grew louder. A strange icy wind slapped Philip's face; it stank of destruction and rot, the stench filling his lungs, treacle-thick. He gagged and fell back, but this was no time to give in to trivialities.

Then a wholesome cloud of sage and sweetgrass smoke enveloped him, so dense his eyes watered. It fought the death-stink, though he could still smell *that*. He dragged out a handkerchief to wipe his eyes, then held it to his nose to filter the air. How could a man *think* with this going on?

"Richard?" He groped with his free hand, but encountered—what the hell?—wet grass? Not snow? He scrubbed his eyes again and blinked at the impossibility, trying to take in the change around him. The earthy howling was the same, even louder, but the fire in the circle of trees had quite vanished along with Iona and Michael. He knelt on open ground, a bleak wind tearing at his clothes and there lay Richard . . .

Oh, no . . .

Richard fought off the physical shock and tried to rise, but the angles were wrong, and the more he struggled the greater the screaming from below. He paused, remembering his real body was elsewhere. The pain eased, but he was still stuck fast, his blood pouring out. For a moment he thought he heard Bourland's voice, distant and harsh, calling to him and tried to respond.

Where was Charon?

"Richard!" Bourland again, sounding scared. He had every right.

He called back, but could hardly hear himself. Charon had stolen all the air.

A dark shape began to tentatively emerge on his right. Charon again? But it was taller, less certain in its movements.

"Philip?" He could only mouth the name, but a name had power. *Philip—over here!*

The shape came closer, seemed to suddenly kneel, feeling its way on the ground.

Philip! Thinking of him made him more real on this Side, though what it would do to the man's sanity . . .

And he was there. Most of him. Staring around, dumbfounded.

Then horrified, when his gaze fell on Richard.

Richard gestured weakly at the *thing* pinning him to the earth, pleading, hoping Bourland would understand.

"You're not really here," he said. His form wavered. Richard could see through him to the red clouds above. "Neither of us . . . we *can't* be."

Take it out! Richard's gaze pressed hard upon his friend. He struggled and managed to mouth the words. He *knew* the sword was not real; he should have been able to will it away on his own, but the agony and terror were too distracting. He needed help.

Bourland hesitated, then visibly made up his mind. His ghostly hands solidified, grasped the hilt, and pulled in one awful effort. The shrieking din ceased. Substantiality traveled up Bourland's arms, finally encompassing his body. He was now fully on this Side, white-faced and frightened. "My God, if I've killed you . . ."

"I'll be fine," Richard gasped. But to make a lie of it, he heeled over and began coughing. It's a damned nasty business to drown in one's own blood.

Bourland stared as Richard grimaced and groaned through a difficult healing. "But you've been run though!"

"The rules . . . are different . . . here." It was slower going this time. The pain didn't leave him as it should have. He felt as weak as when recovering from that bridge fall, less able to concentrate. "Where's Charon?"

"No sign of him."

That couldn't be good, but there was no going after him for the moment. Richard tried willing his lost blood back into himself again. God, but it was hard to think, to visualize. The longer he was here, the more real this Side became to him, and the more damage he could suffer. "The others?"

"In the clearing by the fire, standing with their eyes shut the same as you. Only you fell . . ."

"Remember that place. It's our anchor. If things get strange, picture Michael and Iona, picture *that* place in your mind and go toward it."

"*If* they get strange . . . ?"

Richard missed the rest, if any, doubling over again.

"Whups," yelped Sharon, as the serpent god made a sudden move in a direction opposite to where they'd been traveling. Fortunately the walls formed by his body were somewhat flexible. She was bruised, nothing broken. She maneuvered over to the opening. The light was brighter, flickering, and the air that beat against her face was an uneasy mix of ozone and rotting meat.

They were in the midst of churning clouds, lightning flowered everywhere. One tremendous bolt shot from side to side of her measureless horizon, and this time there was noise. The boom thrummed right through the god's body and hers. He shifted. Sharon pushed back in time, getting her hands clear from being crushed. Her long narrow window sealed up, shutting her in the dark again.

She still felt the thunder or whatever was out there. In here it wasn't loud so much as deep, and the vibration very unpleasant, like a boom box set on maximum. Too loud to hear, you only felt it. Putting her hands over her ears helped. Kukulcan didn't seem to like it either, for he made a lot more moves than before, and she pitched from one point of her sphere to the other.

What was going on out there that would so agitate a god?

The blast of sound knocked Charon completely off his feet. He somehow kept hold of the Grail, pulling himself in tight like a tumbler, protecting it from seeking hands with his body. No one and nothing tried to make a grab, though he felt *something* buffeting him around like a soccer ball.

Earth Mommy is pissed as hell, he thought, when he finally stopped rolling.

It had been quite a near fall. He was partway down one flank of the tor, and had only stopped by twisting to one side on a marginally broader section of the maze path. The top was a hike and a half distant. He had the energy for it now, but suspected his time was short, especially with the weird weather banging around overhead.

NOT *my fault.* That was just a byproduct resulting from taking his Realside corporeal body through to Otherside. You weren't supposed to do that. It weakened structures, ripped veils, and messed up all kinds of other inconvenient crappola. Well, too bad, he was here and would leave only after he got what he wanted. Deal with it.

He had to get to the top again. That last bout with the jock had opened a window of enlightenment. After the business in Chichén Itzá with Big Snaky's blood doing such a world of help, Charon had an insight on how to accomplish the same thing here, but better. This time the healing would be permanent. He could go back to Realside hale and hearty enough to enjoy the fun and games that would take place when some of the more dangerous denizens of Otherside found their way through.

Predators were always looking for fresh hunting grounds. He had no problem with that since he would be the one at the top of the food chain. He would feed from them, while they fed from all the little pink monkeys that had taken over the planet. They were over-populated anyway. Not that they weren't efficient at thinning their own numbers down, but there were other, more fun ways of going about it. In a couple of months the chaos would set things back to a nicer, slower time, maybe about half-past the Dark Ages, with no Renaissance to haul them out of the muck. Hell, he could probably start up another religion again. It'd been a couple thousand years since the last time he'd played that game. He could introduce an inside-out Rubik's cube of conflicting dogmas for them to fight over then kick back with the remote and a six-pack to watch the fun.

Charon began climbing. He tucked the Grail into his pocket again, so he could use his hands when needed. He had to crabwalk to get up the steeper bits, but that was faster than taking the maze path.

After a few minutes exhaustion swooped on him and he paused, pulled the Grail out and used it to replenish himself. Jeez, the stuff was leaking out as fast as he could pour it in. There would be no second chances on this gig. He'd have to make it work right the first time.

Now . . . about the jock. How in hell had *he* gotten here? Never mind surviving his dip in the river and what it must have done to him. He'd pulled through it somehow and waltzed into Otherside easy-peasy, all ready to kick ass and take names.

And that had created no further disturbances to the windy climate . . .

Which meant he'd done it the Boy Scout way and followed the rules . . .

Which meant his *real* body was someplace else.

Which meant he had help.

But his witchy girlfriend was deader'n Dixie. Of that Charon was certain. He'd sucked her so dry in the hospital that even divine intervention from her hot shot Goddess wouldn't have brought her back.

So who else was out there directing the show? Had Dun recruited a gaggle of dippy New Agers to dance nekked in the woods for him? Nah, not his style to bring in a group. He was too much the loner. Maybe he had another girlfriend waiting in the wings. He did love to spread himself around and once they spread for him they tended to be devoted for life. Even Sherry-pie had screamed his name before big Wormy caught her. What was it about the guy? The baby blues or his aftershave?

Another girlfriend . . . and she was probably someone close . . . a blood relation, perhaps?

Charon looked at his hands. Well-well—Dun's gore was *all* over them, how about that? It was messy business, killing, but in this case he didn't mind. He was pretty sure he could improvise something. It wouldn't take much to backtrack. Dickie-boy wouldn't trust his safety to just anyone.

"Come on," Charon whispered. "Talk to papa. Tell me everything you know."

He rubbed his hands against his face, breathing in, smearing the red over his eyelids. The psychic link of the blood here to its Realside originator would be very strong. Yeah, that gave him a fix . . . follow the blood trail to . . . a cozy little cabin in the back of beyond. The same one he'd burgled. He could see it settled in a nest of white drifts, like one of those water globe scenes with the fake snow swirling inside. Very tiny, lots of detail . . . a light over there . . . a fire with four figures at the compass points. Jeez, were they predictable or what? One of the figures was down, that would be the jock, another had left his appointed spot to look after the fallen. The balances would be dangerously off because of that.

So who else was there? A kid? Not him. And that woman . . . who was . . . ? *Well, I'll be dipsy-doodled.* The bitch that clawed his eye out was running this ride. Wow, look at her working it. She wasn't used to this kind of load. The others weren't carrying their share, either. She wouldn't be able to hold out against . . . ah, just surprise her. Something quick and dirty. Then maybe he could get *on* with things.

Oh, yeah: Keep It Simple, Stupid.

They were usually very hung up on symbolism. Yank one thing out of place—that should be enough to buy him protection against more interference.

Charon shut his eyes, cupping his hands before him and imagined the cabin and the woods squarely in his palms. When the image was fixed and strong, he blew hard, like it was a birthday cake with countless candles to snuff.

The fire in the clearing went out.

"Nighty-night," he said, then clapped once.

"Your bleeding's stopped," said Bourland.

Richard had noticed. As soon as he could get up, he would. It felt good to lie here, even if it was freezing and on wet grass. He imagined the strength of the land flowing into him. Not the same as fresh blood but it would do for the time being.

The storm seemed to be in a kind of holding pattern, still full of fury, but not growing worse. Perhaps the blast of sound resulting from Charon's last attack had also knocked him for six. If they could find him before he recovered . . .

"Hand me that sword, would you?"

Bourland reluctantly passed it over, the one that had too recently been buried in Richard's chest. Damn, there was a hellish ache there still. Which wasn't real. Just have to ignore—no—remember Iona's face, ruddy in the firelight, the sage smoke playing about her as she chanted. Richard thought he could hear her voice.

The pain ebbed. Finally. Even the stains on his shirt vanished. He took a deep draught of air and did not cough it out again. "Help me up?" he asked.

"It's too soon."

"Not soon enough. Come on."

Bourland hauled, and Richard used the sword like a cane for balance as he came upright. He swayed, lightheaded a moment, then got his legs. He should have been famished, but only felt a nervous restlessness to get going. Quickly, he explained to Bourland a little of what to expect.

"Charon's attempt to heal himself will probably tear open a rift between the Sides, and it can't be allowed."

Bourland worked to take it in. He really was trying. "But aren't there forces in place to head off that sort of thing? Guardians and such? Iona let that much drop. We can't be the only ones to stop him."

"He's from our Reality. It's our job. And I rather think the guardians might be busy." Richard gestured at the storm. The weather in Realside Glastonbury was probably verging on the catastrophic. He stooped then straightened, picking up his own dropped blade. There, the blood rush to his brain wasn't too bad. The migraine-like agony only lasted a few seconds. "Take this."

Bourland accepted the sword readily, but shook his head. "Fencing wasn't exactly my sport at school. I still have my Walther." He touched the spot under his left arm where it was holstered. "Will it work here?"

Richard hadn't expected that. "Maybe. If you think it will. But cold iron will be better, even if it is imaginary."

"I'll take imagined hot brass and lead over imagined cold iron any day, thank you very much." But Bourland kept hold of the sword and looked around. "What about Charon?"

"He might have wrapped himself in darkness again. Put your back to mine and keep your eyes open for movement. We'll work toward the center. He seemed interested in that area."

"Oh, lord." But Bourland did as he was told and they gradually made their way over. "What's with the fancy dress?" He was still in his modern clothes, the long coat and somber dark suit he'd worn to the memorial service.

"When we pass to this Side we have what we need." That would account for Bourland being armed with his handgun. He didn't know on a subconscious level that it might not work here, so it was with him. Richard wasn't sure why he was in his old clothes, but they felt right to him.

"I suppose every place needs civil servants," Bourland conceded. "I'd look damn silly in tights anyway."

"They're not tights."

"People really used to dress like that?"

"Yes."

"My God."

"You over the shock, yet?"

Bourland snorted, getting the message. "Yes, all right. You said it'd be unsettling, I'm unsettled. We're here. Now what?"

"Stop him when he shows himself. And *ignore* everything he says. His voice has power in this place, though he might not use that attack again."

"This is really Glastonbury?"

"For all intents and purposes."

"Is it supposed to smell so bad?" Bourland held the handkerchief to his face again.

"That's his doing. I think he's feeding from the energies here, and it's made an opening that's not supposed to exist."

"Opening to where?"

"Places that are usually sealed. Remember those creatures from Michael's visions?"

Clearly he did.

"I think they're in the storm. There's some nasty things that can come through, so watch out for them. If you get the chance, take the Grail from Charon and run like hell."

"Run where?"

"Back to Iona. Picture her and Michael and the fire in the circle. She'll do the rest."

"My real body's still there, isn't it?"

"Yes. As is mine."

"What about Charon? Where's *his* real body?"

That stopped Richard short. "An excellent question."

"A damned obvious one. Why don't we look for it instead?"

"Because unless he brought it through to here—which would be horrifically stupid—it's probably in Realside Glastonbury and we're not."

Bourland's brief, one-word response fully reflected his Anglo-Saxon ancestry. "Then we take him out here, no holds barred."

"That's the plan."

"But—"

The specifics of Bourland's objection were lost to Richard. In the same moment both men pitched forward. Richard tasted green grass, its sweetness marred by the slaughterhouse stink of the air, then the grass turned into snow.

He caught a strong whiff of sage and blinked against stinging smoke. The red storm clouds wavered, an unsteady projection superimposed upon a screen of tall trees. What the hell . . . ?

Their circle, the fire . . . out . . . how had *that* happened?

Bourland looking around in confusion, Iona chanting, her voice harsh and desperate, trying to hold things together, and Michael . . . bless the boy, he was busy, quickly dropping more wood into place. Was he somehow taller or was that an illusion of his Otherside self? He lighted a fire starter and shoved it into the kindling, then lighted another and another, adding them in until the blaze was nearly as strong as before. Thank heaven for modern conveniences. He returned into his place again. The last Richard saw of him before Glastonbury reasserted itself was the boy flashing a sudden grin and a thumb's up sign.

Bourland hastily lurched to his feet. "Bloody hell!"

"Just a setback, keep your eyes open." How long had they been gone? Long enough, apparently, as time was reckoned here. Charon now knelt in the center of where St. Michael's tower stood on

Realside and with a thick-bladed knife hacked strongly at the earth there. No screams erupted from this activity, though. The Goddess must have done something to compensate or had sealed that doorway off. He'd never find his way in.

Richard murmured in Bourland's ear. "I'll distract him, you come up from behind." Each man split off in a different direction; Richard saw to it he approached Charon from the front, coming up fast.

That got him noticed right away. Charon paused his digging and scowled. "Damn, but you're harder to shake than a case of the runs. I don't have *time* for this!"

"Get up then. You can try for three out of three."

He showed teeth. "Third one's the charm? That's how you guys like to work, isn't it? If you *really* focused, you could get it right the first—"

Richard found a way to shut him up. Charon blocked the attack at the last instant, his knife blade ringing against the extended sword. He followed through, launching a full body tackle and over they rolled. Richard hammered swift, hard knuckle stabs at the pressure points within his reach, getting grunts of pain in return.

The Grail.

In one of Charon's pockets. Richard could feel it through the material. He closed his hand over it to rip it free, but Charon anticipated and hammered right back—using the knife. It startled Richard, and before he could react to the pain he was abruptly tossed clear by a decisive judo-like throw. Charon had ever been strong, but not like this. The storm-troubled sky switched places with the tor several times before Richard came to a stop. He kept hold of the sword and instinctively brought it 'round to block a blow, but none fell. He'd landed in a heap, breathless and sluggish. It was as though his strength had been sucked out, and he dully realized that's exactly what had happened. Charon was a black hole, feeding, feeding, feeding.

Richard didn't dare risk more physical contact, had to keep a distance between. He got up, feeling heavy and clod-footed, willing himself to heal. Where was Bourland?

Two flat pops on the foul wind. Two more. Gun shots. Richard hurried toward the sound.

Bourland was in a shooting stance, braced with left hand cupping the right, his Walther aimed square, point blank range. He knew what he was doing; there was no way he could possibly miss at ten feet, but Charon refused to fall over.

"That's been tried before," he told Bourland. "It didn't work then, either."

Not one to waste time, Bourland obligingly grabbed up his sword. He must have had some fencing classes once upon a time, but wasn't an expert. The most he could hope to do to stay alive would be to keep backing out of range.

Charon shook his head. "Oh, now you've *got* to be kidding." But instead of his knife, he pulled out the Grail, holding it high. Once more his form lit up with a white flash, but the force went outward from him, striking Bourland like a club. He dropped. Charon turned, grinning. "Hey! Dickie-boy! Can I throw a party or what?"

Using his speed, Richard charged forward, but stopped short as Charon raised the Holy Cup again.

"Don't even *think* it or I'll fry you, too."

Richard had no fear for himself, but Bourland . . . he lay prone and unmoving. "Philip!"

He heard a groan. Alive, thank God, but needing recovery time. "Philip! Stay down."

"No problem," came a muffled reply.

Charon's knife had turned into a sword, and he pressed its point into the back of Bourland's black overcoat, making a dent.

"Come on over, or Mr. GQ here gets stapled to the ground, and I don't think he's got your way of bouncing back."

Richard warily approached. "You don't want to do that. The Goddess was less than pleased the last time."

"Thanks for the hint, I'll be sure not to run him through too far, but hey—who'd a thought she'd turn out to be a screamer, huh? And, oh, gosh, where is she, anyway? Haven't heard a peep from her, and I've been doing some major damage to her real estate. Letting her knight-errants do all the dirty work is kinda tough on you. Will she be around to kiss your boo-boos when the smoke clears?"

He's fishing for information. He might not be able to sense her, even with the Grail in hand. "You're restored yourself, just leave.

The longer you're here the greater the risk you run for retaliation. It's not something you'd like."

"I'm touched you care, but life don't work so simple. If it did I wouldn't have had to haul my ass all over creation to get anything done for myself. Do you have any idea just how *stingy* the powers that be are with their healing mojo? We only get the tiniest *crumbs* of what's really out there."

"Meaning if you leave, you're back to dying?"

"At hyperspeed, pal. *Not* on my event horizon. What I've got here is just bandage work. I want a total fix and some extra to get myself back to how it used to be. You and that freaking Injun Josephine did this to me, so don't think I'm unappreciative. I wanna make sure you each get my personal thanks."

"We cured you from having your beast take you over."

"Screw that, you thought you were killing me, which I get from a lot of people, but they never carried it as far as you did."

"Pity."

"Can it. Where's your Mother Nature wanna-be hiding herself?" Charon shifted the sword point to the back of Bourland's neck. "Come on—or I do a tracheotomy the hard way."

"That's a hell of a storm going on, she could be busy with it."

The gale was right on top of the tor. Still no rain, but the lightning seemed to be having a vast battle with itself, yet there wasn't as much noise as there should have been. Unnatural stuff. At this short distance it should have been stitching the earth, but perhaps the Goddess was preventing that, protecting her sacred ground from further harm.

When Charon glanced up, Richard lunged. Even if that damned parasite drained him empty, he'd find the strength to snap his spine first. Richard slammed his blade through Charon's body, the metal violently disrupting the forces bounded within his flesh.

An almighty flash engulfed the three of them, an inhuman shriek, and Richard felt a massive shock tear up his arm and blast through his body. He fell away, blinded, limbs twitching as the current ripped through his nervous system.

Chapter Fifteen

It was hard to think with the ringing in his ears. Nothing musical about it either, just an annoying, high pitched, and constant jing-ling, a querulous phone that could never be answered.

He muttered against it, shook his head, and opened his eyes.

Still on the tor. Storm overhead. Stink in the air.

Work to do.

Richard was fairly sure they'd *not* been struck by the otherworldly lightning. That would have killed even him. Maybe it had, and he'd not figured it out yet.

No, he hurt too much to be dead. And there was that bloody ringing. It seemed to be fading. He swallowed and worked his jaw to make his ears pop.

That helped. Work to do. Things to do.

And chances were the first man on his feet would be the one to walk out of here.

There was Bourland standing over him.

Unless . . . it was all over.

Bourland had the Grail, holding it protectively, but gingerly, as though it might break. He looked worse for wear and shaken, but there was a grim light in his eyes. What was that? Triumph? "You all right?" he whispered.

That was still under consideration. "Charon? Where is he—?"

313

"You got him. He's had it."

He wanted to laugh, but Richard had to see to believe. Bourland helped him up again, and Richard leaned on him to hobble over.

Charon lay sprawled partway on his side, skewered through his chest. Whatever energies he'd pulled in were leaking out along with his blood. His whole body seemed to be slowly deflating, his stolen health turning into extreme emaciation. Only his eyes retained their strength, burning with life and madness. He stared around, bewildered, and singlemindedly reached out.

Bourland hastily stepped backward, still holding the Grail like a baby. "Can we leave now?"

"We kill him first."

Richard looked for and found Charon's sword. He hefted it experimentally, and thought about what he needed for the task. The shape and length of the blade changed, along with its weight. It acquired a wickedly, visibly sharp edge, and the balance felt off, tip-heavy. It wasn't a weapon for fighting, but of execution.

"What are you—?" Bourland stared, horrified.

"Beheading," Richard answered shortly. "Always does the job. Don't look if you don't want to."

"But—"

He gazed steadily at his friend. "You know my history, this kind of violence has been part of it. Take the Grail and get clear. I don't want his blood defiling it."

Bourland got out of range, and Richard raised the sword, two-handed. He glared down at Charon, who yet lived, but only just. His breath rasped hard, and blood bubbled from his mouth. He would likely die within minutes anyway, Richard was only shortening the process with this finality. It didn't seem right, too quick compared to the deaths the bastard had given to who knows how many thousands of others—and one in particular.

Charon choked and coughed blood, and spat out a word: "*Michael!*"

Richard paused, alert for a threat. "What about him?"

"Give him. The Grail."

What the hell . . . ? "Why?"

"Only one with . . . the right . . ."

"What do you mean?" Richard risked coming closer to hear, ready to get out of reach if necessary.

Charon struggled for another breath, eyelids at half-mast. "*We both . . . loved her.*"

Richard gaped in shock, felt ice form in his veins. *Oh, no. Nonono . . .*

He whirled.

Bourland's face was alight with cheerful mischief. He mimed pointing a gun at Richard, winked, and smirked. "Gotcha!"

No! Richard launched like a sprinter, but Charon made a sweeping gesture and smashed him to the side. The invisible force was hard as iron.

"Hoo-boy!" he laughed, twisting Bourland's voice out of shape in a cross between a giggle and a chuckle. "Shoulda thought of this one before, but couldn't do a soul-swap on that Side. Didn't know if it'd work either, but, man-o-man-o, what a delivery. I can do all *right* with this dude, not too old, not too young. I'll find me a sweet little fang-girl to do the honors and just keep going and going. Think Pocahontas back home'll find me sexy?"

Not going to happen.

Charon must have had some knowledge of their way back. A shadowy shimmering began forming behind him, marking the path to the circle and the fire. Iona and Michael would have seen everything, would know what Charon had done. He'd kill them. This avatar here would return to Bourland's Realside body, then he'd use his gun on them both. Michael would die, Iona would be slowed enough by the bullets for Charon to finish her off with a piece of splintered firewood. He didn't dare keep her alive, even to make a blood exchange.

No. Absolutely NOT *going to happen.*

Dazed, Richard strove to pull himself up, find that sword . . . no, it would be useless, think distance. A crossbow? With an iron bolt. Only one shot, but if he moved fast it would be enough. If he could just *focus.*

"A switch like this is perfect." Charon giggled again, giddy. "My old body gets expelled back to Realside, I take off and disappear myself. Your oh-so-important *balance* is restored. Everyone wins.

Even Mommy Nature can't object to that arrangement. Dickie-boy, I *am* grateful! I'll see to it you get a champion's send-off. There's a nice symmetry to it. You and your greatest enemy slaying each other on the field of honor, very heroic. They'll be weeping in the aisles for that one. I'll write an opera about it just for you."

Richard shut his eyes, the better to recall what it felt like to hold a crossbow, remembering the weight, the positioning of his arms. The goddess provided. When he next looked he had exactly what he wanted in his hands.

Charon was unimpressed. "Kill me and you kill your bud."

"He'd want this."

"Yeah, sure, give it your best shot—I mean it!" But he stepped back; the smoky and vaguely circular opening of the path behind him grew larger, much larger than was needed. It dilated twice his height and kept growing. Why was that?

"Wait!"

"Wa'for? I got me a hot date waitin'." The opening began to envelope his shoulders like smoke. He took another step back.

Had to get to him before he went through, had to—

But it went still larger. Very much larger. Enormous.

Richard had no Sight, but good instincts, and he thought he felt the coming of a pressure wave. He threw himself clear and rolled.

Just in time.

He glimpsed Charon being knocked over by the wave, which saved him, otherwise he'd have been struck by the god's passage as it hurtled out of the shadows. The thing was grown far more huge than in Richard's vision, and the portal widened considerably to accommodate a great coiled knot in its body. Its gaudy scales glittered like jewels, reflecting the lightning and seeming to hold its white fire like an afterimage.

With the majestic delicacy of an oversized train coming to a precise stop, Kukulcan slowed and hovered a mere ten feet up, his bulk between the tor and the storm, cutting the wind and creating night shadow below. Richard was right under it. If the thing decided to land . . .

Movement. Only the knot lowered until a portion of it touched the earth, then the coils relaxed, the muscles beneath hypnotically rippling. Their form changed, widened, stretched out, and lifted. Standing where they'd touched was Sharon Geary, looking rumpled, but otherwise alive and well.

"Mother of God!" She puffed, staggering, then caught her balance. She looked unsteadily up at the serpent. "Wherever this is, thank ye, sir! Thank ye!" Then she dropped flat.

Kukulcan, if he heard, made no sign, rising straight up into the thick of the storm. Lightning licked his flanks, seeming to go into him, be absorbed. In seconds he was hidden by the clouds.

Richard was on his feet, dashing toward Sharon. She was conscious and showed no great surprise at seeing him, gazing up with a crazed smile.

"There ye are, ye great clot, looking just like yourself. Where's that bastard Rivers? I'm gonna throttle him."

"Promises, promises," said Bourland. Charon. He was winded, but in charge. He pointed at Richard. "Don't move." There was *power* in the words.

Richard tried to lift the crossbow, but nothing happened. He'd been on this Side too long, its reality had grown too strong . . .

Sharon struggled up, glaring. "You! I know who you are under that skin you're wearin'. "

Charon pointed casually at her. "You—put a sock in it."

Her green eyes seethed pure fury. "To the devil with ye!"

He didn't expect that. "I said shut up, Sherrie-pie, or I'll spank you. *Shut up and don't move.*"

"Bloody idiot." She tried to pry the crossbow from Richard's petrified grasp. "I spend God knows how long in the company of a deity like *that* and you think I can be bothered listenin' to the likes of *you?* Richard, give this damned contraption over or I'll—"

Charon grabbed her hair, yanking her away. "Hey, baby, did you forget who's boss here?"

She snarled and slammed the heel of her palm under his chin. His teeth clicked together and his head snapped up. She broke free and followed through with a sidekick to his belly. He folded and fell back.

"*God, I HATE that man!*" She started after him.

He made a quick, outward-sweeping gesture. That stopped her if nothing else could. She was thrown to one side, made an *oof* sound when she landed and rolled several times from the momentum.

Richard willed himself to thaw. If she could ignore that voice, so could he. He dragged one foot free, then the other. He still had the crossbow, bringing it up, aiming.

But Charon moved nimbly away, apparently choosing flight over fight to be the wisest course. He headed for the opening, which was fast shrinking. It reduced down close to man-size and stopped. The shadows floating on what might be its surface lost some of their darkness. A silvery sheen replaced most of them until it looked like water under moonlight, improbably vertical. The light flared across the uneven ground like glittering mist.

The change made Charon hesitate before going into it, staring up and around, suspicious. "Okay, Big Mamacita—what's your game? Think with Snaky along to help with the cooking you can fry me? Cold day in hell, cooold day in—"

The silver brightened, turned gold, and a tall and lean figure stepped through. The fiery radiance about his body was like a sunrise in that last moment just before the light becomes too intense to directly look upon. Apparently, even at that level, it was too much for Charon, who cried out, and threw an arm over his eyes.

"*Michael*," Richard whispered.

But that was only one facet of the young man's face. In it Richard also saw the visages of his long-dead son Michel, of Galahad, and dozens of others. Many, many lives. One great soul. Richard had known that truth in his heart, but it was quite another thing to see the actuality. This was the boy's Otherside self.

Clad in gold with an upheld sword like his archangel namesake, Michael reached forward and pulled the Grail from Charon's grasp. Charon tried to resist, tried to strike him, but Michael raised the sword but a little higher and the gesture alone knocked the man right over. He howled against the blast of light, rolling as though on fire.

Michael's gaze swept over Richard and came to rest on the wreckage of what had been Charon's body.

Richard thought he understood what was wanted and went over, kneeling by the dying man.

"Philip . . . ?" He hardly dared hope for a response.

Bourland's eyelids fluttered. He had no breath for speech, what remained was shallow and bubbled blood.

"Oh, God. Hang on and remember where your real body is."

Richard grasped the sword and as gently as he could, pulled it clear, but there was no way to make it easy for his friend. It had to be done so the metal wouldn't interfere . . .

Michael stalked forward until he stood between Charon and Bourland, and held the Grail high. Flashing straight down from the storm came a pure white blast of lightning, far greater than the power Charon had ever summoned. It danced within the cup and splashed out shards of brilliance that split themselves, then split again, fanning out, growing, joining.

A dozen yards away, Charon shrieked in Bourland's voice.

One of the shards leapt between him and his cast-off body. Richard caught some of the tingling shock, just the edge, enough to stand his hair on end. He winced and blinked. His sight cleared. *Everything* cleared. He took a breath of air, and it was like spring sunlight and honey.

The effect spread outward from them in a growing ring, following the contours of the ground. The storm in miniature fled from where Michael stood, and where it touched, the earth seemed to ripple and revive. Dead and blasted patches recovered their green life, even the hole Charon had made digging with his knife filled in as though it'd never been.

Charon was the only thing unaffected by the healing. He was back in his wasted body again, glaring venom at Richard. "You fucking pricks, do you know what you've *done* to me?"

Richard didn't care, caught up in the awe of what was happening. It's not every day one gets to see the forces of the universe at work. Then he sensed a swoop of his own restored strength. One of Charon's claws grasped his arm. Feeding, feeding. Richard tore free while he could and went to see to Sharon. She was already on her feet, open-mouthed at the show.

"D'ye believe it?" she asked in wonder. "It's beautiful."

"Indeed," he whispered, looking at her. For an instant he wanted to put his arms around her. A terrific longing washed over him, familiar, once treasured, but now the core of unbearable pain. All that he'd gone through since that night in the hospital was nothing compared to it.

Yes, it was an unlooked-for miracle to have Sharon back, but Sabra was gone.

He searched the sky, hoping. Of all places it would be *here* that she could manifest some sign of her presence. He called to her in his mind, called desperately, but the void within remained unfilled and silent.

Above, the storm abated. The clouds and whatever things might have been hiding or held in them began to dissipate. The bolt of lightning that filled and overflowed the Holy Cup retreated.

Michael stood unhurt, even smiling, and lowered his arm.

Despite the wound and blood loss, Charon made an effort to crawl toward him. He'd gone truly skeletal, panting, struggling with the now sweet air. The only thing keeping him going must have been will alone.

"*Help me*," he rasped.

Michael looked down upon him, his smile gentle yet terrible. "Do you truly want *my* help?"

Charon teetered, doubt clear on what was left of his face. Then finally, "Yeah, kid. Help me."

"You'll have to earn it. And that will take awhile."

"Wha—no, don't . . . don't leave me. Dammit, don't . . ."

Michael turned and walked toward the opening, passing Bourland, who was just sitting up. He stared at the young man, almost speaking, but holding off. What *could* be said?

"Come away," said Michael, his voice carrying to all of them.

Leaving seemed a very good idea. Richard went over and helped Bourland stand. "You all right?"

Bourland had no words, but his expression was eloquent, as in *What a damn-fool question to ask.*

Sharon balked, pointing to Charon. "We just *leave* him?"

"He's to be looked after, I think," said Richard.

Stars shone down steady in the cold, still air. The storm was gone, its stinking clouds quite vanished. In their stead was Kukulcan, his length compressed into a multiple S-shape, improbably floating, watching them with calm, black and ever-open eyes. The air was chill, fresh . . . if just slightly tainted with the scent of snake.

His massive head came lower and lower, body gracefully stretching and twisting, until it was right over Charon, who hadn't quite realized what was going on. The serpent made an almost leisurely strike.

Richard held his breath, expecting a final scream, but none came.

"He won't be back for awhile," said Michael. He looked sad, but oddly optimistic. "Has a lot to learn."

Kukulcan rose high, turning to the west and south, and soared away. It took a long time before he ceased to be visible. Richard saw a last tiny glint of green and gold wink in the distance.

Some things are worse than dying; having your soul eaten is one of them.

"Good riddance," muttered Sharon. She stood next to Richard and somehow or another his arm had come to be around her shoulders. When had that happened?

Michael walked through the opening, vanishing to the other Side. Bourland waited on them, looking drawn, and little wonder. He'd seen, felt, and gone through things he'd rather not learned about.

"Shall we go home?" he asked.

The clearing behind the cabin was the same, but the fire had died down, and instead of clouds, a butter-yellow full moon shone upon them. It was still very cold, which was the subject of Sharon's first comment, once she picked herself up out of the snow within the circle and dusted off. Her clothes were fine for the Yucatán in winter, but not here.

Richard came to himself standing exactly in the same place where the sage smoke had swirled around him. He rocked on his feet when he opened his eyes and it took a moment to orient to his home reality. What a trip.

Bourland was also the same, his expensive suit no worse for wear, which could not be said of what happened to its Otherside version. He blinked and looked around, clearly unsettled again. "Is it over?"

Iona opened her eyes and stiffly lowered her arms. "Pretty much." Acting as their anchor on this Side had obviously exhausted her. She slumped, and Michael—minus the sword, but with the Grail in hand—went to her, catching her just in time.

Dammit—he *did* look taller.

They trooped tiredly into the warm kitchen. Sharon looked about with curiosity, then pounced on an open bag of cookies on one of the counters.

She scarfed down two and began a third, but paused to clear her throat. "Ye'll be tellin' me what this is about, right?"

"In detail," Richard promised.

"Good. Wouldn't have it any other way. Where are we?"

"Just north of Toronto."

She took it rather well, considering.

Michael slid into his favorite chair at the kitchen table and placed the Grail in the center. They spent a long, quiet, somber moment looking at it. It showed no sign of change, no damage, shining in and of itself in their midst. Flawless, constant.

Then Michael looked up, beaming at them all. "Hey—was that totally *cool* or what?"

Hours later, Richard dressed silently in the pre-dawn dark, not wanting to disturb Sharon, who was asleep in his bed.

It could be *their* bed. Sharon had made it clear she could be persuaded to settle down for good with him now. She'd not been ready before. Her recent experience had sharply delineated her priorities.

Richard's, too. He'd fought his last great battle; he would fight no more.

Things would be just fine, he thought.

Bourland and Richard had talked many things over during the drive back to Toronto from the cottage. They'd each been too wired to rest, and so they sketched out that which had to be done. Most of it would be in Bourland's yard. He had the talent and contacts for it.

Sharon had dozed in the back seat of the van. Michael had elected to stay at the cottage with Iona. Apparently they also had much talking to do. The boy was elated from his sojourn to Otherside. He wanted to know more. He was in good hands.

As was the Grail. Safe once more.

With Bourland's help, life would indeed get back to a more or less normal footing. For the time being She-Who-Walks would take up residence in Sabra's cottage under the name of Iona Walker. Michael and Bourland looked to be regular and frequent visitors.

The Rainbow bridge explosion would doubtless continue as a media mystery, but would fade from the public consciousness as no new leads were discovered. The luckless cab driver would be memorialized with an educational fund set up in his name; the identity of the man who went tumbling into the Niagara river would remain unknown, his body never to be recovered. The people who participated in the rescue effort were already sworn to secrecy for reasons of national security. Bourland's friend Frank would also be very supportive about obtaining the cooperation of his own people. The sunglasses group were silent by nature and necessity and would vanish from the radar entirely.

They'd worked it all out by the time Bourland dropped them at Richard's Neville Park house. It was good to have things all tidied.

He and Sharon trudged arm in arm up the steps, went in, went upstairs and collapsed. He did not sleep, though. His heart and mind still thrummed as he lay next to her.

Richard rested, considered, mourned, and decided to carry on with the decision he'd already made for himself. He'd fought his last battle, he would fight no more, nor would he live on without Sabra. There was much comfort in that for him.

He looked at Sharon; sadness welled up in him. She was very beautiful, long limbs and red hair and bright spirit sprawled artlessly in the tangled sheets. They'd rested together, but not made love. Too exhausted, mentally and physically by their respective ordeals, the both of them, but it had been nice lying wrapped around her warmth in the dark.

He had vast regret about what this would do to her, but the others would be there for her. She was a strong woman, well on her way to swiftly getting over her experience. Much if it was already fading from her mind like a dream. She said she'd slept through most of it, which was likely for the best.

Richard left her, moving quietly as only he could, and crept from the bedroom.

And what of Michael? Well, he would be cared for and loved by Bourland and Iona, little to worry about there. Of all of them Michael would be the one who would understand Richard's actions the best. The likely irony was that *he* would comfort *them*.

Richard paused downstairs. No fire in his hearth, an unthinkable lapse in pre-modern times, now hardly anything to bother about. From the mantel he took down a heavy ceramic urn. Sabra's ashes. He hugged them close and went outside, hatless and coatless, carefully and quietly shutting the door behind.

Cold. Very cold it was. It would be colder still, shortly. He looked forward to it.

He trudged along the sidewalk to the end of the street, using the stair rail to the steps down to the beach, one at a time, slow. Silly, really, to take such care, but if he slipped on the ice and broke something it would delay him, and he'd waited long enough.

He labored across the mix of snow and sand, making his way to the cement groin. The beach was thankfully empty. This was a private thing. He wanted no witnesses, no well-intentioned interference.

He went to the very end of the cement construct and, without ceremony, without prayer, slowly poured Sabra's ashes out over the water.

The Goddess knows her own.

A freezing wind from landward swirled them away from him, scattering them wide upon the lake's dark, gently surging surface.

Perfect. Sabra of the Lake, gone home again at last.

He gave a sudden painful shiver from the cold, but that was all right. Just part of the process. Life was harsh and laborious and the Otherside would be all the sweeter after his earthly strivings.

Richard put the urn carefully down and sat on the glacial cement with the wide metal edge, his long legs dangling over the chill water. It was very black in this pre-dawn dimness, hiding its mysteries well, but he would soon discover them. He faced east, patiently watching the horizon. He noticed the cold; it seemed unnaturally bitter to him, his shivering nearly constant, his teeth chattering violently. Not long. Not long...

All he had to do was wait. The sky was cooperating, free of clouds. All he had to do was wait and let the light work on him, weaken him. Even winter's pale orb was more than enough to overwhelm him, given time. He would resist it as long as possible, of course, resist until he was too wearied to sit up any longer. Then all he had to do was slip forward into the water ... there were worse ways to die. Too weak to struggle against the acidlike burn of free flow, he would drift to the bottom and be content to stay there, welcoming death.

All he had to do was go to sleep and wait. He knew how to do that.

He breathed in the cold, cold air and held it for as long as he could, then puffed it out again, his starved lungs sucking in the fresh automatically. A little practice for what was to come. He'd hold his breath just this way down there, release, then pull in a draught of water. A painful shock at first, but he was confident in his ability to fight off the instinct to rise to the surface as he'd done before.

The horizon got lighter. He shut his eyes against the growing glare.

His bouts of shivering lessened, almost as though things were shutting down already. He'd not been out here long enough for his body temperature to drop, though. Perhaps his subconscious was being helpful.

He drowsed and smiled as the peace settled on him, smiled as the sun crept up, its deadly light saturating him.

But from the wrong direction. It seemed to be on his right, not in front of him. He blinked slowly awake and without much surprise saw Sabra sitting next to him. She was in her favorite jeans and a soft jersey the color of wheat. After all this waiting, all this silence, there she was, as though she'd turned up to take a morning walk with him.

She was a dream, of course, a last defense mechanism thrown out by his mind to talk him out of taking this path. In life he could deny her nothing, but this time, this one time he would have to refuse her.

But there is so much more yet for you to do, she whispered.

"Not without you," he said.

"Of course not. I will always be with you." Her supposedly ethereal presence had a physical effect, for he felt her grasp his hand. That was odd. "Our souls are still linked beyond all other mortal ties, you will never be without me."

"Why now?" he demanded. "Why have you not come to me before? I was in agony for you."

Her form wavered suddenly. Faded. He held his breath, for a different reason now. "Wait—don't leave!"

Gradually, she returned. Her brown eyes were sad. "*That's* why. Your grief blinded and deafened you to me. The peace you feel now has at last opened you up. You must go on, my Richard. You *will* go on."

"I cannot. The pain is gone from me only because I know I'll be with you again. The Goddess must see that and allow it."

"She sees more and farther than you have. The time has come for an ending, but not the one you think."

"What do you mean?"

"It's time for you to take the road you were denied before. You've been on such a long side-journey with me, but now the two roads are converged. As you move forward it will just happen."

"I don't understand."

"That night long ago, you gave up your original life, the original closing of your circle as a living man."

"If you'd not come to me that night, I'd have lived with defeat on my head for yielding, or I'd have died—by my own son's hand, no less."

"That would have been bad," she agreed. "But you and circumstances have changed over time."

"More than I can stomach. I will close my circle well enough in *this* manner. It serves." He watched the sunrise, loving the deadly heat.

I will love the coming heat, I will even love the burning.

"No, my Richard. You will have children, and pass yourself and your memories on to them as other men do. You will help raise

Michael and prepare him for *his* future. Dear Philip can't do it all on his own."

"Such matters are forever beyond my reach. They are not to be. *That's* the path I took that night."

She asked, "How long since you last fed?"

He shrugged. "I don't know. That woman in the lab . . . a long time."

Sabra smiled. A light shone from her, sweeter and more piercing than the sun. "Are you even hungry?"

He was, vaguely . . . but he would not be distracted. Today he would feed on thin, cold lake water and be glad of it.

"No, you won't. Not today or tomorrow," she said, responding to his thought with absolute certainty. She little by little shifted from sitting by his side, and hovered between him and the rising sun. She and it were of the same brightness. It was very like the glow Michael had given off on the Otherside.

Richard stood up, bathed in that loving warmth, spread his arms to it. He gloried in it until the light was too bright to bear, then shut his eyes to feel its heat pulsing upon his body.

The air was cold on his face. The chill was cleansing, like throwing open a window to sweep stale air from a sickroom. He felt like he'd never really breathed before, and gulped down great draughts of it. He waited for the flames to kindle, to overtake, to overcome him . . .

But they never came.

What was wrong?

He opened his eyes. It wasn't a dream, the sun was truly up now, and he'd stood long in its glare, long enough to summon the weakness, long enough for the fire to begin its consumption of his flesh.

But he continued unharmed.

Why?

He suddenly knew the answer. The Otherside battle. Michael holding the Grail, using its true power as it was meant to be used. It brought transformation to them all in one way or another, to a greater and lesser degree.

"It seems," he murmured, "It seems . . . I've been living in the past."

Sabra had told the truth. Ahead of him was a life he could never otherwise hoped to have. A life for himself, for Sharon, one with *their* children, and grandchildren . . .

It was all before him now. And Sabra would be there, too. In her own way, as ever she'd done before.

He felt laughter bubbling up within, a kind of joy so great he could burst from it, the kind of eager elation that saints spoke of in awe and gladness. He wanted to tell someone about it, anyone, even if they thought him mad.

Oh, my Richard, I know about it.

He saw a shimmering along the beach like a cloud of tiny crystals catching the sun. Laughter made visible. Dancing as though in celebration. Was it a swirling of snow particles . . . or Sabra, beckoning him to come and make a start on the new day?

No matter.

He quit his place and hurried his way back. He and Sharon had much talking to do, many plans to make. Happy plans.

A young man . . . he was only thirty-five . . .